CLAN OF THE ARCHANGEL SERIES
BOOK 3

True Vengeance

GRACIE MITCHELL

Copyright © 2023 Gracie Mitchell

This book is dedicated to my husband, who
encourages me to follow my dream.

To my amazing friends and family for their
endless support. Lastly to the reader, who stays
up late, trying to finish one more chapter.

MIRAGE
Satan's Domain
RED CITY
Decimate Mountains
IANUA
CYPRIUS
Mt. Nofri Sai
UMBRA
West River Basin
Leviathan's Domain
TALIA
FUN CITY
East River Basin
South River Basin
ATLANTIS
the Demon Realm

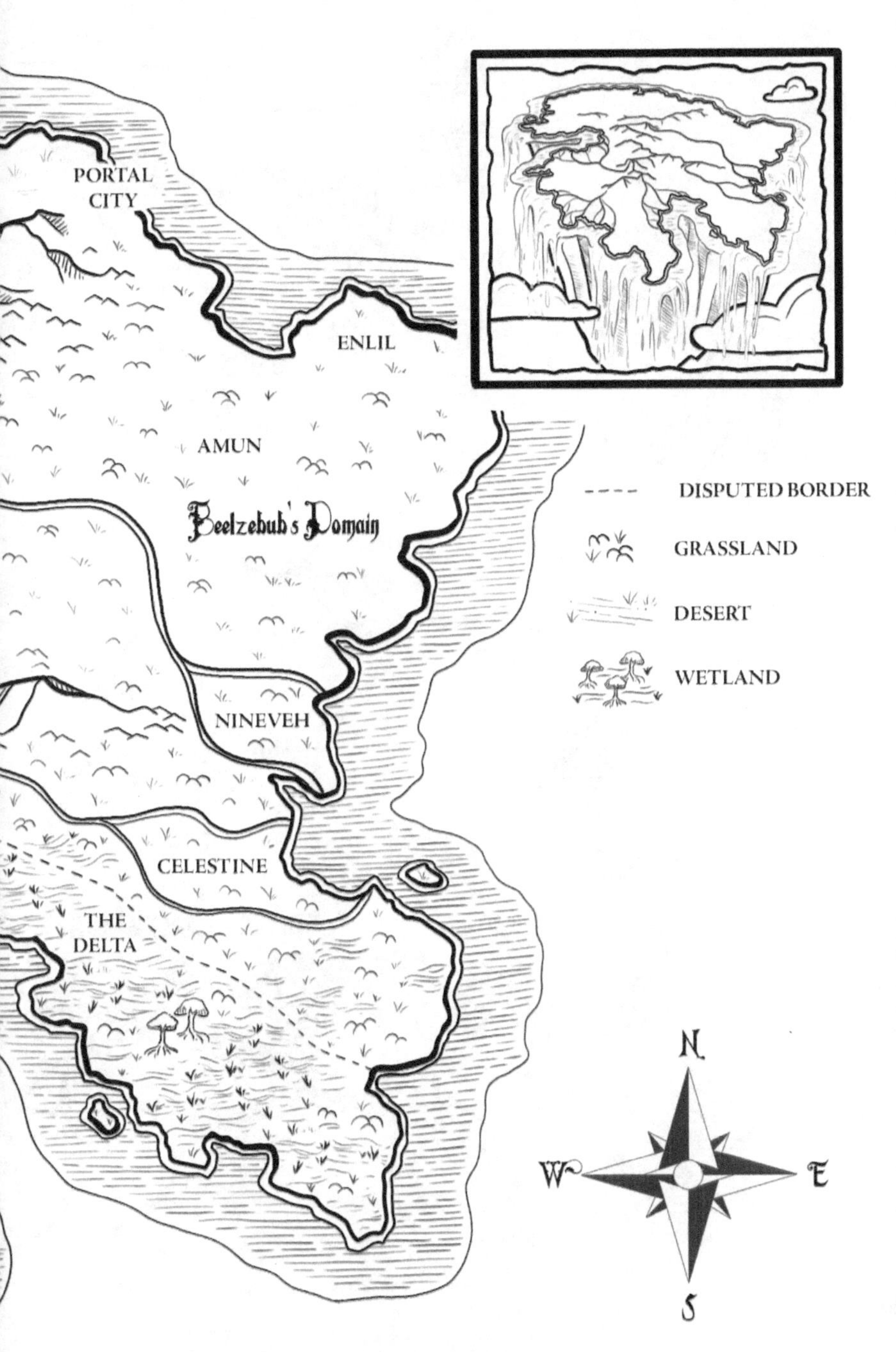

PORTAL CITY
ENLIL
AMUN
Beelzebub's Domain
NINEVEH
CELESTINE
THE DELTA
DISPUTED BORDER
GRASSLAND
DESERT
WETLAND
N
W
E
S

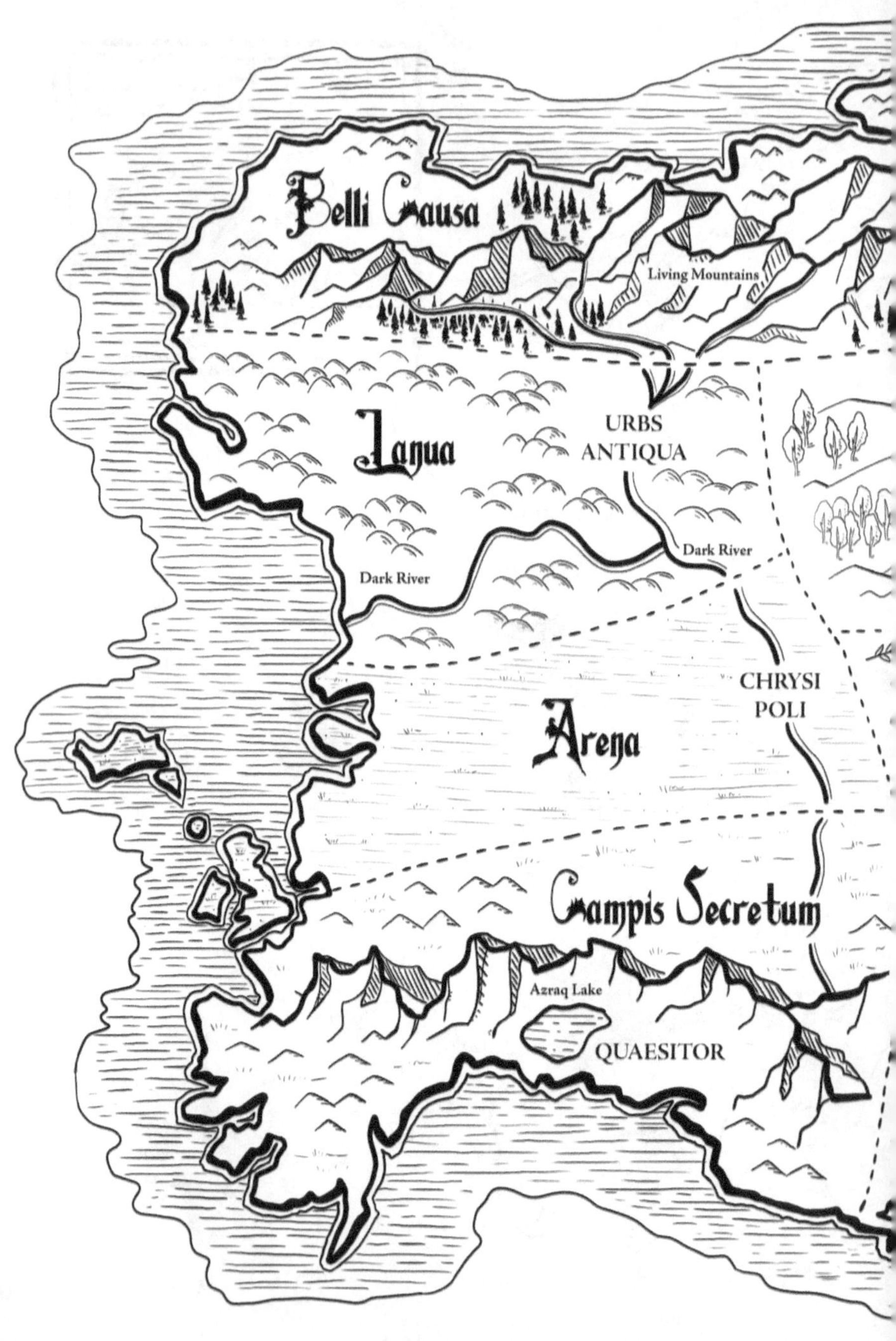

Belli Causa
Living Mountains
Ianua
URBS ANTIQUA
Dark River
Dark River
Arena
CHRYSI POLI
Campis Secretum
Azraq Lake
QUAESITOR

Silva
VENTUS
AQUAM
CAPUT
Elementa
Vallis
Coal
Mountains
MORTEM
N
W
E
S

Chapter 1

Present day...

Clarissa's stomach hollowed as Amos' words reached her ears. A plan. Finally, a plan to fight back! Sparks twinkled along her fingertips, and her wings vibrated. She had wanted to fight back for so long...

A light breeze swirled around her hair. Isabella.

Clarissa glanced over to see her younger sister fidgeting. Isabella's eyes wandered Joshua's large private library. Dark red and black accents painted along the walls created an ominous atmosphere. Amos' eyes shined with passion as he talked.

"—Along with your two kids, can weaken everyone within the vicinity while Joshua creates an illusion that renders them into a mental loop, immobilizing them." Amos' gaze shifted to Clarissa.

Her skin crawled.

"When that's going on," he continued. "Clarissa and Isabella: destroy everything you see but, most importantly, the portal within the city center."

Clarissa raised her brow. *There was a portal in the city center?* Now that Amos mentioned it, Barmen had explained there being portals within certain cities but they were always heavily guarded. *Was it too dangerous to involve Isabella?*

Amos nodded, drawing her attention.

"You and your sister can create a fire tornado," he continued. "Burn the entire city to the ground and leave nothing left of Matthew's little assimilated cult stronghold. Once that's done, Nineteen and Twenty can open another portal so we can escape."

"What about my people?" Nineteen, also known as Gabriel Sr. and the Head Arch of the Gabriel clan, said. They had to start numbering the Head Archs because the Gabriel clan upheld a tradition of naming the ruler and heir the familial name. Considering Archangels lived for a long time, it's very confusing when more than one Gabriel sat in the same room.

"I can get them back," Noah Salutem spoke beside her. His ivory wings flared. "I know where they're going. I can join them."

Clarissa resisted the urge to roll her eyes. Noah reminded her of Flynn in some ways. A pathetic bleeding heart for the freaks and un-naturals of the world. A stupidly misguided superior.

"The jail cell the demons are holding everyone is a maze, idiot." She fired back, not bothering to hide her disdain. "There's no way you'd know your way around."

"Silence," a cold hiss sent shivers down her spine. Snakes sounded nicer than Sewall Ajudtor, Head Arch of the Azrael clan. "We aren't doing your plan." His black eyes narrowed onto Amos.

They argued, but Clarissa's mind wandered to another plan. She had wanted to utilize money from the demon realm to fund her city's reconstruction. She shuddered as thoughts of the alternative brushed against her psyche. She needed to get more money and resources; but how?

Heat spread from her arms to her neck and shoulders.

Her wings twitched and flared as she struggled to come up with a plan. She missed her chance when her meeting with Beelzebub, one of the demon lords, turned crazy. She wanted to create a trade business with the demon lord to generate revenue for her people, as Barmen did.

She winced at the sharp pain piercing her heart. Why did his betrayal hurt so much? She barely knew the heir to the Raziel clan. At 35 years old, nearly 10 years her senior, they never gave each other a second glance when growing up. Barmen Scio was just as mysterious to her as the other heirs in their world. Nonetheless, during the brief time he escorted them through the demon realm, she'd thought…

Another breeze drifted through her hair. Isabella again.

She glanced at her sister to ensure she was safe. Isabella curled in by her wings while tapping her fingers together. Her ombre hair started as red at the roots and faded to nearly blonde at the ends, making her green eyes stand out. The two physical reminders of the mother little Isabella never met. A memory flashed through Clarissa's mind: the first time she'd met her baby sister a few months after turning seven.

Their mother had just died from childbirth complications. Their father, stricken with grief, refused to hold Isabella and forbade anyone from touching her. The nurses had left her, unattended, on the changing table while she cried. Isabella cried and cried for so many hours Clarissa thought her ears would explode. She had marched into the room, fed up with her crying, and held Isabella close. Her baby sister immediately stopped crying in her arms. Isabella opened her eyes and pinned Clarissa in place. That was the first time Clarissa felt the warmth of her fire. The glow started from her heart and spread to her entire body as she clutched her sister. Isabella had been born during a horrible storm that raged on for hours, but when she stopped crying, the storm ceased, disappearing as if it never happened. Clarissa had been stunned by Isabella's power and her own.

Her father stormed in, flames sprouting from his hands, ready to reprimand her when Clarissa brought forth her flames. Shocked by her ability to call upon her power, her father's mouth dropped. He'd forgotten his anger at her for disobeying orders and replaced it with pride. He had the 'fiery' heir he wanted. Back then, she had been too enraptured by the tranquility of holding her baby sister and the newfound warmth in her body to notice. From then on, her life changed forever. They never left each other's sides.

Returning to the present moment, Clarissa's lips twitched as she thought about how their lives had been since that moment. Isabella's gaze darted between faces as the arguments in the room continued. The wind picked up ever so slightly, telling Clarissa more than words could say.

She reached out and grabbed Isabella's hand. Clarissa sensed Isabella's eyes on her as Clarissa turned back to the arguing Archs. The wind died down, and the twitching stopped, but the fire still burned within her. Blazing heat grew with every waking moment.

Off to the side, Amos gasped, clutching his head. His eyes squeezed together as if in pain. Clarissa opened her mouth to ask him what was wrong when something burst through the door. She flared her wings and bolted in front of Isabella. Flames erupted from her hands as she moved into a fighting stance.

A full minute went by as Clarissa registered the face before her. Barmen. Her flames sputtered and dwindled in her hands as he stepped forward. Blood painted his body; some dripped onto the floor as if he'd been swimming in a pool of blood, while a large hump of something hung over his shoulder. Barmen walked into the room with squelching sounds. His icy-blue eyes found hers with eerie accuracy. Her heart fluttered in her chest as he stopped his advance. Her eyes never left his.

"Glad everyone is here," Barmen panted.

Why was he out of breath? she thought. Before she could wonder further, Barmen threw a large hand onto the coffee table with a sickening, wet sound. Her jaw dropped as she turned back to notice a person, not a hump, was over his shoulder. Atarah's pale face came into focus slowly. *Atarah?!? What was she doing here?* She should've been back at their villa healing under Charlotte's careful watch. *What was going on?*

While they were stunned into silence, Barmen grabbed the drink Amos had set down earlier and shot it back in one gulp. His eyes found hers again as he set the glass down.

"There's something you should know before you go into the demon realm," Barmen spoke softly. His voice sounded as smooth as ever, a contrast to his horrific state.

She found her voice before any of the others.

"Where have you been?" She gritted, clenching her fists.

Barmen's eyes wandered up and down her body as if taking inventory. Usually, eyes crawling on her filled her with disgust, but for some reason, not his. He frowned ever so slightly.

"I've been busy trying not to get screwed over by dumbass heirs," Barmen murmured.

He gently lowered Atarah's body to one of the reclined couches. She lay limp, bleeding, and pale. A dagger was stabbed right into her heart. Noah, Clarissa, and Isabella moved to her side as soon as Barmen stepped away. Atarah had been under their roof and protection. What had happened to her?

Anger snaked its way through her limbs, sprouting fire in its wake. She crouched next to Atarah but didn't touch her. *Who had done this to her?* More fire sprouted along her head. *Whoever did it will pay,* she silently vowed. Isabella's horrified face turned to relief as she put pressure on the wound.

"She's still breathing!" Isabella exclaimed. "I sense the air moving in and out of her lungs."

Everyone in the room released a breath, except for Amos,

who sat still with eyes closed in concentration.

"Finished reading my mind yet, Selaphiel?" Barmen scoffed.

Amos' brow furrowed but he remained quiet. That didn't stop everyone else.

Joshua moved so fast that no one knew he was on Barmen until it was too late. He stepped mere inches from Barmen's face.

"It's always something with you, isn't it," Joshua scoffed. He spoke in a low voice, but Clarissa didn't hear an ounce of warmth or relief in his tone. "Go on, tell us what you've done."

Joshua's wings remained by his side while Barmen's flared wide.

Something in Joshua's stance bothered her. An uncomfortable twist entered her stomach; something was not right with Barmen and Joshua's relationship. She reacted before realizing what she was doing. Clarissa stepped to Barmen's side and allowed her flames to come forward. Blazing them so hot, Joshua had no choice but to step back from Barmen.

Both Archs frowned at her. Joshua in frustration from being forced back and Barmen in confusion.

"No one cares about your family drama," Clarissa proclaimed, pinning Joshua with a glare. "Isabella, keep pressure on Atarah's wound. Noah, is there anything you can do for Atarah?"

Noah lowered himself to Atarah's side, his lips pursed. "I'm not as skilled as the rest of my family, but I can keep her from dying."

His hands glowed over Atarah's still form. Clarissa and Barmen sighed.

"What do we need to know before going into the demon realm? Start with that," she demanded, drawing back her fire. A twitch of Barmen's lips gave Clarissa the briefest idea that he was amused with her. She shook the thought away, along with the feelings that came with it.

"Yes ma'am," Barmen murmured. He faced the group again with his wings relaxed. "Mikael, Arick, and Matthew were captured and taken by Satan, the strongest of the demon lords."

He indicated to the bloody hand on the table.

"Mikael threw the staff he had been given and got his hand chopped off as she teleported them out of there," he continued, "I barely made it out alive with Atarah in tow."

"The staff he had been given?" Sewall raised an eyebrow. "Explain."

"The staff that Ben made a deal for with Beelzebub and Leviathan," Clarissa hissed.

"Oh right," Nineteen murmured. "You were each roped into a one-sided deal. At any time Beelzebub or Leviathan can demand a favor from any of you."

Nineteen peered at his son, Twenty, who kept his gaze to the ground.

"Nearly all of the heirs, the future generation of leaders," Sewall sneered. "Owe a favor to two demon lords? The stupidity of youth amazes me sometimes."

Zewal and his sister, Tariel, stiffened at their father's scathing words.

"Never mind that," Twenty lifted his gaze to Barmen. "Why was Atarah in the demon realm in the first place? Where's Charlotte? Is she in danger?"

Barmen pursed his lips together. "She's not safe if that's what you mean. I swam out of there as soon as Satan arrived, my ability to use my powers can weaken around her."

"Was Elijah or Mikael around them?" Nineteen asked.

"Mikael was subduing Arick, who was going berserk—"

"Arick went berserk?" Noah's head popped up from concentration.

"Doesn't surprise me," Clarissa mumbled. *Of course, the halfling would go volatile and violent.* That kind of aggression was simply in his nature.

"Not the point," Barmen shook his head. "Mikael was comforting Arick when Satan arrived. Matthew was taken down by Arick and Ben..." His voice drifted off. Amos winced.

"I was leaving, so all that remained, I think, was Charlotte, Ben, Ava, Elijah, and a dozen or so of Gabriel's soldiers who were taken and experimented on. They were still in the deep depths of the prison when I left."

"Why did you leave them?" Venom melted into her voice before Clarissa could stop herself. The memory of Barmen's abandonment surfaced and stung. His gaze shifted to her.

"I do what's best for the realms," Barmen's voice deepened as his eyes pierced her again. "Don't be surprised if it doesn't align with what you want."

Her heart fluttered in her chest while fire coiled around her. *How did he have this much effect on her? Was this an illusion too?* She narrowed her eyes at him. *He's probably manipulating my reality now*, she thought. Barmen could never be trusted.

"We can still do the plan," Amos murmured with a furrowed brow. "If half of us attack from the north and the other half from the south, we could cause the city to crumble."

"Aren't you worried about the others?" Twenty cried accusingly. "We need to save them!"

"Were you not listening?" Amos rose from his seat, raising a hand to his head. "We attack the city, rescue those in need, and then return home promptly. It's about as simple of a plan as I can make it."

Clarissa liked this plan. Fire swirled around her veins, eager to be unleashed. A way for her to funnel this bubbling anger within her.

"The time to sit and twiddle our thumbs is over," Amos said vehemently. "It's time we fight back."

Sparks flickered from her fingertips.

"Who exactly are we fighting?" Isabella murmured under her breath.

"And who exactly is fighting back here, Amos?" Nineteen put a hand on Twenty's shoulder and pulled his son back to him. "The heirs need to stay here where it's safe."

Gabriel Jr. shook his head, but it was Tariel who spoke up.

"Atarah and Charlotte stayed back, but they still ended up in danger." Tariel crossed her arms.

"We don't know the full story of how they ended up in the demon realm." Joshua moved to pour himself a glass of amber liquid as he continued, "They probably were two disobedient heirs like the rest of you, going off on their own."

"Or," Twenty shook his father's hand off. "They were in danger and forced to the demon realm!" Twenty pivoted toward his father, quivering. "I'm going back to the demon realm and to find Charlotte. Don't try to stop me, father."

Nineteen's mouth opened partly, his hand frozen in the air half-reaching for his son.

"You can't possibly think—" Nineteen stuttered. "I'd never let you—"

"I can and you will." Twenty's wings trembled. While they faced off, the Azrael sibling duo stared down their father.

"You need our help, Father," Tariel said smoothly.

Sewall scoffed.

"The day I let my children into the demon realm will be over my cold, dead body. You two—" He jerked his chin. "—will return home, where you belong."

Zewal's wings slumped to the ground while Tariel squared her shoulders.

"*We* are going to the demon realm to fight for the ones we love." Tariel's eyes narrowed on her father as dark entrails swirled. Shadows shrouded around both of them as a silent struggle unfolded between them. Seconds ticked by like a steady drum, hammering at their hearts.

Finally, Sewall grunted and averted his eyes, his shadows falling in line behind him.

"You will stay close by, young lady," Sewall grumbled, "One move out of line and I'm throwing you through the portal with no warning."

The tiniest of smiles twitched along the corner of her lips. Zewal's black eyes darted back and forth between their father and Tariel before shaking his head.

"The baby gets away with everything," Zewal murmured so softly, that Clarissa wondered if she heard him right. Amos' voice pulled all of their attention as he stepped closer to Clarissa.

"That settles it. You, Twenty, Zewal, and Joshua are to go south of Ianua City." Amos turned to Nineteen. "Myself, Nineteen, Sewall, and Tariel are to go north of the city for the attack."

"Why are we splitting up?" Nineteen questioned. His hands clenched into fists.

"Because we need a Gabriel at both entry points for each team to escape. Joshua, Zewal, and Clarissa are going with him. Each of them is a powerful Arch, they'll be fine together." he indicated to Noah. "Get Atarah to a secure place since you're the only one who can heal her."

Noah gave a grim nod, his eyes furrowed in concentration. Barmen, somehow, shifted closer to her. His wings flared.

"I'm going with the team to the south." Barmen declared.

Joshua gulped the drink he poured down his throat. He loudly swallowed before setting the glass down.

"Oh?" Joshua raised an eyebrow at Barmen. "You think going is a good idea?"

Barmen's lips pursed together but remained silent.

"All the same. The more on our teams, the less likely things are to go bad." Amos removed his hand from his face.

Clarissa saw dark circles under his eyes and a depth of emotion in his brown eyes that had her pause. *Was he ok?* She wondered.

"Are we all in agreement then?" Amos sighed, looking each of them in the eyes. "It's a simple plan to execute."

"Guerrilla warfare style," Tariel nodded.

"We're ready." Clarissa stepped forward.

She forced her flames back as she grabbed Isabella's hand. Her little sister's head darted between her and Amos. After a few seconds, Isabella nodded.

"As long as I'm with you, I'm ready," Isabella whispered.

Amos frowned. "We need Isabella to come with my group."

Seconds ticked by as his words sunk in. Clarissa chuckled. A short huff of air of disbelief. Amos didn't think he was going to split them, did he?

Amos nodded his head with a solemn expression.

The flames threatened to erupt from her chest. She released her sister's hand as her body temperature rose. Her wings vibrated as she opened her mouth to rebuke Amos, but he held up his hand.

"Clarissa," Amos said softly, "Hear me out. With Isabella in the north, she can cast a wind current around the city. When you attack from the south, the heat from your flames will meet the cold wind from the north and create a fire tornado in the heart of the city. Remember, we want to cause as much damage as possible, that means you need to be in opposite directions."

A wind gust swirled around them. A few papers flapped in the air, adding noise to the chaos. Twitching hands and wings called her attention and pulled her back from anger.

Isabella needed her to be strong and calm.

She relaxed her face to something more soothing before turning to her little sister. Isabella's wings were flared and vibrating. Her hands picked at her nail beds, while her eyes were glued to the floor. Her breathing was steady and even, which was a good sign. They were rarely apart from each other, because, together, they gave each other strength. Separated was equivalent to going into battle with one arm chopped off. No one knew the truth of this except them.

However, Amos was right. Their combined attack of a fire tornado required them to be on opposite sides of the battlefield. This was the largest tornado they would ever create, which required more distance. Clarissa gritted her teeth as Isabella's green eyes searched for guidance. A word from her was all Isabella needed.

"Amos is right," Clarissa started in a strained voice. "We'll have the most impact if you go north."

Isabella's wings faltered for a moment as she raised her head. "Will you be disappointed if I can't do this?"

Isabella's eyes widened, waiting for Clarissa's answer.

"I'll be disappointed if we don't do this plan," Clarissa answered honestly. She wanted to fight back so much her flames threatened to burst from the top of her head. She couldn't hide that from her sister.

"Do you think I can do this?" Isabella murmured. "This will be the biggest wind manipulation I've ever done."

"I know you can do this." Clarissa didn't hesitate. "You've done bigger ones before. Keep breathing."

The wind died around them. Isabella's shoulders and wings relaxed away from her ears. All the fear she saw in her little sister's eyes faded away. A word from her big sister was all she needed. Warmth spread to every corner of her body. The faith Isabella had in her kept her going. She vowed to always live up to those expectations.

She faced Amos again. The fire from within reached her eyes.

"We're ready," she exclaimed.

Amos nodded. "Very well. Everyone gather around their Gabriel angel."

Barmen stepped closer behind her. His wings brushed hers ever so slightly, shooting goosebumps along her arms.

Her heart skipped a beat as the smell of smoke and amber drifted to her nose. Though they stood eye to eye in height, his wing span was larger than hers. Encasing her. She waited for the disgust and slimy feeling that came with someone coming too close to her, but none came.

Her flames glowed warmer. Soothed.

"Zewal, Joshua, Clarissa, and Barmen," Amos drew her attention back to the present. "Gather around Gabriel Jr.— oh I mean Twenty. Isabella, you'll come with me, Nineteen, Sewall and Tariel. We'll reunite with the teams back here, in Joshua's library, in no time."

Isabella's gaze darted between her and Barmen a few times before shuffling closer to Amos. Clarissa forced her face to remain expressionless but failed. The fire within her eyes gave her away.

"If anything happens to my sister..." Her eyes were on Amos nodding as her flames sprouted from her hands. "I understand."

Barmen's lips twitched. "Trinity, help anyone who crosses you."

Joshua chose that moment to move to the other side of her very closely. She stiffened as the sensation of worms crawling beneath her skin spread. She sensed his eyes scanning her from head to toe. She flared her wings and let her fire spring out from her skin. Joshua stepped back, his wings flared.

"Trinity, help anyone who tries to befriend you either," Joshua said.

Barmen moved to her back so his chest was nearly touching her fire. He showed no fear of her flames, only slight annoyance at his father. The withering sensation beneath her skin disappeared. Much to her surprise, she felt...protected.

Her wings relaxed.

"Come along now," Zewal huffed, "We don't have all day."

Nineteen grabbed Twenty by the shoulders firmly. "Don't

do anything rash, son. You transport them there and come straight back here, nothing else, you hear me?" He gave his son a shake.

Twenty grimaced. "I will try, Father."

"Don't try. Do!" Nineteen gave another shake. "If anything happens to you, our line is lost."

Twenty sighed and gave a reluctant nod. "I understand."

Nineteen jerked his son into a tight embrace for a few seconds before moving to the opposite side of the room. Twenty shuffled closer to her, Barmen, and Joshua. Once everyone was in their respective groups, the two Gabriels clapped their hands together and glowed.

A bright light shined between their hands. A thin, glowing strip quickly turned into a large, blazing portal as they pulled the portal open. Its heat blended into her flames, blasting heat into the room.

"I'll see you soon, Izzy," Clarissa called out to her sister. She infused confidence into every word. She *would* find her sister again. If she had to destroy everything in her path, she would. Her words had the intended effect, as Isabella straightened her shoulders and lifted her chin high.

"On the count of three, jump through!" Amos yelled over the rushing sound of the portals. "One! Two! Three!"

On three, Clarissa dashed through the portal, Barmen right behind her, followed by Joshua, then Zewal, and lastly Gabriel Jr. The free-falling sensation of traveling through the portal caused her stomach to clench. Gravity pushed and pulled her, stalling the air in her lungs. For a few long seconds, she wondered if she'd throw up without the ability to breathe. *Was that possible?*

Mercifully, traveling through the portal didn't take long. Like falling in a dream and being jerked awake, they were there. She stumbled forward as her stomach heaved. She hunched over breathing in through her nose and out through her mouth. She needed to get it together. She closed her eyes.

"That's right, you and your sister get travel sickness," she heard Gabriel Jr. mumble. Now that there was only one Gabriel angel around, they could call him just Gabriel for simplicity's sake. "The more you move around the faster the sickness will go away."

Walking was the last thing she wanted to do. She slowly straightened up and put both hands on top of her head, taking deep breaths. The deep breathing helps with the motion sickness and prepares her body to manipulate her flames. She needed to focus. She remembered her training, gathering her flames into the pit of her belly, building the pressure needed to shoot through her arms.

"Hmmmm," Zewal's low tone peppered with disapproval. "Where in the trinity are we?"

Her eyes shot open.

A dense tropical jungle surrounded them, buzzing with noises from all around. A loud chorus of cicadas echoed along with the croaks of frogs and chirps of birds. Large trees and thick brush reminded her of her home, Aqua Caput. Beady eyes peered at them from between large banana leaves. The sound of rushing water drew her attention to her left. She saw a large, murky delta teeming with large dragonflies.

They all turned to a red-faced Gabriel Jr. with clenched fists.

"Where did you bring us, Gabriel?" Clarissa said through gritted teeth.

"I—I don't...I thought—" he stuttered, his face somehow growing redder. "I'm not used to teleporting to the demon realm. It's like jumping with your eyes closed."

"What?!?" She roared. Flames sprouted from her arms and head.

"I'm s-s-sorry I...I—" Gabriel Jr.'s voice drifted off. His head hung low.

Clarissa froze. If they weren't south of Ianua City, she and Isabella couldn't create the tornado. They couldn't go through with the plan if they weren't there! Her stomach clenched again for an entirely different reason now.

A loud cough to her right drew her attention. Barmen lifted a finger into the jungle. Following his hand, her eyes widened at the sight before her. A turquoise metropolis stood before them. Flowing aqueducts moved boats to and from the city at a rapid speed. Large buildings connected with vine bridges and extending branches. Creatures and demons in the distance walked around the city, oblivious to their arrival.

The sound of flowing water…

A slithering sensation arrived under her skin again. This time, she didn't bother to hold back her anger. Her fire honed itself to a laser point. Her breathing technique from earlier built the pressure from inside her. The color red bled from her periphery into the center of her vision. She heard her name being called out, but she barely registered it. As if someone was yelling underwater, it sounded muffled.

Her green tunic, made with volcanic rock, melded to her body as her fire grew hot and engulfed her. The smell of ash and burning leaves drifted into the air. She expanded her wings, smoke following her movement. She launched herself into the air, blasting heat and black soot in her wake. Her fire encased her, protecting her, shielding her first. With her fire propelling her forward, she reached the first tall building within a minute.

She heard a single scream and then nothing as she unleashed her flames. Her body was pure heat. From the flames she was born from, she burned.

She torched. She destroyed.

Shooting her flames from her hands and feet, everything close to her turned to ash. She saw the building crumble and the horrified expressions of demons, but the red haze of her vision skewed everything. She needed to burn more. She needed to blaze hotter.

She moved on to the next building and the next and the

next. Her flames burned so hot that no one could come near her. Smoke billowed from her path of destruction. A voice called out her name, and she paused. There was something important in the voice, but she couldn't remember why. The nagging feeling that something was wrong surfaced, but she wasn't sure why.

The voice called out her name again, and her red vision cleared some. She cooled her flames.

"Clarissa!"

Blue eyes, she thought. *Do those eyes belong to someone important to me?* She reached a hand out to the one with icy eyes.

A violent hiss came at her from behind.

"You're not getting away with this that easily, *Arch.*"

A hard blow to her head. The blue eyes shone with rage before darkness engulfed her vision.

Chapter 2

Weeks earlier...

Mosquitos buzzed in the sweltering heat, swarming around him and his team. Flynn grunted as he shoveled the last of the dirt out of the construction zone. Sweat dripped from his brow as he slumped against one of the coconut trees to catch his breath. His team of rangers was in no better shape. They clustered together under the shade of the trees for a small break. Heat exhaustion took over, leaving everyone tired and thirsty at the end of the day. The rangers had been doing manual labor for a week now. They worked in 16-hour shifts in an effort to help rebuild Aquam Caput. Hammering, sawing wood, shoveling dirt, cleaning roads and the riverways, everything to get the city back on its feet. Flynn's back ached so fiercely, his wings dragged behind him.

Jose, who leaned against the tree next to him, gulped down the last of his canteen. He groaned when no more water came out, no matter how much he tipped it back.

"I just came back from the water station," Jose complained. "I don't wanna fly all the way back again."

"You could always walk," Flynn mumbled as he leaned his head back against the tree.

His own water jug needed to be filled, but he was too tired to move. Sahra shuffled over and extended her canteen to Jose.

"Here," she murmured. "You can have some of mine."

"Hey!" a voice yelled from above.

He squinted his eyes at the angel flying above them. It was a Uriel angel carrying a bag of cement.

He glared at Flynn before sneering, "Get back to work, freaks!"

Flynn wondered for the hundredth time: *why bother helping the angels rebuild their city?* It's not as if he or any of the other rangers lived there. Worse, the angels that lived in the spirit realm treated them as if they were slaves to their bidding.

The fire within him burned, baffled that he once thought such treatment was normal. *Not anymore*, he reminded himself. Gritting his teeth, he rose to his feet.

"I think I'll make a trip over to the water station after all." Flynn's hands steamed.

"Hey," Jose called out, "It's ok, Flynn. Let's just ignore them."

Flynn paused. "Do you want me to refill your canteen or not?"

Another stretch of silence passed before Jose answered.

"Yeah, here you go." Jose's hand clasped Flynn's shoulder.

Standing so close, Flynn had no choice but to tilt his head to look at Jose. Flynn grabbed the canteen as Jose's brow furrowed.

"Don't do anything reckless, brother," Jose whispered, lifting his hand away.

Flynn gave a crooked smile. "No need to worry about me," he replied before taking off into the sky. The wind was a welcome relief from the blazing sun, but it only lasted for a few seconds. Once the breeze disappeared, he regretted volunteering. Without the tree's shade, the sun gave its undivided attention. Heat waves rolled over him, sapping the energy from him.

Sweat pooled down his face as he flew to the water station. Today's priority was rebuilding the docks of Aquam Caput, to set up trade once more. Nothing crippled a city faster than economic stagnation. The citizens of Aquam Caput set up water stations everywhere in the city, but very few near the docks where the rangers were stationed.

He landed on his hands and knees along the hillside, panting for breath. Droplets of sweat rained from his face as he recovered. The nearest water station was a mile into the city. He still had about half a mile to fly.

He brought his knee forward to launch himself again when a motion out of the corner of his eye caught his attention. He tilted his head to see a young angel, kneeling in the shade of a tree. She had short, red hair that went along with her red wings. She peered at him over a large banana leaf that expanded larger than her body. Flynn wouldn't have seen her if she had stayed still. She extended a hand.

Flynn shook his head, thinking she was begging for money when he saw she held out a cracked coconut. The liquid contents sloshed around as her thin arm trembled. Flynn's throat burned with the need for water. Her eyes shone with sincerity and concern for him.

His wings hummed as he reached for the coconut.

As his hand made contact, another Uriel angel swooped from below and knocked the drink from both their hands. "Dumb brat, you can't share with rangers. They're traitorous freaks."

The young angel squealed, ducking behind the banana leaf. Flynn rose to his feet to regard the Uriel angel hovering a few feet from the ground. The stranger possessed white hair and red eyes that intensified the glare delivered to the young girl. Wind danced around his wings.

"I'm...I'm....I'm" The young angel stuttered, her wings shaking behind her.

Her knuckles whitened from clenching the large leaf. The only form of protection she had.

The newcomer didn't wait for her reply. The stranger brought back his hand to strike the female. She whimpered and ducked her head, waiting for the blow. Flynn moved at lightning speed, grabbing the male's hand before he could strike her.

"Don't start trouble where there is none," Flynn whispered back to the stranger.

The wind whirled around them as the stranger's face shifted from one of disgust to rage.

"You filthy little—"

"Ah, ah, ah. One wrong move." Flynn snapped two fingers from his free hand. A flame flickered to life. "And you'll encase yourself in flames."

Tension held for long seconds before the white-haired angel shook him off.

"Can't wait till you weirdos are out of our country." The angel scoffed before flying away. Once he was out of sight, Flynn extinguished the flame from his hand. A soft gasp drew his attention back to the young female. She couldn't be more than 8 years old but he second-guessed himself as he spotted her thin limbs. Starvation tended to stunt growth as he knew all too well.

"Here you go," he said softly, extending the empty shell. "I'm sorry."

Her green eyes flickered between the coconut and him. With trembling limbs, she walked forward to take the coconut. She wore a ragged, green tunic with patches around the joints.

"You didn't knock it down," she murmured. "No need for you to apologize."

Flynn's lips twitched.

"I'm going to the water station," Flynn started. "Want to come with?"

Her wings jumped. Uncertainty swam in her eyes with the same question he had when he grew up in Aquam Caput. *Can this person be trusted?*

"I'll bring the water instead. How about that?" Flynn proposed.

Relief filled her eyes as she nodded. Another movement from behind caught his eye. A smaller angel emerged from behind the banana leaf. Flynn didn't see all of the angel's features.

"What are your names?" Flynn gazed back at the young female.

"My name is Raya, and behind me is Jym."

"Is he your little brother?"

Raya shook her head and scooted back. Flynn frowned. They weren't far from the makeshift orphanage Clarissa erected. These little ones were probably from there.

"I'll be back," Flynn said softly.

Raya ducked behind the leaves again.

"That's what they all say." Raya's small voice drifted to him from the foliage.

His wings twitched as his heart squeezed for these two children.

He launched himself into the sky. He vowed to send Sahra over to the orphanage tonight. Aquam Caput possessed many problems before the demons attacked, one of them centering around the children. The Elementa region didn't have many laws that protected children, thus making exploitation easy. Since the city had been sacked, many children had been left to fend for themselves even more so. Without the protection of parents, it was a free-for-all. The orphanage was the only safe place for them.

Flynn ground his teeth together. He remembered all too well how Elementa treated their children. Old wounds and memories of starvation, beatings, and long work days flashed through his mind. Memories that reminded him of why he escaped to join the rangers.

The water station came into view as he curved around the last building. Dozens swarmed the table; everyone shouted over one another, trying to fill their jugs. Two exhausted-looking water benders panted as they maneuvered the water. Flynn's eyebrow rose in surprise.

Angels who controlled water were in high demand to fix the ports. Malachi wanted their trade system back up and running as soon as possible. Flynn was surprised any water benders would be spared to dispense water. Normally, the job fell to the angels who manipulated the wind. Those angels were the fastest to transport clean water to the people. Were the ports back up and running?

As the question floated through his head, a large shadow flew over the crowd. All eyes turned to the blood-orange wings descending upon the water stand. Malachi Ignis, the Head Archangel over all of Elementa, landed on top of the table. A hush came over the crowd as everyone waited for their leader to speak.

Malachi's bright red hair pooled around his shoulders. His face, covered in soot, scowled at the two water users.

"What are you two doing here?" Malachi howled at the workers.

"We…we…ah," one of them sputtered.

The other angel stepped forward.

"We heard there was a desperate need for water," he paused. "We came to help the people."

Malachi's voice dropped, "And you think I'm not helping my people?" Flames licked along his hands as he hopped from the table and slowly approached the two. "You think you know what's better for my people than I do? That following my orders isn't within the best interest of the people at large?"

Every step Malachi took, the angels took two steps back until their backs hit the side of a building.

"No—No, sir," one stammered as Malachi towered over them. "We just tho—ought to—"

"Thought that disobeying me was the better alternative, eh?" Malachi sneered. The flames flickering in his hand sharpened to a torch-like point from his fingertips. "Do you know angels who step out of line cause worse problems than demons ever could?"

Both angels trembled with fear. The sour stench of terror reached Flynn's nostrils, spurring him out of his bystander daze.

"Please, please, my lord," one pleaded while the other whimpered. "We meant no offense!"

"Then you should've followed my orders!" Malachi raised his hand, torched with fire, to strike.

Flynn had enough.

He dove down, dashing past the silent crowd. As Malachi's hand swung down to strike, Flynn darted to his side and snatched his wrist, inches away from the angel's neck. Their fires clashed, fighting for dominance.

"Enough, cousin. You need every water bender you can get to work on the docks." Flynn's arms shook as his muscles threatened to give out. "Don't get hot-headed now."

Something flickered in Malachi's eyes as the anger receded. An emotion Flynn didn't have time to identify. The flames died as they lowered their arms.

"Get back to work," Malachi growled. "If I see anyone else slacking, I'll toss them into the demon realm to get eaten. Or worse, drop you off at a seraphim's feet."

"Yes, my lord!" they shouted in unison.

Flynn smelled the urine that must have been dripping down their legs. He shook his head in pity. No citizen should ever fear their leader. Flynn missed his teammates back in the human realm and missed Luke's odd but fair leadership style. He craved peace from being part of a safe family, despite the surroundings.

A memory of the little orphan from earlier flashed through his mind, and anger slowly burned in his chest. He clenched his fists as he faced Malachi, who peered down at him.

"It's been a long time since you've called me that," Malachi murmured.

"What?" Flynn scoffed. "Hot-headed? A bit of an understatement if I do say so."

Malachi's lips twitched, further infuriating him.

"No," Malachi grunted. "Cousin."

Flynn paused. It had been years since he'd acknowledged his family line.

"It won't happen again," he muttered. "Besides, I need to speak with you."

Malachi scoffed back at Flynn, before turning his heels and walking away. "Make it quick. I have work to do."

"You asshole," Flynn whispered as he scurried after him. He had to take three steps to keep up with one of Malachi's. "We need to talk about the rangers going back home before we break our backs fixing yours."

Flynn huffed as they marched south to the docks.

Malachi snorted. The crowd parted as they stormed by. Citizens' heads hung low, never daring to make eye contact with the Head Arch.

"And you need to give water and supplies to the orphanage close by."

Malachi slowed his pace.

"Orphanage?" he raised an eyebrow at Flynn and chuckled. "That thing Clarissa set up?"

The anger burned hotter in his chest.

"Yes, the thing Clarissa set up," Flynn growled.

His cousin held the same beliefs as the rest of the elites in Elementa. Children were tools, not something to be cared for. They came to a stop just before the harbor. Dozens of merchant vessels shined with new engines and modern designs lined the shipyard in front of them. The stern was narrow with a wide port and starboard for loading items and goods. The power of their ships came from the water benders, the stronger the bender the faster the ship would be.

Flynn's eyes narrowed as he spotted the strongest water

bender in all of Elementa. Flames licked at his fingertips.

Paul turned around as if sensing his glare.

"AY!" Paul bellowed. "Brother! I was just looking for you!"

Paul didn't acknowledge Flynn.

"I had them go back to their stations," Malachi murmured, lowering his gaze to his feet.

Paul clicked his tongue and shook his head.

"You should have burned a leg off or two to punish them." Paul pat Malachi on the back again. "But you've always been a softy."

"Bastard." The word slipped through Flynn's teeth before he could stop it.

A loud silence stretched as Malachi and Paul slowly turned their heads to him. Paul peered down his nose at him before stepping into his personal space.

"Oh, cousin, I didn't see you there." Faster than Flynn could react, Paul ruffled his hair and smirked. "Long time no see buddy. Why don't you come to visit more often? Probably because you're just as much of a failure there as you were here. It's always something with you, isn't it? Poor Aunt Jen. She can never be proud of you. No one can."

A mixture of shame and anger swirled in him. The flames moved from his fingertips to his whole hand. Paul had a way to disarm and cut you open with a few words. Paul kept his face tranquil and jovial to trick others into thinking he was a nice guy, but it made his stomach churn.

Flynn scoffed. Paul was the serpent and Malachi the flower. He smacked Paul's hand away.

"Keep my mother's name out of your mouth," Flynn's voice deepened as disgust and hatred pooled in his gut.

The lowlife had the nerve to look concerned.

"Oh? This weak ranger still likes to cause problems, I see." Paul sighed. "I had hoped the rangers would make you more grateful for the life given to you here, but I can see,"

Paul whispered as he grinned at Flynn. "You haven't changed at all, little bit. You're the same inconsiderate brat."

Malachi must've heard the snap in Flynn's control, for Malachi stepped between them before Flynn torched the bastard.

"That's enough Paul," Malachi growled. "Go back to the docks while I talk with Flynn."

"Whatever you say, big bro. You're the boss." Paul smirked at Flynn as he backed away.

Flynn's wings stayed flared until Paul was out of sight.

"You can't start fights every time you come back here, Flynn." Malachi groaned, turning to face him.

"You need to figure out who the real bad guys are," Flynn pinched the bridge of his nose. "You think everyone else is the problem but the ones responsible for it."

"No, Flynn," Malachi grumbled. "You're the problem. Paul has done nothing but help this family and this city."

"Oh, through his oh-so-generous heart, right?" Flynn drawled. "What did he want in return for the money he put toward rebuilding the city, Malachi? Why do you think Clarissa's so desperate to find another way to fund the rebuild of the city?"

Flames erupted from Malachi's head.

"Do not bring my daughter into this!" Malachi nearly roared.

"She's already been brought into this!" Flynn flared his wings; heat spread along his own scalp. "Dammit Malachi! You could be so much better, but you're choosing the easy way out as a leader!"

"I'm choosing the easy way out?!" Malachi's face screwed into a sneer as he crouched mere inches from his face. "That's rich coming from someone who abandoned us! Left us for the rangers. I'm the one trying to keep everything together here!"

"At the expense of your citizens?" he countered. "At the expense of your daughters?"

Fire sprang all along their wings. Heat coated him from the inside out. They glared at each other as their fire crackled around them. Flynn held his glare. For so long he'd thought he was the problem in this family. Only when he lived with the rangers did he see what a real family was. When he witnessed how Luke led, he understood true leadership.

Memories of the rangers brought him down from his anger; the rangers reminded him of his main objective in searching for Malachi. Just because his cousin refused to become a better leader didn't mean he couldn't be better. Flynn sighed as he pulled in his flames.

"We need to return home." Flynn huffed. "Ask Gabriel to take us, and we will be out of your hair."

"Done!" Malachi hissed.

"And," Flynn paused to soften his voice. "Those kids need supplies, Malachi."

"They're Clarissa's project." Malachi sneered. "Take the issue up with her."

"She already has enough on her plate, don't you think?" Flynn dropped his voice as he nodded to the docks. "She can't do everything for you."

"She should've thought of that before putting up that damn building!" Malachi growled.

Without warning, his cousin turned his heels and stormed off, flames still sprouting from his head. Once Malachi was out of sight, Flynn slumped his wings to the ground. He ran his hand through his hair to pat out his own flames. He was just as much of a hothead as Malachi. Maybe Paul was right?

Flynn shook his head fiercely. *No*, he thought, *Paul lies no matter what.*

The abrupt movement moved his gaze down to the empty canteen by his side. Flynn groaned. He told Jose that he would return with water, and instead, he got sidetracked as usual. The others must've wondered where he was. He turned to head back up the hill, once again for the water station, when something caught his eye. A large, brown bag flew at him.

He jerked his arms up to catch each of them. The bag was filled with coconuts.

"Don't say I didn't do anything for ya!" Malachi bellowed from the docks down below.

Flynn's lips twitched. Despite his anger, Malachi remembered the water. Flynn's smile dissipated as he turned to face that god-forsaken hill…again.

He launched himself into the air, ignoring his aching, tired body. He was needed by the orphans and his own soldiers. They were finally going home.

He didn't have to fly far to reach where Raya hid. The children were in plain view talking to another person Flynn didn't want to speak with. Another family member, Clarissa.

Clarissa's red wings reflected the sunlight as she raised them high to provide more shade for the children. Raya, while apprehensive with him, embraced Clarissa with warmth and excitement. Flynn's descent to the ground drew Raya's attention. Raya shyly waved and smiled while clinging to Clarissa's leg.

"Never thought you had a way with children." Flynn landed a few feet from Clarissa, who raised an eyebrow at him.

"Never thought you were that shitty with them." Clarissa fired back.

Raya gasped as she peered up at the heir.

"Oops," Clarissa mumbled. "I mean bad."

"We aren't supposed to say bad words." Raya scolded her. Clarissa crouched to Ray's eye level.

"You're right Raya," Clarissa replied softly. "We need to use words that show how smart we are, not how mean we are."

"If you're real smart, you'll learn to do both," Flynn murmured as he dug one of the coconuts out of the bag. "Here Raya. Take this and share it with the others."

Raya's eyes widened.

"You're giving us a whole coconut?" Raya gasped.

Her hand reached out tentatively, as if afraid. Flynn frowned.

"Yes." He pushed the coconut into her arms.

She was so tiny, that the coconut took up much of her torso. Flynn's frown deepened. He will command his troops to hand over every ration they have to the orphans before they leave.

"Thank you!" Raya cried out before turning around. "He really came back, Jym!"

A small head popped out from behind the banana leaf. The small angel, Flynn presumed to be Jym, scrambled to grab hold of Clarissa's other leg, peering at him.

"They told me a red-haired male tried to coax them to follow him." Clarissa narrowed her eyes. "You should know better than to be a creep."

Flynn scoffed. "I forget how messed up your society is when a lone child can't trust someone of the royal family."

"We trust Clarizzzza." Raya crossed her arms. "She's good."

Clarissa glanced at the little girl beside her. Something in her expression softened at Raya's defense.

"Yes, she is good." Flynn conceded. Clarissa and Isabella might be the only two good souls in the entire royal family. "I'll send one of my troops to bring supplies to the orphanage before we move out."

"You're leaving," Clarissa said more in a statement than a question.

Flynn nodded.

This time it was Clarissa's turn to scoff. "You're that eager to leave us?"

Bitterness coated her words and stabbed him through the heart. Flynn winced. Clarissa and Isabella were two of the biggest regrets he had. He stuck around for a few years after their mother died and would have stayed if not for their assholes of an uncle and father.

"Please Clarissa," Flynn pleaded. "Come join the rangers."

"Again with those freaks." Clarissa sneered. She lowered her wings to cover the children, who looked at her with wide eyes. "They only want for themselves. They have no real loyalty."

Flynn opened his mouth to protest when a loud gong signaled the end of the day. His soldiers needed him to return with water. Flynn's wings slumped to the ground. He's run out of time. Clarissa picked up the two children and held them close.

"Come on little ones," Clarissa flared her wings wide. "Let's get you home."

Without another word, Clarissa launched herself into the sky. Raya peered over Clarissa's shoulder; her small hand waved as they disappeared over the clouds, leaving Flynn in despair.

Chapter 3

Red sand stretched as far as the eye could see. If they were lost out in the ocean, they'd drown, but out here in the desert, Charlotte was sure they would wither away. The sun blazed down on them without mercy nor a cloud in sight.

While the sun was horrible, the thirst was driving her insane. Charlotte lifted a tender hand to her throat. Her lips blistered from a lack of water. She smacked them together in a vain attempt to produce some saliva. Her dry tongue yearned for any kind of moisture. Her skin reddened with the signs of sunburn on her shoulder and, no doubt, her face. She moved her hand to touch her face and winced. A stinging, burning pain radiated from her cheek to her nose and forehead. She pulled a torn part of her tunic to cover her head again and hissed in pain. They needed to find shelter soon.

Charlotte raised her head to see how the rest of their party was doing. Her father, Elijah, and her sister, Ava, trudged ahead on the large sand dunes. They'd been leading their group ever since they landed in the open desert, searching for any form of shelter. A single day had passed traveling, and the sand dunes appeared endless.

Last night, it dropped to freezing temperatures while the day proved to be scorching.

Makoto and a dozen other Gabriel angels had gathered enough power to transport them out of that underground prison. While away from immediate danger, now she worried that they'd die slowly of dehydration. She drained the last of her water a few hours ago and was desperate for more.

Makoto and the other angels' bodies were in a weak state. Each of them had been tortured, bled, and experimented on for who knew how long. Their wings were withered and damaged to the point where flight was impossible, and their thin limbs trembled with every step, with exposed skin blistered worse than her own.

Charlotte knew they needed to get to safety before she and her family could tend to their wounds. She peered at Makoto's shoulder. Blood seeped through his torn tunic, but he remained silent. None of them spoke a word. Only their panting breaths reached her ears. She chewed on her bottom lip.

Maybe they should stop just for a few minutes? She thought as she watched the remaining feathers fall off their wings. They were nearing the top of a sand dune when one of the angel's knees buckled, sending him tumbling into the sand. Charlotte jerked forward to stop his body from slipping all the way down. She grunted as she dug her feet into the sand, barely stopping herself from sliding.

A shout alerted the others to their stumble. A hand from behind lifted her gently.

"Stand steady," Canaan's hoarse voice rasped.

As she helped the Gabriel angel to his feet, she

peeked back at Canaan and Ben. Her stomach curled.

Ben's ears were crusted with blood that drained to his face, shoulders, and chest. His sunken eyes appeared devoid of life as his wings dragged across the sand. Dried blood coated his tunic, arms, legs, and wings. Atarah's blood.

Charlotte paled as a sharp pain stabbed through her heart. Atarah.

Canaan winced right as Ben stiffened. His dead eyes jerked to hers as Canaan stepped away. Her blood ran cold as his gaze narrowed on her. A spark of something ignited in his expression but disappeared within an instant.

A rush of wind drew all of their attention.

"Are you both all right?" Elijah landed softly beside her. He grabbed the angel's arm and hooked it around his shoulder to lift him. "Do you think you can keep going?" he asked in a gentle tone.

"I think we need to stop, Father." She huffed.

"No," The Gabriel angel rasped. "I can keep going."

Elijah frowned but nodded. "I'll help you the rest of the way. Lean on me."

"Father—" she protested.

"We're almost there, Charlotte." Ava's voice called down from the top.

"Almost there?" Canaan's eyes widened.

A few heads popped up, and hope shone in every face.

"We saw a building on the other side of this large dune," Elijah explained, "We'll seek shelter there tonight."

"Finally," Makoto sighed a few feet away. "Some

luck on our side."

"Maybe we can find out where the hell we are," another chimed in.

They trudged up the dune with more urgency. She panted as she hiked up the dune. Her feet sunk deep into the sand with each step. Two steps equaled one step forward with sand. Her calves burned fiercely by the time she made it to the top. The wind picked up around them, blowing sand in their faces.

Ava stood at the peak, peering down the other side with squinted eyes. Charlotte followed her gaze to see a white building against the red sand, no more than two levels high. Nothing moved below. Was the place abandoned? She surveyed the area and saw nothing. Not even a bird or bug scurrying about. Was this place safe?

Canaan joined her, followed by Ben. Neither looked impressed.

"I should go first and scope the area to make sure it's safe," Makoto spoke out first as the last of their party arrived at the top.

"Hang on, wait," Elijah turned to Canaan. "Can you hear anything from here?" Elijah asked, easing the Gabriel angel onto his own feet.

Canaan frowned. "I hear thoughts, but it's not exactly words or dialogue. It's more just pictures flashing through their head."

"Pictures of what?" Charlotte asked, her wings curled in close to her body.

"The house and," Canaan paused, "Strange-looking animals."

"Any animals with sharp teeth or spears in their hands?" Makoto sighed.

"I don't see any weapons…" Canaan said with hesitancy.

"That's good enough for me," Makoto ambled down the dune. "We need shelter or else we'll fry out here."

"Canaan, go with him," Elijah indicated to Makoto.

"You'll be able to hear any danger long before he will."

Canaan glanced at his little brother. Ben stood there stoically, tilting his head whenever Elijah spoke but otherwise remained motionless. Charlotte frowned. He'd screamed that he couldn't hear anyone, not their thoughts or spoken words, but he appeared to hear her father.

She stepped closer to him as Canaan nodded to Elijah.

"Best to get going then," Canaan murmured with a furrowed brow.

He slid down the steep dune, catching up with Makoto in no time. While the others watched their journey, Charlotte's focus stayed on Ben.

His dead eyes stared ahead. His wings wilted behind him from being dragged along the ground. She lifted her hand again to his ears. He didn't protest or push her away. He didn't acknowledge her at all, as if she wasn't there.

She focused her energy to laser in on his ears. The cool touch of her powers flowed from her arms to the sides of Ben's head. She concentrated on finding the spot where the blood flowed. Her hands glowed as she regenerated the damaged tissue. Piece by piece, she repaired further into the ear canal, traveling deeper into his skull. The bleeding through his ears stopped.

She frowned again. The damage wasn't just in his ears but somewhere in his brain. She lowered her arms and waited. Ben's gaze didn't falter. Within a few minutes, blood spilled from his ears again; the wound refused to close.

"Same as before?" Her father's voice drew her attention. She nodded solemnly.

"I can't get the bleeding to stop." She sighed. "I heal as far as I can without risking further brain damage, but it doesn't help."

She'd tried to heal Ben when they first escaped the prison, but the result was the same. She couldn't fully heal him. All the other cuts, scrapes, and bruises on his body healed except for his ears. The rest of the blood on him remained from lying in a large pool of blood, trying to save Atarah.

Another sharp pain stabbed through her heart.

She gasped as tears sprang to her eyes. A heavy hand rested on her shoulder.

"Easy there, little Charlotte," her father soothed. "One day, sometimes even one breath at a time."

A single tear fell from her face. She clutched her chest to keep herself from breaking down into a sobbing mess. She lost her best friend, her family. Now, she couldn't do anything. She gritted her teeth as frustration sparked through her.

"Breathe, daughter." Elijah's hand on her shoulder tightened. "Breathe. I know it hurts, love."

She gasped. Air rushed in and a dam within her burst. She crumbled to the ground and sobbed. Arms and ivory wings circled her before she hit the ground. She curled her face into her father's shoulder as she released a sob. Tears fell one after the other, like a waterfall. In the back of her mind, she didn't think she had enough water in her body to cry this much, but here, she knelt in the sand.

Her body shook as sorrow took hold of her heart. Inside, she experienced waves of emotion. Mostly a defeated kind of anger. Outrage at the choices others made. The decisions of Ben, Atarah, Matthew, and even her father.

She pushed away from him.

If it weren't for her father, they never would have been in such dangerous situations. If not for Elijah, Atarah and she never would have been taken into the human realm to face off with Matthew. She would still have her best friend by her side if they all left them alone! Matthew, her father, and Ben, all of them played a part in Atarah's death.

She glared through blurry eyes at her father.

"Stay away from me." She hiccuped. "You've hurt me the most."

She rose to her feet with shaking knees, hugging her body.

Elijah lifted his hand to touch her but stopped halfway. His mouth opened and closed several times as if unsure of what to say. There was nothing he *could* say. She was right. Her father sold her off to be married without her knowledge, all for the sake of bringing the 'family' together. He'd misled, lied, and used her. A pained expression fell across Father's face as her vision blurred again.

A softer hand landed on her shoulder. She flinched as Ava stepped beside her. She blinked a few more tears to clear her vision as Ava's wings came around her. She turned into her sister's embrace to stifle her sobs.

"I've only wanted what's best for you two," Elijah's voice sounded thick with emotion. "Everything I've done has been for you."

"Why didn't you ask us what we wanted then?" Charlotte turned her head to glare at him.

"Because I know what's best." Elijah lowered his brow. "As your parent, I always know what's best for you."

"As my parent, it's not your job to make decisions for me. It's your job to guide *me* to make my *own* decisions." She clenched her fists as more tears poured from her eyes. She whispered, "You took that from me, with no remorse or thought either. And *your* decisions left me in danger, barely escaping with my life."

Elijah winced as she stepped away. Ava's arms came around her once more, but Charlotte shook them off. She couldn't anymore. Not when her family had hurt her the most. Elijah opened his mouth to speak again when a shout alerted them.

Charlotte's eyes widened.

Down below, a hooded figure held a long knife to Canaan's throat. Behind the figure, Makoto lay on the ground with his hands tied behind his back. *Where did that person come from? Did anyone see what happened?*

Canaan raised his hands in front of him as his captor

spoke.

"All of ya are to come down slowly, with yer hands and wings raised," a high-pitched voice yelled up to them, "Or else I'll slit both of yer friends' throats."

The Gabriel angels, who had been sitting in the sand, were now on their feet and wings flared. Elijah stepped forward with his wings extended.

"Easy now!" he called out, "Easy. We don't want any trouble. Please return our friends unharmed."

"Ya take me for a fool? I know ya know there's no more shelter for miles. Based on how yer friends look, the lot of ya are desperate folk," the figure paused, "Desperate folk make desperate decisions."

"We are desperate," Ava exclaimed, stepping forward. "We're injured and tired, trying to seek shelter." Ava walked further down the dune.

The hooded figure tightened her hold on Canaan who hissed in pain. A droplet of blood fell from where the knife was held. Ava paused.

"Please," Ava pleaded. "We don't mean any harm. Please, you could tie us up the entire stay if that makes you feel more comfortable. We don't intend to stay long."

"Stay long?" The figure jerked Canaan forward. "Ya shouldn't be 'ere at all."

"You're right," Charlotte chimed in, "We shouldn't be here, but we're here nonetheless. We're trying to go home."

The figure faced her. "Home? Where's exactly yer home, *Arch*?"

The word was hissed as if a curse.

"Please if you could just—" Ava started but stopped at Ben's movement.

Everyone froze as Ben walked down the dune. Charlotte's stomach clenched with anticipation. Silence stretched uncomfortably as the stranger dug the knife deeper.

"I'm warning ya!" the unknown person yelled. "I'll slit

his…"

Ben lifted his head to look at the person threatening his brother. The figure paused as it took in Ben's appearance. Covered in blood, with more pouring from his ears; his dead eyes found hers.

They stared at one another for a long minute. No one spoke. Charlotte didn't dare breathe as she watched their standoff. Ben stood a little distance away. Not enough to reach her in time but farther than the rest of them. He stopped at the base of the dune, where the ground flattened.

"Canaan," Ben rasped. His voice sounded weak as if it took him enormous effort to speak. "She's not going to hurt us."

"How do ya know that?" The figure scoffed.

Ben tilted his head to the side, his brows furrowed in concentration. "Your eyes… aren't cruel enough to kill,"

The knife faltered away from Canaan's neck.

Ava crept down the dune to join Ben at the base.

"Please." Ava pleaded once she stepped next to Ben. "We don't mean any harm. We promise we won't hurt you or any of your family. We just need shelter for the night."

The figure glanced between all of them before landing back to Ben. Lifting the one free hand, the figure loosened the button of the cloak and allowed the hood to fall around her head.

Charlotte's eyes widened.

Jet black hair shined against the sun, while her brown eyes watched them for their reactions. *She was…normal,* Charlotte thought. Her oval face possessed a moon-shaped scar along her temple. Peaking through the cloak, Charlotte saw brown wings curled in close. Charlotte shook her head, certain she was seeing a mirage. *Was she an angel like them? What was she doing here?*

"My name's Rhea," Rhea called out, lowering the knife away from Canaan's throat. "We best get inside 'fore the patrol comes through."

"Patrol?" Elijah asked. He moved closer as Canaan stumbled away from Rhea.

"Her ladyship ensures the soldiers check all through these parts." Rhea faced east and nodded her head to a cloud of dust in the distance. "They're comin' this way now."

"How do you know it's them?" Elijah questioned. The other angels gathered behind Ava and Elijah at the base of the dune. The building sat several yards behind Rhea.

"They always disturb the sand," Rhea replied, turning her eyes back to them. "Come. They're not as nice as I am."

She waved them over to the building.

Charlotte and the others hesitated, but Ben followed. Rhea bent and cut Makoto free of his bonds. He scrambled to his feet with his wings flared. His eyes narrowed on Rhea's retreating form.

"Can we trust her, Elijah?" Makoto asked as Elijah and Ava stepped closer.

"We have no choice," Elijah grimaced. "This can give us the time we need to heal everyone."

"When you and the others are feeling up to it, Makoto," Ava said. "You can combine forces again and open a portal."

Makoto frowned. "We might end up trapped somewhere else. A worse place."

"Right now, it's our best shot at getting home." Elijah pivoted on his heels to face the building. "Stay behind me in case she tries to attack again. If she does, Ava, get the others out and run as fast as you can."

"We can't leave you behind—" Ava started.

"Yes, you can," Elijah interrupted. "And you will."

They watched as Rhea pulled out a long, pronged wooden tool. She slid the tool into the side of the building, jiggling it to and fro for a few seconds before a loud click echoed. Suddenly, a slit appeared in the middle of the building as the doors pulled apart. Ben faced the entrance. His eyebrow rose at the doors' appearance as the only indication of surprise. They froze, wondering if anything was going to burst out at them and swallow them whole.

"Ya better get in 'fore the patrol gets here," Rhea called out.

Not a second later, a horn blared in the distance, coming from the dust Rhea pointed out earlier. This spurred them into action.

Charlotte ushered the others to follow after Ben. Canaan scrambled after his younger brother. Darkness greeted them. Shielded them from the unrelenting sun. Charlotte waited for the fear to arise as they walked past the doors into pitch black; except, the apprehension never came.

She sighed in relief as her burning skin fully healed in the shade. Her father and sister's hands glowed as their power coursed through them, easing their discomfort.

A sharp whistle sailed through the air.

"Ay! Fig! Turn on the lights!" Rhea yelled.

A loud click and the entire space lit up. Light illuminated from the ceilings through small circles. The lights reminded Charlotte of her time in the human realm. The room was large and tall. Along the sides of the room were wooden platforms that loomed high above her head. Various eyes peered down at them from those platforms. Dozens of wary eyes. Glaring eyes and a few curious ones. With the light focused on them, Charlotte couldn't see any other defining features of the new arrivals.

"Rhea," A voice called from the platform. "What are ya doing invitin' them in?"

Sound and grunts of agreement rang around the barn-like structure. *They sounded like children's voices,* Charlotte realized. However, their faces were still obscured.

"What happened to that one?" another child's voice exclaimed. A thin, talon-like finger pointed down to Ben. A spotlight spanned to him and Canaan "He's lookin' like one of the dead."

A few giggles echoed around them.

Charlotte swirled around to see more eyes surrounding them from above. Elijah and the others huddled together in the center. Backs to each other while their gaze remained forward. If whoever was up on the platforms decided to attack all at once, they were doomed. They were weak, tired, and outnumbered. The same thought must have crossed Elijah's mind for he slowly raised his hands. Makoto and the others mimicked his movements except for Ben.

Ben's gaze remained glued to the floor, and his wings dragged against the ground. He, once again, didn't appear to hear the jeers and laughter at his expense.

"EH!" Rhea bellowed. "Enough of tha! Patrol's comin' this way."

Charlotte's wings twitched as Rhea's accent thickened. Upon a closer look, Rhea's skin took on a slightly gray color while her eyes possessed a shade of dark yellow. Her scar arched around her eye, curving close to her nose.

"What about 'hem?" Another voice yelled out.

Rhea's gaze narrowed to Elijah and Makoto. Her wings underneath her cloak twitched.

"They're fine for tonight," Rhea concluded.

Murmurs of disapproval echoed around them. Charlotte frowned. *Were these children demons? Or were they…?*

Stepping away from the shadows, a figure jumped from the balcony above. Charlotte gasped. Large brown feathers fanned out wide to drift a small boy down to the main level. Wings, this demon had wings? Charlotte thought back to all of her lessons on the different types of demons. None of them mentioned demons that possessed wings, like angels.

The boy landed on light feet. His yellow eyes peered at them with suspicion. A single horn grew from his head. The skin around the horn cracked as if split open. Otherwise, his face was round and adorable. Charlotte scanned the rest of him, curious if he truly was an angel.

"I don't like the look of them two," The boy lifted a finger to indicate to Makoto and Elijah.

No—Charlotte shook her head. It was a talon the boy pointed with. His hands were blackened and curved with talons at the end instead of fingers. Elijah and Makoto's eyes widened as they took in the small boy.

"What in the Trinity*are*you?" Makoto sneered, his lip curled in disgust.

"Exactly why ya should've just killed them, Rhea." The boy's wings flared. "Now we have them and patrol to deal with."

"Or we could just hand them over to patrol 'stead?" A high-pitched voice called from the balcony.

Ava stepped forward to the young boy. Within the blink of an eye, he retreated with his wings flared and hands behind his back as if to draw a weapon.

"Easy now, Alan!" Rhea sprinted between them. "They don't have weapons. I've already checked."

"Doesn't mean they won't kill us in our sleep," Alan hissed. "We have more reason than the demons not to trust them!"

More reason than the demons? Were they not demons? Charlotte wondered. Behind her, her father gasped. His face relaxed in realization.

"You're halfling children, aren't you?" Elijah slowly moved forward. It was Charlotte and Ava's turn to gasp.

"Are you really?" Ava grabbed both of Rhea's hands, pulling them to her chest. "Are you halflings?"

Ava's eyes glossed as tears pooled in her eyes.

Alan scoffed. "What's it matter to*you*? So long as we're not in your world, you couldn't give too much crap about halfling business."

"Um, yeah, we all are." Rhea flared her wings and snatched her hands back. "Maybe we should leave them to the patrol."

"No, wait." Charlotte lifted a hand. "We're trying to find a halfling."

"Why?" Alan pulled out a dagger. "So you can kill 'em?"

"No!" Charlotte nearly screeched. "We—we don't mean any harm. Ju—just—"

Three loud bangs at the front door caused everyone to jump. For a second, no one moved or talked. Charlotte's heart raced loudly in her chest. She was surprised no one heard.

"Eh!" A voice boomed outside. "Open up rats! We're doin' rounds!"

Rhea ground her teeth together as Alan faced her.

"We can't be caught with the likes of them, Rhea," Alan whispered, "We'll be thrown in prison just for bein' seen together."

Charlotte's stomach clenched. *Would they turn them over?* She didn't understand who or what the patrol did, but if these halfling children were afraid of them, they should've been afraid too! Charlotte turned to Rhea, with tears in her eyes, silently pleading.

"Please," Ava whispered to Rhea. A single tear fell from her eyes. "Please."

Rhea clenched her fist as another loud bang echoed around them.

"I mean it, girl!" The voice outside yelled. "Open up!"

"Alan, hide them." Rhea sighed.

Charlotte's heart skipped a beat.

Alan's eyes widened. "What?"

"Now!" Rhea whispered to him.

Another loud bang.

"I'm comin' sir!" She called out to the patrol officers before dropping her voice back to a whisper. "Everyone else here scatter. Don't let them see ya."

Rhea bristly walked to the door, giving a pointed cough to Alan.

Alan tensed his jaw but put his weapon back into whatever hiding space he possessed in his cloak.

"This way," he grunted.

Charlotte sighed. Her wings slumped around her in relief.

"Now!" Alan whispered harshly.

Charlotte scurried behind him as he led them down a dark corridor. The others followed, finishing up with Elijah at the end. A glow from underneath the floorboard allowed her to see where he was going. There were no doors, only doorways to signal a changing of rooms. Alan stopped at the last doorway and pulled a rug to the side. A latch appeared. Alan gave a quick tug, lifting the latch open to reveal a hidden room.

"Hide down there until Rhea says so," Alan gritted.

"How do we know you won't kill us if we go down there?" Makoto mumbled.

"Makoto, quiet!" Another angel hissed.

Alan's eyes narrowed. "If you get caught, then we all get punished. Now, get inside."

They all heard the creaking and groaning of the large door opening again.

"Here ya go officers," Rhea called out behind them. "Nothin' to see here."

Charlotte hopped into the cellar, tucking in her wings tight. The room wasn't too far down. Enough room for her to stand. A single light illuminated the back of the cellar. Otherwise, there was nothing in there but dirt and stones on the floor. Small thuds alerted her to the others' arrival. One by one, they filled the room, cramping in together like sardines. Her heart raced as the lid to the cellar closed with a resounding click. She made out her father's silhouette, lifting a finger to his lips to indicate silence. A moment passed by in long, drawn-out breaths. They waited out the muffled conversations.

Charlotte held her breath as thundering boots stomped above them. She froze. They all held on to each other tightly as they waited. No one uttered a sound. A pit in her stomach grew every second she heard the soldiers maneuver around the room. Her heart pounded in her chest so loudly, that she worried the patrol might hear. Would Rhea keep her word? Or was she about to sell them out to the patrol? The others sounded keen on the idea of turning them over. Could they be trusted?

A loud smack resounded around them, followed by a sneering remark. Charlotte strained to make out what was being said above them but heard only the stomps from the patrol guards. Time drifted by slowly before they heard the latch click.

The door creaked open to reveal five faces staring down at them. Alan and Rhea, she recognized but the others were different. One child was tall and long with black eyes and no lips. Razor-sharp teeth lined the mouth, reminding her of a shark. Another child appeared to be albino, with white everything. Hair, skin, and nails glowed a white iridescent color. Except for the eyes. The eyes of this child were blood red. Charlotte shuddered and turned her gaze to the last child.

The last child's eyes caused Charlotte to jump. This child's eyes were incredibly large, in proportion to the face. Long, straight brown hair pooled around the shoulders, creating a dark curtain.

"You can come out now," The albino child mumbled, "Patrol's gone."

"One at a time though," Rhea called out.

Charlotte gasped when her gaze fell back on their host. A large bruise bloomed along Rhea's cheek. Was that the loud smack she had heard earlier? Charlotte flowed her powers back into her hands as concern swam through her.

Rhea had kept her word. She hid and sheltered them, strangers in this world, from guards who would've likely killed them at first glance. Instead, she protected them, even when the others told her to hand them over and at the expense of a blow to herself. Rhea was…

Tears formed in Charlotte's eyes as she lifted her glowing hands to Rhea. Her power flowed out of her to Rhea's throbbing cheek. Rhea jerked, drawing curious glances from her companions. Charlotte healed the bruise on her cheek within a second but sensed other injuries.

She frowned. Rhea was in a lot more pain than she let on.

"You didn't have to do that." Rhea lifted a hand to her healed face. "I don't need any help."

Ava moved to the latch's opening first, her eyes brimming with tears. "You saved us when you didn't have to. Let us help each other. I have a feeling we have a lot to learn from you."

Rhea's eyes bounced between her companions and their rag-tag group for a moment, pondering. Alan eyed Charlotte and Ava with suspicion but no hostility like before. After a few seconds, Rhea nodded. Her eyes softened as she extended a hand down to Ava.

"Let's get everyone some water and food first," Rhea murmured.

Ava grabbed her hand with a smile. Alan slowly lowered a hand down to Charlotte.

"I'm very interested to find out how a group of angels ended up in the Red Desert." Alan's eyes glistened with curiosity but his wings remained flared.

Charlotte latched onto his small hand. She almost jolted. *His hand was much too thin,* she thought.

With strength she didn't think he possessed, Alan lifted her as if she weighed nothing. He quickly stepped away and reached for another hand.

"Here," another small hand touched her own.

Charlotte turned to see the small albino child.

"This way to the kitchen." The child pulled on her hand, leading her down the corridor. The others trickled after her, one by one, to the next step in their adventure.

Chapter 4

Wind sprinkled dust and sand on Arick's face as he slowly roused. Reality blurred as sleep released its hold on him. A sound caught his ear, a noise of pain. Arick peeled his eyelids open. He blinked a few times to clear his vision before the scene in front of him jerked him awake.

Biting on a leather strap from his clothes, Mikael pressed his left arm onto the embers of a burning log. A pained grunt accompanied the smell of burning flesh that made Arick heave. Mikael released harsh, erratic breaths as he pulled his arm away from the fire. He bit hard on the leather strap in his mouth, groaning as he held his arm close to his body. Arick reached for his father but was jerked to a stop. The clinging of metal hit his ears first.

He glanced down to see chains around his wrist and feet, anchored to a large pole that dove deep into the ground. Arick's stomach clenched with dread as he scanned the area. His memories floated back to him as he surveyed his father.

They appeared to be in an open tent with a single fire in the middle as their only source of light. Figures in full length tunics moved around them, walking from tent to tent. None of them spared him or his father a glance. *Judging by the yellow eyes, they must be demons. We may still be in the demon realm,*he thought.

"Father," Arick whispered. He leaned as far as his restraints would allow. "Are you ok?"

Sweat pooled around Mikael's face. His brows furrowed in pain as he nodded, still clutching his arm. He spit the leash piece out of his mouth.

"I'm still alive," Mikael groaned. "Son, what's your status?"

Arick peered down at his own body. How was he?

"You're a crazy bastard, kid." A familiar deep voice echoed in his mind. Arick's lips twitched.

"Long time no talk, old-timer." Arick thought back. *"What happened?"*

"You don't remember going berserk, kid?" Azazel scoffed. *"It was like your mind was experiencing an earthquake."*

"It's all a blur." Arick pondered. *"I remember…"*

His mind drifted. A memory of Atarah's shocked face as a blade plunged into her heart caused a sharp pain in his own. Arick gasped as his chest constricted. He doubled over and clenched his hands as sorrow and failure washed over him in waves.

"Breathe, kid!" Azazel's voice faded as if he was shouting from a distance.

This time, he failed. Atarah couldn't get away. With another twist in his stomach, he heaved. Why was he such a failure? Why was he the one alive right now?

His heart pounded in his ears, like a slow time clock. Each tick mounted more pressure within him. Arick tilted his head up as tears filled his eyes. The stars and moons blurred in the sky, indistinguishable.

"Breathe, kid!" Azazel's voice bellowed in their shared mind, bringing him back to focus.

Arick gasped. Air rushed into his burning lungs, releasing the pressure building in his chest. Arick drew in another gulp of air, and his thundering heart quieted.

"Son!" A harsh whisper in front of him. Arick aimed his attention back to his father.

His father strained against the chains around his arms, reaching for him. Mikael's eyes darted all around his face, frantic.

"Son!" Mikael repeated in a hushed tone. "Speak to me! What's going on?"

"I'm ok—" Arick nearly wheezed out the lie. "I.."

He was far from okay.

"Father, I...I can't," he quivered. "I can't do this anymore."

He slumped forward, curling in on himself as if that would lessen the pain in his heart. Mikael lurched for him, his chains rattled as he stopped a few feet from him. A muscle in Mikael's jaw jumped as he gritted his teeth. He pulled against the chains, in vain; his own eyes glazed with tears.

"I'm right here, son," Mikael huffed out, his voice thickened. "I'm right here with you."

Arick buried his head to the ground before releasing a sob. Grief consumed him, drowned him. If grief was an ocean, it was his self loathing that pulled him under. It was all so vast, so heavy, it was hard to breathe.

"Come on, breathe Arick," Azazel's voice gently. *"Let it out and then breathe again to let it out some more."*

Blood rushed to his bowed head as he sobbed. He heard his father's voice but didn't register what he was saying. Not even Azazel's words fully reached him. Arick allowed the sorrow. He didn't have a choice, because he wasn't strong enough to hold it back any longer. He broke down, for how long he didn't know. His breaths consisted of short gasps and coughs. He cried until he ran out of tears and then cried some more.

Why was he still alive? Why did he bother trying? He wondered if he could sink into his psyche and let Azazel rule over his body. He wasn't doing anything good or useful with it anyway. Another flash of Atarah's shocked face blinked through his mind. Another failure. A loss of someone who would've accepted him.

"*Arick,*" Azazel murmured.

Arick shook his head.

"*Please, let me just sink back. You can take over Azazel. You can have my body completely. Here you go.*" Arick closed his eyes and sunk further back into the recesses of his mind.

"*Arick!*" Azazel yelled this time. "*Lift your head and open your goddamn eyes!*"

Azazel moved forward in their psyche and controlled his head and neck. Arick's head jerked up and his eyes shot open.

"*Look at who still fights for you!*" Azazel barked.

His father had tears streaming down his face like small rivers. His eyes were full of sorrow, while his arms still reached for him. He'd never seen his father cry before.

"I'm right here with you, son," Mikael choked out, "I'm right here."

"*Atarah wasn't the only person to accept you for who you are, halfling and all.*" Azazel blubbered. "*Your father is here, fighting for you. Your mother was there, fighting for you! Many more!*" Azazel paused as if he was biting his tongue. "*Don't give up on yourself when there are still others fighting for you.*"

"*I didn't ask for this!*" Arick pushed against Azazel's control.

"*No one ever asks to be loved, dumbass! You just accept it.*" Azazel countered as his control weakened.

"*I just don't care anymore.*" Arick sobbed. "*I can't take it anymore.*"

"*You can't just give up, kid.*" Azazel strained to hold his control of his head.

Arick was done trying. He wanted to give up.

"*Why not? You did.*" Arick replied, offhandedly.

Silence.

Pure silence stretched throughout their shared mind. A quiet that would marvel Arick, if he wasn't too overtaken with sadness. The turbulent waters of his mind stilled like floating on calm water.

"You can give up, kid," Azazel retreated to the back of their mind. *"If that's what you want,"* he paused, *"But not a day goes by that it doesn't haunt me. Will giving up haunt you, Arick?"*

Arick froze.

A movement behind his father caught his eye. Arick's wings twitched and then flared wide. His father whirled around, tucking his wings back in to assess the new arrival. From the shadows, Matthew limped closer to the fire. His face was battered, with a swollen eye, crooked nose, and busted lips.

A burning sensation ignited in the pit of Arick's stomach before spreading. Within seconds, his body was on fire with something he couldn't place. Something powerful.

It was anger, so much anger. His lips curled on their own accord; his face twisted with hatred.

"You," Matthew hissed. "I oughta kill you right here and now for what you've done. You nearly ruined all our plans with Satan! Ungrateful nuisance." Matthew stopped by the fire, still out of arm's reach. "But you still have a role to play."

Arick groaned as he lurched for Matthew. Red filled his vision. Matthew laughed cruelly as his hands stopped short. Matthew pulled out a poker from his cloak and stuck it into the fire.

"You have to be alive, but you don't have to be whole to finish your role." Matthew sneered. Mikael flared his wings.

"Don't you touch *my* son!" Mikael's face changed to one of pure anger.

His chains groaned against the post he was anchored to, wings flared wide.

"Your son?" Matthew tilted his head to the side, peering at Mikael. "Nothing will ever change the fact that he's from my bloodline, not yours, little brother."

It was Mikael's turn to laugh. Except he sounded more like a huff of air than a chuckle.

"If you think bloodline means anything," Mikael replied in a hushed yet firm tone. "You'll be sorely mistaken."

Matthew turned away from him.

"It doesn't matter what you think," Matthew murmured, facing Arick. "I'll show you that he's my son soon enough."

In the back of his mind, Arick heard Azazel calling out, cautioning him. Warning bells rang in his head as Matthew's words penetrated his mind, but somehow he was falling. Azazel's presence stretched and grew within their mind. His vision shrank as he was thrown back into the depths of their mind.

Arick saw the poker return to Matthew's hand, raised and ready to strike before he sank into a deep slumber of darkness;

a shadowy depth, a void he'd welcomed minutes ago but now denied.

Without thinking, Azazel yanked Arick back, shutting the kid far behind any conscious awareness. He expanded, filling every corner of Arick's body, as the scorching poker slammed onto his shoulder.

He cried out as the flesh burned and seared, and the poker's hook lodged itself into his shoulder blade. The bastard pulled the poker out, twisting as he went. He gasped as the stinging, burning pain radiated down his arm. A faint tug in his mind reminded him how mentally resilient the kid was.

He'd pushed the kid far back so there was no way Arick could feel the torture Matthew dealt. He squeezed his eyes tight, gasping against the pain. The smell of burning flesh filled his nostrils. Gritting his teeth together, he resisted the urge to gag from the smell. A yelp of pain and the sound of chains thrashing drew his attention.

Off to the side, Mikael thrashed against his chains, yelling obscenities at Matthew, who smiled. The crazy assimilate put the poker back in the fire, waiting and grinning, while his stomach formed knots. He braced for the next blow, tensing his muscles and curling in on himself. He fortified his mind to ensure Arick wouldn't feel anything.

A minute passed before Matthew landed the next strike at his back. This time the bastard delivered several blows one after the other. He bit his lip to prevent crying out and tasted blood. A sickening thud echoed around them as Matthew beat him. Blood rushed through his ears, and his stomach heaved a few times as the beating went on. Excruciating pain like he hadn't experienced in centuries spread across this body. His nerves were on fire. His skin burned, and bones cracked. His breathing turned erratic as his willpower trembled. But he refused to give in.

Finally, Matthew lowered the poker back into the fire. This asshole was planning to have this go on for some time. The sounds of rattling chains alerted him back to Mikael. The Arch's muscles bulged significantly as he fought against the chain. *A fight he may win*, Azazel thought dizzily.

The chains groaned as Mikael reached for Matthew with murder in his eyes. Another tug in the back of his mind reminded him to strengthen the wall between him and Arick. He erected another mental barrier and curled his arms around his torso.

Matthew raised the poker up again with a sadistic glint in his eyes. Azazel's body shook as he stared at the red, sizzling poker. Matthew pointed it under Azazel's chin to lift his face, smiling.

Azazel glared at the bastard, silently promising to make his life a living hell if he and Arick made it out of this situation. Emotions poured over him in waves, his own emotions, not the host's. For the first time in years, he felt a body react in tandem to his emotions. As angry as he was right now, it felt good to have a body to direct his emotions. He sneered up at Matthew, vowing to draw out his death.

Matthew paused. Poker raised, he tilted his head and frowned at him.

"What's wrong with your eyes, boy?" Matthew lifted the rod closer to his eyes.

Azazel jerked Arick's head away from the glowing light of the poker.

Shit! Azazel thought, ducking his chin to his chest. He'd forgotten Matthew wasn't aware of his presence in Arick's body. He needed to keep it a secret to ensure Satan didn't try to manipulate them. A rough hand yanked his head up, pulling at his hair.

"I asked you a question, son." Matthew sneered, shaking his head around. "Or else I'll dig your eyes out with this thing."

The end of the poker blazed within an inch of his face. The rod sizzled as a drop of his sweat landed on the point. Though his body trembled with pain, weakness, and fear, somehow Azazel kept the barrier erected between him and Arick. He sensed taps along the boundary as Arick's mind pressed against his, but he refused to loosen.

The kid deserved better than this, Azazel thought, staring up at the deranged assimilate. The poker moved closer to his face.

A loud clinking sound snapped around them.

He and Matthew didn't have time to turn around and see. Mikael moved like a cannon, with speed and power. He collided with Matthew like two boulders making an impact. Azazel heard Mikael more than saw him as he collapsed. With his head in the sand, he listened as Mikael pummeled Matthew. Each punch he connected echoed around them in loud booms.

Azazel coughed, trying to get his breathing under control. The pain radiated everywhere around him. His arms, shoulders, back, and wings all hurt. He groaned as he forced himself into a kneeling position. He focused on the battling brothers with knots in his stomach. Would Mikael win? Could they escape?

Azazel darted his gaze around the encampment, hope blooming in his chest as the thought of freedom dangled in front of him.

The image crashed, and his lungs stalled as dozens of figures surrounded them. They were covered head to toe in dark red tunics with only their eyes showing from a small slit. Rows of them stood shoulder to shoulder, watching Mikael and Matthew fight it out. Azazel frowned.

Why weren't they intervening?

With them standing so still, in formation, Azazel inspected them. No outlined insignia or lettering of any kind. Were they…?

Azazel's eyes widened. Those were the elders, dressed in all red; they served directly under Satan's rule as her enforcers. They were her police, doctors, teachers, and judges. The elders allowed her to control her citizens without controlling everyone's mind. Instead, she only needed to distort a few thousand minds to manipulate the rest of the herd, without a thought of their own.

Azazel grimaced. She might have been nearby to have this many in one encampment. Any hope of them escaping dashed at that thought. He'd seen her work over the years as a watcher. He'd seen the torment and faked happiness enforced upon her people, stifling out any thought of rebellion. Snapping the minds of the most intelligent demons ensured no deviation. Her domain was known as the sands of silent suffering. No one could trust their own thoughts or emotions because she rewrote reality for them.

He'd always been grateful she didn't have the ability to control him…until now. He shuddered. He possessed a body, making him no longer untouchable. He'd been reluctant to allow Arick into the demon realm because he'd feared Satan more than anything else. Now, this mistake might have bit him in the ass.

Another tug on the wall reminded him to reinforce it. Azazel groaned as he strengthened the barrier. As much as he didn't want to admit it, the damn kid grew on him. Sharing a body, he knew every emotion the kid experienced. Whenever Arick took over in the past, Azazel dug deeper into the depths of his mind to explore his memories. The memories of Arick growing up, learning how to fly and swing a sword. The first time Mikael begrudgingly told Arick he did a good job. Memories of growing up with Atarah, toddling after him, eager to keep up.

None of these memories particularly stuck out to him except how perceptive Arick had been. Arick saw the fear in his father's eyes whenever he picked up a sword, so he got up earlier than everyone else to train. So no one would see or fear him. The congratulations from his father on how well he managed his swordsmanship came years later. How Arick hung around his sister because he saw the bullies waiting around the corner for her. The memory of him pretending not to be cold, giving his mother his jackets, during the cold winter months.

Over and over again, Arick played as a jokester, never taking anything seriously, but it was all a ruse. Arick would throw himself in front of any threat to protect the people he loved. Azazel's heart clenched as another tug pulled on the barrier. Arick was trying to get out.

That damn kid, Azazel thought, he's gonna be the death of me.

In the short time span of a few weeks, Azazel's life turned from a life of endless, gray wandering to a vibrant, heart-racing adventure. The complexity of emotions coursing through him was overwhelming compared to the muted pain of his existence.

Emotions flashed through him, like bolts of lightning too fast for him to understand. His own feelings crashed down on him as if a dam burst. He gritted his teeth as he forced their body from its fetal position. Pain radiated everywhere with the slightest movement. He couldn't believe Arick endured this amount of pain for this long.

He shook his head.

No, he thought grimly, *that's exactly what Arick would do.*

A grunt followed by a pained groan drew his attention.

He turned his head to see Mikael, panting and bleeding from his face, kneeling over Matthew's crumbled form. Powerful wrath were the words to describe him at that moment. His wings flared wide, casting a vicious shadow in the sand from the flicking flames of their campfire. Transfixed, Azazel couldn't tell which brother was the demon and which was the angel.

Blood poured from a wound on Mikael's head and dried on his tunic, he looked terrifying. Despite his cut-off hand, power rolled off him in waves that made Azazel shudder. Energy vibrated off of Mikael, humming in the air around them. A mixture of fury and hurt etched into his features as he glared down at his brother.

Mikael's eyes swiveled back to him. The hair on the back of Azazel's neck rose as if coming face to face with a dangerous animal. Unhinged anger swam in those golden orbs for a moment before Azazel saw the raw emotion underneath.

Fear.

Mikael blinked, and the power receded… a little.

Goosebumps rose along his arms as Mikael approached, slowly as if he was about to bolt, which was not far off. Azazel had assumed Mikael was the weaker brother, but watching him now, he'd underestimated Arick's father.

He rose to his feet, wincing at the sharp pain shooting through his back. Azazel whispered a silent prayer that the Raphael blood Arick inherited worked fast. He straightened to his full height, ensuring he was eye-to-eye with Arick's father.

Mikael paused a few feet away, staring at him. He narrowed his eyes.

"My son," Mikael rumbled. "He's not here right now, is he?"

Azazel jerked.

Mikael had been staring at his eyes this whole time, he realized. The eyes were the only clue that Azazel took over Arick's body. Mikael knew that his son's body was possessed. Azazel flexed his jaw, berating himself for being too careless. He debated about denying it until Mikael stared at him like a bull about to charge.

Best to stay truthful. He cleared his throat.

"The kid deserves better than him." He jerked his chin to Matthew's beaten body.

Mikael released a long exhale, considering the weight of his words. A long moment passed before he reached for the chain around his wrist with his right hand. With a powerful yank, the chain snapped. Azazel's eyes widened. A moment ago, these very same chains were holding Mikael at bay. Now he was breaking them like twigs. Did Mikael….

Mikael broke the last chain around his wrist before speaking.

"Don't let him out," he commanded, his voice thick with emotion.

His heart clenched as Mikael's words pierced through him. Don't let the kid get hurt. That's what his father was really saying. Azazel nodded as he rubbed his wrist.

"Don't overdo it." Azazel narrowed his eyes at Mikael. "The kid needs you alive."

For a quick moment, a sad expression came over Mikael's face before he hardened it again.

"Well, I don't plan on dying," Mikael said dryly, "Not until everything's set right."

A loud whistle followed by a slow clap made Azazel

jump. The power from Mikael hummed louder and faster than before. They both pivoted to see Satan, standing in front of all the elders. She wore a flowing wrap dress that tied tightly around her narrow waist. Sheer sleeves ruffled as she clapped with a plastic smile on her face. His stomach dropped.

"Great little... uh tussle you had there with your brother." Her high-pitched voice grated on Azazel's nerves. However, it was her plastic smile that made him shudder. "But I'm afraid I need both of you alive. So you cannot harm Matthew under any circumstances." She tilted her head at Mikael. "You understand, yes?" she asked, but her tone conveyed a command.

Immediately Mikael stiffened. Muscles along his face flexed as if he was fighting. This lasted for a few seconds before his face went slack. Mikael nodded with glazed eyes at Satan.

"I understand," Mikael droned.

Azazel's eyes widened. That fast, she disarmed and controlled the strongest angel in all of the realms. Knots formed in his stomach. They didn't stand a chance. Satan clapped her hands and smiled.

"Perfect!" Her cold green eyes fell on him as his arms and legs trembled. "Now for you, I need you to chain both you and your father back up."

Something wormed and slithered through his mind. In his head, he felt the overwhelming need to follow through with what she wanted, but his body tensed. Fog entered his mind as he tried to remember something important. He needed to... do something. Protect someone, but who was it again?

The desert faded around him, and his vision focused on a boy with round cheeks standing in front of him. The boy smiled up at him and lifted up a rope.

"Come on Dad!" The boy exclaimed excitedly. "Tie this around the tree so I can swing."

He grinned, picking up the rope. "You have to be patient now, son."

A tree stood a few feet away from him, a low branch within his reach. The boy grabbed onto his leg in a tender hug.

"I'm so happy to play with you!" The boy gleamed up at him.

His heart swelled, feeling whole for the first time in a long time. He moved to tie the rope around the branch.

"*STOP!*" a yell echoed around him.

He froze and blinked. Walls were all around him, stretching high. This was... his mind? Some of the fog lifted, and the boy faded. A tug on one of the walls in his mind alerted him that someone was here. There was someone else on the other side of the wall... Arick.

Azazel blinked.

In his hands, he held open chains, about to lock them around Mikael's waiting wrist as he came to his senses. Mikael remained frozen in place with unfocused eyes. Whatever illusion the she-devil placed on him was still in full effect. Speaking of which, Satan commanded him to lock them up, he remembered.

Arick's shout pulled him out of Satan's illusion. *Arick...*

The wheels of his mind churned as he thought of a way for them to escape Satan's grasp. He peered through his eyelashes at Matthew. He knelt in the sand, with the same glazed over expression as his brother. *Was he under Satan's control?* He wondered. He'd heard rumors of them working together and always thought it odd.

Satan doesn't work with anyone. She gives orders and waits for them to be followed.

Like she did now.

His hands trembled, rattling the chains that were supposed to be locked around their wrists now. Beads of sweat dripped down his brow as his heart pounded in his chest.

Her eyes narrowed on him. Waiting.

Crap, he thought. *Play the part.*

He closed the chain around Mikael's wrists and bent

down for his own restraints. Each heartbeat resonated within him like a ticking clock. He would keep the pretense that he was under her illusion while he waited for a chance to escape. With caution, he folded some fabric between him and the chain, jamming the locking mechanism. He gave a small shake to ensure the clasp held before standing. Should he need to escape, this would be easier to break out of.

"Finally," Satan rolled her eyes. Turning on her heels, facing her followers, she shouted. "Move out for Portal City."

That place? He jolted. She was going to the spirit realm now? With this brigade? His mind whirled with the possibilities of why, unaware of another, stronger tug on his mental wall. Arick pushed against his own restraints, and Azazel let him through.

"About time!" Arick's angry voice echoed through their mind. *"Why did you switch with me? What happened? Felt something...weird happening to my brain."*

Azazel tucked his chin down so no one saw his face. The elders scurried around the camp, gathering and packing items up to move out. In the distance, a faint glow of dawn approached.

"We're in big trouble, kid," he whispered back.

"We're always in trouble," Arick drawled. Azazel sensed him rolling his metaphorical eyeballs at him. *"What's new?"*

"Satan's around and has control of everyone in camp, including your father and Matthew," he explained.

"Do you think she's... had control of Matthew this entire time?" The hope in Arick's voice made his heart clench.

The poor kid, who'd broken down less than an hour ago, now sounded optimistic. Azazel didn't have the heart to take that away.

"Maybe, kid, maybe," he conceded.

A horn blared as dawn broke, signaling it was time to move out. Large hoofed beasts yawned as the last of the camp was packed onto their backs. Glass jars of a dark liquid were loaded onto the animal's backs. On the far side of camp, Aza-zel spotted Satan mounting a white stallion with two horns erected straight up in the air. At the back of the line, Azazel groaned at the march ahead. It was a long way to Portal City, the most northern point in the demon realm, but once there they might have a chance to escape.

"Listen, kid," Azazel began, *"So far no one has caught on that we broke the illusion, and we need to keep it that way. We are heading for a place called Portal City. It's the north-ern point of the demon realm and where an active portal sits. When we get there, we can figure out a plan to escape."*

"Why is she heading there? What about the Gabriel an-gels?" Arick fired off question after question. *"Where's dad?"*

Concern bled into his voice at the end. His earlier depres-sion was gone in the face of more danger ahead. He sensed Arick squishing his emotions in the far corners of their mind and didn't blame him.

He pivoted his gaze behind him where Mikael shuffled with a blank expression.

Inside their mind, Arick shuddered. *"He looks like a zom-bie."*

"When she gives a command, trust me he won't look zom-bie-like," Azazel explained.

"This is all my fault," Arick started, *"If I had gotten my act together faster, then we wouldn't be in this situation."*

"Never mind that now," Azazel huffed. *"I don't know what her plan is, but it's nothing good."*

Another horn blared. This time, in unison, the elders marched. A sharp pull in the chain caused him to stumble. He scrambled to keep up. Pain shot through him like lightning from Matthew's earlier beating. Since the poker had been hot, it cauterized any wound that could seep blood, but that didn't stop the stinging sensation. His shoulders and back screamed in protest against any movement. He gritted his teeth as he walked. His stomach rolled, threatening to heave.

"That's right!" Arick exclaimed. *"The last thing I re-member is Matthew coming at me with a hot poker stick."*

"Forget about it, kid."

"What did...?" He paused.

"Never mind that, kid," he grunted. The sun's glow radi-ated heat, driving away the cold night. Azazel grimaced, not looking forward to the desert heat. *"For this plan to work, we need to work in tandem."*

Arick stayed silent for a moment. Emotions swirled around inside. Now that Arick wasn't behind the mental wall, the feelings were harder to discern. Azazel didn't know who was feeling what and why. Only that his chest tightened, and a new determination bloomed.

Chapter 5

With closed eyes, Isabella doubled over. Hands on her knees, she threw up the last remaining contents of her stomach. Nausea rolled over her in waves as the 'travel' sickness faded.

"Move around," Gabriel Sr. barked out somewhere behind her. "It'll get rid of any queasiness. We need to hurry."

"Ugh," she groaned.

Fatigue plagued her joints while her stomach knotted up, no longer because of travel sickness but because of the task at hand. Her wings trembled, as the sense of impending doom grew. She breathed deeply, urging the air to fill her up, to give her strength. The air swirled around her. She filled her lungs again. Goosebumps rose along her skin in anticipation.

"Keep breathing," Clarissa's voice whispered through her mind. *"You've done bigger blasts before."*

Isabella nodded to herself. *That's right, she'd done this before; that meant she could do it again.* She gulped another breath of air, filling her chest and belly. She hissed out the air through gritted teeth, clenching her abdomen and pelvic floor tight. Blood rushed through her body, energized and oxygenated. Deep breaths were different for her. She was in her element. She was wind, air, and light.

To her, inhaling and exhaling were like the first glimmers of morning light. A new beginning. Breathing meant energy and strength. It helped her focus more than others. Many breathed mindlessly, but not her. Her lungs and her spirit lifted with each inhale, building pressure and power. Each exhale was a release of what no longer served her, loosening tension and stress.

Opening her eyes to peer at the others, she noticed their tension. The city of Ianua stood a few miles in the distance, unaware of their presence…for the moment. Gabriel Sr., Sewall, and Tariel faced the city with flared wings and arms crossed, waiting on her. Amos crouched by her, concern marred his face.

"Are you all right?" he asked. A frown deepened on his face as she gave a half-hearted thumbs up.

"Yeah," she murmured, pulling at the ends of their sleeves.

Was she all right? Could she do this? The questions whispered in the back of her mind like snickering classmates. She took another deep breath.

"I mean, yes." She nodded. Her voice sounded firmer.

"Well, get it together," Sewall hissed. His black eyes sent shivers down her spine as he glared at her. "If we get the timing wrong, you and your sister won't create the tornado."

"We haven't seen any flames sprout up yet," Tariel frowned, staring at the city. "She should have started by now…" her voice drifted off.

Gabriel Sr.'s wings twitched.

"Tariel makes a good point," Gabriel paced. "Why hasn't your sister started to light up the place?"

"We should start without them," Sewall grumbled.

A dark, oppressive air gathered around him that made

Isabella jump behind Amos.

"I agree," Tariel chimed in.

The veins along her temple rose to the surface as more shadows whirled around them. Isabella's breathing turned to short bursts of air. Gasping, the wind picked up speed around her.

"Calm down," Amos growled as he spread his wings out wide. "We don't want to rush into anything."

"Maybe Isabella should get the wind going first," Gabriel called out from where he paced. "Clarissa is probably waiting for her to start."

Isabella's trembling body froze

Was Clarissa waiting for her? Were her flames not present because her wind didn't support her? Was she expected to start?

The knots in her stomach tightened painfully. She needed to help, now!

She inhaled deeply, twisted her body, and lifted her hands to the sky.

"Wait, hold on!" Amos boomed.

She released her breath and unleashed her wind. Roaring around them, like turbulent rapids, the air rushed to the city before her. The mountains in the background allowed for a natural path for the wind to blow. The whooshing of the wind drowned out any noise the others may have shouted. She gasped another breath, desperate to keep the momentum. Clarissa was waiting.

The others ducked to the ground as soon as she released her wind to escape the risk of being blown away. As she sent another gust of wind to the city, she glanced at the others. Still, on the ground, their expressions were either one of annoyance or strained control. Was she too close? Maybe I'll move away from them so they won't get sucked into the tornado, she thought.

She released a burst of cold air to keep the momentum

going and allowed the air current to lift her as she leaped with flared wings. From here, she could create a better vortex.

However…something was off.

With her arms extending, the air returning to her from the wind tunnel she created remained as cold as the first blast she'd sent. Where was the familiar heat of Clarissa's flames? She curved the current around the city again in another powerful blast. From this high up, she scanned the city floor. Searching for any signs of flaming red hair.

There were none.

Only running, crouched gray bodies of demons ducking for cover. A few rallied together, pointing their fingers at her flying figure and moving their mouths. She froze. She didn't move or, worse, breathe. They saw her! What was she supposed to do? The knots in her stomach reappeared with more force.

Her fingers trembled as she tried again to swirl the wind around the city, silently praying to feel her sister's flames. The air in her lungs stalled, causing the current to weaken. Doubts grew in her mind from quiet whispers to audible jabs. *Oh no*, she thought. She needed to keep going…right? Didn't Clarissa need her help?

If she did, why wasn't she sending out her flames to meet her wind current? Did something happen to Clarissa because of her? Tears sprang to her eyes. What if—if she took too long to get ready and demons attacked her?

Her wings tucked in as she wrapped her arms around her waist, lowering to the ground. She shivered while more demons, dressed in armor, gathered to their spot at the edge of the city. The demons' glowing, yellow eyes glared at them. Without her manipulation, the wind died down, while other sounds grew in volume. Shouts and cries echoed from the city in confusion and chaos. As her feet touched the ground, a jerk on her shoulder turned her face to face with an enraged Amos.

"What in—Why would you—" he paused as if lost for

words and ran a hand through his hair, tugging on the strands. "Y-you just…"

Isabella's shoulders slumped, as the urge to disappear into the ground consumed her.

"Screwed us," Tariel interrupted.

Her cold voice pierced through Isabella's last remaining piece of confidence. Gabriel appeared to be torn between disgust for her and panic at their situation. Sewall's eyes darkened as the gathering demons marched toward them with weapons around their waists.

"We came here to fight, didn't we?" Sewall hissed as shadows coiled along his arms. "Let's wipe out as many as we can."

"Wait!" Amos boomed this time, still clutching his head. She flinched. "Isabella," his voice softened. "Your sister's flames were nowhere to be seen, right?"

She nodded, keeping her gaze glued to the ground. Too much shame and guilt entrenched itself inside her heart to speak.

"I didn't hear any of their thoughts when we first landed," Amos explained, turning to the others. "Something may have happened—"

"To my son?!" Gabriel whipped around with flared wings. Panic seeped into his voice. "You can't sense my son?"

Amos grimaced as if in pain. "The only thing I know for certain is that your son, Clarissa, and the others aren't on the other side of the city."

"Which means our plan has failed," Tariel sighed.

"No!" Sewall growled. "We can still take them!"

"Until more soldiers come?" Amos yelled back with flared wings. "We needed the sisters' combo attack to distract the majority of them. We can't take on all of them! We need to retreat."

"I need to find my son," Gabriel murmured while Sewall glowered at Amos.

"I can hear your thoughts," Amos crossed his arms. "You know I'm right. Live today to fight tomorrow."

Sewall and Tariel clenched their jaws tight. Both were stubborn enough to fight but smart enough to know they wouldn't win. They shared a look with each other before nodding.

"We'll fight another day," Sewall grumbled, "Whoever messed up owes us another fight!"

They turned to Gabriel, who paced in a circle with a wild look in his eye.

"I knew I shouldn't have let my son go," he mumbled under his breath. "I never should have let him—"

"Gabriel!" Amos urged, grabbing him by the shoulder. "Snap out of it! We need to get out of here."

Gabriel stared at Amos as shouts from the demon guards came closer.

"You're right!" He nodded. "We need to leave to find my son!"

"Take us to Mortem," Sewall pulled Tariel behind him, never turning his back to the approaching party of demons.

"Why there?" Tariel cried out.

"So we can drop you two off," Sewall indicated to her. "It'll be better if you two were safe inside our home."

Isabella slumped further, as her cheeks burned; she didn't bother to protest. He was right. She was useless and only caused them problems.

"No!" Tariel protested.

A shout from one of the demons spurred them into motion. They were within spear-throwing distance now. Amos grabbed her while Sewall pushed his flailing daughter closer to Gabriel's glowing hands. As Gabriel pulled apart the portal to escape, Sewall pushed his daughter through despite her enraged cry.

A shout from behind made her pause.

A demon, dressed in armor, waved his arms above his

head to signal her. He repeated his shout in a language she couldn't understand. Tilting her head, she took a step closer to him before Amos stopped her.

"Let's go. Now!" Amos urged.

She watched the demon as Amos pushed her through the portal, confusion flitted through her mind. The demon didn't have its sword drawn, nor notched an arrow that would have undoubtedly reached them at this close of a distance. *Why didn't he attack?* She wondered.

She didn't have time to answer her question before the bright, white light of the portal consumed her. The warmth of the opening created goosebumps along her skin as she descended.

The dichotomy of rushing movement while remaining still caused her stomach to clench again. Instinctively, she reached for the air and wind, finding nothing. No pull, no strength, pure absence. Panic climbed its way up her throat, as she collapsed to a white floor, coming back to center. On her hands and knees, waves of nausea rolled over her.

She gasped, welcoming the air into her lungs. The wind lifted her, aided her, and rescued her all within that one breath. She curled in on herself as a shudder ran through her, threatening to break her apart.

"Come on, get up!" A harsh voice barked at her. The wind swirled closer to her.

She pivoted her head to the side to see Gabriel glaring at her. His wings flared wide, and his body was in motion. He paced across a stark white hallway with no pictures, colors, or plants. Only a lone black bench in the middle. *Where am I?* She wondered.

"You are in Sewall's estate, currently in the foyer," another voice answered.

She turned her head to see Amos crouched near her. His face was a mixture of emotions. His brow furrowed, and a deep frown marred his face. The dark circles under his eyes deepened, making him look older than his age. Opening her wings, she used the wind to lift herself to her feet. Once standing, she fought another wave of nausea and wrapped her arms around her midsection. The wind curled in, and she took another deep breath for reassurance.

An outraged cry made her jump. Tucking her wings in tight, she lifted her hands up, the wind swirling tightly along her fists, ready to fight. She searched the area, finding nothing but white walls and black furniture scattered here and there. Gabriel continued to pace with tension around his eyes. Amos sat on a bench not too far away, rubbing against his temples. No threat or demon loomed anywhere.

Behind her, another shout alerted her to an alcove. Tariel, with flared wings, argued with her father inside. Sewall's sneering would have made her tuck her tail and run but not Tariel. The young Azrael heir appeared intimidating in her own right. She inched closer to Amos, to potentially hide behind him when their voices drifted over.

"You're staying here and that's final, young lady," Sewall hissed.

"Final my ass!" Tariel's eyes narrowed, and her lips curled into a sneer, her voice sounding as cold as ice. "You can't keep me here now that my babysitter is gone."

"We'll get Zewal back faster than you can come up with a plan to sneak away," Sewall countered.

They both crossed their arms and glared at each other, looking like mirrored images of each other. Isabella held her breath as their standoff stretched. Who would win? Tariel made the first move.

"Arick is important to me." Tariel's voice added a hint of warmth at the mention of the young heir.

But it had the opposite effect on Sewall. His wings flared, and his sneer deepened.

"You are going nowhere near that halfling." Shadows swirled along his side, agitated and menacing.

Tendrils gathered around Tariel. Dark veins popped out along her head, eyes, and arms, making her look like the terrifying angel of death.

Isabella squeaked as she ducked behind Amos, who sat on the bench. Her wings quivered as she watched their standoff once again. Shadows withered within the alcove, and the temperature dropped as their powers pushed out of the room. Isabella shivered while the shadows suffocated the air from the room.

"That's enough," A high-pitched, firm voice called out from the other side of the room.

Immediately, all the shadows descended back into Tariel and Sewall's bodies as if they had never appeared. Isabella gasped as warmth and airflow came back into the room, breathing in as much air as possible to calm her nerves.

Heart pounding in her chest, she pivoted to see who'd spoken. An Azrael angel stood underneath an arched doorway. Her pale, leathery wings lay relaxed by her sides but her black eyes narrowed at Sewall and Tariel. A black tunic covered her from head to toe, leaving only her pale face to be seen.

Sewall's demeanor changed. His wings dropped, and his face softened as he slithered over to the new arrival. Isabella's eyes widened as Sewall knelt before the mystery angel, drawing out a thin, pale hand to kiss.

"My love, shadow, and life," Sewall murmured while kissing her hand. The reverence in his voice was palpable. "Please, my shadow, my wife, forgive me."

Isabella's jaw dropped. *His wife?*

"Fatima, my shadow," Sewall continued, his voice soft and soothing. "What shall we do for our children? It's not safe for Tariel to join us."

Fatima turned her eyes to Tariel, who refused to meet her mother's gaze. Sewall rose to his full height, nearly towering over Fatima, which would be intimidating if it wasn't for the affectionate glow in his dark eyes. Isabella was awestruck.

The love Sewall had for his wife was…beautiful, not scary.

"Tariel." Fatima drew everyone's attention. "Is what you said true? That Arick is important to you."

Tariel's face flushed red. Silence stretched as everyone waited for her response. Isabella's face blushed in secondhand embarrassment. *What an awkward conversation to have in front of others*, she thought as she brought her hands to her face.

"Yes," Tariel admitted through gritted teeth.

With wide eyes, Isabella swiveled back to Fatima and Sewall, whose eyes narrowed. A sneer grew on Sewall's face but Fatima placed a hand on his cheek, and the sneer faded.

"That's settled then," Fatima said softly.

Sewall sputtered, darting his gaze between the two females. "Bu—but, that's not—no, I must object—"

Fatima stopped him with a small grin.

"Tariel isn't someone who chooses lightly, my love," Fatima said, cradling his face with her hand. "We must trust her to find her shadow, like we trusted in each other."

Sewall melted into her hand. His wings cradled around her protectively. The sight made Isabella's heart flutter. Tears swelled in her eyes at the beauty of their love.

"With that said," Fatima continued, turning to face Tariel. "You're staying with me."

"Wh—what?" Tariel mumbled. "But you said…"

"I know what I said. You'll stay with me and help me study this book," Fatima narrowed her eyes at Tariel as she lifted an old, black-covered book format from the folds of her tunic. "A book written in the language of the dead."

Tariel's eyes widened. "How did you find that book?"

Fatima's lips twitched. "You left it open on your desk in plain sight."

A faint blush spread across Tariel's face as she crossed her arms. "You didn't have to go snooping."

"It isn't snooping if it's within my own house," Fatima

replied.

Sewall flipped through the book with a furrowed brow.

"There's nothing written in that book," Isabella murmured. Why did they act like it was so important?

"The book's written in a language very few can see and read," Amos answered, "The writer wrote the book while dead. Only those with 'soul-seeing' eyes can see and decipher the text."

"Then Fatima and Tariel have soul-seeing eyes?" Isabella asked, fascinated by the book now.

What hidden messages did the book possess? Could the book help them fight against the demons? Isabella stared at the book Sewall held in his hands. His eyes squinted as if he was trying to read the book until he shook his head in defeat.

"That gift was passed down to you and our daughter," Sewall sighed. "But I don't want either of you to be exposed to something that'll be upsetting."

Fatima gently took the book back from Sewall. "Everyone in this family needs to stop acting like I'm made of glass."

She frowned at Sewall, who mirrored her expression. *Was reading the book dangerous?* Isabella wondered. This time Amos didn't reply but grimaced.

Another standoff in the Azrael family, but this one didn't make Isabella as nervous. Concern shone in their eyes more than anger. Much to Isabella's relief, the shadows that withered around them weren't suffocating…more comforting.

"None of this matters!" Gabriel's face flushed from pacing, his wings flared as he spoke.

Everyone paused.

"We need to get back there and find my son! I never should have agreed to let him travel alone." He ran a hand through his hair. "He's not ready to travel through the demon realm."

"He already has once before." Amos pointed out.

"With two Head Archs and a larger group! If he gets captured by the wrong demon, who knows what they'll do to him? We still haven't found the soldiers taken from my region!" Gabriel pinched two fingers on the bridge of his nose, taking shaky breaths. "We need to rescue them. Now."

Sewall raised an eyebrow. "Where might he have gone?"

"I don't know," Gabriel answered softly.

His jaw flexed as his teeth ground together. A knot formed once more in her stomach. Clarissa was with Gabriel Jr… Where could they be?

"My son's not used to traveling through the demon realm," Gabriel explained. His fingers stayed on the bridge of his nose, eyes closed. "So the portal he opened could've led anywhere."

Amos pursed his lips together, while Sewall appeared disgruntled. Isabella glanced around at the defeated expressions. She frowned. Clarissa would know what to do…but she wasn't here now. So what could they do?

"Get my father before going back," she heard herself speak up.

All eyes turned to her. Goosebumps rose along her arms at their stares. She hunched her shoulders and leaned behind the bench Amos sat on.

"What?" Gabriel scoffed.

She slumped further.

"You need more help than what we can offer," she mumbled, keeping her eyes on the ground as shame swam through her. She was too useless to help out, especially without her sister."Take my father with you and you will have more heads and strength to fight your way through the demon realm to find everyone."

"That's a good plan." Amos' eyes widened. "Better than anything we've come up with so far."

Gabriel crossed his arms. "We could use another Head Arch to fight. He'll be more useful than you at least."

She flinched at the jab. What could she say? He was right.

"I need to get our son." Sewall gave a grunt as his approval and turned to Tariel. "Stay home and stay safe."

Tariel bristled but it was Fatima who answered.

"You stay safe," she said in an arctic voice with her eyes narrowed and wings flared. "If you get yourself killed, I'll raze through Hell and drag you back."

A shiver ran down her spine at the sudden deadliness of Fatima's voice. Her wind gathered around her as if a new threat entered the room. Isabella shuddered as the room grew cold once again. *Fatima's not one I want to mess with*, she thought.

The shadows around Sewall swirled and shrank back within him, as his face softened.

"As you wish, my shadow," he replied, lips twitching.

"She's so freaking scary," Tariel murmured under her breath.

"It's settled then," Amos stood, wings wide and a new light to his eyes. "We recruit Malachi and head back to the demon realm. Pray tell where should we start?"

"We can try Atlantis first," Sewall proposed, "The Azraels and Leviathan have had a…lengthy history together. We may have a shot of finding out more information out there."

"Plus, she shouldn't go back to cities within Beelzebub's domain." Gabriel shuddered. "He'll know to attack us faster than we could escape the next time we set foot on his land."

"That leaves for you to go only to either Satan's or Leviathan's domain." Fatima sneered.

Her eyes glowed with anger when she mentioned Satan's name. Sewall grabbed Fatima's hand.

"I'll ensure you get vengeance, my shadow," he whispered in her ear.

The shadows danced together around them. Another shiver ran down Isabella's spine.

"Then Leviathan's domain it is," Amos concluded. "Barmen said Satan showed up and took Mikael, Arick, and Matthew. If she's the one supporting Matthew and his attack on our realm, we'll need to avoid her domain as much as possible."

"I was taken to her domain," Fatima hissed, "with red sand as far as the eye could see."

"We'll start in Atlantis and see what we can find!" Gabriel said, his wing trembling.

Sewall grabbed Fatima's shoulders. "Meet with the other Arch ladies. Ava, Rachael, Farah, and anyone else who can hold their own."

Isabella startled.

This would be the first time in a long time all Head Archs were not within their own realm. Once her father left with them, there were only a handful of them left to defend. Unease crawled its way through her body as she prayed nothing happened while they were away. They weren't enough. She wasn't enough.

"We'll keep our realm safe," Fatima promised.

Chapter 6

Voices reverberated across the room. *Raised voices*, Clarissa corrected. She hissed as pain shot through her head like she had been hit with a blunt object. She gritted her teeth and lifted her heavy eyelids as the voices hushed.

Peering through one eye, she saw Barmen's widened blue eyes first. Sweat dripped from his brow, worry etched onto every line in his face. This was the most expressive she'd seen him. His hand touched her head and prodded with care.

"Does this hurt?" He breathed softly, feeling along her head and neck.

Clarissa's body stretched on the ground with her head laying in Barmen's lap. Her face grew hot as he leaned in, watching her.

She opened her mouth to protest when he touched a tender spot on the base of her skull. She winced. Frosty anger glimmered in his narrowed gaze while his voice sounded unaffected.

"She may have a concussion." Barmen looked at Gabriel and Joshua.

While Gabriel's wings twitched nervously, Joshua frowned at her with crossed arms. *Where were they?* Clarissa wondered. She moved to get up but Barmen stopped her.

"Stay down for now," Barmen commanded. "You took a pretty nasty blow to the head earlier."

She groaned as the sore spot throbbed.

"What happened?" she asked.

Her hoarse throat itched with dryness. The air felt thick and heavy with each word she spoke.

"You went berserk." Zewal grimaced down at her with disgust. "Now we're being held prisoner and lost a full day because of you and your temper."

Barmen tensed around her, his wings flared.

An ember of irritation ignited in her stomach at Zewal. She opened her mouth to defend herself when some of her memories came back. She froze. Gabriel teleported them to the wrong city in the demon realm and then…the sound of rushing water sent her over the edge.

She shuddered at the memory. Barmen frowned, staring at her.

She remembered his blue eyes pulling her back to safety when someone hissed in her ear. Then everything went black.

"Someone hit me from behind." She rasped. Her throat burned for water.

"Leviathan didn't take too kindly to you destroying his city." Zewal scoffed.

Barmen lifted a ladle up to her lips, tilting her head back. "Drink this."

She gulped eagerly, not caring that the water tasted like minerals.

Zewal continued, "You wrecked a good portion of the city."

"Many demons are angry at us," Joshua mused.

He lifted a finger to his chin while his eyes were on his son. He tilted his head as if trying to figure out what was going on in Barmen's mind.

Clarissa scoffed as she finished the last drop.

"At least they still have a city." She looked around the room. "Plenty of their kind demolished mine."

If they were prisoners, this was the oddest jail cell she'd seen. She expected a dark, dingy cell with three stone walls and iron bars to cage them in. Instead, green, fluffy moss covered the ground, and they were surrounded by small trees and shrubbery. The air was dense and moist while the temperature was warm. There were no guards anywhere around them. She glanced at her wrists to find them bare. No restraints either. No one was tied up or locked away.

Off to the side, brightly colored frogs the size of large dogs sat by a small pond. Her eyes widened as she tried to scramble away.

Those were poisonous Slaadi frogs.

"Easy now." Barmen held her closer. "We've been keeping an eye on them and holding them back."

Zewal huffed. "As long as your illusions hold up. Otherwise, we're screwed."

Screwed indeed. Every direction she turned there was a frog, outnumbering them by nearly a dozen. One touch on their skin and they were done for. Her lessons on these frogs described there was no cure; you could only try to lessen the severity of the symptoms and pray you made it. These types of frogs were much smaller in her region back home but preferred to stay in specific areas in the jungle. She never knew the demon realm possessed larger ones.

She furrowed her brow. Why haven't they escaped yet? They were surrounded, yes, but Joshua and Barmen could've made illusions to get out by now. She glanced at Gabriel's twitching wings. Though he'd placed them in the wrong city, it would make sense if he'd teleported them out of here. What was the holdup?

"You were injured." Barmen saw the questions in her eyes. She paused, startled he could read her so easily. Something in her chest fluttered at his words. "We didn't want to risk injuring you further."

"*You* didn't want to risk injuring her further. Besides, who knows where else this idiot might land us?" He indicated to Gabriel, who flinched.

"Where's Leviathan? We should escape now that I'm awake." Clarissa stood up.

Barmen helped her this time, keeping a wary eye on her.

"We haven't seen him since he placed the lid on." Joshua's fingers tapped along his leg. "We…" Joshua froze, his eyes dilating. Clarissa counted ten heartbeats before Joshua finished his sentence. Joshua shook his head and then smiled. "We can try to escape now."

"Oh no," Barmen murmured, frowning at his dad.

Zewal and Gabriel exchanged a glance.

"He's been doing that since we've arrived." Zewal glared at Barmen. "What's going on with your dad? He's acting strange. One minute he's serious and the next all jovial, trying to talk with the frogs and shit."

She swirled on Barmen, eyes wide. "I thought he was…"

"There's nothing going on with him" Barmen moved to his father's side, lips curled in a sneer. "He just needs to sit down for a moment."

Gabriel and Zewal exchanged another glance, one that said they doubted Barmen. She furrowed her brow as she watched him. Her heart squeezed.

He whispered in Joshua's ear, too low for anyone else to hear. His father's eyes widened and narrowed several times before a calm expression overtook his face.

Barmen pulled away and pointed to a small bump in the moss. "Sit right there for a moment, Dad."

"Ok." Joshua smiled widely.

He bounced—Clarissa's jaw dropped—over to the spot his son indicated to and plopped down as if he was a little kid again.

Gabriel frowned while Zewal looked downright outraged.

"What the hell is going on here, Barmen?!" Zewal stormed up to him. "Don't give me some crap of 'there's nothing wrong'. Look at him!"

Joshua swung his legs back and forth while humming a

cheery tune.

Zewal jerked a wing in his direction. "That isn't the same Arch as before."

"Careful." Barmen hissed with narrowed eyes. "You don't know a damn thing about my dad."

"Maybe we don't." Clarissa shifted closer to Barmen's side. "But we deserve to know the truth."

A sharp pain pierced her heart at the last time Barmen tricked her. Back when he'd led them to Beelzebub's office and abandoned them with an illusion. *That's right*, she reminded herself, *he's a really good liar.* She didn't want to be fooled again.

Something passed over Barmen's face as he watched her. It was gone in a flash, but she thought it looked like remorse.

She shook her head. *No, that wasn't possible. Was it?*

"My father just needs his meds. That's all. He's perfectly normal." Barmen's calm gaze at her transformed to glaring at Zewal and Gabriel. "With how much time has passed, he needs his next dosage soon."

"Needing meds is *not* normal dumbass." Zewal scoffed, eyes flashing with irritation. "How much will this set us back? Did you ever think about that?"

Clarissa's flames sprung forth, causing the Azrael heir to jump. Heat radiated from her. The moist air combined with her fire to create more fog around them, but she didn't care.

"Don't bring your own daddy issues onto Barmen's," she hissed. "We have enough going on without you, adding to it."

Zewal's wings flared wide, his eyes flashing with animosity. She'd guessed correctly then on the source of his anger. Sewall's last words to his son were pretty harsh; it'd reminded her of her own father.

Still, she thought, *he had no right to attack Barmen or Joshua.* What was happening with Barmen and his father was his own business, not theirs.

Barmen's face softened as he gazed at her.

"Oh," Zewal's voice dropped low. "You're not one to talk about daddy issues."

She flinched. Barmen's wings flared. His icy eyes frosted over as they landed on Zewal.

"Whoa, whoa, whoa." Gabriel stepped between them, both hands extended out. "Come on, guys. We need to work together here. Not fight with each other."

"Hmmm, you're right." Barmen straightened his clothes, composing himself. "Bickering like children will get us no-where."

Clarissa wondered if the others noticed the wall coming over Barmen's eyes like she did. The wall that shuts down all emotions to get stuff done. To move on to the next action.

"I'll handle my father. What we need is to get out of here." Barmen faced Gabriel. "Will you be able to open another por-tal?"

"Open a portal….yes, technically." Gabriel blushed sheepishly.

Zewal huffed and raised his hands in the air.

"You'd gotten us to the demon realm before," Clarissa interjected, crossing her arms. "What was so different about the last time?"

"The first jump was just a blind jump to a new realm." Gabriel ran a hand through his hair. "This time, there was a specific destination in mind, and I…I don't know the demon realm well to pinpoint cities. If I can't see where to go, the portal could open anywhere in the demon realm."

Clarissa ground her teeth together. "Why didn't you say anything earlier? We could've planned better. My sister was expecting me to be there for her."

Another flash of irritation burned through her. Her flames swirled around her hands while the heat floated around her temples, threatening to erupt through her hair. She took a deep breath, in vain. Anxiety clawed her chest at the thought of Isabella by herself. *Was she all right?* Her sister was powerful but needed to be looked after. Isabella wasn't strong enough on her own, not without her.

Clarissa clenched her fist. She will return to Isabella's side, no matter what.

"He's already tried to escape this place." Zewal glanced up. "And he couldn't open a portal in here."

Clarissa followed his gaze and gasped. A glass dome stretched before them with a large cork-looking bulb at the top, locking them in there. They were in a gigantic terrarium, filled with poisonous frogs.

They could fly up there, she thought, *but how would they lift the cork lid? If they had a Michael angel, they'd stand a chance. Even Atarah could be of some help*, she thought begrudgingly; none of them had super strength.

She had her flames. Barmen possessed illusions, Gabriel with teleportation which was useless while in here, and Zewal had his ability to suck the life out of anything.

She paused. The wheels turned in her mind.

"What do you know about Leviathan?" The question tumbled out of her mouth. Zewal made a sound of disgust.

"He's a flashy lizard who's an attention seeker." Zewal rolled his eyes.

"He possessed the powers of all of the elements, healing, and death," Barmen answered with a hand to his chin, his eyes looking over her and Zewal. "He has the ability to out-manipulate both of your powers and any Raphael angels if they were present."

Zewal's eyes glimmered but he didn't contradict Barmen's claims. Clarissa had only seen Leviathan for a brief period of time when she met with Beelzebub. He acted like a partygoer and lazy but how quickly he took her down sent chills down her spine.

However he'd taken the time to bedazzle his staff, something he didn't necessarily need. *Leviathan was a demon who appreciated appearances,* she pondered.

"Zewal, could you—" she hesitated as his permanent glare shifted to her. "Could you wilt everything in here?"

He raised an eyebrow.

Clarissa continued, "I'm just guessing here but Leviathan likes pretty things. If you use your powers and things dry up, then he'll have no choice but to come in here and put a stop to it."

"Oh!" Gabriel's eyes widened. "That's a good idea."

"It is," Barmen murmured. The wheels in his mind still turned. "I'll create an illusion to hide us from his view so he'll have no choice but to open the top and come in."

"And then what?" Zewal jeered. "We have no chance in hell of stopping him. He'll nullify mine and Clarissa's powers. So, what then?"

Barmen frowned. "I may be able to create a powerful enough illusion on Leviathan to give us a brief window to fly out of here, but…" he paused. "If he's familiar with his sister's work, he'll pick apart the illusion in no time."

"We'd have to be fast, very fast," Clarissa replied.

"As soon as we're out of here, I'll open a portal too." Gabriel's wings stopped twitching. "I'll aim for Joshua's library again. I won't mess that up."

Zewal glowered at each of them before sighing.

"All right," Zewal drawled. "We'll go with this plan, only because we have no better option right now." Zewal swiveled on his heels, facing the frogs. "I may accidentally kill the frogs though."

Clarissa's heart skipped a beat.

"Wait!" she cried. "That'll piss him off. Don't do that."

Zewal peered over his shoulder. "What did you think my powers were? Putting things to sleep? I'm the angel of death."

Before she could answer, Zewal's cold shadow expanded, stretching and decaying everything it touched. The springy, green moss withered beneath him. Tendrils grew from the shadows and wrapped around the frogs and shrubbery. Groans and weak croaks resounded around them. A sudden wave of exhaustion forced her to her knees. Though Zewal wasn't directing his powers at them, she still felt the effects of his life-sapping abilities.

Her flames around her arms and torso dwindled as if a cold hand gripped her shoulders and pushed her down. Cold hands…She whimpered and curled in on herself. *She was… safe-ish*, she reminded herself. *She still had her flames. She still had her flames.*

She repeated the mantra in her head as more decay spread.

Zewal was right. He was death. Cold, decaying, and stifling the air around them, he shrouded his powers around them. She shivered weakly in an attempt to call forth her fire. A small flame from within heated her body enough. If Zewal drained her of any more power, she wouldn't be able to stay warm.

Something drifted over her huddled form. Too weak to lift her head, she pivoted her eyes to the side to see Barmen hunched over. His wings extended over her as if to protect her from Zewal's abilities. His face looked ghastly pale, and his limbs trembled with effort. In his kneeling position, his brow furrowed as he watched the cork, waiting for Leviathan to come by. Clarissa prayed the demon lord entered soon to relieve them of this suffocating death.

She whimpered again. Barmen's wings tightened around her. The frogs, once vibrating with color and life, appeared dead and withered. The smell wafting around them reminded her of soil and stale air. Nothing moved. She wondered if Barmen had an illusion around them but didn't have the energy to ask.

It was as if all of her willpower was being sucked out of her by someone. No—by Zewal. All the color pulled to Zewal, leaving everything else gray and dull. He sapped the strength and life out of every living thing. A warm glow radiated around his face. Energized, the Azrael heir looked…

handsome. However she'd rather die than admit that to him.

She feared if there was ever going to be an end to this suffering when a hiss resounded through the terrarium. She mustered up enough energy to roll on her back to see the large cork lift. Numbly, she watched the cork roll to the side and a small figure jump through the opening.

This was their chance to escape, but she was too weak to lift her head, let alone fly out. She groaned. Zewal took too much from them.

The small figure grew bigger as it careened toward them. Blue scales glistened against the surrounding light, along a lizard-like torso. She thought Leviathan would land with a loud thud but she was wrong.

Leviathan floated to the ground with the grace of a ballerina or gazelle. He twirled a purple cape around him and struck a pose. His gold eyes flashed to Zewal, slithering their way up his body as if he planned to eat the heir. She shuddered, feeling grateful those eyes weren't on her.

A smile curled on Leviathan's face, stretching almost from ear to ear. Goosebumps rose along her arms. She resisted the urge to cower away from the demon lord, forcing herself to stay strong. Leviathan raised a hand and snapped his fingers together. A few seconds passed in silence but energy returned to her. Color seeped out of Zewal and back into the ground and surrounding area. Breathing was easier, lighter than before. Her fire filled her limbs with life and strength. She rolled herself to stand, lifting her wings to take off.

"Not so fast—fire girl," Leviathan pointed a claw at her. His eyes stayed on Zewal. "You're still on my shit list after what you did to my beautiful city and people."

His eyes narrowed and the fire in her veins sputtered.

"All of you are to blame for my suffering. There's so much work to do, I haven't been able to get high for a full day now. A day! Rebuilding the towers, buildings, waterfalls." He put his hands on his hips and scoffed. "None of you brats know what it's like to rebuild a city."

Flames erupted from her head. Indignation spread through her like wildfire, raising her body temperature.

"Rebuild? You call that rebuilding a city?" She released a mirthless laugh. "Try having nothing left, not even a tree to shelter you from the rain, and then talk to me about rebuilding a city, *demon.*"

She spat at his feet. Leviathan hissed in disgust and coiled his body away from her.

Her flames flickered high on her head. Narrowly, she controlled her fire from shooting out of her arms by concentrating on her breathing. They needed to escape, she reminded herself, not start a fight they couldn't win.

"What the hell are you talking about girl? Never mind, it doesn't matter. What matters is that you'll be punished for attacking my people. Properly punished this time!" Leviathan's voice softened as he turned back to Zewal. "The offer still stands with you, Zewal."

"Offer?" Clarissa raised an eyebrow at the Azrael heir, who frowned.

"Leviathan offered me a ridiculous punishment—" Zewal started.

"Punishment!" Leviathan placed a hand on his chest. "I asked you out on a date! Not a—"

"Punishment all the same," Zewal scoffed. "One I won't be taking."

Leviathan sighed. "Your ancestor played hard to get and I still won in the end."

"I'm not Azrael." Zewal glared at the demon lord. "We aren't the same Archs."

Leviathan rolled his eyes. "You're all the same in one way or another. There's barely any difference between the clans."

Clarissa's brow furrowed. *Barely any difference? What the Trinity?* She thought. The clans have been at each other's throats for generations because of all of their differences and disputes.

"There's nothing different about demons," she retorted. "All of you are the same violent, disgusting scum you'll always be."

Leviathan raised an eyebrow and slicked his tongue out. "For every 1 of you angels, there's 1,000 demons. Do you really think we're all the same?"

Clarissa remained silent, glaring at him. Demons were no different. She had fought and feared them all of her life. Nothing he could say could take that from her.

"Enough of this," Leviathan waved his webbed hand. "I'm not the teaching type and I want to smoke my blunt, so it's time to punish you."

Barmen twitched behind her. She opened her wings to launch into the air when her feet collapsed. She fell to the ground, her flames extinguishing in her arms and legs, weakening. She gasped as she saw Zewal, Gabriel, and Barmen on the ground, the color drained from their faces.

Dammit! She thought. While she was, angrily, chatting away they should've been escaping out of here.

"Not so fast," Leviathan purred. "I'm calling in that favor you owe me."

She jerked her head up, mouth agape.

"What?" Gabriel asked weakly. Leviathan grinned.

"Each of you owe me a favor from exchanging my staff."

"But—!" Clarissa protested.

"But nothing princess," Leviathan countered. "You walked in there expecting a deal. It's time to accept the consequences."

The deal was the three demon lord staffs in exchange of owing a favor to them. None of them used the staffs except Ben. An unfair deal he'd trapped them all into. They'd begged him not to take it and the asshole didn't bat an eye. He agreed to the one-sided deal, damning the rest of them. The other two staffs were who knows where with either Mikael or Elijah.

Neither of them were present. She gritted her teeth, cursing Ben.

"The favor!" Leviathan pointed a claw to the sky, the other hand on his hip. "Is servitude!"

Blood drained from her face, leaving her cold.

"You'll all serve and help my people in Talia and the delta." Leviathan continued.

Clarissa's wings trembled.

"We don't owe you such a favor." Joshua popped up beside Leviathan.

"Eeeeek!" Leviathan squeaked, jumping into the air.

Somewhere behind her, Barmen cursed quietly. Her eyes widened. Barmen must've been creating an illusion around him and his father this whole time. She hadn't noticed him and when he moved it had been simple movements.

"Shit! Raziel angels," Leviathan hissed. "I despise you slippery bastards. Little henchmen of my sister."

Joshua tilted his head and smiled. "Not all rubies are red. Heaven and Hell are delusions within ourselves."

Leviathan tilted his head back at Joshua.

"Hmmmm, you need medicinal herbs don't you?" Leviathan snapped two fingers together and Barmen groaned.

Energy sapped away from him, draining all the color from his face. The world around her swirled, like fog fading away, and a different picture focused. While she'd thought the life inside the terrarium decayed, when the illusion lifted everything was teeming with life and vibrant. Three large frogs croaked on all sides of Leviathan, which she hadn't noticed. Their slick skins rubbed against the demon lord. Their skin…Their poisonous skin! She smiled, opening her mouth to celebrate. Barmen must have created an illusion to ensure Leviathan didn't realize he was touching the frogs. This was their chance to escape while the toxins weakened Leviathan.

She glanced at Barmen ready to leap into his arms but froze. Barmen's face wasn't one of victory but one of frustration. His eyes narrowed on Leviathan.

"The frogs have been rubbing up against you since you landed." Barmen sighed. "How are you still standing?"

"Hmmmmm," Leviathan hummed, reaching up and petting the frogs fondly. "This is my home, Arch, and these are my demons, the Slaadi frogs. I'm immune to all poisons and venoms."

He wrapped his tail around Joshua to prevent him from jumping on the frogs.

"All of them?" Gabriel's eyes bulged, his face ashen.

"Of course. I'm the Demon Lord. Controller of healing, death, and the elements." His eyes flickered between Joshua, who still tried to hop on the frog's back, and Barmen. "Your father here is going through psychosis."

"Psychosis?" She furrowed her brow.

Barmen's wings and nostrils flared.

"That's none of your business," Barmen replied softly before turning to his father. "Dad, you need to come here right now!"

A muscle jumped in Barmen's jaw as Joshua ignored him.

"Tsk, tsk," Leviathan wrapped his tail around Joshua's torso, immobilizing him. "What a nasty side effect from your powers."

"Side effect?" Gabriel murmured, exchanging another glance with Zewal.

"Oh yes," Leviathan drawled. "After so many years of creating illusions and distorting reality, the user slowly can't tell what's real anymore. Becoming crazier and crazier as they grow older."

"My father isn't crazy," Barmen answered through clenched teeth, his hands curled into fist. "Please release my father and return him to me."

"How many drugs have you been pumping into your father?" Leviathan lifted Joshua in the air, turning him upside down. "He's in quite an advanced stage of psychosis if he's stopped taking orders from you. If he hadn't spoken to me, you could've gone on with your little plan."

"Please," Barmen growled. "Stop."

Joshua laughed as Leviathan straightened him and set him down. "I have the herbs and medicine he needs to come back to our reality but you'll have to be cooperative with me."

Leviathan wiggled a claw at him. Barmen's cold gaze flickered from Leviathan and Joshua for a moment.

"Very well." He sighed. Reluctancy in each word.

"No more illusions punk," Leviathan pointed a finger at Barmen. "It's annoying enough when my sister pulls this shit. I'll just kill you all if you do that again."

"Aw and I thought we had something special," Zewal jeered, coming to his feet.

Her flames returned to her as Leviathan withdrew his hold on them.

"I have my limits and standards to uphold, Arch," Leviathan sounded serious. "First thing's first, you'll all serve me in Talia."

Barmen's eyes widened. "Wait, my dad needs that medicine!"

Leviathan coiled his tail tighter around Joshua.

"And he'll get that medicine *after* you do as you're told." Leviathan hissed back.

He swiveled to Gabriel, who jumped.

"No!" Gabriel cried, wings trembling. "Don't drain me to death!"

"You do as you're told and I won't have to," Leviathan huffed. "You're to open a portal to Talia. It's just outside of the south river basin."

Gabriel paled. "I have no idea where that is! I screwed up the last time I opened the portal."

"Have you ever looked at a map before, kid?" Leviathan sighed, pinching the bridge of his nose.

"We don't know what your world looks like," Clarissa

defended, her wings flared at his tone. "Why would we?"

"It's basic warfare knowledge sweetheart." He slithered closer to Gabriel. "If you were going to attack us, I'd assumed you would be much more….prepared, but I suppose you're all as clumsy as you look."

Gabriel tried to scurry away but Leviathan latched onto his ankle and pulled.

"Let him go!" Zewal hissed, encircling his shadow tendrils around Leviathan.

The demon lord peered down at them and snapped his fingers. The shadows disappeared before she could blink.

"Your power comes from me child, not the other way around," Leviathan growled. "All of you have way more fight in you than I thought. It'll be useful when the time comes."

"The time for what?" Clarissa challenged.

She wanted to fly out of here but not without the others. Leviathan captured Joshua and Gabriel within seconds.

How are they going to get out of this? Could they?

"Never mind that," Leviathan purred.

He snapped his fingers again. The ground swelled beneath them, raising them into the air toward the terrarium's opening. She staggered, struggling to balance as they careened upward. The ground shifted as if it was quicksand. However, instead of sinking, they were lifting.

Despite herself, her eyes widened. She knew Leviathan possessed control over all the elements, but it caught her by surprise to see him use earth manipulation. No angel or Arch had the ability to use more than one element. Yet, Leviathan snapped two fingers and used any power all at once. Fire coiled in her belly, flaring into her limbs. She didn't have any hope they could ever kill the demon lords.

However, maybe, she could ensure her people never had to set eyes on another filthy demon.

"We can fly," Barmen said dryly.

"Not all of us have wings, Arch," Leviathan sounded exasperated.

She peered back at them. Joshua remained wrapped in his tail while Gabriel dangled from his outstretched arm.

"What could you possibly need a favor from us for?" Clarissa asked, watching their ascension.

They left the glass dome opening, entering into a different type of jungle. Cooler air hit her first, along with a change in atmospheric pressure, as if she stepped out of a shower or left a greenhouse.

"Truly very little," Leviathan sighed. "There's little you could offer me, outside of entertainment. Even then you—" he waved his other hand around, "—lot are going to bore me soon enough. Whatever happened to that interesting Arch with the brown wings? He looked like fun."

Clarissa jerked, wings flared.

She didn't want to talk about Ben. That bastard could rot in hell for all she cared. Ben screwed them over without a second thought. Worse still, a part of her, a very small part, understood why he did it. He'd been desperate in the same way she was to help her people.

However she wanted to rescue her people and rebuild her city, she doubted Ben had such altruistic motives. His eyes glazed over others as if he never really saw them. She shuddered. She recognized that kind of gaze in her own family, and it made her blood boil.

Heat filled her limbs as another tremor shook her. No, she didn't want to talk about Ben. She glanced up to see Barmen staring right at her. While his face remained expressionless, something in his eyes shifted as he answered Leviathan.

"We don't know what happened to him," his icy, blue eyes stayed on her as he spoke. "But last I heard, he encountered your sister."

Leviathan gave a humorless laugh. "Poor little Arch. There won't be much left of him after my sister's through with him."

They landed on firmer ground, with the jungle echoing

the sounds of birds, croaks of frogs, and other loud sounds Clarissa didn't want to identify. Unlike her home, less gnats and mosquitos buzzed around. The tree canopy towered high above them, reminding her of Aquam Caput. For a moment, her chest tightened as knots swirled in her stomach for her people and Isabella. She shouldn't have been away from them for so long.

"Where are you going?" she asked.

Alarm bells rang in her head as Leviathan dragged Joshua and Gabriel along. The large leaves and dense brush engulfed him within seconds. They scrambled after the demon lord, desperate to keep up. The branches moved out of Leviathan's way as he slithered along the jungle floor.

"Please say it's somewhere close." Zewal groaned close behind Leviathan, who chuckled.

"If your friend," Leviathan jiggled Gabriel, who let out another plea to be released. "Could teleport us, it would be much faster. But alas we'll have to use my method of travel instead."

"What's your method of travel?" Clarissa asked beads of sweat dripping down her face.

The hairs on the back of her neck stood up at Leviathan's smile, stretching nearly ear to ear. He stayed silent as they walked through the rainforest. Dread pooled in her stomach as the sound of rushing water drew closer.

Within minutes, they entered into a clearing to see one of the biggest rapids she's ever seen. The river sounded like thunder from the force. In the distance, a large waterfall stood with a rainbow stretching over the sky above it.

While a beautiful sight to behold, she couldn't admire it. The blood drained from her face and cold sweats spread across her back as she stared at the water. Her wings trembled as her worst fear came to pass. Their travel involved the rivers in some way. She shuddered. She sensed Barmen stepping closer to her, but another sound took everyone's attention.

Large birds screeched and gulled at them from the safety of a high tree branch. Their beady eyes watched them as if waiting for something.

Zewal narrowed his eyes. "They're waiting for our deaths, aren't they? Those birds."

Leviathan frowned at Zewal.

"They're not birds. Those are Malphas, very intelligent and sophisticated demons." Leviathan yelled above the sound of the rapids. He tilted his head to one side. "They wouldn't eat anything as disgusting as you. They stay by the river to ensure no one can overhear them. They're a cautious species."

Clarissa didn't bother looking up. Her eyes stayed on the large river before her. The flowing water…chills ran down her spine. Air lodged itself in her throat refusing to let out a scream. Her fire! She needed her fire! She forced out a breath in one rushed exhale. Her fire spread from her belly into her limbs, warming her. Protecting her.

Her legs trembled as flames sprung from her hands. *You're fine*, she reminded herself, *I'll survive this just like I survived everything else*. Through gritted teeth, she stilled her legs. She wouldn't lose control like last time.

As she returned to her senses, Leviathan's voice drew her attention. She hadn't realized he'd been talking this whole time.

"We'll travel through the basins and the rapids are the fastest way to Talia. After we are done there, we will travel to the Delta—"

"Wait! " She protested. "We're not going anywhere with you!" She narrowed her eyes at him. "Release our friends now!"

"No? " Leviathan raised a scaly eyebrow. "You forget that you, and these two," he pointed to Zewal and Gabriel. "owe me a favor. Each. Trust me girly, you don't want to know what will happen if you don't complete the agreed trade."

"I didn't agree to it." She scoffed, shuffling her feet.

Flames circled up her arms.

"But your party left with three staffs. One of which was mine. The favor you owe me binds you in that agreement."

"Does that mean she'll owe a favor to Beelzebub as well?" Barmen stepped in front of her.

His wings flared and tension around his eyes and shoulders that hadn't been there earlier.

"No," Leviathan purred. "He didn't specify which demon lord you owed a favor to, only that a favor was owed. The perk of making deals with my brother is that he makes them… relatively fair. "

"Compared to you or your sister?" Barmen's lip curled at the mention of Satan.

"Especially compared to my sister, Arch." Leviathan scoffed.

"What happens if the favor is never called upon?" Clarissa asked, thinking of her sister.

Could she keep her from this?

"Since an expiration date wasn't mentioned, that means there is none," Leviathan explained. "We could come to you on your deathbed and demand that favor."

"And if we can't complete that favor?" She hated the slight tremble in her voice.

Leviathan gave a cruel smile.

"Then your soul is ours to control and manipulate for all of eternity." He purred. "Why do you think that Matthew fellow is so annoying for my brother and I? He's our sister's little pet."

They all froze.

Matthew was….Matthew couldn't complete a favor owed to Satan? Was that why he was attacking everyone? Why they attacked their world? The destruction of her city? The havoc and hordes of demons pillaging their towns across the spirit realm?

"Why?" She whispered. "What does your sister even

want?"

Leviathan narrowed his eyes at her, growing serious.

"Now, that's the first interesting question you've asked. But it'll have to be answered some other time." He waved his last free webbed hand. "You're welcomed to stay here and try to survive against the Malphas or the other numerous demons in my region, but I'm taking these two to Talia. You can follow and live or stay and die."

She gasped as he leapt into the river with Joshua and Gabriel. A cry caught in her throat as he plummeted to the water. Barmen launched into the air about to follow them into the water when Leviathan stopped above the water.

Her jaw dropped.

Leviathan hovered above the water on what appeared to be a long and narrow surfboard. He switched Joshua to his other hand and put his tail in the water at the end of the board. The demon lord pivoted back and forth, missing rocks and dips with ease. Using a mixture of his webbed feet and tail to maneuver, he shot down the river like a bird in the sky.

She scrambled into the air, Zewal close behind her, following Leviathan down the river. Barmen reacted faster than them, allowing him to keep up with the demon lord. The large rapids crashed and thundered along the jungle terrain, splashing them though they flew high enough to reach the tree canopies. If they had attempted to travel into the river by themselves she doubted they would've survived. The river would've sucked them under within half a second. The current held such high pressure, they wouldn't be able to swim their way out. Not that she ever planned to swim.

She shuddered, flapping harder against the wind to keep up. If Isabella was at her side, she'd manipulate the wind in their favor. Another sharp pang shot through her chest at the thought of her sister. They've rarely ever been apart, especially for this long. Anxiety gnawed in her stomach as the desire to see her sister spiked.

She glanced at Leviathan to ensure she followed his path. The waves carried him in a way she carried her flames. *The river obeyed him, not the other way around*, she realized. That's why he appeared almost bored surfing through the rapids. She peered at the path ahead and nearly balked.

Nearly hundreds of river pathways lay in front of them as far as the eye could see. Like hundreds of roots spreading from a tree trunk, the river broke into paths leading in every direction. How the hell did he know where to go? She wondered.

She reluctantly flew closer. She couldn't risk losing sight of him. Or else she'd be lost, alone, and doomed. The sounds of the jungle echoed as the sun's heat blazed down and drained her and Zewal. Zewal glided low to the river, looking as exhausted as she felt. His pale face turned grayish before long and sweat coated his neck, shoulders, and back.

For a moment, she was grateful to be acclimated to this type of heat, but the humidity took its toll on her. She hovered low enough for the river to spray on her and prayed they'd arrive at their destination soon.

Chapter 7

The sounds of chattering voices irked Malachi more than usual today. Probably from the person speaking more than what they were saying. The scruffy collar on his tunic itched, prickling at his temper. The flames in his veins roared for release, but he withheld.

Flynn, Luke, and another female angel stood across from him in the foyer of his coastal villa. Each appeared disheveled, but Malachi remembered Luke, the leader of the rangers, enjoyed looking unhinged. He pivoted his gaze to Flynn, his cousin by blood but ranger by choice. Flynn took pride in his clean appearance, leaving Malachi to wonder why so much dirt and hay covered him.

Flynn was the first one to notice he'd stopped paying attention. Flynn pursed his lips and flared his wings.

"Are we boring you, Malachi?" Flynn started quietly, annoyance simmering beneath his tone.

The fire within his belly grew hot at his younger cousin's tone. The large female behind Flynn narrowed her eyes at Malachi, lifting the side of her mouth in a sneer. Were all rangers this bothersome?

"Yes," Malachi scoffed. "Each and every one of you. Particularly you."

He pointed at Luke, but the leader of the rangers regarded him as if *he* was the unhinged one.

"All you freaks are a constant pain in my ass," he complained. "Haven't I given plenty of soldiers for your little group in the human realm?"

The female behind Flynn flared her leather wings.

He continued, "Why are you bothering me with your stupid scouting reports? What does that have to do with me?"

Irritation pricked at his fingertips as flames threatened to spark to life. He had enough on his plate. Worse, he hadn't seen his daughters in days! Clarissa left a half written note about securing money for their people before disappearing with Gabriel's kid.

Dammit, he thought as unease coiled in his belly. Paul was up his ass from dawn till dusk about his 'return' on investments. His daughters were nowhere to be seen, and now Flynn expected him to stay calm and listen to their routine patrol. He rubbed his hand roughly over his face, taking in ragged breaths. Fire crackled underneath his skin's surface, threatening to burst through.

He took another breath, trembling. Now wasn't the time to let his temper get the best of him. His people needed him. His daughters needed him. Everyone needed him. *Shit! Couldn't he have just one minute to breathe?*

A sharp pain pierced his heart as memories of Liliana, his late wife, surfaced in his mind. The hole she'd left grew more with each passing day, consuming him. She'd been the air in his lungs, the wind beneath his wings, and the light in his life. She'd been his equal in every way. If she were alive, she'd be standing beside him, calming him down from Flynn's provocations, welcoming everyone to sit...

Maybe that was it? He sighed, peering back at Luke, who appeared concerned by him. As if he was a wild animal about to attack.

Another flare of irritation caused him to clench his fist, smothering the flames that sprouted forward.

"Sit and explain to me what is so important," he said through clenched teeth.

Crap! He thought. He couldn't even pretend to be hospitable. The female reached for her dagger.

"It's all right, Imani." Flynn put a hand on top of hers. "That was him trying to be…well, not mean I think."

Malachi scoffed. Liliana would've wanted to hear them out and get back to finding their daughters. *Yes*, he nodded to himself, *he needed Clarissa back to help him rebuild.* Then they could tackle Paul's outrageous demands. *Where in the hell was that girl?* Malachi frowned as he indicated for everyone to move outside.

The balcony wrapped around the corner of the villa facing out to the coastline. Reclining chairs were sprinkled along the wall. Malachi welcomed the cool air against his heated skin as he tasted the salt on the ocean breeze.

Leaning over the terrace edge, he searched for patience as he watched the waves crash onto the shore. After a few deep breaths, he turned back to the rangers. Imani glared at him. Flynn shuffled on his feet, always eager to leave, while Luke sat.

Luke regarded him from his seat with a look as if he pitied him. Malachi didn't like this expression any better.

"We had no choice but to come to you with this information," Luke's deep voice carried above the noise of the waves. "All other Head Archs are on missions and unavailable."

"Unavailable?" Malachi raised an eyebrow. "What about the heirs?"

Surely someone would be left behind in charge, to take over when needed.

"We've tried every region," Luke shook his head.

Malachi frowned, a pit in his stomach grew as he remembered his daughters disappearing with Gabriel Jr. and Ben. Amos had written to him dozens of times, telling him to send Ben back home, but he'd been too busy with the city's repairs to think much of it.

"Elijah, Amos, Joshua, Gabriel Sr., and even Mikael were

nowhere to be found," Luke explained. "We've sent a scout south to see if Sewall is present but you're the first Head Arch we've encountered since arriving back in the spirit realm."

The fire in his blood withered at Luke's words. That can't be possible... Where were the others? Hair rose on the back of his neck. *No...* he thought, *he couldn't be one of the few leaders left to defend their realm...*

He shuddered, hugging his wings closer. Why did they come to him? His anger flamed back to life and didn't dwindle. He had enough on his plate!

"We needed to report to a Head Arch what we learned in the human realm," Luke continued, "The demons aren't following Matthew's orders. They're following Satan's. She plans to—"

"Stop!" Flames sprouted from Malachi's hands "Don't tell me anything. I've had enough!"

"Malachi," Flynn pleaded, stepping closer. "Someone has to know and tell the others."

"This affects all of us," Imani hissed. "If you spaceheads do nothing, we rangers will suffer as well."

Malachi gripped the ledge tightly, turning his back to them.

"I can't take anything else on my plate." He rasped.

Flames pulsed along his arms, urging for release. He tightened his hands. Another gust of wind blew against his face. The smell of salt mixed with the moist, cool air aided him.

*Liliana...*Her element had been the wind. Free, caring, and adaptable. Bright green eyes ricocheted through his mind. Lilian's green eyes. His heart clenched. Why did it need to be him? He ran a hand through his hair, patting out any sprouted flames. This was just information after all...he only needed to pass it along and then be done. He sighed.

"I can do that," he murmured to himself.

"What?" Flynn tilted his head.

"Nothing," Malachi shook his head. "I can pass some information along since there's not many Head Archs here. If anything else comes up, pass it to another leader. Someone who's less busy."

Luke smacked the side of his legs as he stood up. A strange smile spread across his face.

"That's more like you. We've made trades with two watchers to gain this information." Luke's irises flashed gold for a moment before going back to black. "Satan wants to combine the realms to subjugate humans and angels alike."

Malachi furrowed his brow. "She should know it'll destroy the realms if she does that."

"She's willing to take the gamble," Luke grinned, joining him at the ledge. "You see, she faces a problem unique to the demon lords."

"What do you mean?" He frowned.

"The demon lords can't leave their realm. Their power is too great," Luke continued. "So she's been using others to do her bidding. Her first victim was Matthew."

Malachi's wings twitched. Matthew was a victim? He released a humorless laugh. *Surely Luke was joking,* he thought.

The ranger regarded him for a few minutes. His expression conveyed a 'matter of fact' sentiment. He dropped his own half-felt grin.

"He's serious, Malachi," Flynn chimed in from his left. "The watchers confirmed everything."

"Watchers?" He scoffed. "That's your source?"

"What would they gain by lying?" Imani fired back. "Once they possess a body, they're as vulnerable as we are."

Malachi opened his mouth to retort but Luke stopped him.

"Never mind that," Luke countered. "The important thing to know is Satan's limitation and how we can stop her."

"Stop her?" Malachi's flames snaked up his arms. "Last I checked, Matthew was leading the charge on my people, destroying everything in sight!"

The volume in his voice grew with each word.

"Don't come to my house and tell me that the one who destroyed it, is a victim here!" He pointed a finger at Luke. "You said Satan can't come into our realm, so why should I or any of the others bother stopping her? We should put Matthew's head on a spike and everything will return to the way it was!"

"No." Luke frowned, shaking his head. "That's not the point."

"Then what's your goddamn point?" Malachi yelled, stepping closer to Luke.

Within a flash, Flynn was there, standing between them. Flames swirled and erupted from both of them. Anger simmered beneath his cousin's eyes while the emotion spewed from him. Were they here to plead with the Head Archs for Matthew's life?

No! He'd never let that happen.

"Malachi," Flynn's voice broke through his red haze. "We need to stop Satan if you want your people to stay safe."

"What's your point?" Malachi repeated through clenched teeth.

Luke placed a hand on Flynn's shoulder, smothering the flames.

Malachi paused. Those flames should've burned Luke. *How did he do that?*

"The point is." Luke's irises grew dark and somber as if shadows were filling in. "She's after Gabriel's angels to transport her enforcers. They call themselves 'assimilates' or 'elders'. She's after Michael angels for their strength and Raziel angels."

His flames calmed as he listened.

Something about Luke's voice…sapped the anger away. "She possesses immense power to create illusions and rewrite reality for some people. She has a limit but we don't know what that is yet."

Malachi relaxed his wings and extinguished his flames as

a numbness fell over his body.

Luke continued, "We know that she experimented with her control on Matthew by having him attack cities in the Spirit and human realms. Now that she knows her reach, she plans to use other angels to expand her territory from afar. Raziel angels to create illusions to keep others in line when she cannot. Use Michael angels for extra muscle when she cannot, and use Gabriel angels to transport her puppets anywhere she needs them to be."

Luke gripped both of his shoulders.

"Don't you see!" The ranger shook him slightly. "She plans to overtake all of us, from this realm to the next, using our very own against us! She'll infect us like a virus and watch the disease spread from the comfort of her home! We *have* to stop her*!*"

Some of the numbness lifted. His fire awakened as he processed Luke's words. Everything he'd studied concurred with Luke's words. The demon lords were known for being incredibly powerful and to be avoided at all cost.

How could they stop her?

"We stop her by banding together," Flynn finished. "We have to gather everyone—every angel from every clan, every ranger. Anyone who can fight."

"I don't know where the others are," Malachi said, dread pooling in the pit of his stomach.

His people couldn't fight. He couldn't ask that of them, not when they've lost so much. He owed Paul too much to ask for more…

"Malachi!" Luke pulled him from his dark thoughts. "The battles aren't happening now but we need to gather. We're heading back to pull all units together and need you to create another summit meeting for all of us. Everyone needs to know and everyone needs to fight."

"Another summit meeting?" Malachi brushed off his hands. "The last time I organized one, my city was hit so hard we haven't gotten back up yet."

"Then host it here," Flynn suggested. "With all of the leaders here, no one will be taken by surprise again."

"Here?" Imani exchanged a look with Luke. "Our troops won't like being back here after their poor treatment."

"They don't have to like it," Luke retorted. "None of us will."

Malachi knew the angels of the spirit realm wouldn't like it either. Angels saw the rangers as beneath them, weak and never fully belonging. Malachi glanced at Flynn. An Arch of a noble clan by birth but a ranger by choice. Despite being one of the few rangers from a pure lineage, he fit in with them more than his own family.

Malachi waited for the disgust to rise for his cousin and the other rangers but none did. Instead, to his horror, admiration bloomed in his chest for Luke and Flynn. They had every right to curse the angels of the spirit realm and leave them to a damned fate. Yet, here they stood, willing to fight for the ones who may not even sit at the same table as them.

He ran another hand through his hair. He wished he possessed the same integrity as them; he truly did. However, creating another summit meeting when all the Head Archs weren't in their region was no easy task. He couldn't locate his own daughters for Trinity's sake! They asked for too much…

"Malachi," Flynn's voice floated to him.

He peered at his cousin with weariness etched into every line in his face. Couldn't Flynn see the burden on his shoulders? The boulder of responsibility he carried. Flynn frowned.

"We have no other option but you," Flynn whispered.

Malachi gave a humorless laugh. No other option…damn if that didn't sting a little. He was the last pick and didn't have anywhere else to run. Another gust of wind blew across his face. The smell of the salty ocean floated around him.

Liliana…

"I'll do it," he grumbled. "I'll set up another summit meeting."

Luke's grin held no joy but grim acknowledgment.

"On the third morrow for us," Luke grumbled before turning on his heels and walking out.

Imani exchanged a look with Flynn before following Luke out. Shooting him a warning glare, she exited. Leaving him alone with his cousin.

Malachi tilted his head at Flynn and raised his eyebrow.

"He means three days from now. Morrow was an old term humans used." Flynn explained with a small smile. "He's odd, but he's right Malachi. We need this chance to go after Satan."

He didn't doubt his claim. However…

"Whose bodies did the watchers claim in exchange for this information?" Malachi grumbled. "Those lowlifes wouldn't give anything away for free."

"Do you care who?" Flynn fired back. "We're just rangers, the 'weirdos', you love to hate."

"Enough of that Flynn," Malachi growled. "You're not one of them, not really."

Flynn's eyes flashed, sparks flew from his hands before he closed them into fists.

"They're my family more than you ever were! I'll die as one of them!" Flynn hissed.

He flinched, shame and the familiar pang of regret surfaced.

"I'm sorry," he whispered, lowering his wings. "That was uncalled for."

The sparks fizzled out in Flynn's hand, but he nodded. Accepting his apology.

"I want to know—" he started.

"If it was me?" Flynn sneered. "If I traded my body for the information?"

"Yes, dammit!" Malachi strained to keep his voice low.

"Why does it matter?" Flynn goaded. "Will that make me officially damaged goods in your eyes? One of the freaks?"

Malachi froze.

The word 'yes' sat on the tip of his tongue, like an arrow about to hit its target. He stopped himself in time but his silence provided enough of an answer. Flynn scoffed, disgusted with *him*. What was wrong if he believed that? As Arch, they were above everything else in the human realm, including rangers. They were stronger, faster, and smarter than those beneath them. What of it? Why did Flynn sear him with a look as if he was the freak?

"It must be so hard to live a life of conditional acceptance," Flynn murmured.

"I—I…there can't be anything wrong with…I still accept you." He sputtered.

Did he? The question whispered in the back of his head. *Could he?*

Flynn shook his head. "Does it matter if I'm one of the bodies then?"

He opened his mouth to deny it but the words refused to come out. If Flynn was possessed by a watcher, would he still allow him in his house? Around his daughters? Memories flashed of their harsh upbringing. Beatings, training, and rules. So many rules to follow. Growing up, Flynn had the hardest time adjusting to the way things were.

Acceptance was never taught. Only learning what to reject was. Flynn faltered too close to the categories of rejection. He'd resented Flynn for leaving them for the rangers but never thought about what it would've cost him to stay.

"It doesn't matter," Malachi said softly. "But I care if the watcher will hurt you."

Silence stretched between them. Mostly from shock if he had to guess from Flynn's expression. His cousin's eyes softened before he spoke.

"I'm one of the volunteers. Luke was the other." He sighed. "And no, the watcher doesn't hurt to…house I guess is the word for it."

"Host, maybe? Since the watchers are glorified parasites," Malachi grumbled.

Flynn released a low chuckle.

"Host sounds like the better term for it." He conceded. "He's…odd but not as bad as I thought he would be."

"He?" Malachi scoffed. "Watchers are its, not anything that deserves a name."

"You can't even give something a name if you don't deem it worthy enough." Flynn's voice turned cold. "For a moment I thought…maybe a part of you changed through this whole ordeal."

"I've become more jaded since my city was attacked," Malachi confessed. "More guarded and callused."

"You hardened your heart a long time ago," Flynn argued. "You've been hiding behind a cheery smile. Pretending, with the rest of the aristocrats, that you're a good person. But now that the walls have been stripped away, you bare the fangs you've possessed this whole time. I've seen it in your city. The powerful prey on the weak without a second thought."

"Not all," Malachi growled back. "Not—"

"You've allowed it!" Flynn yelled. "You've—"

"Can we not have *one* conversation where we just talk peacefully?! How hard is it for you to ask how I'm doing? To wish me and my daughters well?" Malachi lifted his hands in the air and scoffed. "Every time you come around, it's like all you want to do is argue."

"Argue?!" A flush bloomed across Flynn's cheeks.

Suddenly he froze, placing a hand over his mouth as if to stop himself from speaking further.

He raised one finger, breathing deeply. "I need a second."

His eyes oscillated back and forth for a moment before going still.

"What the Trinity?" Malachi crossed his arms and counted.

Taking deep breaths, ten heartbeats passed by with the

waves breaking the quiet.

"I didn't come to argue," Flynn replied in a softer voice. "This family just frustrates me."

"You're not the only one frustrated, little bit."

Sparks flew from his cousin's fingertips.

"I'm sorry." Malachi soothed immediately. "I forgot you don't like that nickname."

"I didn't like what was happening when you all called me that name," Flynn said darkly. "None of it was fun for me."

Malachi rubbed the back of his neck and frowned. "You're right. It was messed up what we did back in the day. I'm sorry for that too."

The sparks fizzled out. Flynn eyed him suspiciously.

"What?" Malachi barked.

"Maybe you have changed. Several apologies in one night?" Flynn shook his head. "Never thought it possible for the great Malachi to admit to any wrongdoing."

He snorted. "The great Malachi? Don't joke."

"No, truly," Flynn continued. "You were the strongest. The wealthy heir who got everything he wanted. The golden child."

"Stop." Malachi sighed.

"No one could tell you no."

"Enough!" Malachi narrowed his eyes. "Not all shit smells the same, cousin. Don't go thinking you know everything."

Flynn frowned, looking at him with a sheepish expression.

"Sorry, you're right I don't know everything." He paused. "I never bothered asking how you were doing because I assumed…"

"Oh yeah?" Malachi raised an eyebrow. "What did you assume exactly?"

Flynn pursed his lips together, averting his eyes.

"Did you assume I ate food from a silver spoon? Did you assume life was full of sunshine and roses with Liliana?" His eyes hardened at the painful memories.

The first few years he and Liliana kept their love a secret out of fear of what their families would do. His parents, no—his father, only wanted a union between fire manipulators. Liliana didn't fit the equation since her ability was wind. Vice versa for her parents. Each set of parents agreed to keep bloodlines 'pure' for the sake of legacy. All the way until she died painfully, giving birth to Isabella. Taken from him far too soon.

He hid the bitterness from that night the best he could from his daughters, but the night the city fell, he couldn't hide anymore. "Did you assume everything was fine when Aquam Caput fell? That since my people escaped to Chrysi Poli all must be well? That my daughters were safe and happy?"

Flynn flinched. His chest tightened at the thought of his daughters. Liliana's last gift to him.

"I feel dumb asking now but," Flynn coughed. "How are you holding up, cousin?"

He ran a hand down his face before answering Flynn.

"I'm barely holding on most moments. Half the time I think about flying away or burning everything back to the ground. I get so angry all the time and I don't know how to squish it down anymore." He sighed. "It used to be so easy to smother it but slowly my anger has been getting harder to… hide."

"Not to me it hasn't."

Malachi let loose a brief chuckle. Flynn had a knack for getting on his nerves the most. Ever since they were kids.

"I know what a piece of shit Paul is," Malachi continued. "I don't need you to tell me."

"You know what he's tried with Clarissa and Isabella?" Flynn asked carefully.

Fired brewed hot in his belly as his anger flared.

"Yes," He hissed, clenching his fist. "I know he assaulted Clarissa when she was younger. She's still scared of water because of his water manipulation. It pains me every day that the city's reconstruction depends on the money he brought in."

The words tasted like ash on his lips.

"I've exhausted every other financial option before going to him. Trust me, Flynn, I looked at every other option before him. I asked Clarissa before I went to him. If it was too much for her…" A lump grew in his throat, making it difficult to speak. "She said she understood, but now she's taken off on some incredibly dangerous mission in the demon realm in hopes of getting more money for the city, and I—"

He lifted his hands again in defeat.

"I'm stuck between finding a new way to fund the city's needs and stopping a demon lord from destroying my city again." He smacked his hands against his legs. "I'm not doing well, cousin. I'm just not."

A hand fell on his shoulder.

"I'm sorry Malachi," Flynn said sincerely. "I had no idea. I'm sorry for the burden you bear and for judging you too soon."

"I would judge me too," he replied. "I—I'm not winning father or leader of the year any time soon."

Flynn scoffed. "Vast improvement compared to your father."

Malachi grinned. "I suppose so."

A breeze drifted to them from the ocean, gentle and assuring. They inhaled deeply, feeding oxygen to the fire coiled in their bellies, warming their bodies. Light mist sprayed against his face when he leaned over the railing. Salt invaded his nostrils and mouth. The taste of home, his home. Liliana.

He tightened his hold on the railing. This villa, the sanctuary, he'd built for Liliana to escape the plots of their family and high-strung society. The vacation home served its original purpose of housing and protecting his daughters. The thought of another threat, another army sweeping through his city like it was nothing…

He shuddered.

Flynn and Luke were right. He couldn't sit here and hide his head in the sand. Clarissa and Isabella needed him; his city and angels in the region needed him. He shook his head roughly, the moisture of the air fluffed his hair out of the bun he'd loosely tied.

"Where the hell do I start?" He murmured to himself.

"You'll figure it out." Flynn patted him on the back. "You always do."

A beat passed by.

"If you need anything, help, angel power, or whatever I'll be there," Flynn replied

He furrowed his brow. "How soon before Luke gathers his people?"

"Three days," Flynn answered.

"Three days to find the other Head Archs, drag them back, and stop another army onslaught." Malachi drawled. "Piece of cake."

"Flynn!" A voice called out from inside. Imani hovered at the edge of the door, watching—no—glaring at him. "We need to go."

Flynn nodded and she retreated.

"Set up the meeting and you won't take on the army by yourself, cousin." Another pat on the back. "Don't go dying on me. We have much to plan."

Flynn walked through the threshold of the home, leaving him with the noise of the waves for company.

Where could he start? He mused. Luke had mentioned earlier that Sewall may possibly be in his region. He pivoted to lean his back against the rail, tilting his head up to the stars. The stars twinkled, the new moon allowed them to shine brighter than before. On a beautiful night like this, he longed for a carefree dinner night with his girls again. Was Isabella staying close to her sister? He shook his head. As long as she stayed with Clarissa, all would be fine. Clarissa could handle herself. He trusted her to pull back if something was too dangerous. Now, he wondered where Amos, Elijah, Joshua, Gabriel, and Mikael wandered off.

He remembered Amos pursuing after his little brother Ben…and Elijah had taken off on some sort of mission with Mikael but—he gritted his teeth. Why was it so hard to remember? *Ah,* he thought. Clarissa was the one who read the messages from the other Archs. She'd been a crucial leader in the first few weeks. She'd organized supplies, food, created clinical stations and orphanages. She read through every report whenever he'd been too busy to look through them and relayed the messages. He'd remembered the gist of the message as they were going on a mission, but he couldn't remember any details.

He rubbed a hand down his face. *What was the other thing she said about Mikael and Elijah?* He struggled to remember.

A loud clap reverberated off the stone walls. Clouds cast themselves over the stars. The balcony grew darker. If not for his ignited flames, he would have missed Paul lurking in the far corner.

"Quite a touching reunion," Paul scoffed. "The little guy just doesn't know when to go away, does he?"

"What do you want Paul?" He sighed, running a hand through his hair.

Paul's eyes narrowed as he approached. "Is that any way to talk to the man who's keeping your city afloat?"

He winced as Paul scanned him from head to toe with disgust.

"I don't know why you bother talking to riffraff like that. You should've burned him for embarrassing the family like that. Being a ranger's humiliating enough but to trade his body with a watcher?" Paul shook his head. "Disgusting."

"How can I help you?" He moderated his voice carefully.

"That's a better attitude," Paul smirked, leaning against the rail. "You have three days to bring me Clarissa."

His flames flared in his gut. Sparks fizzled along his fingertips, threatening to ignite.

"Why her?" he said through clenched teeth. His wings flared. "You have everything you could ever want. Why must you insist on making my daughter's life a living hell?"

Paul turned his back to him, facing the ocean.

"It has nothing to do with her," Paul answered. "You were dad's golden child, graced with fire manipulation while I was nothing."

"You were just one of his bastards and you're doing the best out of all of them!" Malachi's fire broiled in his belly.

"But the damn male didn't care," Paul's wings flared. "All he, and anyone in the family, cared about was who could control fire, which was you and Clarissa."

Smoke bellowed off his skin as his body temperature rose.

"I remember the day she was born," Paul sneered. "And how his face lit up when her fire abilities came in. The pride he took in saying the lineage will continue with her. Torturing her is one of the few ways I can get back at him. Especially when I drown her."

"It ends now," he rasped, clenching his hands. "I won't let you hurt her again."

Paul laughed—a cruel, cackling sound.

"I'll starve your citizens and have you watch the city fall into disrepair." Paul jeered, his blue eyes gleamed darkly. He stepped closer. "You should be grateful I don't do that now with your insolence."

Anger racked his body so fiercely, his limbs shook. It took every fiber of his being to not blast Paul into smoke and ash. Dammit, if his hands weren't tied…

Paul patted the side of his face with a grin. "Bring her to me in three days and I won't crumble this fragile city to the ground."

Paul sauntered away with his hands in his pockets.

"Be grateful Malachi!" Paul called over his shoulder. "I could make both of your lives worse."

Without another glance, Paul shot into the sky, flying into the city.

When he was certain Paul was out of hearing range, he roared into the ocean sky, blasting his fire into the air. Trinity damn that bastard! He threw a fireball over the balcony and into the water.

Hatred and anger circulated in his veins, mixing with his flames in a powerful concoction. *Damn him*, he thought bitterly. *Trinity curse him!* When all his fire was released, he slumped on one of his balcony chairs. Elbows on his knees and hands clutching his head, he released a humorless laugh.

Dammit! Could he get some damn luck on his side for once?

A sizzle sound startled him. Jerking to his feet, the hairs on the back of his neck rose as a small white light swirled in front of him. He stepped back as the small light doubled in size with each second. The warm heat radiating from the portal was nothing compared to the flames he ignited in his hands. He raised his fist, concentrating his fire to a fine laser point, ready to fight. Luke's warning resurfaced in his mind, about demons transporting at will from the collected Gabriel blood.

He darted his eyes over to the double doors leading into the house. Could he make it in time before an attack? He shook his head. No—he would defend this last home for him and his girls. His wings flared and his fire pooled into every limb as he readied himself.

He lifted his hand, ready to strike when he froze. All the fire in his hand dwindled out as his jaw dropped. He stood there speechless as Gabriel, Sewall, and Amos plopped out of the portal, looking as ragged and tired as he did.

Where in the hell had they been?

Amos winced, lifting a hand to his ear before answering.

"We're coming here to get you—" Amos' brow furrowed. "But apparently you have much to tell us as well."

Malachi huffed. "Gabriel, you have impeccable timing."

"Oh," Gabriel raised his eyebrows. "Well, that's what should be expected of an Arch like me."

"You have something to tell us?" Sewall drawled.

The temperature around him dipped as the cold tendrils of Sewall's powers stretched.

"We both have a lot to share—" Malachi started.

"Well," Gabriel interrupted, his wings twitched anxiously. "Can we share on the way? We need to get the others now!"

"No," Amos murmured, rubbing his temples. "We need to hear what Malachi has to say."

Malachi's lips twitched, a glimmer of joy for the first time in a while. "Perfect."

Chapter 8

The breeze cut through Isabella's tunic, chilling her to the bone. Goosebumps rose along her arms and legs as she shivered. She complained about the cold night one time and had been met with such a withering glare from both Tariel and Fatima, she'd snapped her mouth shut. Tariel grumbled about her grueling adventures through the demon realm and that she 'didn't want to hear any complaints' from her.

Isabella dropped her gaze to the ground, her cheeks burned in embarrassment. She wrapped her arms around her midsection and stayed quiet. The nighttime's biting cold air made her miss her sister more. Clarissa radiated heat that not only warmed but calmed her as well.

The knots in Isabella's stomach tightened as they flew.

After Sewall, Amos, and Gabriel left, Fatima wasted no time to fulfill her promise to Sewall to protect their realm. She ordered her and Tariel to wash, change, and get ready to fly to Quaesitor within the hour. While Tariel took the washroom first, Isabella scarfed down the food their staff had brought in. The house buzzed with activity, reminding her of the reverse lifestyle. Staring out the dining room window, she saw dozens of Azrael angels guide glowing orbs of light deeper into the mountains. She'd asked Fatima what the glowing orbs were and she answered with 'the dead'. No specifics of who or what, just the dead.

When she'd mustered enough courage to ask again, Tariel

came out of the washroom, cleaned and in a fresh black tunic with long sleeves. One barked order from her sent Isabella scurrying into the bathroom. Washing off the dirt and grime of the demon realm, the cold water calmed some of the uncertainty swirling inside her. In the scramble to get ready, she had to borrow some of Tariel's clothes, which were comically long. The sleeves stretched far past her hands and the pant legs flapped as she flew. The dark linen material made her look like a proper wraith.

She followed Fatima and Tariel blindly in the night. She'd never been to the Coal mountains and her chance to see them was impossible in the darkness. Would she have the chance to see them in the daylight? She gathered a small strand of wind around her hands to remind herself that she wasn't powerless and silently vowed to find her sister. Clarissa would know what to do.

They flew for hours without rest before a distant light came into view. On top of one of the mountain peaks, a flickering light shined bright. *A signal?* She pondered. Fatima and Tariel veered toward the beacon without hesitation; she followed.

As they ventured closer, she realized it was a lighthouse. Lighthouses were used in the mountains to help angels find their way, like a northern star. *Were they close?* She thought. The loud wind drowned out any question she tried to yell, forcing them to fly in silence.

Tariel and Fatima landed at the mountain's peak, right beside the lighthouse. As she landed, Fatima walked to the door and knocked. A slit cracked open in the middle of the door.

"Who is it?" someone growled from the inside.

"Fatima Adjutor of the Azrael clan." Black smoke and tendrils swirled along Fatima's hands as she pointed a finger at the slit. "If you know what's good for you, you'll open this door."

The slit closed with a muttered curse. A loud click signaled the door unlocking before it cracked open.

"Apologies, my lady," an old angel stood inside, holding up a lantern. "Victor at your service."

In the lantern light, Victor's face was lined with wrinkles. His hair gleamed white with old age and his gray feathers appeared faded. While he stood at the same eye level as Isabella, Fatima towered over him.

"Take us to Farah, immediately." Fatima narrowed her eyes at Victor. "Is this illusion necessary?"

"Apologies again," Victor answered. "Force of habit."

The person before them shimmered and melted away. A gasp lodged itself in Isabella's throat as a new face emerged. This one was younger. An elven-like face stared back at them with blonde hair tied up in a high ponytail.

"How did you know it was an illusion?" Victor raised an eyebrow, opening the door wider for them to cross.

Fatima stepped inside first. "It was a guess. Living next to Raziel angels my whole life, I've never trusted the first image shown to me."

Victor grinned. "A wise choice I suppose. Follow me."

They walked through the damp tunnel with Victor's lantern as the only light. Isabella's heart pounded in her chest. Somehow he knew where to step without tripping on the rocky terrain.

She shuddered. The air was stale and lifeless down here. Her lungs turned gummy with each breath. While warmer within the lighthouse, she longed for the breezy, cold air outside. She wanted the flow and freedom of the sky, not this condensed, old oxygen.

More knots tightened in her stomach as she stumbled down the hall. Her insides churned, threatening to throw up everything she'd eaten back at Fatima's house. She called the wind to her hands again, gasping a short burst of breath into her lungs.

Her hair lifted as the wind picked up around her. With nowhere to go, her wind-ruffled feathers.

"Stop it!" Tariel commanded harshly. "You'll create a wind tunnel in here and blow us out!"

"Sorry." She gasped, trying to calm her racing heart.

They came to a fork in the tunnel. One led further down and another spiraled upward.

"Follow that path down and it'll lead you to Quaesitor," Victor explained. "I can't leave my post beyond this point."

"Thanks," Fatima replied, somehow making the simple gratitude sound unfriendly. "I know the rest of the way."

Victor lifted the lantern high up to her. "Take this, I know my way around these tunnels but newcomers might struggle without a light."

"We're Azrael Archs," Tariel huffed. "We don't need as much light as other angels."

"Quiet, Tariel," Fatima chided. She took the lantern. "Thank you, Victor. That'll be all."

With a single bow, Victor silently disappeared down the path they came. The hairs on the back of her neck stood up as she wondered if Victor had been an illusion.

"Here Isabella," Fatima's long, skinny arm extended the lantern toward her.

Surprised, she muttered a thanks as she grabbed it.

"I forget others can't see as well as us in the dark," Fatima replied to the questions inside her head.

She clutched the lantern tighter. The warmth of the flame reminded her of Clarissa and some of the knots in her stomach loosened.

"Thank you," she said with more sincerity.

The winds around her shrunk to just her hands.

"We're almost there." Fatima walked down the path Victor indicated to.

Tariel glided close behind.

"Where are we going exactly?" Isabella scrambled after them.

"We're going to Joshua's private villa," Fatima answered.

"To look for Farah? Who's that anyway?" She asked.

With the lantern in front of her, it was easier to follow after them.

"Farah is…well she's someone important to the Scio family."

"Weren't you good friends with her, Mama?" Tariel inquired.

"We're still good friends," Fatima replied.

"You haven't gone to see her since…" Tariel's voice drifted off.

While she couldn't see the young heir's face, she heard the sadness in Tariel's tone.

"Yes," Fatima sighed. "Since I was captured. I haven't had the willpower to visit her."

A shiver ran down her spine. She didn't know what happened to Fatima and the other females captured, and it didn't feel like her place to ask. Her wings dropped as tears pooled in her eyes. A cruel fate her family and people might have been subjected to, if not for the Selaphiel angel's aid.

"I want to make a world where cruelty like that is never allowed." Isabella's voice didn't waiver or shake.

For once she felt a fire in her chest, that Clarissa always talked about. It was a dream she and her sister shared for Elementa but she couldn't think of a reason to not extend it to every region.

A light chuckle pulled her attention.

"Same here, girl." Fatima peered over one shoulder, giving Isabella a sad smile. "We're here."

They had walked out of the tunnel and were steps away from Quaesitor. Her jaw dropped. Carved into the mountain, the city stood fortified and strong with little evidence of a siege. Was this an illusion or did the citizens repair the damage done by Matthew's army?

She shook her head. That wasn't important. Now…why were they going to see Farah? What did she have to do with anything?

She turned to Fatima to ask and nearly squealed. Fatima and Tariel were on the move, walking through the city. She scrambled after them again, quietly cursing their long legs. She saw little of the city in the darkness but spotted the library immediately. The large intimidating building drowned out everything else. Drawing her eye to the Head Tree and building, she nearly missed the turn Fatima and Tariel made to Joshua's villa.

Hidden in plain sight, she noticed the house carved out of the side of the mountain, behind the library. Easy to walk past despite being next to an eye-catching monument. She wondered if Joshua put an illusion over the house to make it more unnoticeable.

She followed Fatima up the steps, coming to a stop at two guards. They both wore burgundy armor; cloths covered their heads with only an opening around the eyes. They said nothing as Fatima approached.

"I'm here to see you, Farah." Fatima huffed.

A moment of silence passed. The guards didn't move, not even to blink.

Another beat passed by before she spoke again, "Damned succubus! I know you don't sleep, so don't bother pretending."

The guards exchanged a look with raised eyebrows. A laugh echoed on the other side of the door. Suddenly, it creaked open and the guards melted like puffs of smoke.

Her jaw dropped again as a beautiful angel with long, blond hair and gray eyes answered the door, grinning at Fatima.

"Overgrown crow," she scoffed back. "I wasn't pretending to sleep. I was reeling in shock, seeing you here! Get your ass inside!"

Fatima chuckled and a tightness around her eyes loosened. Isabella looked back and forth between them in bewilderment. Weren't they offended by the names they called each other? Fatima and her status demanded respect, not this tactless greeting.

"Hello, Auntie Farah," Tariel groaned.

She appeared used to this kind of behavior! Isabella sputtered in shock, entering behind everyone else. The door closed and locked into place behind her with a loud snap.

Once inside, Farah yanked Fatima into a hug, wrapping her wings around her. Fatima shuddered, peering at the Raziel angel.

"How long do I have to endure this hug?" Fatima sighed.

"Until I feel like it!" Farah replied, muffled against Fatima's tunic. She tightened her grip. "I was worried about you!"

Fatima scoffed. "You're as fussy as my husband."

Farah took a step back, tears brimming along her eyes, threatening to spill over. The shorter angel glared up at Fatima fiercely enough to make her flinch.

"I've known you longer than your husband," Farah huffed. "And we have every right to fuss."

A servant scrambled to meet them in the foyer area. Sweat dripped profusely down his neck as he bowed low at the waist.

"Apologies, we weren't expecting guests so late," the servant sputtered.

The moment Farah looked away from Fatima, her face changed. Her open, teary eyes turned to distant and cold within a second. Though nothing moved, goosebumps rose along Isabella's arms as she wondered if Farah was friendly to anyone else. Her wind twirled along her feet.

"Get some water and meet us in the nursery room, Issac." Farah's voice turned to steel.

No warmth or giving tone like before. A stone command, leaving no room for questions. With trembling wings, Issac muttered an agreement before scrambling down the hall.

"Is she to be trusted?" Farah raised an eyebrow at Isabella.

She opened and closed her mouth. How did one respond to that?

"She has to be trusted for the sake of our realm," Fatima answered.

A beat passed by before some of the frost in Farah's eyes melted.

"Come," Farah addressed them. "Let's join the others in the upstairs room."

"Others?" Isabella squeaked.

No one answered. Instead, they filed behind Farah up the stairs. The soft pad of their footsteps was their only sound.

The stone stairwell led to a hallway full of mirrors. Mirrors of different shapes and sizes attached along the walls, while bright fluorescent light bulbs shined down upon them. Peeking a glance at herself, she froze. The lighting created harsh shadows across her face, making her appear ghoulish.

She gazed ahead at the others and jumped. If she looked ghoulish, Fatima and Tariel were downright terrifying. The contours of their faces sharpened and their figures reminded her of snakes. She shook her head. *Fatima and Tariel wouldn't hurt her*, she reminded herself as a cold sweat broke out against her back.

They didn't have to travel far. Surprisingly, this three-story house was small. If she had to guess there were no more than five rooms. Why was Farah living in such a confined space? Her status as an Arch would provide her with better accommodations. Questions swirled in her head, while her wind gathered closer to her chest.

Farah stopped outside of an arched doorway, knocked once, and entered. Isabella tilted her head as the others followed after her, blocking her view of the room. Why would Farah knock on a door inside her own house?

She stepped inside and froze. Her jaw dropped open and the air in her lungs stopped.

Atarah sat up in a twin bed, dressed in a white nightgown, laughing with another male angel no more than 10 years old. He had the same blonde hair as Farah but iridescent, crystal blue eyes that struck her speechless. The young angel sat on the edge of the bed, his small legs dangled and…

He's sick, she realized. Other than his cherubim face, the rest of his body appeared withered and weak. His legs were thin to an unhealthy degree and his bony ribs poked through the neckline. *Who is this boy?* Isabella wondered.

"Jack." Farah's icy expression melted when she locked eyes with the young angel. "We have some guests."

The affection in her voice was palpable. Whoever this boy was, Isabella guessed he was someone close to Farah.

Jack grinned at Fatima and Tariel, small dimples popped up on his cheeks.

"I remember you this time!" Jack said excitedly. "You're Fatima and Ariel!"

"Close enough," Tariel muttered under her breath.

Farah sat next to the boy and covered him with one of her wings.

"Close but her name is Tariel." Farah smoothed his hair down. "It's important to call people by the name they prefer. It's how you show respect."

"But I was close," Jack whined.

"You were close." Farah grinned. "Now, you have one more name to remember."

She looked up at Isabella's gaping expression. She couldn't take her eyes off Atarah. She'd been on the brink of death when she'd last seen her dumped on Joshua's library table. Now, here she sat, sipping tea!

She opened and closed her mouth, once again unsure of what to say.

"Jack." Farah's voice floated. "This is Isabella Ignis, from the Uriel clan."

"I—Ig—Nes," Jack attempted her name. "Does that mean you control an element?"

Curiosity shined in his eyes as his gaze dropped to her hands. She peered down to see her sleeves flapping in the breeze she'd created.

"Is it wind?" Jack asked with wide eyes. His own small wings hummed in excitement. "Will I get to see her wind, Mama?"

The air in her lungs ceased. The swirl of wind stopped as her mind restarted. Mama? Farah? She scanned her memory to see if Farah had ever been married, engaged, or even courted someone at some point. Everything came up blank. More importantly, she had a child!

Children, having a child, was a huge ordeal. Many angels, especially Archs, had difficulty conceiving children. Age gaps or single-child households were common because of how difficult pregnancies were for angels. How did Jack's birth go undetected? Unreported?

She shook her head.

The Uriel household should've been informed. Farah's aristocratic standing demanded recognition. Farah sat as an advisor and region official on Joshua's council. When Farah's late sister, Nadia, married Joshua, increasing their family status, she'd solidified their importance. However, after Barmen's birth and Nadia's subsequent death, no other Raziel births had occurred. Jack had to be added to the line of succession and much more. She jerked back to Jack, intrigued by him. Who was the father?

"Uu—huh," Her words lodged themselves in her throat.

First, Atarah survived…whatever she went through, and now, there's a child in the folds. Tariel and Fatima knew about the boy, so why didn't anyone else?

"Well?" Jack tilted his head back to look at her. "Can I see your wind manipu—elation?"

"It's manipulation and Isabella's taking in a lot right now, so let's give her some time. Are you getting cold?" Farah pulled a blanket around his shoulders and placed a hand on his forehead. "You aren't feeling sick again, right?"

"No, I don't feel sick." He pinned her with his puppy eyes.

"Are you sure she can't show me?"

Farah opened her mouth to respond, but Isabella shook herself out of her stupor.

"Ye—yes! Of course." Lifting her hands, she gathered the wind, concentrating the whirlwind on the boy.

"Oh!" Jack giggled.

Using a gentle but firm hold on her wind, she lifted Jack a few feet above his bed.

"I'm flying! Look at me, Mom! I'm flying!" Jack cried out in excitement.

He opened his small wings, using her wind current to hover in the place.

"Yes," Farah strained through a tight smile. Her arms lifted up, ready to catch him should he fall. "I do see. Good job, Jack. I think it's time to come down now."

"I'm flying," Jack murmured to himself, not hearing his mother's words. "This is the best feeling ever."

"Isabella," Farah rumbled low, giving a warning in her tone.

Her eyes widened with worry. Slowly, she lowered Jack back to the bed. She'd orientated him to land on his feet, but he crumbled into the sheets. His wings trembled with effort as if trying to fly while his face shone with joy and sweat.

He can't fly, she thought. His wings are too small and weak to lift him.

When the last of her wind died off, Farah pulled him close and placed a hand on his head.

"You've overdone it," she frowned at her son. "You need to rest up and gain your strength back."

"Tell Isabella to come back," Jack murmured, his eyelids fluttering shut.

Within seconds he slumped down, fast asleep in Farah's arms. Her eyes widened in alarm.

"I'm so sorry!" She gasped. "I—I didn't think it would—"

"You're fine. Jack overdoes it all the time, not just with

you." She gently tucked him into bed. "He'll be fast asleep for a long while. Nothing will wake him; it'll give us a chance to talk."

Farah patted the blankets in place and pulled out cylinder-like ottomans for them to sit on. The furniture, no doubt made for the child, sank when they sat down. Atarah straightened as everyone settled. Isabella glanced at Fatima wondering if this was the reason they'd come here.

"What's happening out there?" Atarah's hoarse voice drew everyone's attention. "Where's my brother?"

That halfling? She shuddered.

"A lot's happened since you last woke up, I think," Tariel spoke first. "Tell me what you remember and maybe we can connect some dots."

Atarah exchanged a look with Farah, who curled around Jack.

"I didn't lie when I said I knew very little of what happened to your family." Farah frowned. "Barmen rescued you and brought you back to the Spirit realm."

"But how?" Atarah pinched her chin. "The last thing I remember was destroying this weird machine Matthew had built, collecting the blood of other angels. After we—"

"Who is *we*?" Tariel and Isabella asked in unison.

"Me, Arick, and Canaan. Matthew had brought Charlotte and me to the demon realm. We'd managed to free ourselves and the Gabriel angels in the prison. My mother and Charlotte stayed to heal them while I went to find a way out." She paused. "I ran into Arick and Canaan in another room by that strange machine Matthew built, so I helped them destroy it. Matthew showed up right after and…"

She lifted a hand to her chest. Pulling the gown to the side, Isabella gasped. A bulging scar stretched over where the heart lay.

"He stabbed me through the heart, and…next thing I knew, I woke up in this bed with Farah looking after me."

Atarah finished.

"How are you alive?" Isabella asked in a hushed tone.

Fatima and Tariel's eyes widened at the sight of her scar but stayed silent.

"I—" Atarah started. "I'm not sure. I feel…different in a way. It's hard to explain."

"Different how?" She tilted her head. "This is the second time you've nearly died."

Atarah gave a humorless laugh. "I feel like I've come back from the brink of death too. But after I recovered from your villa, Isabella, I—I came back stronger. Fighting with Matthew was easier compared to the first time and I was able to deal out more damage."

"If he was easy to fight, how did you get stabbed through the heart?" Tariel raised an eyebrow.

"I said he was easier," Atarah scoffed. "Not that fighting him was easy. He snuck up on me at the last second."

"Are you saying you powered up?" Isabella pivoted her gaze between Farah and Atarah. "Is that possible, Farah?"

Raziel angels were renowned for their knowledge and education. If there was a mystery solved and documented, a Raziel angel probably made the discovery. The caveat was that Raziel angels were reluctant to share information. Isabella guessed it had to do with the superiority complex they got from withholding information. However, after talking to Barmen, it may have to do with the capitalist incentive. Paying a hefty price for the information.

Farah's frown deepened.

"After Noah stabilized her and handed her off to me. I researched further on Atarah's lineage. I suspect her recovery process had to do with her mixed heritage," Farah answered, "Her mother is an advanced healer from a strong family line and her father's familial blood mixed and formed a soldier that's hard to kill."

Atarah paused. "But that doesn't explain how I've gotten

stronger."

"Doesn't it?" Farah inclined her head. "When a bone is broken, the body repairs that part of the bone stronger than it did before. Isn't it safe to say that's what your body is doing?"

Atarah opened and closed her mouth. She saw the wheels turning in Atarah's mind of the possibility. No, the *truth* of Farah's words. To heal and recover stronger than she did before...

She shook her head, wishing she had Atarah's powers.

"The wound from Matthew?" Tariel raised an eyebrow. "Didn't kill her?"

"No, but it was damn close to." Farah indicated to Atarah. "The armor your family can call forth—does it come consciously or unconsciously?"

"I thought it came forward consciously." Atarah frowned. "What are you suggesting?"

"From what I've studied," Farah explained. "Researching how to take care of a Michael angel. I came across scrolls about the armor a few families possessed the ability to create."

"My family being one of those families," Atarah nodded, not surprised.

"Correct," Farah continued. "The scrolls described how the armor comes forward from the skin hardening as a protective mechanism. The way it was written gave me the impression that there's a subconscious component to the armor."

Atarah tilted her head to the side, raising a finger to her chin. "Jamor the shield was the first Michael angel on record to create the armor many years ago but..."

"No one knew how he developed this new ability." Farah straightened up and clasped her hands together. Her face turned solemn. "There was another scroll...that suggested the ability came from him being a halfling."

Isabella's eyes widened and the air in her lungs froze. All halflings had been either killed or forced back into the demon realm. There's no way a high-ranking Michael angel was a halfling. Was there?

Her gaze pivoted back to Atarah, who didn't appear disturbed at the thought of having demon blood running through her veins. Isabella shuddered, thankful she was a pure-bred angel from the Uriel clan.

Farah continued, "I believe that's why you survived. Because of your body's protective reaction and its ability to heal faster than any other Michael angel before you."

"How does this tie into us protecting the realm while the Head Archs are gone?" Isabella asked, not wanting to discuss Atarah's questionable heritage anymore. "Sewall wanted Fatima to meet with the other Ladies of the clans, but I don't see how that'll help us."

Farah's cold gaze sent shivers down Isabella's spine. She regretted speaking for a second before squaring her shoulders. This is what Clarissa would do. She wouldn't cower from speaking her mind.

"This matters a great deal," Fatima answered. "This makes Atarah our strongest warrior to fight against demons that come our way. The only one we need to speak with is—"

"Rachael," Farah sighed, pinching the bridge of her nose. "But she's reluctant to see anyone at the moment. I've already tried reaching out to her."

"It's all right—" Fatima started.

"It's not all right," Farah snapped. "We're in charge until the Heads come back and she refuses to meet! That's unacceptable! It's—"

"I wrote to her," Fatima interrupted. "And she agreed to meet us."

Farah stilled. A beat later she raised an eyebrow.

"Pray tell, why did she agree to meet you and give me the silent treatment?" Farah's voice was tight with tension and frustration.

Fatima glanced at each of them before speaking.

"What I'm about to say must stay between us," Fatima

whispered. "At least for the next few months, or until everything settles."

Farah lowered her chin by a fraction of an inch while the rest of them murmured their agreements.

"Rachael's pregnant." Fatima sighed. "And she doesn't want to risk anything happening to the baby by traveling which is why I offered for us to go to her."

"Why doesn't she tell everyone she's pregnant?" Tariel tilted her head.

"Because this is her 42nd or 43rd pregnancy, I think," Farah sighed.

Isabella gasped. Over 40 pregnancies?! Her stomach churned at the thought. The physical turmoil of going through so many losses and changes would be enough to drive her insane. No wonder she didn't want to go anywhere.

"How far of a flight will Urbs Antiqua be for us?" Tariel asked.

"Not only that," Farah frowned. "I can't leave Jack all by himself. If I had Barmen with me I could manage, but I can't leave him."

"What about with the servants?" Isabella inquired.

Surely they could take care of him for a week or two?

Farah narrowed her eyes. Goosebumps rose along her arm as Farah's scowl turned fierce. The air in her lungs sputtered, and the wind around her fingertips grew agitated. Farah opened her mouth to no doubt sneer a reply at her but Fatima came to her rescue.

"Little Jack," Fatima interjected. "Shall come with us? Yes?"

Though she spoke her sentence as a question, Fatima raised her eyebrow at Farah as if it was a command.

"Yes," Farah huffed. "Jack will come with us."

A shiver ran down her spine as Farah's cold, steel gaze continued to glare at Isabella. She silently vowed to avoid her bad side.

"I'll carry him," Atarah volunteered, staring at Jack's small sleeping figure with tenderness. "I doubt he weighs too much for me to handle," Atarah quickly included when Farah opened her mouth.

There was a beat of silence before Farah nodded.

"When do we leave?" Tariel faced her mother.

"As soon as they're ready," Fatima answered to Farah and Atarah. "The faster we get to Urbs Antiqua, the better. With all of us, it'll take about two days to fly there."

Atarah nodded while Farah furrowed her brow, clutching Jack's sleeping form tighter.

"The further north we get the less likely we'll run into demons." Fatima pointed out. "The portals open more down south."

Some of the tension around Farah's shoulders eased.

"What happened to Noah?" Isabella asked, blushing. "Where did he run off to?"

Farah shrugged. "He returned to his home region. Something about rallying forces for when everyone comes back. He's sent out troops and healers everywhere to help others."

"I'm glad someone stayed behind," Atarah murmured. "There's too few of us here."

She nodded in agreement. Their home felt too vulnerable.

"Get up, Atarah." Farah sighed. "We leave in the next hour."

Chapter 9

Salty, warm juice dripped down Charlotte's chin as she gulped down the last of her stew. Filled with onion, peppers, couscous, and tomato, the simple dish was heaven in her mind. There wasn't enough for a second helping, but she remained quiet. Her stomach stopped growling, and that's what mattered.

Circling one arm around their bowl, Rhea, Alan and the other halflings watched them from the other end of the long, thin table. They all ate fast, too fast to be satisfied, except for Ben. His eyes glazed over his half-eaten food, somewhere far away. Makoto and the other angels inhaled their food, not bothering with chewing. The water offered to them lasted for 2 minutes before the container ran empty.

Ava spoke the first words as they finished eating.

"Why did those patrol guards treat you so cruelly?" Ava said in a hushed tone. "I'd thought…well, I guess I don't understand what life's like in the demon realm for you."

Alan scoffed while Rhea gave a sad smile.

"We face discrimination because we're seen as impure. Because we're not wholly demon or angel, we're seen as less than." Rhea touched the bruise on her cheek.

Alan winced at the motion.

"I've been hit worse by a much uglier face," she finished.

"What about your parents?" Heat rushed to Charlotte's face as she saw the effect her words had.

Rhea's face darkened while Alan scowled. The rest of the halflings lowered their gaze, dejected.

"What 'bout our parents? Ya say." Rhea murmured in a low, dark tone.

"Killin' us would've been kinder than what they did." Alan sneered.

Ava frowned.

"What do you mean?" Elijah leaned forward, clasping his hands together. "What happens to halflings?"

"We're sold," Rhea answered with a thickness in her voice. "Bartered, traded, beaten', whipped, tormented for amusement."

Tears brimmed in her eyes as she continued.

"We're the best-case scenario because we purchased our freedom or escaped death." She jerked her chin up, indicating to the barn building. "We carved out a life out 'ere in the desert so no one will bother us."

"We'd rather suffer out 'ere," the albino child sighed. "Then take a chance in the city."

"The guards?" Makoto chimed in.

The rest of the angels watched the halflings with wide eyes. A pit in her stomach grew with each word they spoke. The horror they must've endured living in a world that hated them…

"The guards look the other way if we've somethin' to trade 'em," Alan answered, flames burning in his eyes.

From the corner of her eye, she spotted his hands clenched together underneath the table.

"And if you don't have anything to trade?" Elijah asked with a raised eyebrow.

All the halflings' gaze turned to Rhea for a second before looking away. Anywhere but her. Rhea held her gaze on Elijah and said nothing. Silence stretched with tension and pain with each second. The weight of what was left unsaid caused her heart to constrict. They couldn't leave these halflings here.

"Come with us." The words tumbled out before she thought them through. All eyes turned to her. "Come with us and carve out a life in the Spirit realm."

Wings flared and eyes widened as if she'd committed a murder.

"Now..." Elijah started, lifting a hand.

"Hold on—" Makoto interjected.

"I don't think—" Rhea said.

Alan silenced them all by laughing. A dark, cruel chuckle that carried meaning. The other halflings winced at the sound, retreating further into themselves.

"You'd think we'd go to the *Spirit realm*?" Alan spat as if it was a curse, using his words like daggers to her heart. Anger shone in his eyes as he continued, "Think we'd trust ya not to shoot us at first glance? Make no mistake, yer no better than the guards that storm thru' those doors."

"If you hate us so much," she grimaced. "Why'd you let us in?"

Alan gritted his teeth and jerked his chin to Rhea. "We follow her orders."

"We trust her with our life." The halfling, with abnormally large eyes, answered.

Sincerity rang with every word. The others nodded alongside her.

Charlotte settled back to Rhea, who watched the other halflings with fierce protectiveness. If she swayed Rhea to come to their realm, the others would follow.

"You love them with everything." Tears glistened in Ava's eyes.

"Of course I do." Rhea met her gaze with a frown. "I'd rather die than let them feel any more suffering."

Alan's hands clenched tighter under the table, so much she wondered if he was cutting his palms.

"Then consider our offer." Ava's pleading eyes mesmerized them all. "Create a safe haven in our realm."

Rhea's frown deepened. "Our safety guaranteed?"

Elijah coughed, pulling all of their attention.

"You can't promise them that, daughters." Their father had the decency to look embarrassed. "They have every right to be wary of us. Halflings aren't permitted due to their… behavioral issues."

Wings flared along the opposite side. Blood rushed to their faces.

"Behavioral issues?" Rhea hissed. "Is that your excuse to slaughter us?"

"There's no excuse," Makoto chimed in. "Halflings are killed because of how much destruction you cause from a young age."

"Destruction?" Alan scoffed. "That's rich comin' from the ones who destroy whole lives for the sake of *yer* comfort."

"How many halflings do ya know?" Rhea glared at each of them.

"Well," Charlotte hesitated. "We know one."

Arick, she thought.

"And did they destroy anything?" Rhea raised an eyebrow.

It was their turn to be embarrassed. Arick hadn't hurt anyone. Even when her brother, Noah, bullied him and her mother provoked him, Arick never lashed out.

"Well, it's only a matter of time before he does something." Elijah frowned. "It's in his nature."

"Of course," Rhea scoffed. "Yer mind's made up about him. Ya don't know who the real bad guys are."

"Their minds are made up about us too," Alan hissed. "We shouldn't have allowed them in, Rhea. They're no better—"

"We get it. We're no better than the guards, but we try to be!" Charlotte stood up.

Alan followed her with a glare. She put her hands on her hips and glared back.

"My sister, niece and I are trying to make our world a better place because we all deserve better. I admit, we don't know much about halflings, but—" Tears welled in her eyes, making her vision blurry. "I want to live in a world where everybody matters. Hatred's easy to build but understanding's hard to create."

Alan's eyes widened for a second before closing off again. He scoffed, turning away without another word. The other halflings stared at her, with open mouths. She sat with burning cheeks, folding her hands in her lap. Maybe she spoke too loud?

Ava placed her hand over hers and squeezed. Elijah furrowed his brow while Makoto and the others murmured amongst themselves. Rhea's gaze flitted between her and the others, assessing their reaction.

Elijah cleared his throat, and silence descended. He slowly rose to his feet, with his hands clasped together.

"My daughter's right. Hatred's easy, but you didn't pick hatred when you saw a desperate group outside your home." He leveled his gaze at Rhea. "You chose to shelter and feed us when you had every right to turn your back."

He indicated a hand to her and Ava.

"You and my daughters possess hearts full of compassion in spite of the world's cruelty." He bowed his head, bending at the waist. "Please accept my humble apology for my judgment and inconsideration. My clan represents healing, and I've done nothing but cause damage. For that, I'm sorry to you and to your family."

A beat of silence.

Rhea's jaw dropped. Alan glued his gaze to the floor but his jawline softened. One of the kids giggled.

What started as one giggle turned into a cascade of laughter from the other halflings. The albino and the kid with the large eyes laughed so hard, that they leaned on each other for support. Her own lips twitched in amusement at the infectious sound.

From the corner of her eyes, Makoto and the others relaxed their wings. The tightness around their eyes loosened as smiles formed reluctantly on their lips.

"Never seen anyone apologize to us before," the tall halfling with sharp teeth mumbled.

"Never seen anyone bow to us before either." The albino halfling chuckled.

"I—I…" A blush bloomed across Rhea's face. "T—thank ya bu—but that's not really necessary. Get up now."

Elijah straightened up, smiling. "Your forgiveness is necessary—"

"Yeah, yeah ok." Rhea waved her hand, indicating for him to sit. "Just sit back down. I don't like it when ya do that."

"Yes'm" Elijah grinned, sitting.

"Tell us your names," Charlotte chimed in, pivoting between the albino and the lanky halfling. Curiosity burned inside of her to know them more.

"My name's Fig." The tall halfling with sharp teeth and no lips spoke. He pointed beside him to the large eyes halfling. "This is Bugs. She's sharp and quick on her feet."

"My name's Frost," the albino raised his hand.

"Frost?" Makoto asked, tilting his head to one side. "Why is that your name?"

Frost cupped his hands together for a moment before opening. She gasped. His fingertips formed clumps of ice balls in his hands.

"I can make ice," Frost mumbled. "But not for too long."

"That's an amazing ability," Ava replied, grinning. "Is part of your heritage from the Uriel clan?"

Frost nodded sheepishly.

"What about the rest of you?" Charlotte asked, peeking at Alan.

Bugs raised her hand and bounced in her chair. "I can shrink in size to sneak in and scope out places."

"She mostly uses this to warn us when patrol is coming." Fig rubbed the back of his head.

Charlotte jerked her chin to him. "What about you? Do you have an ability?"

"Scares the heck out of poor bastards that walk by," Alan grunted.

They laughed while Fig rolled his eyes at Alan.

"I can…influence people's energy, kinda." Fig put a finger to his chin. "It's not really that useful."

"He can make others drowsy." Bug chimed in. "He helps out against patrol!"

"Please tell us more. Can you all fly?" Elijah leaned forward. "There's so much we don't know about halflings."

Fig opened his mouth to speak but Alan stopped him.

"Tell us about you." Alan narrowed his eyes. "We've introduced ourselves. Now it's your turn. What do you want?"

Rhea frowned at Alan but didn't speak.

"My name is Elijah and these are my daughters, Ava and Charlotte." Elijah waved a hand to them. "Beside them is Makoto and a few other Gabriel angels we've rescued."

Alan jerked his chin behind them. "What about those two?"

They all turned to see Ben and Canaan huddled in the back corner of the room. One food bowl lay empty while the other was half eaten. Ben's face was obscured by the shadows of the room while Canaan kept his back to them. Concern etched into every line of his face, Canaan cleaned the blood spilling from Ben's ears using ripped fabric from his tunic.

"Those two look like they need more rescuing than the others," Alan huffed.

She frowned. Ben and Canaan had remained silent since they arrived. Poor Ben looked…

"Their names are Ben and Canaan," Ava answered.

"We can't stop his bleeding." Charlotte sighed. "No matter how hard we try, we can't heal Ben."

"What happened to him?" Rhea asked eyes on his blood-stained tunic.

She sighed. "Our stories are a little different, but we all ended up kidnapped by a monster we know as Matthew. I'm not sure what he'd be called in this realm."

Alan jolted in his seat.

"The assimilate Matthew?" Rhea gasped, her eyes widened. "He's ranked high in her ladyship's military campaign."

Canaan scowled, calling out from the corner.

"We know, unfortunately. I scouted Umbra's streets for weeks to learn more about him and who was funding his expedition." He shifted his eyes to Alan. "I think you know more than I do."

Alan glared at Canaan.

"I know no one works for tha she-devil for the sake of it. She wants to take over more territory 'cause she 'deserves' it," he emphasized, his lips curled on one side.

"Alan was born in her ladyship's castle." Rhea sighed. "He knows her cruelty well."

"Hold on," Elijah lifted a hand. "Let's start with where we are."

"After we tell ya." Alan's eyes gleamed as he spoke. "How do we know ya won't run off to her ladyship?"

"We have just as much right to hate her as you do," Charlotte chimed in. "We could help each other."

"Be careful with yer words." Alan frowned at her. "Not everyone abused hates the abuser. Many will run back at any given chance."

Blood rushed to her face. "Does that mean you will?"

Alan's eyes flickered between them. "Nah, I'll never go back…alive at least."

He swiveled his head back to Rhea, giving her a pointed look. They stared at each other for a moment before Rhea nodded.

"It won't happen," Rhea whispered so low she almost didn't hear.

Alan loosened his shoulders and faced Elijah. Shadows

covered his small face, making him appear older. *Was Alan a child?* She wondered.

"He doesn't trust us," Canaan called out, nodding to Alan. "He thinks we'll turn them in or sell them as slaves to the palace."

"How can we trust—?" Alan's words were cut off by Ben.

Ben stood from the corner and shuffled to the table. A gleam in his eye that hadn't been there before; a glimmer of life. Ben slumped on the bench across from Alan; his blood-shot eyes never leaving the small boy's face.

"Her staff," Ben rasped, pointing to his ears.

Alan froze.

"You know more about her staff." Ben's voice sounded dry as if he'd eaten chalk.

Alan nodded, eyeing Ben with a new interest. "You were dumb enough to try and use it."

Ben nodded this time.

"Wait," Elijah jumped from his seat. "Ben, can you hear him?"

Ben shook his head and tapped his temple before pointing to Alan.

"So you can hear his thoughts?" Charlotte asked excitedly.

Did Ben have some of his powers back? Ben nodded again.

"Can he hear all of our thoughts?" Rhea pulled away from Ben.

The others followed her example.

"Not sure," Canaan answered, watching his younger brother carefully. "But I can."

Fig's jaw dropped while Frost and Bug gasped.

"That's too cool!" Bug cheered, stepping closer.

Fig yanked her back. Bug flinched.

"No!" Fig yelled. "Mind readers are dangerous and—"

"Outlawed." Alan finished, still facing off with Ben. "They're outlawed 'cause her ladyship has a harder time manipulating them."

"Harder time?" Questions swirled in Charlotte's head.

"Outlawed..." Elijah gripped his chin. "Then we *are* somewhere close to Satan's capital city."

The other halflings jumped.

"Don't speak her name!" Rhea snapped. "It only brings trouble!"

Elijah furrowed his brow, opening his mouth to speak but Alan cut him off.

"We're many miles outside of the Red City," Alan huffed. "It's not like she can hear us."

"Everyone fears speaking that name for good reason!" Rhea clenched her fist. "From now on, just refer to her as your ladyship or anything else but her name."

"What other things do we need to know?" Charlotte leaned in closer. "Why does she have a hard time with mind readers?"

"Cause they can read *her* mind and intent," Alan explained. "She'll say a command and mind readers will know they're bein' tricked and break free from her illusion."

"How do you know this?" Makoto interjected from his side of the table.

"Because he's a mind reader." Canaan tapped his head. "Don't bother lying, kid. You're not the only mind reader here."

Alan flared his wings. "I'm not the best mind reader."

"Best mind reader," Ben echoed.

Alan's eyes widened as Ben gave a weary grin.

"Neither am I." Ben rasped.

"I 'scaped before I could be killed. I got by long enough growin' up but then...one day I did the same stupid mistake ya did." Alan indicated to Ben. "I took her staff hoping to turn myself into a full demon."

"A full demon? Why not an angel?" Canaan inquired. "You look more like us, anyway."

Alan scoffed. "Even if I do, I'd never be accepted 'cause

I'd have come from the demon realm."

"You can't possibly know that," Charlotte argued.

"But I do." Alan grimaced. "T'was a part of her ladyship's entertainment. She'd enjoy bringing in captive angels to torment. Part of the torment involved me."

Charlotte frowned. *What was this kid's life like? How did he heal—? Wait!* She remembered.

"When you used the staff before, did it hurt you? How did you get better?" She fired off each question.

As the wheels turned in her head, more questions popped up.

"Rhea found me." Alan crossed his arms. "She put me back together, piece by piece."

All eyes turned to Rhea, who glanced down sheepishly.

"I...I—" she sputtered, clasping two hands together. "I didn't do much really."

"How?" Ava asked softly.

Rhea blushed.

"It'll sound so ridiculous, ya won't believe me." Rhea sighed.

"Are you part Raphael angel?" Elijah's eyebrows shot up.

"Well," Rhea's hands fidgeted.

Alan leaned back and grabbed them. "It's all right Rhea. Ya were right. They won't attack us so we can tell them."

"Someone's had a change of mind," Fig scoffed. "What happened to 'kill them! 'Fore they cause us any problems!'"

"I still believe that, but they won't cause us any problems for now." Alan exchanged a look with Ben, then Ava and Charlotte. Something in his gaze softened. "A few of them are a lot like us."

A beat of silence, and the halflings settled at the table.

Charlotte's eyes widened. *They must have complete trust in Rhea and Alan,* she mused.

"I'm from Leviathan's region," Rhea began, "I was born from a Raphael angel and siren."

"Siren?" Charlotte gasped. Didn't they need water?

Rhea nodded.

"In Leviathan's region, halflings are treated better. They're not enslaved, but they're separated. We live in different cities along the border, which is dangerous since raids happen all the time." She sighed. "The demon lords have always fought over their drawn borders, but that didn't stop *her* raiders from grabbing me."

A shadow cast over her eyes, darkening them.

"I was taken from my home and sold all across her domain for many, many years. I didn't have much of a home to return to…so I made one here with my made-family." Her eyes softened as she peered over her shoulder.

Bugs squeezed her arm, peering up with pure adoration. "Yer the best thing to ever happen' to us."

"I made this far because of all of ya." Rhea grinned, patting her head. "I'll die fighting for ya."

"Same here," Fig echoed. "We're all we got and that's enough."

Something crackled and puffed out in his figure, reminding Charlotte of a cat puffing up.

"Were each of you kidnapped?" Makoto asked in a quiet tone.

Sadness and anger mixed together in his eyes. After a beat or two, Charlotte realized he was sad and angry *for* them.

"Alan and Bugs were born here." A soft chill swirled around Frost for a second before dying down. "But the rest of us were taken from other regions."

"Is this common?" Charlotte asked, frowning.

Rhea nodded.

"Many raiders along each border take their chances in kidnappin' us halflings," Fig explained. "T'was no point in goin' back 'cause not each camp's…well…a good place."

"Are there any legal protections for halflings?" Elijah asked softly. "Or repercussions against the raiders?"

Rhea shook her head.

"No one cares about what happens to us halflings. The demon lords get offended by their borders being crossed but nothin' else." She indicated her head to Frost and Fig. "Many halflings end up displaced and pulled apart from their family, like us. I'm a lucky one 'cause I got a few years of knowing my family before a raider took me."

A heavy sadness flowed through Charlotte at Rhea and the others' story. How could such cruelty exist? Why haven't we done anything to help?

No, wait. She paused. The angels in her world *had* done something, discriminate and hold onto old beliefs. Tears welled in her eyes as she remembered how wary she'd felt around Arick after finding out he was a halfling. A heavy shame filled her chest as she wished she'd done something different. She should have given more compassion and understanding but…how could she have known? How could any of them know the fate of halflings?

Her vision blurred as her tears overflowed. She sniffled, wiping her face. She didn't have the right to cry; it was their trauma, not hers. A small hand patted her shoulder, startling her for a moment.

Bugs tilted her head to the side, appearing fascinated with her face.

"Those are tears, Bugs," Rhea explained, placing a hand on her head. "Sometimes people cry when they're sad or very happy."

"But she doesn't look happy." Her pupils constricted and dilated several times. "Right?"

"Correct," Rhea murmured.

Fig lifted Bug in the air and placed her on his lap. "Don't mind Bugs. Emotions can be tricky for her."

"Not emotions," Bugs whined. "Just crying. I've never been able to cry before but I see others do it all the time."

Something sharp hooked itself underneath her ribs and

yanked. Her heart twisted as Bugs' innocent statement caused a rippling effect on the other angels. Many appeared visibly shaken.

Charlotte cleared her throat three times before she could form a sentence. "Is there really nothing we can do for them, Father?"

Shaking his head, Elijah opened his mouth to speak but froze. Following his gaze, she pivoted to see Ava had moved around to the other side of the table while they'd been talking. Not even Rhea noticed her until Ava was standing right by her.

Rhea's eyes widened as Ava encircled her in her arms and wings. Ava whispered something in Rhea's ear that turned her eyes glassy. Suddenly, she wasn't the only one crying. A single tear fell down Rhea's face before she buried herself in Ava's shoulder. Charlotte didn't hear a single sound but saw Rhea's shoulders quiver. Whatever Ava whispered hit a mark for all of the halflings, for they huddled closer to her. Alan watched Ava as if she had grown three heads, in disbelief.

Silence filled the room as loud emotions rolled off of everyone. Even Makoto and the other angels held sympathy for the halflings.

"There is something we can do." Elijah's eyes softened as he watched Ava. "Nothing we do will be easy but it's a change we can work toward."

Ava glanced from where she held Rhea's trembling form. A sad smile on her lips.

"Anything worthwhile will never be easy," Ava replied. "That's what my mother said growing up and it still rings true."

Sniffling, Rhea sat up, vigorously wiping her eyes. "I can't believe a few hours ago I was about to slit y'all's throats."

Laughter erupted as the tension in the room lessened. Charlotte's muscles released their hold around her heart. Her spirit lifted as a new light entered Rhea and the others' eyes. She shook her head, marveling at the difference one conversation could have on their group.

"You've been open about your stories," Elijah began. "So let us share ours with you. Starting with this."

Elijah pulled out two staffs. One looked ragged and old while the other was bedazzled and sparkling with glitter. While she had no clue what the significance of the staffs were, the reaction was instant for halflings.

Rhea and Alan gasped while the others looked on with curiosity.

"How'd ya get those?" Alan whispered, eyes wide. "To touch one staff is a miracle but to see three within a lifetime's…almost impossible."

"We have Ben to thank for this," Elijah lifted a hand to him. "Ben conjured the idea to propose a deal with Beelzebub. All three staffs in exchange for a favor for everyone in the the room."

Alan furrowed his brow. "That's it?"

Elijah frowned. "What do you mean that's it? Forming any deal with Beelzebub is risky business."

Alan shook his head. "You're underestimating Beelzebub and Leviathan."

"I've never heard Leviathan agree to a deal where payment wasn't taken first." Rhea chimed in. "Same for Beelzebub. The fact that they let you leave makes me wonder about their real motive."

"Were there any other details to the deal?" Alan asked, grabbing his chin. "Anything strange Leviathan said or did?"

Ben scoffed. Canaan's eyebrow shot up at his brother, and a grin played at his lips.

"Everything Leviathan does is strange." Ben huffed. "He enjoyed messing with Beelzebub for amusement."

Elijah grimaced. "His only interest was messing around and getting high. He didn't strike me as…well, diabolical."

Rhea giggled. "He's very strange, but he has a soft side. He'd come by the outskirts with medicine and picture books for the kids' makeshift schools."

Elijah tilted his head to the side. "We're talking about Leviathan, right? The same demon lord who banished a servant for fifty years because they said the order of his name wrong?"

Rhea shook her head. "Not sayin' he's good, but he's far from all evil."

"Do we risk using the staffs if it brings the demon lords around?" Charlotte interjected. "Also, look at what Sat—er, I mean her ladyship's staff did to Ben's ears."

"Her ladyship," Alan drawled with a sneer. "Rigs her staff so that it has a backfiring' effect. Since she can affect the mind, the staff overwhelms the brain and causes damage."

Alan nodded to Rhea.

"Took her weeks to fix my head. I was wobblin' around for weeks." Alan glanced at Ben. "My guess is that his ears were hit the hardest 'cause he was trying to listen for someone's thoughts while usin' the staff."

Ben nodded solemnly.

"How do we fix it?" Ava turned to Rhea, who frowned at Ben.

"At the time, we were around a body of water so my powers were stronger…" Rhea mused. "I may be able to help if we're closer to moving water."

"We need to leave her ladyship's region as fast as possible anyway," Elijah replied. "We need to get back to the spirit realm and warn the others."

"I'm not leaving until I find Mikael and Arick." Ava sat up, her tone firm.

Charlotte straightened up too. "Same here. I'm not going back without Arick."

That's what Atarah would want her to do. Another stab of pain ricocheted through her chest at the loss of her friend. She vowed she would be there for Arick, for Atarah and Ava's sake.

"Makoto and the other Gabriel angels need to get back to their own homes. They've been gone long enough," Elijah argued, "We're not abandoning Arick or Mikael, but we need to help the others before we can look for them."

Charlotte pursed her lips. The other angels deserved to be home in their beds, surrounded by their loved ones instead of dragged around the demon realm.

"We could use one of the staffs to help," Makoto answered. "What powers do the other demon lords have?"

"Leviathan can control elements, healing and death magic," Rhea answered.

"Beelzebub possesses unlimited strength, mind reading and teleportation." Alan fired out right behind Rhea.

"Teleportation?" Makoto straightened up. "That's it then. The staffs enhanced the power we already have, yes? Then we just need to use Beelzebub's staff to teleport us all out of here."

"There's a risk there Makoto," Elijah sighed. "The deal was made with myself and Ben in the room. If you or the others touch the staff, there's a risk that you'll owe Beelzebub."

"Every option has a risk, your lordship," Makoto replied. "This is the best one we have. None of us Gabriel angels are Archs so we don't possess the power to teleport far. Even with all of us combined, we didn't have the power to get out of here."

"The chance that Beelzebub will go after them is unlikely," Alan mused, "They weren't in the room when the deal was struck, and they're low-level soldiers. He'll have little use for them. No offense."

"None taken." Makoto chuckled. "The boy speaks the truth. We should use Beelzebub's staff to get the hell out of here before anyone finds us."

"You all should come with us," Charlotte faced Rhea. "Come with us to the Spirit realm."

"Charlotte, you shouldn't push what you want," Elijah chided, nodding to Rhea. "You'll have a welcome spot in my region if you and your family choose to come but it's your decision. We won't force anyone to leave."

Rhea and Alan exchanged a glance. Fig, Frost and Bugs watched on, waiting for whatever decision with complete trust shining in their eyes. Alan nodded slowly with tension lining his wings and shoulders.

"To the end?" Rhea whispered.

The halflings nodded.

"To the end." They replied in unison.

Rhea turned back to Elijah, more tears brimming along the surface, as she answered, "We'll go with you."

Charlotte sighed, relaxing the tension in her wings. For the first time in a while, a smile formed on her lips.

"Perfect!" She cheered. "Now all that's next is leaving."

Fig jolted forward, starting everyone with his sudden movement.

"Sorry," Fig murmured. "I need to pack some canteens and jerky. Ya never know what's out there."

Rhea nodded. "Good idea."

"While Fig is doing that," Elijah directed. "Let's gather in the big room for the teleportation. Makoto, are you sure you and your men are ready for the jump?"

Makoto glanced at each of his soldiers before answering.

"Yes, I'm sure." Makoto stood and his men followed.

While he and the others talked, Charlotte scrambled after Fig to help him pack. It'd been so long since hope bloomed in her chest, the excitement sent her nerves on edge. This rough plan might work!

"Here, let me help," Charlotte called out, following Fig to a small side room.

It fits the description of a pantry better. Two rows of rocky shelves were all that fit in the space. Small bags that smelled of onions along with a pile of coconuts were all that were in there.

"Here." Fig extended the bag toward her. "Hold this open for me while I pack the coconuts."

She held the bag out eagerly.

"I'm happy you're all coming," She said with sincerity.

To leave them here…all by themselves, her heart twisted at the thought. She hadn't known them long, but the inexplicable feeling of responsibility washed over her. The halflings deserved to live in peace too.

Fig shrugged at her comment.

"This will just be another place for us," Fig tied off the bag with a single knot, moving his long fingers with delicacy. "We're used to movin' places."

A slight pang shot through her chest. She opened her mouth to assure Fig that her home would be their home but a voice drew their attention.

"Come on, Fig! Let's get goin'!" Rhea called out.

Fig tucked out of the pantry and made it back to the large room. She scampered after him. For every step he took, she had to take five in order to keep up.

In the big room, everyone gathered. Elijah held what appeared to be Beelzebub's staff in his hand while the other gleamed around his belt. Makoto and the other Gabriel angels lined themselves in a formation, placing a hand on each other's shoulders. Every hand eventually led to Makoto, who grimaced at the staff. His wings twitched a few times, as his eyes oscillated between the staff and Ben's bleeding ears.

"It's now or never," he huffed under his breath.

"Everyone stay close," Elijah instructed. "Once Makoto opens a portal we'll need to be quick and jump through."

"Jump?" Rhea furrowed her brow.

Charlotte nodded, moving closer to Rhea and Ava. "The Gabriels teleport by opening a portal and jumping through very quickly. The portal will appear as a bright, warm light, but don't be afraid. You won't be able to use your wings for a moment or two and then we'll arrive."

Rhea's wings twitched while Alan didn't appear fazed in the slightest. Bugs huddled closer to Rhea. Frost leaned in closer on the opposite side while Fig towered over them all from behind.

"Will it be big enough for me?" Fig asked, tilting his head.

"Yes," Makoto answered with a frown, "We're not used to making them for anyone bigger than ourselves, but we can do it."

Fig hunched low, anyway, cuddling close to the others. His arms came around them almost like a cage.

"Ya won't get separated from us Fig," Alan answered. "We're all movin' to the same place."

Elijah grunted in agreement. "Is everyone ready now? There's no telling what will happen after we use the staff, so best be ready for anything."

Charlotte nodded along with everyone else.

"Very well," Elijah sighed. "Grab a hold of the staff Makoto and try to open a portal. Aim for anywhere in my region, Silva. I know precision gets less accurate for lower ranks but try your best."

Makoto inhaled deeply before grabbing onto the staff. A minute ticked by in silence. Nothing happened. No gust of wind or loud whooshing sounds. Nothing but their own breathing.

Makoto's brow furrowed deeply; a bead of sweat formed on his temple. Like a flickering candle, the staff blinked to life, glowing red.

The wind swirled around the room, nearly lifting Charlotte off the ground. If Fig hadn't had his arms out, she would've been blown away. A bright light grew from where Makoto held the staff. The portal started off small but then grew tall. A familiar heat blazed from the opening, offering them an escape. Through squinted eyes, she found Rhea's hand.

Charlotte tugged gently.

"Come on!" She yelled above the wind. "Let's get out of here!"

With trembling wings, Rhea nodded. She indicated for

her group to follow.

They all jumped through. Warmth encased her as the weightlessness took over. She braced herself for whatever they may face on the other side.

Chapter 10

Malachi ran a hand through his hair, patting out any flames that had sprung up. Since Gabriel, Amos, and Sewall stumbled onto his patio last night, they'd done nothing but argue. He'd explained that Luke and Flynn wanted another emergency summit meeting to discuss a new attack plan; however, this only created chaos. Gabriel urged them to travel to the demon realm and find his son and the others. Amos argued they needed to prioritize reenforcing their own territories, while Sewall glowered and brooded watching the debate in the back corner.

Eventually, after hours of arguing, Malachi convinced them to retire for the night. Sewall tipped the scale in his favor, agreeing to rest. Hopefully, Sewall would side with him again.

Amos' cheeks looked sunken and dark circles hung under his eyes when they first arrived. Gabriel's wings had slumped with exhaustion, dragging along the ground. Sewall's growling stomach echoed down the hall. He suspected none of the Head Archs had a proper rest or meal in a long while.

Now, he sat at the breakfast table on his villa's balcony. Waves crashed in the distance but the coast wind helped keep his anger in check. The sunrise passed hours ago as they debated their next move.

A shower and a long night's rest later, Amos arrived on the balcony a new man. Dressed in the green tunics he'd lent to them, the Archs looked more like themselves. Sewall appeared with the same dead-looking demeanor but a quieter stomach. Gabriel showered and hair combed back, continued to twitch anxiously in his seat. He'd understood Gabriel's conflict as a parent and doubted the Arch slept during the night. Sewall told him Isabella was safe and with his wife and daughter at Mortem. Knowing his daughter was close by cleared his head. The priority of the summit meeting outranked the others in his mind.

"Your son's more than capable of saving himself," Amos argued, clutching his temple. His eyes scrunched together as if in pain. "He has more power than anyone except for you to get out of any situation he'd find himself in."

"Oh!" Gabriel sneered, wings flared. "Easy to say considering your brother weaseled him into this farce."

Amos' eyes narrowed. "Don't bring my brother into this."

"He already did the moment he dragged my son along!" Gabriel yelled.

"Hey!" Malachi boomed, fire exploding from his head once again.

Everyone paused as the heat of his flames radiated. He pinched the bridge of his nose, taking deep breaths.

"Our plan still involves the demon realm. We need to go there to grab Joshua and Barmen anyway." He lifted a finger as Amos opened his mouth. "It'll take no additional time for Gabriel to teleport around to look for his son."

"It will take time," Amos countered. "He doesn't know the demon realm as well and it's a larger territory to cover. Opening a portal to the correct location will be less accurate."

"You understand the term 'course correction', yes? I'll get to where I need to go one way or another." Recrossing his legs, Gabriel narrowed his eyes at Amos. "And I'll find my son."

"We've lost a day already sitting here," Sewall grumbled.

"It's not a waste if you need it to recover your strength," Malachi countered. "No one was in any condition to fight."

"Speak for yourself." Gabriel scoffed. "The way I feel, no demon lord or monster should dare cross my path."

"My point is," Malachi sighed. "We need to go to the demon realm regardless. There's no telling where your son teleported to, but there's a good chance it's somewhere in Levithan's or Beelzebub's region, which narrows the possibilities."

"And Barmen went with him." Sewall finished the last of his dosa and soup. "Barmen has a sharp head on his shoulders. He'd keep everyone together and have a plan formed."

"So there's a chance we'd find everyone together?" Malachi asked, sitting forward. "My daughter, Gabriel's son, and Joshua and Barmen."

Sewall nodded. "So long as Joshua doesn't go crazy."

Gabriel's wings twitched.

"Crazy?" Gabriel tilted his head to the side, glaring at Sewall. "I thought that was treated."

"It's not something that's 'cured' and goes away," Sewall hissed back at Gabriel, "It's a chronic illness he has to regulate and manage."

Gabriel clenched his fist. Malachi heard his teeth grinding together before the Arch spoke.

"I never," Gabriel answered in a hard whisper. "Never would've let him go if I didn't think Joshua had his mind under control."

"He does," Sewall argued.

"Without his medicine?" Gabriel raised an eyebrow.

"Our mission was supposed to be quick." Amos grimaced. "I doubt Barmen or Joshua anticipated being away from home this long."

Gabriel huffed and waved his arms. "What the Trinity were you thinking?"

The fire heated in his veins, waiting to be released. Malachi took another calming breath, focusing on the coastal wind.

"He was thinking of fighting back," Malachi answered.

Amos' eyes widened.

"Yes, actually." Amos' lips twitched. "Not used to other people knowing my intentions."

He ran a hand through his hair again. "It's something I would've done when I was younger."

Amos lifted his chin. "Is it something you would do now?"

"We don't have any other choice. The demon lord's coming and she has no plans of stopping until she destroys or rules us all." He exchanged glances with everyone at the table. "We grab our people and come back home to prepare for the battle coming our way. Luke and the others will be here in two days."

Gabriel frowned. "That's not enough time."

"We have to make it enough," he barked back.

The flickers of frustration fueled the flames in his veins. His heart quickened in his chest as he calmed his fire. Now was not the time to let anger rule. It was time none of them could afford.

Again, Sewall had the final say. He clapped his bony hands together, startling them all.

"Very well then." Sewall stood to his full height. "Gabriel, you best open a portal now."

Gabriel sat there for a few seconds, mouth agape before springing to action. He leapt from his chair, bringing his hands together. Electric static buzzed for a second until the thin slit of the portal's light appeared between his hands. The slit opened wide, sending waves of warm air their way.

Sewall walked to the portal, shadows trailing after him. Malachi stood to join him but caught the reluctance in Amos' face.

"We need to do this for our people, Amos," Malachi called out above the sound of the wind.

Amos frowned. "My people will be without their leader for too long."

Malachi patted a hand on his back, nodding to the portal.

"Your people won't be around much longer unless you act now."

Amos' frown deepened. What will it take to get this Arch to come with them?

He thought for a moment before leaning into Amos' ear. "Ben and Canaan are still somewhere in the demon realm."

This sent a jolt through Amos. He rose to his feet, clenching and unclenching his hands. Concern etched into every line of his face. Malachi didn't know much about Ben and Canaan, but they must've been plenty capable to venture willingly into the demon realm. He wondered if Amos thought the same. Amos needed an heir and to bring all the Arch Heads together. Two strong reasons to go into the demon realm.

Amos flinched, hearing his thoughts. The 'brother' argument won. Amos walked over to the portal and stepped through. Malachi followed behind his heels. The rush of traveling through the portal lasted a few uncomfortable seconds. His wings flared out, trying to right himself in a directionless dimension. He flailed until his feet found solid ground.

He landed with a thud, his wings extended out wide and ready to take off if needed. Another thud followed by a groan told him the others made it. A dense jungle surrounded them. The calls and cries of bugs, birds, and animals echoed in a chaotic symphony.

He furrowed his brow. Did Gabriel open a portal to the right place? Anger and frustration shot through his limbs. What the hell was wrong with Gabriel? Can't he do anything right?

Flames sprouted from his hands as he shot a glare at Gabriel, grinding his teeth. "Why are we deep in the Elementa jungle? We're supposed to be in the demon realm!"

Gabriel furrowed his brow.

"We *are* in the demon realm." He stared at their surroundings and frowned. "I know I aimed for the demon realm. This has to be it."

"What city or domain did you aim for?" Sewall's shadows danced and withered around his feet.

"Leviathan's region, close to Atlantis city," Gabriel answered.

Amos raised his hand to him.

"Calm, Malachi. Leviathan's domain is known to contain dense jungles similar to the ones in your region." He glanced at the dense brush to his right. "But we need to be on guard because the monsters are very different here."

The fire in his stomach fizzled out some. He extinguished the flames in his hands but kept the heat close to the surface of his skin. There was never a thing as being too cautious in the demon realm.

"Any clue if we're actually close to Atlantis?" Sewall hissed, scowling at the sun. "I can't stand this heat."

"I'm not positive, but," Gabriel mused, nodding his head to the East. "I think I overshot and opened the portal past the city."

"So we need to travel east? We'll run into Fun City before Atlantis if we head that—" Amos gasped suddenly, clutching his temples with both hands. His face scrunched together as he pointed to their west. "There's another group close by."

"Another group?" he asked, sprouting flames into his hands. "A horde of demons probably."

Anger and heat mixed together cohesively in his mind. The images of his city falling to the destruction of those monsters flashed through like lightning strikes, charging him. Heat cascaded down his body, eager to burn.

"Should we interrogate them first?" Gabriel inquired. "Maybe they'll know something about my son and Joshua."

Amos continued to clutch his temples, curling in on himself. He didn't speak a word, but his wings trembled, conveying his pain. Malachi and Sewall grunted in agreement, already moving in the direction Amos pointed. He wondered if Amos was pushing himself too hard but shook the thought away.

They needed to locate the demon group before they found them first. *An ambush attack would work well,* he thought, creeping low into the brush. Gabriel tended to Amos' crumbled form while Malachi and Sewall disappeared into the thicket. Close behind him, Sewall's cold shadows slithered forward under the canopy's shade. The hairs on the back of Malachi's neck rose as he suppressed a shudder. Maybe having Sewall following him wasn't such a good idea.

Voices drew his attention and he crouched more into the foliage. Taking care not to touch the leaves, he extinguished his flames but kept them ready to burst out when needed. He peered around a large banana leaf to see two drastically different figures with their backs turned, one tall and thin and another short and round. Standing several yards away, he couldn't hear their soft voices, but that mattered little. He'd extinguish them soon enough.

He called his fire to his fist. He'd aim for the taller one and keep the smaller one for questioning. He crept closer, lifting his flame at the taller one's head. Taking a deep inhale, he took aim and fired.

As his fire streamed from his hand, the little demon faced him.

His flame sputtered.

The demon was a child. A child with large eyes and dark, ribbon-like hair on her head. Her wide mouth opened and released an ear-piercing scream. Too late to call his fire back, he could only watch as the last of his flames rained on them.

The tall demon moved with lightning speed. One second, he was there, and the next, he grabbed the smaller demon and bolted deeper into the jungle. The taller demon looked terrifying. All he saw of its face was a dozen rows of razor-sharp teeth and small beady eyes.

Shit, he thought. His hesitation allowed them the chance to escape. Just as he'd cursed under his breath, shadows dashed through the brush.

He'd forgotten Sewall came with him until he'd made his presence known. His shadows chased the two demons with the speed of a striking snake. Another cry of alarm followed by a low groan, told Malachi that Sewall hit the mark.

"Now then," Sewall's cold voice sent shivers down his spine. "You two may be able to help us."

The shadows dragged back the two demons. The smaller one wiggled and fought while the taller one lay limp.

"Let me go!" The small demon gasped.

Her movements weakened by the minute. The tall demon groaned once more.

"Where are we?" he barked at them, sitting back on his heels. "Are we close to Atlantis or Fun City in Leviathan's domain?"

The smaller demon shuddered, curling in on herself, trembling. She looked so fragile…reminding him of when Isabella was a baby.

He peered at Sewall with a frown. "Loosen your grip on them."

"This is as loose as I can be without letting them go." Sewall hissed back.

"Then let them go!" he growled back. "Can't get answers if you drain them."

Sewall scowled but retreated his shadows. The two stayed frozen on the ground. He wondered if the taller demon was rendered unconscious but his gaze focused on the smaller one. Her whole body quaked and her breathing sounded erratic, probably panicked. She refused to look at them but whimpered.

He shuffled closer, staying low to not tower over them. The girl flinched and tried to hide herself more. He paused.

She's waiting for a blow, he dimly realized. He recognized that fetal position. Her arms cradled her large head, not covering nearly enough space. He scanned the area to see if this was a trick and if other demons were about to ambush them.

He swiveled his head, seeing nothing. No ambush or sneak attack. He frowned again, glancing back down at the girl. Were they out here by themselves? He gently moved closer to see the smallest pair of wings he'd ever seen on her back.

He froze. She was a halfling?! He jerked his head to the taller one on his side.

One deformed wing stuck out the side of his shoulder blade at an odd angle. Did Sewall's shadows cause that? He shook his head. No, that wasn't possible. With that angle, they would've heard the loud snap of bone breaking.

He must've been born like that then, he mused, pulling his hand away.

"Let us go if you're not gonna hurt us." The girl's voice quivered.

He returned his gaze to her. She flinched.

One large eye peeked at him. She held her fetal position, her head low and braced. Her eyes widened further as Sewall stepped behind him, towering over them all.

"Please," she whispered, her lips quivering. "Don't kill us."

His heart twisted, as regret and shame filled his stomach. Though she didn't look like Isabella, the small demon reminded him so much of his daughter when she was younger. Isabella had been a tiny, pitiful baby. Staring at him with pleading eyes, begging for something he couldn't name or give. The same eyes this small demon stared at him with.

"We aren't going to kill you." He gave a pointed glance at Sewall. "We're not gonna hurt you either."

Her eyes flickered between him and Sewall, doubt shrouding her expression. Sewall scowled and grunted as if to say 'they didn't have time for this'.

"We need to know where we are," he continued, "Are we close to Fun City? Or Atlantis?"

A groan caused everyone to jump.

"Fig!" The small demon cried. "Are ya all right?"

The taller demon sat up, clutching his chest. Malachi backed away and raised his body temperature, ready to call upon his flames. Sitting up, Fig's head towered over his crouched form, putting him at a disadvantage.

He rose to his feet.

"Bugs?" Fig groaned again. "What happened? I thought I was dyin' back there."

"If you'd kept running, you would have." Sewall's cool voice carried over them.

Fig focused on Sewall and paled.

"We don't want any trouble," Fig said, lifting a shaking hand as if to ward them off.

The one called Bugs crawled over to him like the creatures she was named after. She hid behind him, peering around him every few seconds.

"We're not here to hurt you," he growled, frustrated with repeating himself. "We just need to know where we are."

"Then you'll leave us alone?" Fig's eyes flickered to Sewall.

"Yes. We didn't expect to see uh—children. Even if you're halflings, you're too young for us to have been rough with you." He indicated his head to Fig. "Apologizes."

Bugs gasped while Fig's eyes widened.

"Uh," Fig muttered. "Thanks."

He patted Bugs' head.

"We don't know where we are either," Fig explained, "Our group just got here, so I'm afraid I can't give you a good sense of direction."

He cursed under his breath. Dammit, back to square one. Sewall narrowed his eyes on the two kids. They shuddered.

"How did your group get here exactly?" Sewall asked, slinking closer.

Fig crawled back. "W—we…w-we…umm…"

Bugs clung to his torso, with trembling limbs.

"Our friends got us here, ok?" Bugs blurted out. "They opened a portal and now we're here."

Figs tried to shush her but it was too late. They'd heard her.

He swiveled on his feet, back to the children while Sewall took another step toward them. Shock ricocheted through him like electricity. Opened a portal? Was that Gabriel Jr.? Or Beelzebub?

He pulled Sewall behind him and the children stopped crawling away. In fact, they sighed in relief.

"Opened a portal?" He echoed his thoughts. "How? Did your friend have wings like us?"

Fig gave a reluctant nod. "They appeared out of nowhere by our home."

"We gave 'em food and shelter." Bugs jutted her chin out. "We're going to be friends…maybe but hopefully!"

His lips twitched in amusement.

"Who's in your group?" He asked, crouching to their level. "I think some of them are our friends too."

Bugs retreated. "Are ya going to take our friends?"

Her voice sounded so small now.

"We're gonna take them home," he answered. "We have a bad guy coming to destroy it and I need their help."

"Bad guy?" Bugs exchanged a glance with Fig. "Like the patrol?"

"Patrol?" Sewall snapped, tilting his head to the side. "Let's keep to one question at a time. Answer Malachi, who all is in the group?"

They flinched. Bugs ducked back behind Fig. Malachi sighed, pinching the bridge of his nose.

"Don't worry," he gave a pointed glance at Sewall. "Neither of us will hurt you. We just want to know if our friends are also your friends."

"Umm," Figs wrapped an arm around Bugs, slowly getting to his feet. "One of their names was Elijah and—"

"Yes!" He boomed, causing Fig and Bugs to jump.

Finally some progress in this mission!

"Who else?" Sewall raised an eyebrow.

Fig cleared his throat.

"Another's was Charlotte and Ava…Ummm who else? I'm tryin' to 'member all of their names." Fig rubbed the back of his head.

"Oh!" Bugs said, climbing to whisper in Fig's ear.

"Ah," Fig sighed, nodding. "Makoto was another. He's one of the reasons we were able to open the portal."

"Are there others like Makoto?" he asked. "Where are they?"

He needed to get Gabriel and Amos here so they could track down Elijah. One Head Arch down, two more to go!

"Have you seen an insanely large angel by any chance, with black wings? Or an angel with bright red hair, like mine?" He fired off the questions before they could respond. "Or a blonde-haired angel with a screw loose?"

"A screw loose?" Bugs tilted her head to the side. "What's that mean?"

"Never mind that for now," Sewall snapped. "Malachi, I sent a shadow back to Gabriel and Amos to lead them here. We need to track down Elijah if he's nearby."

"Agreed," he nodded. "Kids, we need to know where our friend, Elijah, is located. Can you lead me and my friends to him?"

Fig frowned while Bugs asked "Friends?"

"You've already met Sewall." He lifted a hand to Sewall and then to his chest. "My name is Malachi and the two others are Gabriel and Amos."

"I won't lead ya to where the rest of my family is." Fig shook his head and whispered to Bugs, "I don't trust 'em Bugs."

"Listen here—" Sewall hissed.

"*We* understand," Malachi interrupted, shooting a glare at Sewall."Simply go tell Elijah that Gabriel, Sewall, Amos, and Malachi are here and we need to talk. We'll wait for them right here."

"Ya won't follow us?" Bugs furrowed her brow.

He shook his head.

"Or attack us again?" Figs interjected quickly, his eyes flickering to Sewall.

He nudged Sewall's arm.

"Fine, we won't attack either of you," Sewall grunted. "Or your family...unless provoked."

Fig and Bugs exchanged a look, nodding in agreement.

"We'll go back and tell the others," Fig concluded. "But we can't promise anything."

"Very well." He sighed.

He doubted Elijah would ignore their names. Now the hard part of gathering everyone started.

Fig clutched Bugs as he walked backward into the thick jungle, eyes never leaving the Archs. Bugs' large eyes stared at them, like prey watching a predator. Malachi thought he'd be more disgusted with interacting with halflings, but nothing arose. No disdain, anger, or repulsion. In fact, he was mildly surprised that the persisting thought in his mind was that they were children. Maybe Sewall scared them too much, he wondered. In a more relaxed setting, halflings would be more demon-like in behavior.

His thoughts wandered to Mikael's heir, Arick. From the reports he read, wasn't he also a halfling?

He frowned, pondering the similarities, or lack thereof, between the halflings. Arick looked and acted like one of them. His wings were intact, whereas these two possessed deformed wings. Arick spoke well whereas these two carried a thick accent. The differences were many but...those two hadn't attacked them. Fig and Bugs tried to run away from them. Arick hadn't attacked anyone either. Why was that?

An uneasy feeling coiled inside his chest as his thoughts roamed. He didn't have any right to judge. Maybe that's why he hadn't reacted.

A branch snap caused him to whirl around. Flames erupted from his hands, ready to launch an attack. He froze, seeing two familiar faces.

"Confound this horrible place," Gabriel scowled, ripping a large leaf from its branch. "As if the heat isn't enough."

"Or the sounds." Amos groaned behind him. "There's so many…thoughts."

"Took you two long enough to get here," Sewall growled. "We caught two demons."

"Halflings," he corrected.

Gabriel and Amos snapped their heads up.

"Pardon?" Gabriel's eyes widened. "Halflings?"

"What happened?" Amos narrowed his eyes on him.

He explained their encounter with Fig and Bugs. As they listened, Gabriel furrowed his brow while Amos continued to rub his temples. At the mention of Elijah and his daughters, they perked up.

"Elijah may know where the others are." Gabriel crossed his arms and grasped his chin with one hand. "My son said he'd gone with Mikael to rescue my soldiers. This is the best lead we could've hoped for."

"My brothers." Amos sighed. "They may be with him too. Canaan will have valuable intel for us after spending so much time in the demon realm."

"If Mikael is with Elijah," he stated. "Joshua's the last one to track down."

"The problem's finding out where my son has been transported to." Gabriel frowned. "Or if he would try to teleport again."

"You're the expert in opening portals and how it works," Sewall glowered at him. "What's to stop your son from going back to the spirit realm?"

Gabriel's face flushed.

"I know opening a portal looks easy to you but it's much more complex than that. There's directional and spatial awareness needed as well as a highly concentrated amount of power many angels don't possess." He sighed. "While my son has the power, his directional and spatial awareness isn't fine-tuned for long distances. He hasn't learned to land properly when traveling the long distance between realms."

"Yet you believed he could do it without you?" He raised an eyebrow, receiving a glare in return.

"I thought since he'd jumped from our world to the human world, he'd be fine." Gabriel sighed. "I was wrong to assume that and it'll never happen again."

Amos winced beside him.

"Your thoughts are like a tornado," Amos murmured. "Too much."

"Amos." Sewall stepped closer. "Can you hear Elijah or any of the others close by?"

"I'm trying," Amos groaned. "It's hard with a dozen of voices shouting all at once."

He watched Amos with sympathy; grateful he hadn't been born a Selaphiel angel. His thoughts wandered to Amos' father, Aesop. He had been a composed and thoughtful Arch in the few encounters they'd shared. He frowned as Amos' grimace deepened.

When he died and his powers transferred to Clarissa, he didn't want her to struggle this much. She'd take over his role as Head Arch and inherit all the responsibility with the title. Since the reconstruction of their city, she'd stepped up in her leadership role more than he'd ever expected. Several of his principalities deferred to her for building layouts and architecture decisions instead of him.

She'd mastered her flame manipulation from such an early age that he'd never been concerned about her ascension into leadership. He shook his head. *No*, he thought, *Clarissa will handle the influx of power with grace. She'll be fine.*

Isabella, on the other hand, was another story. He worried about her role. Without Clarissa by her side, would she fly on her own? Or struggle worse than Amos? That halfling from earlier reminded him so much of Isabella; his chest tightened.

She'd been the loudest baby he'd ever seen. He'd lost Liliana so fast, he'd barely registered his children needed him. Clarissa stepped up then too, he remembered. Isabella stopped crying the minute Clarissa held her.

He grimaced at the memory. He'd been so relieved to push Isabella off to Clarissa, that he hadn't thought of how it would affect them later in life. He shook his head again. *As long as Isabella stays by her sister's side, she'll be fine too.*

Sweat dripped down their faces as they waited for word to get back to Elijah and the others. The sun traveled across the sky. They would've baked if not for the canopy coverage, but the heat circulated around them. The humidity of the climate provided a greenhouse effect.

A rustle of leaves pulled their attention. He called his flames to his hands, ready to fight. The others quieted and followed suit.

Several tense seconds passed by until a hand popped through the brush, cursing his way through.

"Damn, bugs are on every leaf," Elijah grunted, pushing his way through.

He extinguished his flames as relief filled him.

"It could be worse," a soft, high-pitched voice called out behind him.

"Hey!" a familiar voice exclaimed. "Bugs aren't bad."

Despite himself, his lips curled into a grin. Their plan worked! Bugs and Fig brought the others to them.

Elijah brushed debris off his clothes. "Sorry, Bugs. Nothing against your name—"

Elijah paused as he noticed them for the first time.

"Well," Elijah huffed, as a grin spread across his face.

"Aren't you all a sight for sore eyes?"

"Hmmmm." Sewall crossed his arms and tilted his head back. "The same could be said about you."

Elijah chuckled.

"Finally we've found you!" Gabriel sighed. "Are there any others—"

Slowly more and more angels walked into the small clearing they'd created.

Gabriel's eyes widened as his soldiers came into view, their wings intact but wilted. Their clothes were torn and coated with dried blood and dirt. Faint bruises marred their wrists, indicating shackles. Elijah and his daughters looked withered and weak. Their wings hung low to the ground, nearly limp.

What happened to them? He wondered. He took one step forward, but a blur of movement shot by him. Amos sprinted forward, wrapping his arms around two males in the back he hadn't spotted earlier. His wings twitched and the air in his lungs froze.

Ben and Canaan wrapped their arms around Amos, comforting *him.* Canaan looked disheveled but it was Ben that shocked him. Dried blood coated his tunic to the point where a crust formed along the shoulders. Ben's face was hollowed out and his eyes were sunken in.

That kid appeared to be in the worst situation, he mused. He scanned the other figures hovering behind Ava. Fig and Bugs stood the closest, still holding onto one another. However, a girl with black hair and a deep set of eyes closed in on them.

His wings twitched and the air in his lungs stalled. The strange girl possessed wings resembling their own, in better condition than Fig's and Bugs'. Was she an angel or a halfling?

The answer slammed into him as more emerged from the trees. An albino kid walked forward followed by a young boy, a horn protruding through his head. A set of yellow eyes narrowed at him. The boy possessed a pair of dark wings as well. If not for the horn and eyes, the kid could blend in with their society.

Why were they here? Malachi pondered.

He watched the kids huddle closer to the girl with dark hair. They moved together as if ready to defend one another. The girl hesitated at the clearing, observing them all. She lifted a hand, and the other kids froze. All waiting for her command.

He frowned, tilting his chin to the side to address Elijah.

"There are a lot more here than I anticipated Elijah," he drawled.

The girl's face jerked to his. Her curtain of hair moved enough for him to see a large half-moon scar along her face. His wings twitched again. This girl…memories of the children at home echoed through his mind. The ones who needed protecting and sheltering. His heart gave a squeeze.

"Now." Elijah extended his arms out, stepping in front of the children as if to shield them. "These are *our* friends. They don't mean us any harm."

He furrowed his brow. What did he mean by that? Of course, they couldn't mean any harm; they were children. Did he think they'd attack them outright? He nearly scoffed at the idea until caught the sight of Gabriel.

Disgust etched itself on every line of Gabriel's face. His lips curled back as if he was going to gag.

"Are they halflings?" Gabriel sneered, taking a step back.

Sewall didn't appear disgusted but was not happy either. Amos tightened his hold on Canaan and Ben, looking at them reproachfully.

Should he be more disgusted? He wondered. He peeked over his shoulder at Fig and Bugs. Their faces scrunched in fear and uncertainty. The only thing he felt when looking at them was…sorrow. They reminded him too much of his own people. In need.

He stepped to Elijah, lifting his palms up and extinguishing any flames.

"We mean them no harm." He glared at Gabriel and Amos. "Whether they're halflings or not."

"Oh," Elijah sighed, his eyes widened. "That's a relief. I thought it'd be tougher than that."

"It will be," Gabriel huffed, taking a step back from the children.

"For once," Amos joined in, letting go of his brothers. "I agree with Gabriel. Are you sure what you're planning is a good idea, Elijah?"

"Pray tell," Sewall said in a cold voice. "What's this idea you have?"

Elijah opened and closed his mouth several times, no words coming out. They all waited and watched as he struggled for words. The silence worsened the tension, minus Amos who could read every thought going through Elijah's head.

Charlotte stepped in front of her father, head held high as she spoke firmly, "They're coming home with us."

More silence followed. His was one of shock. Gabriel, he guessed from the shade of red on his face, was from outrage. Whereas Sewall…well, he didn't look any different than his usual sulking self. Amos frowned, but his gaze was on the halfling girl who squirmed under his scrutiny.

"Uhh," he mumbled. "Ok."

"It's most certainly not ok!" Gabriel cried out. "Those *things* aren't allowed in our world."

Some of the kids flinched, including Fig and Bugs. His wings flared. Heat flowed through his arms again as something tightened in his stomach.

"They're children, not things!" Charlotte's eyes narrowed at Gabriel. "And they'll be allowed in our region."

"Most certainly not in mine." Gabriel scoffed and pivoted to Elijah. "Your region borders mine. How inconsiderate can you be to allow those things close to my home?!"

Elijah's eyes flashed and wings flared. He opened his mouth but someone else beat him.

"My lord," a voice drew their attention.

They all turned to see the Gabriel soldiers kneeling before their leader. Heads bowed and wings flat. All in unison they spoke.

"Please allow them, my lord." They called out. Gabriel froze, his eyes wide as he took in his troops.

A single voice continued from the kneeling members. "My lord, please show them your kindness. Without these children, we wouldn't have made it this far. We owe them our lives and gratitude. Please!"

Gabriel's jaw dropped. His gaze pinged across their begging forms.

"B-b-b-but…" Gabriel stuttered. "They're…"

"Please, my lord!" They all echoed in unison. "We vouch for them!"

"As do I," Charlotte exclaimed.

Ava stepped forward.

"As do I," Ava said softly, her wings cradling the girl.

His own jaw dropped. He'd never seen such…he didn't have the words for…He shook his head before turning to Gabriel. They all waited for his answer.

A blush deepened on Gabriel's face as he exchanged a glance with Amos. The two stared at one another hard for three heartbeats. Amos gave the smallest of nods; he'd nearly missed it.

"Very well," Gabriel's wings slumped. "You can have your little…whatever they're called."

"Thank you, my lord!" The soldiers called out.

"We have a lot of catching up to do." Gabriel rubbed a hand over his face. "Elijah, what's happened to you? What led to all of this?"

He indicated to the halflings.

"We all better have a seat." Elijah sighed. "It's a long story."

An hour passed by as they listened to Elijah. Charlotte

interjected a few times to share her and Ava's part of the story but otherwise no one talked. The children continued to huddle around the scarred, halfling girl while Ava stood in front of them. Ava's wings flared protectively around the kids.

Sewall divided his glare between Gabriel, himself, and Elijah as if determining who he hated the most. Amos didn't appear to be listening to the story but observed the kids with rapid interest.

Elijah explained how he and Mikael started off on their quest to find the Abbadon but it quickly changed. They'd been transported to the demon realm by accident and eventually made a deal with the demon lords, Beelzebub and Leviathan, for their three staffs in exchange for a favor. He detailed how he, Mikael, and Ben charged Matthew's prison to find Gabriel's soldiers. Ben had obtained his current injuries by activating Satan's staff to find everyone. Matthew killed Atarah, sending Arick into a rage. Mikael had arrived in time to calm Arick, but Satan made an appearance.

Although the halfling kids flinched at the mention of the demon lord, Elijah continued. He explained that Mikael, Arick, and Matthew were taken by Satan somewhere else. Whereas they used a combined effort of soldiers' power to transport them out of the prison. The soldiers could only muster enough power to teleport to a desert close to the Red City. Starving and dehydrated they walked the desert for days until they came across Rhea and her halfling group, who fed and sheltered them from the authorities.

Malachi glanced at the girl called Rhea. She squirmed when all eyes turned to her. Charlotte chimed in and gushed about their bravery and the compassion they exhibited. Rhea blushed while the boy with the single horn scoffed.

Elijah explained how they used the second staff to muster enough power to teleport out of the desert, landing them here in the jungle. Figs and Bugs had gone out on a food scouting mission when they came across them.

"And well," Elijah sighed. "That brings us to about now. We owe these kids our lives and we have one staff left from the deal Ben made with Beelzebub."

"So Mikael was taken by Satan?" Gabriel ran a hand through his hair. "How in the trinity are we supposed to get him?"

Malachi sighed, pinching the bridge of his nose. Gabriel was right. Mikael would be nearly impossible to rescue. They still didn't know where he was taken either.

"Have you seen or heard anything about my daughter or Joshua?" He asked.

Elijah shook his head. "You're the first angels I've seen in days."

"The real question is," Sewall spoke from where he leaned against a tree. "What are we going to do now?"

His eyes squinted down at the soldiers and kids.

"That's a brilliant question," Amos murmured, frowning at Ben and Canaan.

"Well that leaves our part of the story to be told next," he answered. "In a couple of days, I'm holding another emergency summit meeting."

"Another?" Elijah raised an eyebrow.

"Yes," he nodded. "The rangers are joining us and we need to all unite. According to them, Satan's planning on controlling the minds of every soldier she can to attack our world, using Matthew and probably Mikael against us."

Ava's face paled and her wings trembled.

"Their intel's from watchers who've spied on Satan in the hopes of gaining a body." He continued. "Leaving no reason to lie and all the more reason why we need to unite. We meet in two days to prepare for war."

"Why?" Charlotte's voice was barely above a whisper.

"Apparently," he answered. "The demon lords are always fighting for more land and power. And instead of fighting her brothers and their borders, she's decided to conquer our world in order to get more land."

"But her ladyship can't leave our world," Rhea called out.

She slapped a hand over her mouth as if regretting her words. Gabriel opened his mouth, no doubt to sneer at her.

"You're right," he said quickly, cutting off the Arch. "Satan can't leave the demon realm so she's using others to do her dirty work. She now has control over the entire Michael clan as well as any demons in her army to attack our world with."

"Where are they heading?" Ava gasped.

"We don't know," He shook his head.

Charlotte covered her mouth, her wings trembling.

"We need Joshua and Barmen then," Elijah said gravely. "For the summit meeting?"

He nodded, rubbing the back of his neck.

"Going back to Sewall's question," Gabriel chimed in, gazing at his troops. "What to do now? I think the first thing is to return my troops home."

"And my brother Canaan," Amos called out.

The brother in question jerked his head up, mouth open in protest. Amos lifted a hand to silence him. They glared at each other, gesturing their hands every few seconds. While they argued mentally, Elijah frowned at Charlotte and Ava.

"I want you two to go home as well," Elijah exclaimed. "Especially you, Ava. With Mikael gone, you need to prepare the citizens that their leader and his heirs are most likely dead."

A pained gasp escaped Ava. Charlotte dashed to Ava's side as she doubled over, clutching her chest.

"Don't say they're not alive," Ava whispered, tears welling in her eyes. "They're alive, we just have to find a way to release them from her mind control."

Charlotte engulfed her into a hug, murmuring softly into her ear. Elijah exchanged a glance with Amos, asking a silent question. Amos frowned and nodded.

"There's a chance," Amos answered. "But you're right;

she needs to return to her home and prepare the others. She should join the meeting in Mikael's stead."

"That would be too much—" Elijah started.

"I'll do it." Ava interrupted. Her face no longer burrowed in Charlotte's shoulder, Ava's red, puffy eyes flashed with determination. "I'll prepare our people for battle and for Mikael and Arick's rescue before ever conceding to their deaths."

Elijah gave an imploring glance to Ava but she ignored him. Her gaze was on Gabriel.

"Well?" Ava tilted her head. "You agree to take us?"

It was Gabriel's turn to raise an eyebrow.

"Who all is included in 'us'?" He crossed his arms.

"All of us," Charlotte called out, grabbing Rhea's hand. "You'll take us home."

Gabriel pursed his lips. "Those—"

"Kids," he interjected.

Gabriel whipped around to him. "Since when did you become a halfling sympathizer?"

He paused, wondering why he cared. These kids weren't his responsibility or his citizens but…A memory of compassionate green eyes flashed through his mind.

He held his ground and glared at him. "They are but kids Gabriel."

"They're kids now," Gabriel huffed. "But monsters later."

"We aren't monsters," Rhea flared her wings. "You are."

Gabriel's wings flared, his face flushed in anger. Malachi stepped in front of him.

"Gabriel," he snapped. "These are *kids*. I thought you, out of any of us, would understand the value of kids."

Gabriel's red face paled. A sharp inhale of breath told him his comment made its mark.

"Very well, you'll all be transported back but," he pointed a finger at Charlotte, "You better ensure they all stay in your region."

Charlotte nodded. "It'll be done."

Malachi sighed. *One less thing to worry about,* he thought. He turned to see Amos and Sewall watching him with a strange expression. He shrugged. It wasn't his fault Gabriel was being extra difficult today.

He clapped his hands together.

"Well, that settles who all is returning home." He turned to Elijah. "We still need to find Clarissa, Joshua, and Barmen for the summit, and we need your help."

"I can spend a day or so more in the demon realm. It won't kill me…I hope." Elijah chuckled.

A sizzling sound drew his attention. He pivoted to see Gabriel opening a portal with his hands.

"Everyone who wants to go home, better go now," Gabriel grunted. "Makoto, you and your troops go in first."

Makoto bowed deeply before leaping into the portal's opening. The troops followed after, disappearing into the light within seconds. Charlotte nodded to Rhea, guiding her by the hand to the portal. The other kids followed, giving wary glances to Gabriel. Only Bugs spared him a glance. A smile twitched at the corner of her mouth as she gave a small wave to him.

He stared on as Charlotte and the group of kids shuffled through the portal. Ava followed from behind, helping the kids through the back. She speared Elijah with one look before walking through.

"Don't count them out yet," she exclaimed before leaping through.

"Anyone else?" Gabriel called out.

"Yes!" Amos pushed Canaan closer to the portal "You'll go home because you, as heir, have a duty!"

"What about Ben?" Canaan protested.

They both frowned at him. Amos sighed.

"I think I know someone who can heal him here in the demon realm. That's the only reason I'm not forcing him back home." Amos grabbed Canaan's face and brought their foreheads together. "Go home, notify the troops, and learn as much as you can."

Canaan's shoulders loosened and his wings slumped in defeat. He whispered something to Amos he couldn't hear. All three brothers embraced one last time before Canaan jumped through the portal.

Only Elijah and Ben were left from their group.

Malachi faced the forest, wondering for the hundredth time where Clarissa was and if they would gather everyone in time. Knowing that Mikael and Arick were taken shot knots through his stomach. To fight against Matthew was one thing but now they may have to fight three Michael Archs. He shuddered at the thought. They wouldn't stand a chance.

"All right then," Sewall's voice drew his attention. "Where to now?"

Gabriel closed the portal, bringing his hands together in a prayer position.

He grimaced, pointing a finger in the direction he'd hoped was one of Leviathan's main cities. Somewhere out there, Joshua and Clarissa's group roamed. A distance he wanted to close as quickly and quietly as possible. If what he knew of the demon lords was true, they needed to avoid drawing too much attention to themselves.

He silently prayed the others weren't in Satan's clutches. If so, they were doomed and he was double doomed. Clarissa was his heir. Without her, his future—no, his clan's future— was bleak. While he breathed easier in knowing Isabella was safe back at home, as a father, it didn't mean she was his heir.

He took the first step into the jungle, the others falling in line with him. The calls of the jungle crescendoed around them, closing in on all sides.

Chapter 11

"No, silly!" Inu chuckled. "Ya're 'pose to take tha loop under tha knot en then tie it off."

"Ooooh," Clarissa drawled, her lips curling at the ends. "What about like this?!"

She dove for Ina's sides and tickled her ruthlessly. Inu screamed in delight, wiggling as her arm nubs tried in vain to push her away.

"I give up! I give up!" Tears of laughter welled in Inu's eyes. "Please!"

"There we go." She sat back with a grin. "That's the kind of attitude I like to work with."

Inu rubbed her eyes, her tail splashing in the small bucket she was stationed in. Born half siren, Inu possessed one long dorsal fin, gills along her rib cage, and scales along her neck and face. Her round black eyes creeped Clarissa out at first but…Inu liked her immediately.

"Do ya en tha others really have to go soon?" Inu asked, her eyes downcast. "Ya only just gotten 'ere."

She paused to decipher Ina's heavy accent. When they first arrived a day ago, she'd thought the children were speaking a different language. Until Leviathan enunciated each word, she'd guessed what each child was asking for. Now, with a little concentration, she understood full sentences.

She sighed, rubbing a hand along Inu's scaly head. "There's another school further inland that needs our help too."

"Closer to tha city of Talia?" Inu asked the fins along her head curled inward. "Innit tha dangerous?"

Clarissa frowned, glancing back at the scars slashed across Inu's arms and torso in jagged lines, her hands cut off. Since arriving, they'd come across over a dozen children who bore horrible scars or missing limbs. Children of all different kinds and backgrounds. Many still had a sparkle of childhood hope in their eyes, but the teens appeared broken and depleted of any joy in life. The expressions the older kids had sent shivers down her spine.

Leviathan told them they'd be helping at a school that got frequent attacks from raiders, but she never imagined how much this small village would remind her of her people at home. The village consisted of three buildings: the school, the hospital, and the food bank. Otherwise, everyone lived in pitched tents.

She'd asked Inu why they didn't build homes for everyone. Inu tilted her head to the side and told her a big home would be harder to run with when the raiders came. Not if, but *when* the raiders came. The tents the citizens lived in were light and easy to pack. They relied heavily on fruit from the forest trees and fish from the river as their main sources of food. Sometimes the raiders would burn down the surrounding trees as a tactic to starve them. However, according to Inu, that only happened twice in her very short life.

Leviathan explained that many of the families moved to the outskirts to avoid more invasions. The raiders were a variety of demons, usually not from Leviathan's domain. They attacked with quick and cunning techniques, dragging anything and everything of value from the villagers to sell it. Their people, their food, and any supplies they had. Many of the adults lacked motivation. Surviving to the next day was the only goal anyone had in this village.

Inu told her many of the children didn't sleep at night because that's when the raiders struck. Many huddled and hid together in sleep packs. Clarissa had asked where their parents were.

Inu's eyes had darkened. "Dead. Or wanting to be dead"

The hairs on the back of her neck tingled. Clarissa whirled around to see Barmen at the door. His tunic, once cleaned and pressed, was caked with mud and sweat. His face flushed red from the hard labor and sun. He, Zewal, and Joshua were digging trenches and underground passages for the villagers. After being here for a day and a half, they'd completed the trenches, while she'd taught some of the children in the school. She volunteered for the job, pulling from her previous experience.

Now, Barmen leaned against the doorframe watching them.

"Wat's he doin' 'ere?" Inu's fin tipped out of the bucket they'd used to bring her to the school.

"A siren from the stream's calling you back," Barmen said in a soft tone. "She's worried you've been gone too long."

"Ah." Clarissa sighed. "That's my fault. I've been keeping her for too long."

"Tha probably my older cousin." Inu frowned, turning to her. "Can ya take me back 'stead of him?"

Back to the water…a cold sweat broke out against her skin.

She clenched her hands together, forcing her lips into a smile. "Of course I can."

Clarissa hooked one arm under her dorsal fin and the other around her Inu's shoulders. With a grunt, she lifted her out of the bucket and pivoted to the door. Barmen stepped out of the way, careful not to touch either of them. His icy eyes monitored them from the doorway, shuffling on his feet.

Outside, the stream's sounds haunted her. She bit her lip to keep it from quivering. Inu asked her to do this for her. She had to follow through. The stream to drop Inu off at wasn't far. In fact, they'd been surrounded by rivers and streams ever since they arrived. Another shudder went down her spine as the stream came into view. Her wings trembled.

Inu frowned at her. "Ya ok miss?"

"Ummm," Clarissa gasped, taking tiny steps to the water's edge. "Yeah, it's nothing."

Inu furrowed her brow at her, flicking her head fins side to side.

"Ya know," Inu said. "Ya never ask me how I loss mi hands."

"Oh?" She huffed.

The river was narrow but deep. A few eyes stared at her from underneath. She shuddered. Her throat threatened to close as fear slithered up her spine.

"Twas tha raiders 'course." Inu sighed.

Clarissa paused, tilting her head a little closer.

Inu's story helped distract her. "Las' year or so, a raider dragged me from tha water. Chopped mi hands clean off, sayin' somethin' bout how they'll fetch a good price."

"That's horrible." She whispered, kneeling next to the water. "I'm so sorry, Inu."

"Eh! Wasn't your fault. Sides, tha point tis, I was scared and angry for most of tha year and avoided everyone, never leavin' the cavern. Til mi cousin told me I could either be a part of tha change or continue tha cycle of hurt." Inu lowered her eyes to the water. "Cause I was only hurtin' miself by avoidin' everyone."

Inu looked back at her.

"Ya hurtin' too and I hope ya heal like I'm trying to." She lifted her nubs.

Words nudged itself in her throat. Her flames stirred with a warmth in her belly.

"Why are you telling me this now?" She whispered.

In the distance, a scaly head broke the water's surface. Dark eyes stared at them.

"If I'd known ya didn't like water, I'd 'ever would've

asked." Inu murmured. "but seein' ya brave yer fears to bring me back home inspired me to speak up, I guess."

"Inu," the siren called out. "Git back in quick, ya hear!"

"Comin'" Inu answered, turning back to her. Inu wrapped her in a hug. "Tank ya Clarizza. Hope I sees ya again someday."

Inu flopped back into the river, disappearing into its depths. For, once, she didn't hear the sounds of the river. She heard Inu's words.

Her wings stopped twitching as she wandered back to the main school building. *Would Inu be back tomorrow?* She wondered, catching two halflings helping Zewal lift dirt away. Sweat dripped down their backs, and Zewal flushed as red as a tomato working with them. His eyes sank in deeper as the day went on.

Her thoughts drifted between each of the adults and children she'd talked to. Upon arriving, not once had she been scared. The adults in the village were different races and species of demons, yet she'd felt no fear or hatred toward them. The first halfling to greet them, Rogu, possessed one wing and two horns protruding from his head. Rogu's voice was soft and tender as if he was handling small animals. Though he didn't speak much except to explain where everything was and how to help.

While he'd explained their needs, the rest of the villagers swarmed around Leviathan as soon as he arrived. The kids raced from their hiding spots to greet him, jumping around and cheering when Leviathan reached to hold them.

Leviathan's aloof expression changed to goofiness for the children. In the first hour of arrival, he held a variety of children, listening to the needs of the leaders with sharp focus. Leviathan healed and nourished any parts of the land the raiders had destroyed. He played with the young children, bringing out smiles and shy grins for nearly everyone around, including the teenagers.

When she'd assigned herself to the role of helping the students, much of it was due to Leviathan's influence. If not for him, she doubted Inu would've come out of her underwater caverns. She pursed her lips together.

"Why the long face?" A soft, familiar voice asked.

She whirled around to see Barmen. Had he been standing there that whole time?

"No reason," She cleared her throat. "It's just...If Leviathan cares so much why doesn't he do more for them?"

"More for them?" Barmen tilted his head to the side.

"Yeah, his people," she extended her arms to the side. "Instead of leaving them defenseless against the raiders, why doesn't he arm them?"

The edge of his lips twitched. "Arm them?"

"Well yeah," she sighed. "I...I guess I shouldn't care as much because it's not my problem but..."

"This place reminds you of your home," Barmen concluded.

She lowered her eyes to the ground, nodding.

"Seeing Inu and Rogu's scars and their lack of resources—" She rubbed a hand across her face. "It just doesn't sit well with me."

"No," Barmen stepped closer, merely inches from her. "It shouldn't sit well, but it doesn't bother many people."

"Well, it bothers me," She narrowed her eyes.

Barmen chuckled.

"You're different from everyone else I've met," he whispered, his mouth inches away.

Her gaze focused suddenly on how soft his lips looked and she struggled to string a sentence together. "I'm not that different really. I was just born in the right family."

Barmen grinned. "You haven't once referred to Inu or Rogu as halflings."

A blush crept up her face.

"Well...they're just different," she defended, her heart

thumping loudly in her chest.

"Different than Arick?" Barmen tilted his head to the side.

"Uh," She muttered. Suddenly the air was hard to breathe. "I thought that…"

Barmen leaned in, their noses touching. She gasped, reaching for him.

"All demons are the same, right? Hmmm? What interesting tension I see between you." A hissing voice said from behind.

They jerked apart for each other, wings flared to see Leviathan perched on top of the tree they'd been standing under. He curled his body around a large branch, his head poking out.

"Why are you spying on us?" Clarissa's fire raced to her face, threatening to burst through her head.

"Oh my," Leviathan gasped. "Don't think you're important enough to be spied on, my dear." From down below she saw his wide grin. "I was here first."

"You—I—but," she sputtered, opening and closing her hands. "Did you hear everything?"

"Hmmmmm," Leviathan purred. "Why? Are you scared I'll spill your secret hidden romance?"

She crossed her arms. "It's not a romance."

"It's not a secret," Barmen murmured at the same time.

He rubbed the back of his head as she gaped at him. Sparkles ignited around her face, from her blood rushing. Her heart raced at Barmen's words.

Did he mean they had a romance then?

"Oh, young love," Leviathan cooed, uncoiling his body to stretch along a tree limb. "I remember the first shivers and fires of romance. How the butterflies fluttered in the belly. How the heart races. What an unlikely couple, you two are."

"N-never mind that!" She stuttered. She had no desire to have this conversation with him. Maybe alone with Barmen but not with anyone else. "What defenses will you give these villagers?"

"Defenses?" Leviathan hummed, lounging back on a branch. "Have any suggestions, dollface?"

Her wings faltered.

"Why not erect a wall or give them weapons to defend themselves?" She argued.

"Tsk, tsk, tsk," Leviathan shook his head. "Walls are impossible to build without damaging something crucial in this ecosystem. As for weapons…" he paused, his eyes slithering to her face. "You, an Arch, would suggest arming halflings? I thought you wanted them all dead."

She opened her mouth to protest but froze, remembering her words a few weeks ago.

"I don't want them dead." She sighed. "I believe we should arm them, so they can defend themselves against the raiders. That's all. No one deserves to live in fear."

"Hmmmm, well even if I wanted to, I can't." He clapped two hands together. "There was a written agreement between my siblings and me that we wouldn't arm the halflings."

"Why not?" Barmen stepped closer.

"Because of you, Archs." Leviathan pointed a finger down at them. "When halflings started pouring into our world, we'd thought your ancestors sent them over here with the purpose of espionage or to take over our cities. So we decreed to leave them abandoned in the corners of our realms with no weapons allowed."

"That's cruel!" She cried out.

"Why not send them back to our realm?" Barmen tilted his head.

Leviathan rubbed his eyes. "There's no simple answer to that question."

"Then, what's the point?" She glared at him. "Why keep them here? Why not change the decree?"

Leviathan narrowed his eyes at her, sending shivers down her spine. His face furrowed into sharp lines that made him downright terrifying.

"You truly know nothing of our world, dollface." He hissed. "Our agreements and deals are binding and solidified unless *all* parties agree to modify or change it. As of right now, my other siblings benefit from halflings."

"Ah," Barmen exhaled, his eyes widening. "That leaves halflings as unprotected citizens."

"In Satan's domain, they're not even considered citizens. They're simply slaves or indentured servants." Leviathan sighed. "Beelzebub uses halflings as cheap labor."

"Is that why Inu said they were lucky to be born in this domain?" She asked.

Leviathan nodded.

"My domain—" Leviathan slithered down from the tree. "—is the most open-minded. I don't say that gloatingly but as the truth. My people are free to be whoever they want, whenever they want, with *whomever* they want as long as it's consensual. The only things I won't tolerate are disrespect toward me *or* how I choose to run my domain."

He slunk along the floor before rising to his full height, with his hands on his hips and a sneer on his scaly face.

She stepped back so that Leviathan wasn't towering over her and ran into Barmen's chest. Her back lined to his front perfectly. She murmured an apology and moved to step away when his wings engulfed her. Warmth spread from the outside to her inside. Another blush crept along her neck and face. While she struggled to compose herself, Barmen wasn't fazed in the slightest.

"What is it that you want most in this world then?" Barmen asked in a soft tone.

Leviathan's face softened, and his tail unfurled. She leaned forward, interested in his answer. Did Leviathan want more power? Land? Or Influence?

"Interesting question, young Arch. I've had eons to ponder this question and yet I've found peace and chaos without having an answer." Leviathan's eyes scaled Barmen's body. "What about you? What's something you Archs want? Hmmm? More power or influence I suppose?"

Her wings jerked. *Did Leviathan read her mind?* She shook her head. *No, he didn't have that ability,* she reassured herself.

"Did you ever ask the original Archs that question?" Barmen lowered his wings and gently stepped around her. "If so, what did they want?"

"Ohhh," Leviathan put a webbed hand on his cheek. "It feels like just yesterday I met Azrael and Raziel."

He peered at Barmen.

"They were very different from you Archs today. They wanted…" he moved his hand to his chin. "I suppose in the end they wanted perfectly defined lines. They wanted order. Not all of the Archs saw the worlds in black and white but they definitely wished for a world to call their own."

"Why does this matter now?" She murmured, glancing between Barmen and Leviathan.

"Depending on who's asking. It doesn't have to. However—" He jerked his head to the jungle, eyes narrowing. "—we have new guests arriving."

Their wings flared.

"Raiders?" She called her flames to her hands and scanned the dense foliage around her. "Where?"

She whirled around, ready to fire.

"No," Leviathan crossed his arms, his eyes still on the jungle directly in front of him. "Not raiders, but not people I'd welcome either."

Tense seconds ticked by, with her heart pounding in her chest. She measured her breaths to ensure her flames stayed hot. Barmen crouched to the ground, with his wings flared. A strange haze hovered over him, making her guess it was his power.

Leviathan stuck out his hip and tapped his tail impatiently

on the ground.

"Come on now, people!" Leviathan called out. "You're not fooling anyone with your pathetic sneaking around."

A beat of silence passed them before a sharp curse signaled their arrival.

"Don't harm Clarissa! And we'll come out nice and slow." A familiar, deep voice yelled out.

Her flames sputtered out as she lowered her fist.

"Dad?" She asked with wide eyes.

A shuffling of leaves revealed her father walking out of the jungle with his hands raised. Her jaw dropped. Her father was in the demon realm. Not back at home.

"What are you doing here? Don't you know how dangerous it is? You could be killed!" She crossed her arms, narrowing her eyes at him. "Why did you—?"

"I can say the same for you, young lady!" Father yelled back, crossing his own arms.

"Dad!" She protested. "Who's watching over our people? I left on this mission because you were supervising everyone while I was gone."

"While you were gone?" Malachi scoffed. "It's my city, not yours."

"Not yet," she snorted. "It will be soon enough if you don't explain yourself this minute."

Flames erupted from his head. "You don't tell me what to do!"

"Not unless you mess up!" Flames erupted from her own head. "At least tell me Isabella's safe and in charge."

"Isabella's safe." Malachi huffed. "And I'm *your* dad and you listen to me!"

A sharp whistle resounded around them, causing them all to flinch. Leviathan lowered his two fingers from his mouth, satisfied to have their attention.

"I'm not high enough for this family drama," Leviathan hissed. "What are all of the Head Archs doing here?"

"Head Archs?" Barmen chimed in, rising to his feet. The ripple of haze around him faded.

"Yes." Leviathan snapped his fingers. "Come out, all of ya."

Curses and groans echoed out of the brush. Emerging from the foliage, Elijah, Sewall, Gabriel, and Amos came into view. Ben shuffled in last, sending shock waves through her spine.

"*You,*" she sneered. "What do—"

She paused, first seeing the blood pouring from his ears, then the rest of his face and body. *What happened to Ben?* Her anger fizzled out when his eyes met her own.

"Tsk, tsk, tsk," Leviathan clicked his tongue. "You used one of the staffs I see."

"You can heal him, can't you?" Amos stepped forward; his eyes searched Leviathan's.

"Of course I can." He waved. "But why would I?"

"Because," Ben's hoarse voice shocked her. "You don't want your sister's plan to succeed."

Leviathan tilted his head to one side.

"You're as interesting as I remember you to be." He grinned. "No wonder Beelzebub liked you. You have another plan don't you?"

"Not much of a plan." Ben rasped. "More of a goal."

"How come he can hear you and not the rest of us?" Sewall grumbled.

"He can hear those with healing abilities, that's why." Leviathan slithered forward until he was nose-to-nose with Ben. "Hold still."

Leviathan placed his hands on either side of Ben's ears. A faint glow hummed around them for a moment. For a breath, no one moved or spoke. They watched as Leviathan pulled his hands away. The bleeding stopped.

Ben winced.

"I can hear everyone's thoughts more clearly now." Ben

sighed.

Amos released something that sounded like a chuckle and scoff before yanking Ben into a large hug. "Glad you're back to normal."

"Normal is relative." Leviathan purred. "To what do I owe the pleasure of having five Head Archs coming into my region?"

Her father stepped forward. "We need everyone to come back home with us. Satan's planning a full-scale invasion of our lands and we need every Arch to join us for an emergency meeting."

"Hmph." Leviathan lifted his nose in the air. "You're so dramatic."

"It doesn't matter if you believe us—" Sewall started.

"Oh, I believe you." Leviathan raised a finger in the air. "That's definitely something my sister would do. However, it'll fail because she can't leave our realm."

"She's not planning on leaving," Malachi continued. "She plans on controlling her army along with other angels and Archangels to conquer land for her."

Leviathan raised an eyebrow. "Come again?"

"She has control of the entire Michael clan," Malachi explained. "She'll use Matthew and Mikael to take command of the Michael clan and then strike against any clan who won't bow to her."

"What a clever idea my sister has," Leviathan purred.

"You're not surprised in the least." Ben narrowed his eyes on him. "You expected this."

Leviathan grinned. "*Expected* is a strong word. I'd say I guessed this was her goal when she got a hold of her little pet Matthew decades ago."

"Where's Joshua?" Malachi redirected. "Barmen, how's your father?"

Barmen nodded. "I'll go get him."

"Hold on!" A sharp command from Leviathan. "You may

take Joshua and Barmen but Clarissa and Gabriel still owe me their favor."

"You have my son?" Gabriel Sr's wings flared, his eyes wide. "Where is he? Is he ok?"

"Their favor?" Father pinned her with a frown. "Is that because of the deal you got yourself into?"

Flames whirled in her stomach, eager for a release. "You go straight to blaming me as usual, I see."

"I'm not blaming you," Malachi defended. "I'm just trying to understand it all. You usually sort everything out quickly."

"And I am," she answered sharply. "I'll be back home in no time."

"In no time?" Leviathan hummed. "Remember when I said there was no time restriction?"

Her eyes widened. "W-w-what do you mean? I've done—"

"Everything I've asked." Leviathan hissed. "I didn't add a time stamp to your task. I can have you working for as long as I'd like."

Blood drained from her face. The world tilted on its axis for a moment. His favor consisted of helping the citizens along his border but he hadn't specified how long she was supposed to offer aid. Her stomach bottomed out.

She...was trapped here? For however long he wanted? Her throat constricted as the weight of his words hit. *What about Isabella? What about her city and people?! The children at the orphanage needed her. Her sister needed her! She couldn't stay here!*

Her wings trembled. *No, no, no, no, no, no!*

"Leviathan," she rasped. "Please!"

The demon lord narrowed his eyes. "Don't go crying, dollface. I was just starting to like you."

"What about my son?" Gabriel Sr. asked; his wings trembled. "Is he alive and well?"

"Go by the river and see for yourself." Leviathan jerked his chin down the path she'd come from earlier. "But be warned. You can't take him before he's fulfilled his favor to me."

Gabriel Sr. bolted in the direction Leviathan indicated, his eyes wide. He didn't appear to hear the demon lord's warning. The Head Arch was gone within a matter of seconds, disappearing within the thick brush. Sewall groaned while her father pinched the bridge of his nose, breathing deeply.

"Trinity give me strength," Malachi muttered before turning back to Barmen. "Bring Joshua here as fast as you can. Then we can…figure out the rest."

Leviathan smirked but said nothing else. Barmen snuck a glance at her, concern in his eyes. She gave a shaky nod. Her father was right. From the sound of it, they needed Joshua present.

Barmen launched himself into the air at her signal. His eyes never left hers until he passed over the trees' canopy, leaving her alone.

She needed to find a way back home. She refused to leave the fate of her citizens in the hands of Paul. Some of her fear receded, replaced with determination. With a sigh, she turned back, only to encounter her father's frown.

"Is there something I need to know, Clarissa?" He crossed his arms, giving a pointed glance at where Barmen flew off. "Or are you gonna disappear again?"

Blood rushed to her face at his implication.

"What does it matter?" She hugged her stomach.

Malachi raised an eyebrow. "It matters because you're the heir. You can't marry someone without a political strategy."

"Oh," Leviathan yawned, leaning back against the tree. "What a dull way to live."

Malachi shot the demon lord a glare. "What business is it of yours?"

"Malachi please!" Sewall hissed. "Stay focused on the task at hand. You can save this conversation for another time."

"I agree with Sewall," Amos chimed in.

"I second that," Elijah sighed. "Now's not the time."

Ben approached Leviathan, drawing everyone's attention. His expression remained blank, leaving her no clue as to what he was thinking.

"I need to speak with Beelzebub again." Ben's voice no longer sounded hollow but clear.

Leviathan smirked.

Amos' wings flared. "Absolutely not!"

Ben didn't flinch or break his gaze with Leviathan.

"I knew you were the fun one. Not many creatures have the balls to want to meet with my brother, let alone a second time." Leviathan's thin pupils scanned Ben's figure. "I'm curious, why do you want to see my brother again?"

"Now, Ben." Elijah extended a hand. "I don't think that's wise considering last time."

"Don't go with him if you're smart." She scoffed. "Or else you'll get roped into his mess."

"Silence!" Leviathan hissed, sending shivers down her spine. Everyone quieted. "Let him speak."

A beat passed by before Ben opened his mouth again.

"I need to offer him a chance to change his mind," Ben answered.

Another beat of silence echoed by. Then another and another. Two full minutes ticked by until, finally, Leviathan broke the tension.

The demon lord's eyes widened and his lips twitched. Some huffs of air came out of his mouth escalating in speed. She realized a moment later that Leviathan was laughing, with huge gulps of air and clutching his belly. His chuckles came out in low hiss-like sounds with the occasional crackle as if he was coughing.

Amos clenched his fist, staring daggers at his younger brother. Ben flinched once, possibly hearing whatever Amos was mentally yelling at him, while Leviathan continued to cackle.

"Ben," Elijah said imploringly. "Please don't approach Beelzebub again. He'll never agree to any deal you have in your head."

"I'm not going to make a deal," Ben answered Elijah but glanced back at Amos. "Trust me."

"Trust a Selaphiel? Ha! Never again." She snorted.

The nerve he had, asking to meet with the demon lord when she was dealing with the consequences of the first encounter! Did he have no shame?

Her father frowned at her again. He opened his mouth but was cut off by Joshua and Barmen's arrival. They landed without a sound. Barmen's piercing eyes found her with eerie accuracy. Taking one glance at her scowl and trembling wings, his own wings flared.

"What happened?" He asked, stepping closer to her.

Her father's frown deepened. Leviathan's cackling increased, causing him to double over.

"I—I can't!" Leviathan laughed, clutching his stomach. "It's too much!"

Barmen scanned her head to toe before facing everyone else. When his eyes landed on Ben's, she spoke.

"Ben wants to go see Beelzebub again." She sneered.

Barmen's wings twitched.

"By yourself?" Barmen asked Ben, raising an eyebrow.

"As Clarissa pointed out," Ben answered, indicating to her. "Anyone who joins me will be dragged into my mess."

"Hmmmm…" Barmen glanced back at his father.

Joshua moved to Leviathan's side with a furrowed brow but Elijah and Sewall wasted no time.

"Joshua!" They called out in unison.

"How are you?" Elijah asked, stepping closer to Barmen.

"What the hell took you so long?" Sewall hissed.

Joshua's steel-colored eyes narrowed at Sewall. "Receiving treatment for my…ailment takes time. The mental state of mind is nothing to rush."

Leviathan straightened from the tree.

"Tis true. Now, all of you should get out of my region before my patience wears thin, " A threatening hum vibrated from his chest, and his eyes illuminated. "I won't tolerate another disturbance."

Malachi and Elijah raised their hands.

"*None* of us," Malachi emphasized, shooting a glare at Sewall. "Mean you or your people any harm. We'll take our people and go. Come, Clari—"

"Are you deaf *Arch*?" Leviathan hissed. "She and the other boys can't go with you."

Sewall's wings twitched. Black shadows withered along his figure.

"Who are you to keep me from my son?" Sewall's voice chilled the air.

The hair on the back of her neck rose and her wings flared. Clarissa braced herself to flee if Sewall activated his powers.

Leviathan tilted his nose in the air while peering at the Arch, a small smile curved along his lips.

"Try it, Arch," Leviathan purred. "And find out what happens to those who overstep."

The air staled, and the temperature dropped. The shadows around Sewall withered and shrunk away from Leviathan. The trees and shrubbery bent toward the demon lord, curving to his will.

Barmen stepped between them, extending out his arms.

"Easy now," Barmen pleaded to Sewall. "Fighting won't resolve anything."

"But it'll feel good," Leviathan smirked.

Sewall scowled.

A rush of air brushed by them followed by a thud. Gabriel Sr. and Jr. landed on either side of Barmen. Their black wings extended wide as if to block any attacks.

"Enough of this," Gabriel Sr. narrowed his eyes at Sewall. "The others need to get back as soon as possible."

Sewall crossed his arms. "What's with the sudden change of mind? You were obsessed with finding your son an hour ago. What's changed?"

Gabriel Sr. turned to Leviathan, a somber expression filled his eyes. Amos jerked, bringing a hand to his temple, while Ben's eyes widened.

"My son showed me what you're doing for these…vermin," Gabriel Sr. said softly.

Leviathan's nostrils flared. Gabriel Jr. elbowed his father with a fierce frown and Gabriel Sr. shook his head.

"Er—I mean, children. Yes, they're children." He corrected, nodding to Sewall. "Our sons threatened to never come back if we took them now."

"My son, Zewal, wants to stay…here?" Sewall uncrossed his arms. "With these…halflings?"

Gabriel scolded while Clarissa flinched. Why did that name not sound right anymore? Halflings was too harsh a word for Inu and Rogu.

"These halflings," Leviathan scoffed. "Are tougher and kinder than any of your kind."

She flinched again.

The demon lord was right. Every halfling she'd met had been through so much torment and pain. They'd been born into a world where their survival wasn't guaranteed. She hugged her side, as some of her fire dwindled, shame taking root in its place.

They'd been hurt and hated because…they were seen as less than. *She'd* seen them as less than. She dropped her gaze to the ground as shame spread.

She'd seen firsthand how reality mixed harsh cruelty with the beauty of hope. She saw that hope in Inu's eyes. The hope that one day, the world would be a little easier to live through. Her mind flashed to when she last saw Raya, one of the orphans in Aquam Caput, left abandoned to fend for themselves. Her heart twisted.

Flynn had been one of the few angels to extend a helping hand while many others walked by without sparing a glance. She'd known their way of life in Aquam Caput wasn't perfect, but she'd only felt the burning desire to change it when the city was in shambles. When she saw their society's most vulnerable plowed or pushed out of the way, it drove her mad. The same way Inu was treated infuriated her.

She glanced at the path leading to the river that held Inu's family. What could she possibly do when society was set on treating them so poorly? Her wings slumped, and her fire shrunk to a small flame within her belly. She'd struggled against the people, her father and her uncle to get the funding for the orphans and elderly citizens. Even then, the reluctance to change had been strong. She'd been shocked seeing her own people not wanting to help one another. What did that mean for the ones like Inu or anyone else who was vastly different than them?

Knots coiled in her stomach while her heart twisted. Was she any different than her own people?

"My point is!" Amos' voice drew her back to the present conversation.

He was red in the face arguing with Sewall, Gabriel, and Elijah.

"My point is," he repeated. "We need to transport who we can back to our realm."

He pointed to Malachi.

"We need to gather as many as we can. If we have to fight against Mikael and Matthew, we're fighting an uphill battle." Amos exchanged a look with Malachi, Sewall, and Gabriel Sr.. "Your children will be fine. Looking through Leviathan's mind—"

"Rude," Leviathan snorted.

"He has no intentions of hurting anyone."

"I could be faking these thoughts," Leviathan rolled his eyes. "I've had to deal with my siblings long before you were born. A little mind reading doesn't immune you from trickery."

"You're honest," Ben rasped. "You have no interest in trickery or cruelty."

"How would you know what my real interests are?" Leviathan raised an eyebrow.

Ben pointed to the river. "You would've killed or traded them by now. But you haven't."

The two stared at each other for a long time in silence.

Leviathan scoffed. "You may actually cause a shift, you strange Arch."

"You're the strange one." Ben tilted his head. "You could have ordered a number of cruel things to call in as a favor but that's not you. Beelzebub would sell them as a way to earn profits while your sister would've used them as puppets to do her bidding."

Leviathan flared his nostrils but Ben continued.

"But that's not you." Ben coughed. "Deep down, we all know this."

Leviathan narrowed his eyes. "What's your main motivation for seeing my brother?"

"To change his mind," Ben rasped.

"Hmmmm," Leviathan tilted his head before swiveling to her. Barmen flared his wings. "I'll take you to see him."

The tension in Ben's wings eased.

"Only," Leviathan continued. "If Barmen goes with you."

They all froze.

Joshua whirled around, his voice sharp and cold. "Why him?"

Leviathan smirked. "That's for me to know and for him to find out. I know how you Raziel angels like to dig for information."

Joshua frowned.

"We can't leave our children here," Malachi pleaded to Gabriel Sr..

"We aren't children," Gabriel Jr. chimed in. "Also, Ben's

right. For as…eccentric as Leviathan is—"

"I'm not that eccentric." Leviathan defended, rolling his eyes again.

"He's not holding us here as hostages." Gabriel Jr. pivoted to Leviathan, who shrugged.

"I mean I kinda am holding you hostage," Leviathan mused with a grin.

Gabriel Jr. chuckled.

"But," Gabriel Jr. replied. "You're not going to keep us forever, right?"

"Why do you little archs keep thinking that?" Leviathan huffed. "I could have this favor dragged out for years on end."

Shadow tendrils slithered around them, ruffling the leaves. A cold breeze blew by them, sending shivers down her spine. Soft footsteps drew everyone's attention as Zewal entered the clearing.

"Leviathan," Zewal's cold voice cut through the air. His black eyes glimmered with an emotion she couldn't name. "Do you plan on keeping us here for the years to come?"

Sewall froze while Leviathan smirked.

"When did you…"Amos' eyes glazed over as thoughts, no doubt, poured into his mind.

However, Zewal watched Leviathan.

"You brought us here to show us them," he indicated to the river, where a few siren heads popped up. Dark eyes watched them with curiosity. "Your true goal was—"

"Ugh! Enough with the mussiness. My real goal was for the next generation to take responsibility for the halflings so that they stop dumping them on my front door." Leviathan hugged himself and shuddered. "Stop looking for some kind-hearted intention, it makes me squeamish."

A small frown inched its way onto her face. Though Inu and the others had captured her heart, she didn't expect to stay in the demon realm. She hadn't forgotten her responsibilities and passion for her people. Gabriel and Zewal must've felt the same. They'd been as eager as her to leave at the next given opportunity until a day or so ago.

"Yes," Leviathan sighed dramatically, sticking his nose to the sky. "You, along with Clarissa and Gabriel, will be released soon but not yet." He rolled his eyes at Malachi and Joshua. "But you and the other Head Archs should go."

"How long is not yet?" Amos murmured, shooting a pleading glance at Ben.

Gabriel Sr. clenched his fists as he stared at his son. Gabriel Jr. crossed his arms, jutting his chin out. Clarissa mimicked his stance, giving a determined look to her father.

"That'll be determined by them," Leviathan nodded to Barmen and Ben.

"The sirens by the river. I overheard them talking about Satan and her plans for overtaking our realm." Zewal narrowed his eyes. "Is this true? Are you going to keep us here while our people suffer at her hands?"

They all waited. Leviathan's eyes darkened.

"Your citizens will lie in a warm bed tonight and tomorrow night. None of you have learned nor fully understood your role in this world," he hissed as he indicated to the river. "Especially regarding the halflings."

"Things are changing," Elijah raised a hand, drawing their attention. "We came from Satan's domain, and we wouldn't have made it out if it weren't for halflings. I've offered them a safe haven in our world."

Zewal's face softened but it was Gabriel Jr. who spoke.

"Dad," Gabriel Jr. said. "What about our home—"

"Our people aren't made for that," Gabriel Sr. snapped. "Neither is *my* son."

Disgust coated each word. Gabriel Jr. frowned but didn't budge. The father and son held a silent standoff while she pivoted.

"Father?" She turned to Malachi. "What about our home?"

Malachi grimaced, shaking his head. "I have to agree with

Gabriel on this. Our place isn't ready for halflings. Not even you."

She flinched. If their citizens could just see the others maybe they could learn to accept them.

"It doesn't work that way," Amos spoke aloud, his eyes on her.

Her wings slumped. There had to be a way.

"There is a way." Ben chimed in. "It starts with us. With me talking to Beelzebub and you all returning to our realm to defend our people."

"That's something I can agree with," Elijah grabbed Malachi's arm. "We have Joshua. We do need to return home and prepare our citizens."

Malachi nodded, a quick and solemn jerk of his head. "You will handle yourself?"

"I can take care of myself." She sighed, releasing her arms.

"Good," Her father grumbled. "You're living not just for yourself but for your people. Never forget that."

How could she? She thought to herself. She'd known since birth she'd been born for the benefit of others. Appearing satisfied, her father turned on his heels. Speaking of which…

"Where's Isabella?" Her heartbeat quickened. If something happened to Isabella, bargain be damned.

"She's fine," Malachi answered "I left her with Fatima and Tariel before coming to the demon realm."

She let out a sigh. Good, that was one less thing on her conscience.

"Get together," Malachi commanded, waving a hand to the other Archs. "Joshua, Amos, Sewall, Elijah and Gabriel. It's time to head back."

Only Elijah appeared eager to leave. Sewall and Gabriel glared at their sons while Amos placed his forehead to Ben's in a quiet goodbye.

"How's Tariel and Mom?" Zewal shot out, ignoring the glower his father sent his way.

Sewall paused, his wings lowered. "I told them to meet with the other Arch females, to gather as many people as they can."

"Good," Zewal didn't smile but lessened his frown. "When Mom wants to do something, it'll get done."

"Don't die or else she'll drag you back to life," Sewall called over his shoulder as he walked away.

She let out a chuckle until she realized Sewall was serious. Zewal would indeed get dragged back to life. A shudder ran through her at the implications.

Sewall stepped behind Gabriel. "Come, we can't waste any more time."

Gabriel Sr. didn't break the glare he shot at his son. "When you get home, we'll talk more in-depth about this nonsense."

"Yes." Gabriel Jr. sighed. "We will."

Clarissa paused. Did Gabriel Jr. seem taller or something? She'd never seen him so…sure of himself until now. She shook her head. It was probably her imagination. There was too much going on around her.

Elijah, Amos, Gabriel Sr., and Sewall walked down the path to the river and vanished from sight. Joshua pointed a finger at Barmen.

"No funny business," Joshua said to Barmen.

"No funny business," Barmen echoed, giving the smallest of nods.

With that, Joshua walked through the trail. The brush was so thick that the leaves engulfed his figure within seconds. Her father was last. He spared her one glance, concern painted deeply in her fiery eyes. She understood. He needed her to ensure the line of succession, and to have a strong leader for their people.

Malachi marched down the trail, with his brow furrowed and his wings twitching. Their footsteps were drowned out by the sounds of the forest. Soon, she was left alone with Barmen, Ben, Zewal, Gabriel Jr.…and Leviathan. A few beats of silence passed before anyone moved. Leviathan stared down the path the others walked down as if waiting. Some sort of silent signal must have happened, she guessed, for Leviathan turned his attention back to them.

The demon lord slinked closer to Ben.

"Now that the rest are gone." Leviathan purred, "It's time for you two to take your leave."

He pointed two fingers at Ben and Barmen. The latter ignored the demon lord, walking past him as if he didn't exist.

"Clarissa," Barmen spoke in a soft tone. "How are you doing?"

Her wings twitched as blood and her fire rushed to her face. "I'm fine enough."

Barmen frowned.

"Let me clarify," Barmen stepped closer. "How are *you* doing? Not Clarissa the heir. Not Clarissa the older sister or caretaker. How are *you*?"

Her heart raced in her chest. No one had asked her in that manner. She'd never considered such thoughts. She'd just assessed herself on two things: If she could keep going or not. Did she even know how she felt?

"I think," she paused, noticing the others' gaze for the first time. More blood pooled in her cheeks. Her flames flared out of her head as she stuttered. "I—I—I…j-j-j-just need a—a moment."

She put her hands to her face, taking in deep breaths. Her heart hammered so loud that she wondered if everyone could hear it.

Pull yourself together, she thought, shaking her head. *He just asked you a simple question.*

"Hmmm," Leviathan purred. "While the two love birds say their goodbyes—"

"We're not lovebirds!" Her voice rose an octave. "We're just friends."

"Friends?" Barmen tilted his head, his lips twitching.

Her heart sputtered.

"Well…no but…" More heat built inside her face, fanning the flames in her blood. "It's just that—"

Gabriel Jr. patted Barmen on the back.

"I get it." His blue eyes softened. "The girl I love doesn't love me back either."

Barmen's twitching lip turned into a grin, changing his face. She gasped. *Barmen looked very handsome when he smiled,* she thought, watching his gray eyes light up with amusement.

"Tsk," Zewal scoffed, ruining the moment. "Simpering fools."

"Now, now, Zewal. Don't give up on love yet." He slithered around Zewal. "After all there's still a chance for you and me."

"Maybe when I'm dead." Zewal drawled, stepping out of reach.

"Don't guard your heart too closely or no one will get in." Leviathan coiled himself. "Besides, I wanted you all to accompany Ben and Barmen on their journey."

Zewal put a hand to his chin, his black eyes flickering back and forth. "Is this a trick?"

"No trick," Leviathan hummed.

"Why all of us?" Gabriel chimed in.

Her blood and flames cooled enough for her to follow their conversation.

"Didn't you say we still had to stay here?" she asked Leviathan.

This demon lord was all over the place. Wanting them to stay then kicking them away. What was his deal?

Leviathan grinned.

"Ben's onto something," Leviathan peered down at Ben. "If my sister's making her move now with the Michael angels, then you'd serve my people better by going to see Beelzebub."

"How would we?" Clarissa furrowed her brow.

Beelzebub was his brother. Leviathan was far more powerful and influential than they were. What could they say that would help the halflings and preserve their own sanity? A shiver ran down her spine at the thought of seeing Beelzebub again. That demon lord would try to find a way to manipulate them again.

"Hmph." Leviathan swirled his fingers in the air. Rushing wind gathered along his fingertips along with sparkles. "Try not to strike any more bargains, Archs. It'll be annoying to deal with."

At the snap of his finger, the bedazzled staff appeared in his hands. The wind picked up speed, lifting them off the ground. The wind roared around them, like a typhoon. Clarissa flared her wings wide to maneuver but to no avail. She was used to Isabella's wind but Leviathan's slammed into her like a crashing wave. The trees and leaves shook as a bright light shined from the staff.

The air in her lungs lodged itself in her throat. The pressure built around them, pushing them further and further away from the ground. She met resistance as she strained to tuck her wings. Her muscles locked into a flight position she couldn't get out of. As if the wind was knocked out of her, her lungs burned and didn't move.

She shot a glare at Leviathan but saw nothing but bright, warm light.

"Safe traveling, Archs." Somehow, Leviathan's voice reached them from the ground. "I hope we see each other under better circumstances."

Zewal snapped back some remarks that she couldn't hear while Gabriel flailed around. She tried to right herself in the air, straining for control. Until a firm tug on her shoulder caused her to hit something solid on her back. She peered over her shoulder to see Barmen wrapping his arms around her waist.

"Tuck your wings in!" He shouted in her ear.

His wings knocked into hers, pulling hers in enough for her to tuck in. Once she curled them in tight, Barmen flared his wings wider, carrying them higher. The wind gust carried them like a rip current, forceful and fast.

"Hold on!"

She barely heard Barmen's shout above the wind as they careened through the sky. Dozens of trees flashed below them in a blur. The terrain shifted as the color of the ground changed from dark green to light green.

Her neck muscles bulged as she tried to keep her head steady against the wind force. She clenched her teeth to help against the pressure. She clung to Barmen, not knowing when this whirlwind would stop. After a while, they stopped flaying for control, accepting the current and their position.

The hot air circulating around them dropped to a cooler temperature. The humidity shifted, no longer clinging to their skin. Barmen's arms tightened as the current changed direction. A downward trajectory. The muscles in her wings flexed instinctually to catch her but the pressure was too great. Her wings couldn't open, as if a boulder descended upon their backs, careening them toward the ground.

"Brace yourself!" Barmen shouted in her ear.

She curled into his chest, preparing for the impact, the pain. The sound of shattering glass echoed and she closed her eyes.

Then everything stopped, the rushing wind and the immense pressure. She heard two thick thuds and flinched. Her wings twitched with the urge to cover herself.

Wait...they moved, she thought. She extended one wing and then the other to test. Both followed her command.

She peeled open one eye to see white tile on the ground. She jerked her head up.

Beelzebub sat at his large desk, pen in hand, a few feet away. Hot air brushed against her skin. She turned to see Barmen panting, wings flapping. He hovered them a foot off the ground, which would explain the lack of impact. His arms cradled her with no signs of loosening as his icy eyes glued onto Beelzebub's frame like the demon lord would pounce at any moment.

A groan to her left drew her attention. Gabriel, Ben, and Zewal stiffly sat up, their wings flared wide. Gabriel rubbed a hand through his hair while Zewal cracked his neck.

"It's been a long time since I've had whiplash," Zewal murmured.

"Ughh," Gabriel groaned again.

A loud sigh caused them to jump. She swiveled back to Beelzebub, eyes wide.

Steam blew from nostrils like missiles. He peered at them with glowing red eyes, his mountain of a frame dwarfing the size of his desk. His gloved hands continued to scribble on a piece of paper on it. Bulging muscles were barely contained within the button-down shirt he wore. The aura around him grew dark and angry, rolling off of him in waves. His stern face appeared composed, but she wasn't fooled for a second.

Beelzebub faced them, and Barmen's arms tightened. He lowered them to the ground, his wings curling around her protectively.

She didn't need protection.

The fire in her belly crackled and boiled, eager for release. She inhaled deeply, fueling her flames. Her body temperature increased. Barmen must have noticed because he released her. When her feet hit the ground, she didn't hold back. Flames sprouted from her hands and wings, ready to defend herself.

"I see my brother still doesn't respect my space," Beelzebub grumbled. "As usual."

Ben approached first, moving a few feet in front of her and Barmen.

"He sends his regards." Ben rubbed the back of his neck. "He's…strange, your brother."

Beelzebub scoffed. He wrote a large, aggressive signature

at the bottom of the paper, turning it over before she could see. Setting the pen down, he rose from his desk. Her head tilted back as she looked upon the giant demon lord.

His hoofed feet clicked as he walked toward them, causing her heart to pound with each step. Her fire coiled up her arms, as sweat beaded along her brow.

They were here to talk; they were here to talk, she reminded herself.

"Get out of my office," Beelzebub growled.

Shivers ran down her spine at the depth of his voice. His eyes glowered at them so fiercely that her flames sprouted all over her body. This wasn't like the last time. Now she called upon her flames, eager to defend herself.

Ben didn't flinch but his wings twitched once.

"I've come here to talk one last time," Ben answered in a hushed tone. "About your family."

Beelzebub tilted his head to the side. His large horns seesawed to one side as he blew more steam from his nostrils.

"What makes you think I have any further use for you? I may have use of him," Beelzebub scowled, jutting his chin to Barmen. "Besides, I only talk business, not family."

Her flames grew in size and temperature at the mention of Barmen.

"You're not taking him," her voice sounded harsh, guttural.

Beelzebub's red eyes flickered.

"Hmph." Beelzebub crossed his arms, busing his muscles more. "I see your illusions are still strong. Who are you hiding, Barmen?"

"No one you need to know," Barmen answered smoothly.

His hands tucked comfortably in the pockets of his tunic. If she didn't know Barmen, she would've guessed he was relaxed. However, the smallest flex of his jaw told her a different story.

"Humor us," Barmen continued, stepping closer to Ben.

"With one conversation"

No, she realized. *He's trying to draw Beelzebub's attention away from her and to Ben.*

Beelzebub's eyes scanned each of them slowly, from Gabriel's trembling form to Zewal's stoic gaze to, lastly, Ben's determined stance.

The demon lord frowned. "Release the illusion and I'll agree to a one-minute conversation. My time's money, and you're spending more than you can afford."

"Actually." Barmen moved another step. "Thanks to the trade agreement you and I arranged, we can afford five minutes of your time."

Beelzebub's lips twitched.

"I'll address the bill to you then," Beelzebub turned on his hooves, stomping back to his desk. "Sit!"

They scrambled to the sitting area set up behind them. The glass window they'd been blasted through stood before them. A few glass shards scattered over some of the furniture. Either Beelzebub didn't notice or care about the damage done to his window. He plopped behind his desk again and folded his hands together, leaning forward.

"Now, let's talk."

Chapter 12

Water, Azazel thought, *I need water.*

The sun blazed on him without mercy. With each passing minute, the heat intensified as if focused on draining every last bit of liquid from his body. He smacked his lips, peeling his dry tongue from the roof of his mouth. Nothing helped.

Worse, the march before them was endless. On and on and on, they trudged through the desert without an end in sight. Only stopping at night. Adding insult to injury, a few wounds from Matthew's beating healed incorrectly. Every breath he drew in caused aching pain. His ribs creaked with effort and felt jagged along his sides. Some of the bones healed at odd angles. For two days, this endless suffering continued. Azazel hadn't switched with Arick. This was the longest run of time he'd possessed control over their shared body…and it was awful.

But it could be worse, he reminded himself. At night, Satan ordered a few select elders to pitch a tent for her, while during the day, she was carried in a canopy. He considered himself lucky to not have to carry her hefty carrier around. He struggled enough on his own two feet.

Arick's endless chatter distracted him from this marching torment. However, on this third day, Arick ran out of things to talk about.

"*I'm surprised kid,*" Azazel drawled in their shared mind. "*You ran out of words for your mouth to say. I'd thought this day would never come."*

"There's only so many embarrassing stories I can remember." Arick mused for a moment. *"I could get started on some of Atarah's embarrassing moments, if you're that desperate. Like the time she started her period when the guys from training camp came over—"*

"Ay, ay," Azazel interrupted. *"I'm not that desperate. I don't think I'll ever be."*

Arick chuckled.

"At least you weren't there. Mom and Dad weren't around at the time. So we had to grab her stuff." Arick laughed again. *"None of us knew what to look for, so we ended up buying her the entire aisle of women's products to pick from."*

"Poor girl," Azazel huffed. *"I only had a son, so I never had to worry about that."*

Arick's consciousness shifted up as if perking his ears.

"That's right," Arick called out, *"Was that your son in the illusion Satan showed you earlier? I didn't know you had a son."*

"Yeah, that was him." Azazel sighed. *"I never thought I'd talk about him with you either but here we are."*

"Is this another thing about your past you don't want to reveal?"

"No," he paused. *"It's just difficult to talk about...what happened to me and my family."*

A beat of silence passed by. Arick waited. He didn't prod or push, simply waited for when he was ready to speak.

Azazel groaned as he waddled through the thick sand, debating about how much to tell the kid. He might as well start from the beginning.

"My son was the smartest, kindest and goofiest kid I knew."

"Was?"

"Yeah, kid. Was." Azazel flinched as a sharp pain pierced his heart, as it did every time he thought about Jamal. *"You*

would've loved Jamal. Everyone did."

"What happened to him?"

Another slash through his chest.

"He was killed because his mother was human and I... well, I'm obviously not."

"Ah..." Arick sighed. *"They taught us that the watchers didn't obey orders and went into the human realm with rebellion in their hearts. Is that true?"*

Azazel scoffed. *"Oh? You doubt your own history books?"*

"I'm starting to...question things because..." Arick drifted off.

"Because everything written about halflings is skewed too?" Azazel finished for him.

Arick grunted in agreement. *"Everything I thought was true—isn't. It's like I've built an entire tower of beliefs, only to find out the bricks I've been using were wooden sticks instead of stone. A foundation of lies."*

"More like a foundation of misconstrued truths," Azazel replied. *"At least there was a hint of truth in the stories they told about watchers. Most of it was bogus, but there's a tiny element of truth."*

"What's the truth then?"

"First off, none of us wanted to go to the human realm in the first place. How can we have a rebellion to take over a place we dreaded? The squad I overlooked was ordered to go to the human realm, but not because we had rebellion in our hearts."

"Why did you dread the human realm?"

"Back then, there were no rangers or encampments for us to station in." He explained. *"We regarded the human realm as dirty, beneath us, and...well the entire assignment was an embarrassment. As soldiers of high status, it was mortifying to be given the task of an animal sitter. Which is what we considered the humans back then: nothing more than delusional animals."*

Azazel grimaced as he thought back to his earlier years. He'd been prideful and arrogant in his youth. His troops were no better, only worse.

"We were stationed in a highly fought-over area for the humans. We were to report back any demon activity and ensure the animal population didn't dwindle too far," Azazel continued. *"If the population decreased too much, it'd create an imbalance between the energy that transfers between realms, thus causing chaos. A simple enough assignment but we were too prideful to see its importance."*

Arick waited in silence, listening without judgment.

"Little did we know that humans were trying to wipe out all living things, including themselves." He scoffed, remembering the early days. *"We stationed ourselves in an area where there were constant wars causing famines and drastic changes in their food supply. I never understood why humans fought against one another but I suppose they'd think the same of us if the roles were reversed."*

The pain in his legs eased as the story poured out of him. A calmness smoothed the tension in his back and shoulders as he talked with Arick.

"For weeks we camped out, watching humans from afar. We—I—really was bewildered by their tendency for violence and bloodlust. I made the decision to camp further away from the humans' larger settlements because as the battles went on, they grew closer and closer to us. To avoid this, I moved my troops."

"Hmmm, that's different than you showing yourselves to humans."

"...We did eventually meet with the humans. Merely a week or two after I'd moved my troops, my lieutenant Arakiel acted without my command. One of the human's warring parties attacked one of the largest villages and slaughtered many of the men, women, and children. A pile of dead bodies stacked taller than the walls of the city. Since one of our or-

ders was monitoring the human population, Arakiel dispelled the warring party and rescued every person he could find."

"Uh-oh."

"Yeah, exactly," Azazel sighed. *"By the time Arakiel came back to camp to report, it'd been too late. Many humans on both sides saw him and some of my other troops joined him. To make matters worse, many women and children clung to their sides, desperate to stay safe."*

"Hmmm, that's different." Arick drawled.

"I have no doubt you were told we'd forced women into our camp as a source for our own enjoyment."

"Was that true?"

"Not in the slightest," Azazel confessed. *"We didn't force them to our camp. Many came of their own volition, seeking protection for their families and children to escape the war. Weeks turned into months, months turned into years and we protected and watched over them, earning us the name Watchers. Families thrived and enjoyed our small makeshift village, which soon grew into a bustling city center. For a decade or so, life was good. While a few of my troops looked down on humans, many others' viewpoints on humans changed after living with them. Several even took wives and built homes for them."*

A soft warmth filled his chest as he remembered Abigail.

"I met a strong, beautiful woman named Abigail. She wanted me to teach her and some of the other girls how to fight so they could defend themselves. For weeks, she pestered me, trying to bribe me into teaching her about weapons.

"Finally, I caved and taught a class that turned into two, then three, and many more. I taught the women about physical and spiritual weapons, how to wield them, and how to fight against men and demons alike. I taught them everything I knew. Abigail and I had grown to love each other and I asked her to marry me and build a life together. I'd thought surely the higher-ups would understand and look past prejudice."

He winced. *"Which is why my punishment was so severe. I shared 'classified' information with an unfit group. Another crime was having my son. On top of the crime of showing ourselves to humans and quote-unquote disobeying orders."*

A familiar bitter taste filled his mouth as resentment bloomed. The council of Head Archs had taken everything from him and his troops, damning them without hearing their side of the story. The trial had been black and white. They'd disobeyed orders and were deemed guilty, nothing else. The Archs hadn't cared about learning from the humans or trying to integrate a life with them. Only that once esteemed, highly trained soldiers lowered themselves to the same level as humans.

"They killed my son and every child my watchers had with their human wives. Soon after that, they killed every human in the city simply for knowing us, burning the city we'd built to nothing but ash."

"Who is 'they'?" Arick's voice was barely above a whisper.

Azazel glowered, hatred and pain mixed together in his heart as he answered. *"The Head Archs' heirs. The sons and daughters of the original Archs had determined that status quo and tradition were more important than anything else."*

"What about protecting lives? To ensure the balance of the realm was maintained?" Alarm rang in Arick's voice.

"Those orders were from the original Archs," Azazel grunted. *"While my troops and I were away, the new Head Archs had ascended. The few troops who'd held onto their prejudice throughout the years went to the newly ascended Head Archs to demand they put a stop to our integrated city. It was agreed upon unanimously by the Council of Heads and for their first diplomatic act, we'd been given a choice. Abandon everyone we'd come to love and face punishment or watch as they burned us all."* Azazel grimaced. *"We fought till the last of every bit of our strength. Those of us left alive were*

bound, gagged, and brought before a seraphim to be cursed to wander the realms and land, never again settle or build a life. Only to ever sit back…and watch. Another reason we'd been dubbed the Watchers. Once a title we'd bore with pride and now a title reminding me how I failed my family, my troops, and my people. A title that's forever seared into my soul with shame and regret."

Silence echoed in their mind, like a gaping hole, swallowing them as memories of Abigail and Jamal swam through Azazel's mind. He'd pushed away every memory, emotion, and feeling behind a mental wall as a means of self-preservation while in Arick's body. In watcher form, he had no choice but to suffer. Surrounded with no outlet but his mind, he'd drowned with no way to die or escape. Constant anguish, his punishment for loving someone different than himself.

He flexed his jaw. The familiar weight of grief pressed against his heart. Despite the brisk hike through the hot desert, a chill ran down his spine. A reminder of the suffering that would await him if Arick died.

No, Arick said in unison with him.

"I won't let that happen to you. I may be young and inexperienced but whoever condemns a person for loving someone different than them, doesn't understand love at all." Arick's voice shifted, growing gruff. *"I don't believe you committed any crime, old man."*

"I'm not innocent, kid. I'm technically guilty but…I don't think it should've been a crime in the first place." He scoffed.

"When I'm—" Arick paused. *"If I'm ever the Head Arch, I'll change that."*

Azazel grinned. *"We could use more leaders like you, kid."*

"We gotta make it out of here alive." Arick mused. *"Think we can take the manipulative broad out?"*

A horn blared from the front. He peered ahead to see the carriage holding Satan lowering to the ground. Another barked command from one of the guards rippled down the assembly. They were camping for the night, he realized, startled.

A flurry of movement from guards in front caught his eye. Poles, lines and tents were erected within a few minutes. Shouts of commands sounded off around him as the elders got ready for the night.

"What's going on?" Arick asked, his voice sounding further away.

Azazel hadn't noticed he'd pushed Arick further back instinctively.

"We're camping for the night." He relaxed his mental barrier.

"The sun doesn't set for a few more hours though."

Azazel lowered his head as guards approached. He needed to look as dazed at Mikael and Matthew or else they'd know something was up. Matthew, who had marched in front of him, pivoted to jerk his chains forward.

What was going on? Azazel wondered.

Matthew grabbed Mikael's chain as well and yanked them ahead. Azazel shuffled along, getting shoved anytime he veered off whatever invisible path Matthew pushed him along. He noticed quickly that Matthew was leading them to the tent near the front of the marching line.

Oh no.

Alarm bells rang off in his head, alerting Arick.

"Think it's time to bust out of those chains?" Arick whispered.

"Remember, kid, you don't need to whisper in our mind. No one can hear you except me."

"Oh right." Arick mumbled, *"Still it may be time to escape."*

"Kid, we're in the middle of the desert." He drawled. *"We'll make our escape with your dad once we're at the portal."*

Arick sounded nervous. *"But what if she tries to mess with our mind again?"*

"You gotta pull me out, kid. Every time the fog rolls in, you clear it, ok?"

Arick murmured a reluctant agreement as he approached the largest tent. Two guards flanked them on either side. There was no escaping another encounter with Satan. He ground his teeth together, keeping his gaze down as he was marched through the tent's entrance folds.

Long, flown currents draped across the back. Off to the right, another draped opening stood. Possibly an exit? He wondered. Satan herself lounged on a large throne of pillows in the center. She held a small rabbit-like demon on her lap, stroking it absentmindedly. She wore a light blue dress that hugged her curves. A slit along each side hiked the fabric high on her thighs. Her pale skin glistened without a single blemish, scar, or wrinkle. The dress possessed a deep v-cut neckline, covering the bare minimum of her chest. She stared out a small window opening, not paying them a single glance. The sun hadn't touched the horizon, yet a ray of light danced across her face. A halo-kind of effect glowed around her head. She was stunning.

"Kneel." A harsh command from behind.

A swift kick to the back of his knee sent him crumbling. He bit back a groan as he wormed his way to a kneeling position. Another thud told him that Matthew kicked Mikael down too. Once they were both kneeling, Satan faced them. He didn't have the slightest clue what was going through her mind.

Would she order them to kill each other? Or tell them to sing or dance? What could she possibly want?

Her green eyes scanned them. Maybe assessing them? Her brow furrowed as she waved her hand at them.

"Come out of your illusions." She commanded, her high-pitched voice sounded light and soft.

Mikael startled, gasping for air. Azazel quickly mimicked him, praying she didn't notice his hesitation. Mikael blinked, his brow furrowed in confusion. The Head Arch's eyes landed on his, for a breath, and released a sigh. Azazel gave the smallest of nods, hoping he'd get his silent message.

Arick's safe.

"You two," Satan called their attention forward. Azazel kept his head bowed, avoiding her direct gaze. "Do you know why I need you?"

A beat of silence. Azazel didn't dare speak and risked drawing more attention. Instead, he lowered his head, peeking at Mikael from the corner of his eye. Mikael glared at her.

"I don't suppose you had a change of heart and decided to let us go," Mikael's voice dripped with sarcasm.

A sharp thud followed. Azazel peeked again. Matthew stood over Mikael, some blood on his knuckles. Mikael groaned as he lifted his face from the sand. Blood poured from his nose, but it didn't look broken.

Satan shifted her eyes from Mikael to his, as if this type of violence was normal.

"And you?" She sighed. "Do you have any idea why I need you?"

"You don't need us," Azazel said, keeping his gaze down. "You just need our bodies."

"Hmmm…One is smart while the other one has a smart mouth," she paused, "You said Mikael is the current Head Arch and this is his son, yes?"

Matthew stepped forward and knelt. "Yes…but, Arick is my son, my lady."

"Sure, sure," Satan huffed, waving a hand in the air. "But he's the next in line for the succession?"

"Correct, my lady."

"Perfect," She sighed. "There's only two more I want, Matthew. Gabriel and Barmen. Grab those two and bring them to me."

"Not Joshua, my lady?"

"No," she sneered. "Not that one. He's used up. Grab the

next in line."

She paused.

"*Can* you do that? The last few times I've sent you to grab him or Gabriel, you come back with strays or beaten to a pulp." Her voice tightened. "Should I send Mikael instead?"

Matthew's jaw flexed. "No, my lady. I can deliver them to you."

"Good," her voice lightened. A single clap echoed around them. "The guards can leave and you two…hmmmm. How can you entertain me tonight?"

A chill ran down his spine. A cold sweat broke out along his head. This couldn't be good.

"Mikael," she snickered, glancing at his bowed form. "Let's dig through your mind."

"Ah!" Mikael shouted, reaching for his head. His face scrunched in pain.

"Hmmmm," Satan smirked at him. "Let's play the game of favorites since I have everyone here." She snapped her fingers at Mikael. "Tell Arick how you really feel about him."

Mikael's eyes widened for a brief second before a glazed over shadow fell across his face.

"He's disgusting," Mikael answered, with little emotion. "I've always hated and resented him from the day he was born."

A sharp pain pierced their chest, as Mikael's words hit the intended target.

"That…that's not true…right?" Arick's voice whispered in the back of their mind.

"No, kid," Azazel urged. *"She's just messing with his mind. He loves you."*

"It's true," Mikael faced them, his eyes narrowing while his lips curled into a sneer. "You know deep down it's true, Arick."

Azazel flinched. Satan's smile widened.

"I'd rather be by my *own* child's side than sit here next

to you." Mikael continued. "Why do you think everyone at home likes Atarah better than you? Because *she's* my heir. Not you. Never a disgusting bastard of a half-breed, like you."

A dark turmoil boiled within their stomach. Inside their mind, thunderclouds formed. Azazel's wings trembled as Arick's emotion rolled through their body.

"Arick! Nothing he's saying is true! You're the heir to the Michael clan." Azazel reassured.

"Because I'm Matthew's bastard?" Arick's consciousness darkened.

"What else?" Satan giggled. Her shrill voice grated on his nerves.

"He's always been a disrespectful—"

"Make him stop." Arick rasped.

"Ungrateful—"

"No."

"Inconsiderate—"

"Please!"

"Worthless burden I never wanted!" Mikael sneered.

Something hooked onto Azazel's heart and yanked viciously. Knots grew in his stomach, threatening to empty its contents. The tremors migrated from his wings to his body as he saw the fierceness in Mikael's eyes.

"You'll never be one of us," Mikael finished, spitting at him.

In the back of his mind, something withered. Like watching a small flame, barely holding onto life, disappearing into the darkness. Arick's mind whirled with shadows and memories of his childhood, becoming shrouded in doubt.

"It...can't be true, can it?" Arick's pained whisper barely came through.

"Snap out of it kid! I need you to focus so she doesn't control us!" He urged. *"I know it hurts but don't let her distract you!"*

A beat of silence stretched across their mind before Arick

grunted in agreement.

"I'm here."

"Good kid."

"Hahaha," Satan cackled again, clapping her hands together. "That was fun! Now, how about I show you both something horrific, yes?"

The sweetness in her voice sent knots through his stomach. Arick will pull him out of whatever nightmare she showed him but Mikael…

"Your brothers spoke about you," Azazel said with a shaky voice.

He peeked to see her eyes narrowing on him.

"Oh?" She raised one eyebrow and crossed her legs. "Go on? What did they say?"

For once he was grateful for his years as a watcher. He'd learned quite a bit about the demon lords from a distance. Now, he needed to play the cards right if he was to spare Mikael and Arick some torture.

"They said you were the favorite of their parents," Azazel spoke in a low tone. "That you were spoiled rotten when little and that you always got whatever you wanted."

Her nostrils flared and her eyes narrowed into slits. The corners of her face sharpened, revealing a small glance of her true form. Though she appeared picturesque of beauty for a human, he knew it was nowhere near the truth. Her brothers were the bull and the serpent while she was…

"They also…" he hesitated, worried if this would take it too far.

"Yes?" Her face screwed, distorting like rippling water.

Her brothers were indeed her weak spot then, he mused.

"They made fun of your ears," he whispered.

A humming sensation ricocheted around the room, buzzing around until fanning out of the tent. Goosebumps raised along his arms, and his heart pounded inside his chest. If he angered her too much, they'd all suffer.

"Do you want to switch?" Arick murmured darkly. Something didn't feel right with Arick's emotional state. *"You can feed me whatever you want to say."*

"No." Scared as he was, he didn't want to risk Arick having control. He sensed Arick's fragility, remembering the kid's loss of control when Matthew killed his sister. *"Stay back and be ready to pull me out in case she goes crazy."*

A fire burned in her green eyes as they glowed brightly with narrow-slit pupils. Her cheekbones lengthened and stretched down her face. Slowly, like water settling down, some of her real face revealed itself. Her ears popped forward and her lips curled in a quiet snarl.

A beat of silence.

"She's a fox?" Arick questioned in their mind.*"Why is she masquerading as something more like us? Or a human?"*

That was the demon lord trio. The serpent, the bull, and the fox. Each represented their region and their power with what they were. Satan's true form resembled the desert fox. Cunning, quick-minded, and deceitful.

"Dammit, just the thought of them makes me lose my composure." She grimaced, lifting a hand to her tall, pointed ears. "I'll make them pay for that."

The coldness in her voice sent shivers down his spine.

"I thought they were mad," Azazel interjected. "I told them, there's no way someone as beautiful as you deserved such harsh words."

Her eyes narrowed on him, scanning him. She waved a hand across her face. Her ears disappeared and her cheeks rounded, setting the illusion back into place. A tingling sensation moved its way through his scalp. Fog entered his mind from the sides.

She twirled her hand in front of him again.

"Tell me everything my brother's told you," she said, her voice dropping an octave. "Matthew forgot to mention, you'd met with them. Was it both of them or just one?"

Azazel opened his mouth to speak but stopped as an invisible hand clamped around his throat. He choked, hunching over. The air in his lungs froze. He tried to breathe but his lungs refused to work. A mixture of fog and panic crept in as his lungs burned and begged for oxygen. Was she trying to kill him?

"Azazel," A faint voice called out.

Who was that?

His hands twitched and clawed at the invisible hand around his throat, struggling to break free.

"Azazel!"

There's that voice again. This time it was louder.

The fog lessened and the grip around his neck loosened.

"Azazel! It's me, Arick! Snap out of it!" Arick yelled out again.

Azazel gasped. The sweet, cool relief of air rushing through his lungs caused him to collapse into the sand. He coughed and gasped, struggling to calm his ragged breathing.

"Did she attack?" Azazel groaned to Arick, sand stinging his eyes.

"No, It was just an illusion. You just stopped talking and started choking. The same fog from before rolled just like you said."

"Next time, pull me out faster kid." He groaned.

"That was so fast, I didn't notice until you went down."

He sat back on his heels and peeked at her. Satan rested her chin against her hand, glaring at him. Her jaw flexed and the rabbit on her lap squealed. She'd wrapped her hand around its neck and squeezed. The small creature flailed in her grasp, trying and failing to get away. She gave a quick jerk of her hand and a loud snap echoed around the room.

A second later she opened her palm and the rabbit flopped to the ground, dead.

"Throw it out." She commanded, deadpan.

Her eyes were cold and unmoving.

A red-cloaked elder swiftly grabbed the dead animal and exited the tent without a word. A shiver ran down his spine at her callousness. She'd inflicted an illusion before he'd spoken his piece. Maybe he shouldn't try to talk his way out of this?

"You got her attention," Arick murmured. *"and we have nothing left to lose."*

"Our sanity!" He scoffed back.

"Between the two of us, she can't drive us both crazy."

"She already has! Never underestimate the psychiatric powers of a woman, Arick." He shot the kid a mental glare but dammit! The kid was right. He had to try.

He cleared his throat and attempted to speak again. Her glare sharpened as he opened his mouth.

"I didn't end my illusion." She pursed her lips together.

Azazel froze. *Crap.*

"Aw, dammit that's right." Arick mused.

Satan sat up and snapped two fingers together. Guards grabbed him on either side, yanking him to his feet.

"Bring him forward." She pointed her finger at him.

Dragging him a few feet forward, they slammed him onto the ground, causing him to groan. His body protested. His back and sides were still sore from the beating. His wounds had closed up but were not fully healed. Another good kick or shove to the ground and his wounds would re-open.

Please, Trinity, let me make it out of here, he prayed.

"Me too, Trinity!" Arick chimed in.

A hand roughly yanked his hair. Satan leaned into him, her face mere inches from his. A waft of her overpowering jasmine perfume invaded his nose. He turned his nose up, holding his breath to avoid the smell.

She grabbed his chin, forcing him to look directly into her eyes.

Crap. Crap. Crap. He thought. *"Kid, I think our plan is screwed."*

"Uh-oh, that look on her face is scary."

The lines around her eyes tightened and a thin smile spread across her face. Her green eyes flashed with anger, sending shudders through him.

"Is that a watcher in there with you?" She asked, her voice tight. "Which one are you?"

The air in his lungs stalled. Beads of sweat formed on his brow as he scrambled to think of a way out of this situation. He peeked behind him, at Mikael. Arick would fight for control if he tried to leave without his father. So he had to think of a way to get all three of them out of there.

A sharp pinch at his chin drew his attention back to Satan, whose eyes glowed. Claws sprouted from her fingers, causing them to pierce his skin. Otherwise, the rest of her illusion held.

"If I have to ask again," she purred. "I'll force it out of you and believe me, it won't be gentle."

He narrowed his gaze at her, mentally pushing Arick farther back into their mind.

"It's Azazel." He grinned. "Your brothers were right. You're a bit slow on the pickup."

Sharp pricks penetrated along his jawline. He bit his lips to keep from crying out in pain. She dug her claws in deeper, relishing his silent grimace.

"Why are you in this brat's body?" She sneered. "What do my brothers have to do with anything? They know better than to get in my way."

"Your brothers aren't dumb." Azazel released a pained scoff, squinting through one eye. "I bet my existence that you've found other Archangels lurking about in the demon realm."

Her hands twitched.

"And you never thought to wonder why?" He grinned as her jaw flexed. "You never wondered why Barmen's been so hard to catch?"

Satan's eyes widened for a fraction of a second before closing off her surprise.

Got her! He triumphed.

"What do you know about Barmen?" She squeezed the sides of his head between her hands.

Though smaller than him, he didn't doubt the strength she held as a demon lord. She would smash his head in if she wanted to. Pressure built along his head, proving her power.

"Well?" She pursed her lips together. "Don't shut up now, watcher. Go on."

She hissed the title. His stomach knotted.

"So you can kill me right after?" He huffed. "Get me and Mikael to the portal and I'll tell you everything."

She raised an eyebrow. "You and Mikael?"

He nodded.

"You already have a powerful Michael angel to do your bidding." He indicated to Matthew behind them. "You don't need two."

She grinned. "It's not about needing them, watcher. It's the principle."

She dug her claws in once more, this time higher on his face. He cried out in pain as her ten fingers stung like needles. She jerked her hands away, ripping flesh as she went.

Blood dripped down his forehead and into his eyes, and mouth. The metallic taste of blood spread across his tongue. He cursed as the pain radiated to his neck. Dark spots glimmered in his peripheral vision, unconsciousness threatening to take him under.

No, he shook his head. *He had to secure the deal.*

"If you kill me or Mikael, you'll never get your hands on Barmen." He threatened.

She froze, her eyes assessed him as if wondering if he was lying.

"I offer you this proposition." The blood from his face created a puddle around him. With dark spots growing in his field of vision, he needed to act fast. "I'll tell you what your brothers have been up to all these years, but I want security that you will take us to the portal *and* that no harm will come to us during that time.”

Her eyes glowed as the only clue to her feelings. Otherwise, her face remained expressionless. A long minute passed in silence.

“Very well,” she purred, wiping the blood off her hands from a cloth a servant handed to her. “I accept your deal.”

She grinned, showing a row of bright, white teeth.

“I best make sure you don’t die then.” She snapped her fingers.

Her mouth moved, but he no longer heard the words. His vision tunneled and darkness crept in. In the distance, he heard the echoes of Arick’s concern. The last thing he saw as he slumped over, was Matthew standing over him, frowning. The rest faded as he fell into a deep sleep.

Chapter 13

The cold air greeted her hands with gentleness. The night sky twinkled above them as they flew. Isabella used the wind to aid their travels, like a current guiding them along their path. A full day of traveling passed without incident.

She'd used her powers as an excuse to stay at the back of the formation when, in reality, she was too weak to keep up. Atarah zoomed to the front, carrying a sleeping Jack without breaking a sweat while the rest of their group scattered in between. Tariel and Fatima flapped their wings with effort. At the start of their journey, Farah had been concerned for Jack's sake, but now Farah's eyes flickered behind her every few minutes to check on the Azrael ladies.

Fatima and Tariel's faces burned bright red during the day as they traveled. Sweat dripped down their faces as they panted to keep the pace. However as the sun drifted below the horizon, their faces paled drastically, causing them to stick out at night. She'd debated asking to break for their sakes when Atarah called from the front.

"We'll stop here for a moment," Atarah shouted above the wind.

She nodded in agreement. Using her wind, Isabella aided Fatima and Tariel to the ground. The two Azrael angels slumped the moment her wind took over their weight, too exhausted to protest.

Fatima curled a wing around Tariel when they landed on

the ground. Farah scurried to her friend's side.

"Here!" Farah shoved a bottle into Fatima's face, leaving no room for argument. "Drink this!"

Titling Fatima's head back, Farah poured the vial's contents down her throat. Isabella mimicked Farah's movement and did the same for Tariel.

Before leaving, Farah packed a variety of medicines for them and Rachael. This vial contained a number of electrolytes to help with energy levels. Fatima and Tariel had already gone through nearly half of these vials throughout their day's journey. During the last few hours of the trip, Fatima refused to take another vial to save them for others which caused her depleted state. Tariel, just as stubborn as her mother, rejected the vial as well.

Now they lay exhausted to the point of passing out! A few minutes passed before Tariel's eyes flickered open.

She grunted, rolling over to her side. "How much farther do we have left?"

Atarah stood, cradling Jack within the crook of one arm while staring into the distance. Rolling green pastures stretched as far as the eye could see.

"Not much," Isabella patted Tariel's back. "We only have a few more hours of flying."

"We've made amazing time thanks to your wind, Isabella," Atarah exclaimed, lowering Jack next to Farah.

The young angel snored lightly as he curled closer to his mother. Tariel's wings slumped.

"Dear Trinity…hours…" Tariel whispered.

Fatima, for her part, put on a brave face.

"Good," she grunted, using her arms to sit up.

"You dumb wraith." Farah crossed her arms, glaring at Fatima. "You worried me there. You're supposed to tell us when you're at your limit."

"Overgrown nerd." Fatima huffed a short laugh. "I'm too tired to fight with you."

Isabella shook her head, marveling at their dynamic. They took each other's insults as compliments.

"Let's rest for a few more minutes and then keep going," Atarah said, sitting with the rest of them. "We need to get to Rachael's as soon as possible."

Farah opened her mouth to, no doubt, protest when Fatima cut her off.

"Atarah's right." Fatima sighed. "We need to get there fast."

"We spent all day yesterday and the day before flying," Farah protested. "Surely we can take a longer break."

Tariel shook her head.

"Dad's still not back yet," Tariel said, rising to a seated position. "Which means *we* need to be ready to fight any demons that come into our world."

"All the Head Archs are gone…" Atarah clenched her fist. "If it wasn't for me, my dad and brother would probably still be here. Defending our home."

"Umm," Isabella murmured hesitantly, "No one will accept Arick as the heir now, Atarah. That makes you, Tariel, Jack, and I next in the line of succession."

Atarah's wings flared and her eyes narrowed, but it was Tariel who spoke.

"Zewal will kill me before he lets me lead our region," Tariel scoffed.

"Why?" She asked, furrowing her brow.

"He thinks the leader should have all three dark abilities." Tariel rolled her eyes. "I only have two."

"So does your brother." Fatima raised an eyebrow. "He possessed the same two your father had when he was his age."

"But he thinks once Dad passes, he'll get the third and qualify to be leader over me."

Farah frowned. "There have been plenty of other Azrael Heads before him without all three dark abilities."

"Try explaining that to him," Tariel retorted.

"What happens if the third ability goes to you?" Atarah tilted her head to one side.

"Zewal's still the oldest, so the line of succession will continue with him, probably," Tariel answered with a shrug.

"Is there something similar with the Michael clan?" She asked Atarah. "A test of strength, or is it whoever's the oldest that's next in line like everyone else?"

"The oldest," Atarah nodded. "Is next in line."

"Same here." Isabella hugged her knees into her chest and shuddered. "I'd probably throw up if I was *really* next in line."

Farah's frown deepened as her arms closed tighter around Jack's frame.

"You seem…different than before, Isabella. Why is that?" Atarah asked with a furrowed brow "When we were fighting the Abaddon you weren't this scared."

She gave a humorless laugh. "Because when I'm with Sissy, I know everything will be all right. She won't let anything go wrong."

"Anything go wrong?" Atarah raised an eyebrow. "Like what?"

She lowered her gaze. "I can get a little out of hand if I'm not careful."

"Out of hand?" Tariel chimed in. "You're so quiet."

"I haven't fully controlled the range of my powers," she explained. "When I was little, I caused typhoons and tornadoes by accident."

"Oh," Atarah exclaimed. "But you seemed in control when—"

"Clarissa was there," she interrupted.

"What does she have to do with anything?" Tariel inquired. "You're just as capable of controlling your powers without her."

She shook her head. "I need her by me to keep me and others safe."

"Why?" Atarah asked.

"I just do."

Atarah and Tariel exchanged a look.

"I don't understand," Atarah mumbled.

"No one does." She sighed. "Sissy does."

Fatima frowned at her. "Is that why you stay quiet? Because you don't think others will understand you."

"Well…" she drifted off. "No one else has."

"Help us understand why you need your sister." Tariel leaned closer. "From what I saw in the demon realm, you were plenty capable on your own."

"We failed that mission." She pointed out softly.

"Your wind gusts were strong enough to encase the whole city," Tariel defended.

Isabella shook her head again, frowning. How could she get them to understand? Atarah pinched the end of her chin, looking at her with a pensive expression.

"Is this the longest you've been away from Clarissa?" Atarah asked.

She nodded.

"Hmmm," Atarah pondered for a moment. "Were you scared to use your powers when we were flying all this time?"

She paused. "W-well…no—but that's different because it was easy."

Atarah nodded knowingly. "What's something harder for you to do?"

"Um, never really thought about it before but…It's the directional changes." She lifted her hand toward the night sky, palm up. "Wind is free and formless with no concrete structure. Just pressure."

She closed her hand into a fist and brought it to her chest.

"When I channel that pressure in one direction, it's super easy. Effortless." She glanced back at Atarah. "But when I have to concentrate on multiple wind directions, I—I—"

"You get overwhelmed by the pressure." Tariel breathed softly.

"Yeah!" Her eyes widened. "That's exactly it."

Atarah nodded again. "Clarissa's fire helps with your air manipulation because the heat causes air to rise naturally. That's one less direction for you to deal with."

"Yeah." Her wings relaxed.

Maybe they did understand?

She never expected them to grasp her elemental concepts so quickly. Her father had grown frustrated with her lack of… everything really. Her inability to control the wind in various directions. Her inability to lead with conviction. Or communicate with others outside of her family.

"We've all been there," Atarah murmured.

Tariel gave a grunt of agreement, peering at her hands.

"You two are naturals," she scoffed.

She remembered their mission to Belli Causa to fight the Abaddon. Atarah led them without hesitation. She'd held it off to give them enough time to escape. While Tariel… she shuddered. She didn't need to see Tariel use her powers to know how strong she was. Not to mention, the Azrael heir possessed other incredible abilities to see the written word of the dead. There were so many signs of how special they were, while she showed the opposite.

Isabella hugged her knees closer.

She caused trouble from the moment she'd been born. Killing her own mother during childbirth and nearly a dozen more. She'd been told for as long as she could remember that no one wanted to touch her out of fear because of the horrific windstorm she'd caused that day. A bitter taste filled her mouth at the memories.

Unleashing her wind powers, she'd wreaked havoc on their family's villa and the city. Citizens had to stay indoors, locked in their bathrooms. The ships had to dock because her wind currents had manipulated the currents in the water. They destroyed dozens of ships and buildings, carrying away anything not deeply rooted in the ground.

Ever since, Clarissa had watched over her to make sure she didn't lose control. Without her sister, she was a liability. A burden to be guarded. A lost cause.

"The hell do you mean?" An irate voice drew her back to the present.

She jerked her head up to see Atarah standing before her, hands on her hips and glaring. Tariel mimicked her stance except she crossed her arms.

"Natural at what?" Tariel hissed, narrowing her eyes at Isabella.

"I—I mean, it-t-t's just that—"

"Natural doesn't mean a damn thing! Do you have any idea what it's like to be the smallest, weakest and slowest angel in her class?" Atarah raised an eyebrow. "In a clan that values strength above all else?"

"Or being constantly compared to your older sibling?" Tariel sneered.

"Well, yes," Isabella answered, rising to her feet to join them.

"We've *all* been compared to our siblings. Doesn't make it right, but it's something we've each had to deal with." Atarah crossed her arms.

The hair on the back of Isabella's neck rose. A tingling sensation snaked down her spine as she listened to Atarah's next words.

Atarah sighed, softening her gaze. "Only we can determine our own limits. Don't let anyone, not even your family, tell you otherwise."

Her eyes widened.

Her own limit? What did that mean? Atarah and Tariel looked so fierce and full of conviction in speaking. Where did that come from? How were they so sure of themselves? They reminded her of Clarissa. She paused.

Could she rely on them too?

"Not even us!" Tariel retorted harshly.

Isabella jumped, curling her wings around herself.

"We've had to learn the hard way to trust ourselves through our mess ups," Tariel explained, "If you see your value through someone else's lens, they'll set your limits."

"I agree, don't do that! If I'd done that, I never would've left Sanctum or met either of you." Atarah gestured to Tariel and her. "I would've missed out on life, following other people's limits."

A warm feeling spread from her chest to her belly. Could she really be like them? Or was this only a reality for certain people?

Atarah tilted her head, furrowing her brow. "Aren't you... angry, Isabella?"

Her heart sputtered. The wind picked up speed. "A—angry? W—what do you mean?"

"Hmmm, I can't put my finger on it, but I sense...pressure building inside of you." Atarah shrugged. "I don't know. That would make me angry, so it only makes sense."

Isabella's mind stalled and then blanked. Something pierced her heart, slicing through her toughest barrier from the question. *Was Atarah right? Was she angry?* She didn't get a chance to ponder her thoughts long before Farah spoke out.

"They remind me of us when we were younger, Fatima," Farah said softly, rubbing Jack's back.

"Hmph." Fatima rose to her feet. "They're nicer than how we were back then."

Farah laughed. "You're saying we've gone soft?"

A smile twitched at the corner of Fatima's mouth. "We got soft the moment we married and had kids."

The two exchanged a smile before moving closer to them.

"We best get going," Fatima called out, expanding her wings. "We'll reach Rachael's villa just outside of the city by dawn."

Atarah and Tariel nodded, while Isabella twiddled her thumbs together waiting for the lift-off command. There was no way she had what it took to go off on her own, right? Maybe it wasn't a bad idea to see how much of her wind she could control.

"Let's go!" Fatima commanded, launching herself into the sky.

Atarah carefully took hold of Jack before lifting off as well. Followed by Farah and then Tariel. She stayed on the ground. The last one, making up the tail of their formation.

"It's ok," she murmured out loud into the quiet night. "It's in one direction." The voice coming out of her mouth didn't sound convinced. Isabella crossed her arms and copied the stance Atarah had earlier. "You said so yourself, it's easy. You don't want to be scared for the rest of your life, right?"

Right, she nodded to herself. Isabella expanded her wings and launched herself into the air. Dawn was many hours away. Glancing at Fatima and Tariel, they'd most certainly tire out many times before arriving. Could a stronger wind current help them like before? She brought her hands in front of her face.

Knots coiled in her belly, as her brain screamed at her dumb idea. It was too risky to put more power behind it without Clarissa, her mind chastised. But she could save Tariel and Fatima from exhaustion.

She clenched her fist with a stern nod. *I need to set my own limit.* She could start with a new minimum, at least.

Isabella inhaled deeply, calling the wind to her hands and fingers. Building the pressure within her lungs, air expanded. The atmosphere around her twirled and moved. In the sky, she possessed a greater understanding of her wind.

She eased the flap of her wings, conserving her energy. After one quick prayer, she exhaled and released the current building from within. A strong gust of wind propelled her forward.

She gasped, tucking in her wings tighter.
Keep breathing!

Cries of surprise called out ahead of her. The others tucked in the wings, extending them enough to glide within the current.

The wind she created was stronger than the last but not overwhelming. Isabella's heart hammered as she flattened her wings enough to surrender to the current. Taking in another breath, she released another burst, propelling them further across the land. The air blasted against them on all sides, rougher but manageable.

She extended her arm out as a directional test. The wind— no—her wind followed her direction. Her fingers trembled but were greeted by cool air. They were heading in the right direction!

"Yes!" Isabella cheered.

The knots in her stomach loosened little by little as she maneuvered them through the sky. She could control this! She could do it. This could be her new minimum.

"Ok!" She huffed, reaching her hands forward. "Breathe."

Tension eased along her shoulders and back as her body realized she was safe to use her powers. The others were safe. She used the stars to guide them throughout the night, testing the air temperature to ensure their direction. Antiqua was just before the Living Mountains with very cold winds. The moment she came in contact with warmer winds, she veered their direction.

The others huddled their formation together. No longer in control of their flight pattern and orientation, they stiffened their bodies; like kites to the wind, she was the one with the string to guide them along the path. Using her breathing techniques to calm her racing heart, she kept chanting she was fine.

With each passing moment, the air grew colder yet softer, like flowing water through her fingertips. Her heart hammered for a different reason. Excitement and exhaustion. If the elevation weren't so high and the wind died down, she would've had beads of sweat dripping down her face. She was too happy to care. Her shoulder and arm muscles burned but she maintained her hold. Neither Tariel nor Fatima signaled for a stop. Atarah and Farah appeared to be enjoying the ride. One hour passed by without incident. A whole hour! Her lungs ached and her muscles quivered with fatigue. She debated about stopping, for her own sake, when a strange scent drifted through the air.

Closing her eyes, she sniffed deeply.

A sweet, floral smell filled her nostrils. The refreshing scent was familiar somehow and sent tingles down her spine. Her head grew fuzzy and light. The pain along her muscles eased while a numbing sensation overtook her lungs.

Her eyes shot open. The flowers!

She lowered her arms, reducing the strength of the current. They descended to the ground slowly, flaring their wings wide. Like walking downhill, she pulled back the strength of her wind and slowed its speed. This built pressure along her lungs and arms, but she didn't care.

Her focus shifted to the others. She needed to guide them carefully. If she managed to pull this off, this could've been a new milestone for her.

Atarah was the first to land, followed by Farah who grabbed Jack from Atarah's arms. Tariel and her mother landed after, leaving herself in the sky. She stopped her wind and tucked her wings. She landed with a light thud, crumbling onto her hands and knees with exhaustion. Isabella's ribs and lungs ached with each small breath she took.

"Ugh," she groaned, gently clutching her sore sides. She'd be fine within a few hours. "At least no one was hurt."

"Isabella!" Atarah exclaimed.

She looked up to see Atarah's excited face crashing onto her. Atarah squeezed her tight into a large bear hug. Her cry of pain wasn't heard over Atarah's loud praise.

"You did it! You got us here a half a day early!" Atarah

cheered, doing small bounces.

"Ahh!" She meant for her scream to be loud but it came out as a hoarse, pained gasp.

Her ribs creaked before a loud snap finally caught Atarah's attention.

"Oww…" she whined.

"Oh!" Atarah cried out. "I'm so sorry! I didn't realize…"

She didn't hear the rest of Atarah's apology, too consumed by the pain in her sides. Why did Atarah have to be so freakishly strong?

More voices talked over one another. She peeled one eye open to see Tariel and Farah lifting her. Fatima was nowhere to be seen.

Atarah's brow furrowed deep with worry, her hand gripping the top of her head. "I didn't mean to hurt you. Here, let me help."

Atarah grabbed her legs and hoisted Isabella over her shoulder like she was a rag doll.

"Ughh, oww…" she said through clenched teeth.

Atarah was on the move before the words were out of her mouth. "Hang on, let's get you inside."

Wait, inside? She thought.

She raised her head to see a large building on top of the hill. Rushing water echoed around them, meaning a stream or river was close by. Dawn was hours away, providing too little light for her to gather her surroundings. From the jarring steps, she glanced down to see Atarah walking up cobble steps.

Floral scents of lilac and lavender threatened to overwhelm her senses. The fragrance grew stronger with each step, along with voices.

"We're almost inside," Atarah said, "Fatima went ahead of us once we landed, so I'm sure she's waking Rachael and the others."

She grunted, not wanting to draw in too much air to speak. Atarah reached the top step and nearly jogged through what looked to be a garden. Based on what she smelled, flower bushes were arranged on all sides of the garden. She heard the sounds of a water fountain close by, but Atarah's heavy footsteps drowned out all other sounds.

She lifted her head again. The villa was several stories high with vines climbing all around the corners. Shadows moved through the light illuminating the downstairs windows. She wondered why there were so many shadows, but shifted her attention back to Atarah.

"Slow down." Tariel and Farah huffed in unison.

Farah carried Jack, who was waking after so much commotion. Jack rubbed his eyes with both hands, groaning.

"Are we there yet?" He yawned, peering at his mother.

"Almost, buddy!" Atarah called over her shoulder, reaching for the door. "Fatima and Rachael are just through this door—"

Everything froze. Atarah's leg suspended in the air.

Isabella wondered if she was breathing. Atarah's eyes widened so much that she thought they'd pop out of their sockets. Her wings flared wide before slumping to the ground, feathers falling.

"Atarah?" she rasped. "What's going on?"

She wiggled her way off of Atarah's shoulder, keeping one arm wrapped around her side. The others stopped just outside of the door frame, peering around Atarah's frame.

"What's wrong?" Tariel's eyes swept the room.

Her gaze stopped as they landed on something or someone.

Braving her face, Isabella turned around. Her jaw dropped.

On the opposite side of the room, along the long table, Ava, Charlotte and Canaan sat with Rachael. Their faces showed variations of shock and disbelief. Behind them, along the window sill, sat the strangest children she'd ever seen! Their eyes glowed yellow. One had a horn protruding from his head. Another boy didn't have any lips, just rows and rows of sharp teeth. An albino child with red eyes sat beside him.

What in the Trinity were those things? A shiver ran down her spine. Everyone appeared to be in so much shock that no one moved or spoke, gaping at each other with slack jaws and flared wings.

What the Trinity was going on here? Isabella puzzled.

Atarah's eye flickered between Charlotte and Ava. The two in question gazed back at her as if they were seeing a ghost.

Isabella jolted. *That's right.* She remembered.

Charlotte and Ava thought Atarah was dead. They all did except for Farah and Jack. Charlotte stood slowly.

"A—Atarah?" Tears brimmed in Charlotte's eyes, threatening to spill over. "Is that really you?"

Within the blink of an eye, Atarah engulfed Charlotte in a bear hug.

"I'm so sorry," Atarah murmured, her voice quivering. "I meant to come back, I swear!"

The room filled with Charlotte's quiet sobs as they embraced. Ava rose and cradled them with her wings.

"We thought you were dead." Ava rasped, with tears streaming down her face.

They all clung to each other for a minute, their wings trembling every few seconds.

"What's going on here?" Isabella directed her question to Rachael, who sat with flared wings at the table.

Fatima stood behind her with a strange expression. However, Isabella couldn't take her eyes off the strange kids on the window sill. *Who were they? Were they....halflings? Here?!* She wondered.

A girl, who looked about her age, stepped in front of the others. The new girl had brown wings and a semi-circular scar running down one side of her face. She flared her wings wide enough to block the other kids from her view.

"These...children are with Ava and Charlotte." Disapproval oozed with every word as Rachael scrunched her nose. "They won't be staying long."

Atarah peered from the huddle formation, eyes wide as if seeing the children for the first time. Behind her, Farah tightened her hold of Jack.

"Hey!" Jack wiggled in his mother's arms. "Let me down! I wanna see them."

Farah frowned but lowered him to the ground. Jack poked his head around the others, waving.

"My name's Jack!" He pointed to a small girl with impossibly large eyes. "What's yours?"

The girl blushed crimson red, curling closer to the older girl. "My name's Bugs."

Jack grinned, shaking the bottom of Farah's tunic. "Mama, can I play with them?"

Farah's frown deepened. "You know that's not possible, Jack."

It was Jack's turn to frown.

"I'm strong enough." He whined. "I can play."

Farah exchanged a look with Rachael, whose hesitation was evident in her furrowed brow. Farah opened her mouth no doubt to deny Jack again, but Tariel spoke.

"I can watch over them." Tariel tilted her head to the side, entering the threshold.

The kids jumped at the sight of Tariel. Her black eyes tracked each movement.

"I won't hurt you…unless you misbehave." Tariel added, her lips twitching at the sight of Bugs' paling face.

"I don't know about that," the girl with the scar chimed in.

A boy with a horn protruding from his head poked around her, glaring at Tariel.

"She looks like she'll hurt us." The young boy scoffed. "Just like that Arch who hurt Bugs and Fig."

Tariel tilted her head. What other Arch?

Jack wobbled over to the children. His legs shook with

effort and his breathing labored. Isabella wanted to move to help him, but Atarah raised a hand to stop her.

Farah and Atarah's eyes widened at the sight of Jack walking. Now that Isabella thought about it, she'd never seen Jack walk. He'd either been lying in bed or carried by someone. He wobbled like a baby learning how to walk, but he made it to the table before gripping the leg to steady himself.

"W-Will…y-y-you play with me, Bugs?" Jack panted, a bead of sweat forming on his brow. "I—I don't…get many-y chances to play with others."

Bugs' eyes somehow widened further. A small smile formed on her lips.

"S-sure!" Bugs cheered, glancing at the older girl. "As long as it's ok with ya, Rhea?"

The older girl, called Rhea, glanced between them before nodding. "We'll all go outside while the grown-ups talk."

Rhea gave a pointed glance to the other kids.

"The garden will be perfect," Tariel murmured, opening the door.

Rhea paused for a moment but Ava encouraged her.

"Go on," Ava nodded. "We'll be in here if you need us. We won't leave without you."

Rhea gave a grunt of acknowledgement before ushering the kids outside. With slowed movements, Tariel followed them out last, shutting the door.

Isabella wondered what the Azrael heir was thinking but pivoted back to Ava and Charlotte. Those two would have more answers.

"I think we all need to have a seat and drink some tea." Rachael sighed, pinching the bridge of her nose. "I don't know what my husband was thinking in sending those things here."

Charlotte and Ava stiffened but Fatima spoke.

"Now, now," Fatima exclaimed, taking the first seat to Rachael's left. "Let's start at the beginning. There's much for *each* of us to go over."

Atarah's gaze switched back to Ava and Charlotte after watching the children move outside.

"What happened while I was recovering?" Atarah murmured as Charlotte guided her to the table.

Isabella sat next, while the others found their seats. Everyone was in a daze, almost a shocked state.

"Start with you!" Charlotte huffed, her hands still wrapped around Atarah's. Her nail beds were white from her grip. "What happened? We—We thought the worst when Arick freaked out."

"Arick freaked out?" Atarah's eyes widened.

Ava nodded.

"By the time we got to the room, Arick was a hysterical mess. Blood was everywhere and your body…" Ava drifted off. "We couldn't recover your body from the rubble."

Atarah put a hand to her chest. "Last thing I remember was Matthew driving a dagger through my heart."

"How did you survive such an attack?" Charlotte leaned closer, her brow furrowed.

"Barmen got me out of there, but Noah and Farah stitched me up. I woke up in her place next to little Jack. She said that—maybe— I lived because I solidified armor around my vital organs." Atarah rubbed the back of her head. "Also possibly from the healing skills you taught me."

Charlotte's eyes widened. "I—"

"Never mind that! There's a more pressing issue than that right now," Rachael interrupted, bringing a hand to her temple. "On the topic of Matthew, my husband told us his next move."

Fatima leaned forward. "What news comes from them?"

After a few cautious glances outside, Farah finally approached the table. "Any news about Barmen or Joshua?"

"What about Father and Arick?" Atarah's wings flared.

Rachel scowled. "One thing at a time, please."

"Rachael's right," Fatima barked out. "You speak first,

Rachael. Tell us what you know."

"Gabriel's with the other Head Archs—" Rachael started but froze, her eyes staring into the distance.

Isabella followed her gaze to see a growing white light in the hallway. She gasped as the portal expanded and figures walked out.

With a grunt, Elijah, Amos, Malachi, Sewall and Joshua stumbled into the room one after the other. Her father landed with a thud and his eyes downcast. Her wings stiffened. If he was here…

She peered behind him, eyes searching for her sister as her heart hammered. The air in her lungs caught as she waited for the sparkle of red hair or the sensation of flames to drift into the room.

Her heart sputtered when she saw Gabriel coming through the portal and her wings flared when he closed it.

Clarissa wasn't coming.

Her world tilted. The wind shifted, agitated.

The air around them picked up as she curled her wings to hug her stomach. Knots formed and twisted in her belly. She had to survive a little longer without her. She exhaled shakily, tightening her arms.

"Speak of the devil," Fatima murmured with a small grin. "Rachael was just talking about you."

Amos winced as everyone's eyes turned to them.

While Sewall replied, "Only the bad stuff I trust."

Fatima's grin grew. "Care to join us?"

"I'm afraid we don't have much time," Malachi frowned, stepping forward. "We need to ready our troops and prepare for another summit meeting at Aqua Caput."

Her wings twitched. *At home? Why?* Her thoughts screamed inside her head.

Her mind whirled with questions, but fear gripped her throat shut, chastising her. It wasn't her place to speak. Malachi walked within a foot of her and placed a hand on her shoulder. Warmth from his hand eased the knots in her stomach a little bit.

Everyone else shifted to various spots in the room after the portal closed. Sewall knelt by his wife's side, clutching her hands while Gabriel rushed to Rachael's chair. Joshua joined Farah by the back wall but stayed a few inches away, his wings brushing hers.

Canaan, who'd sat quietly in the back, wrapped his arms around his older brother. He murmured something in Amos' ear before placing a pair of headphones over his brother. Tension in Amos' face and shoulders released once the headphones were in place. Gratitude shone in his eyes as the brothers nodded to each other periodically, silently communicating with one another.

Elijah froze upon seeing Atarah, his arms outstretched. His face paled as if he'd seen a ghost. "I-I'd thought—"

Atarah embraced him. He enclosed his arms around her, staring at a tearful Ava and Charlotte with a dumbfounded expression.

"Is this a trick of some kind?" Elijah asked his daughters, who shook their heads.

"We're just as surprised as you are." Ava chuckled, wiping a tear from her eye. "We arrived just a few hours ago and as we were telling Rachael about our adventures, Atarah came through the door right as rain."

"Noah and Farah nursed her back to health." Charlotte chimed in, eyes shining. "Barmen saved her from the rubble."

"Barmen?" Amos' head popped up.

Canaan turned his gaze to everyone as well.

"It appears we'll have to make time for this discussion," Malachi sighed, running a hand through his hair. "Everyone have a seat. Keep the recap quick and to the point."

Isabella waited for everyone else to sit before moving away from her father.

Would he explain why Clarissa wasn't home yet? Did he

find her?

She bit her tongue to keep her questions at bay, waiting for the explanation she desperately needed. Her father leaned against the chair, gripping the handles tight enough to make his knuckles go white. The wrinkles along his forehead deepened as he tilted his head to one side. His wings stiffened and twitched every few minutes, exposing his displeasure. She frowned.

He was about to share bad news, she internally groaned.

"I'll go first." Malachi grimaced, lifting his gaze to the others.

The knots in her stomach tightened with her father's every word until she was certain she could never eat again.

Chapter 14

Shouts and obscenities echoed as protests and objections burred together as a unified voice. The moon shined bright as the rangers gathered in an abandoned stadium. The abandoned Avanhard Stadium in Pripyat, Ukraine, created the perfect meeting place for the rangers from around the world to converge.

"Why should we fight with those spaceheads?!"

"They haven't done anything for us!"

"Those elitist shitheads!"

"Leave them to deal with their own consequences."

Flynn waited for the jeers and shouts to die down, but Luke's patient gaze frustrated them more. Imani hovered behind him, ready to move if a fight broke out. The rangers from his group all stood by him, much to his relief.

After imploring his cousin to gather the Head Archs, he'd spent the past two days gathering the rangers from factions around the world. They all came out of respect for Luke. However, the tricky part came in trying to convince them to fight for the Spirit realm.

Luke hadn't said beyond explaining the facts. Satan and her troops were coming and the Spirit realm needed help. They'd stood for most of the hour listening to the frustration of the people. Flynn was beginning to wonder if it would ever end.

"Eventually, everyone gets tired of speaking," Arakiel

mumbled in their shared mind. *"Listening's the wise thing."*

Flynn shuddered, cursing the sensation that slithered through his head each time Arakiel spoke. He changed his thoughts to numbers, counting the amount of people in the room.

"It doesn't have to be this way, Flynn," Arakiel implored. *"We can benefit each other."*

Flynn ignored the watcher, continuing his counting. He refused to speak a word to Arakiel; if he did, that meant…

He shook his head. *No, he refused to acknowledge the shame.*

Arakiel sighed and Flynn sensed him burrow to the far corners of their mind. He couldn't stop the revulsion from working its way up his spine. His wings trembled and his stomach heaved, threatening to empty out its contents.

Imani placed a concerned hand on his shoulder when he lurched forward. A few of the others glanced at him from the corner of their eyes, confused. Only Imani knew the truth of the deal he'd made with the watcher. The rest of the rangers were in the dark; he'd go to his grave with this secret.

After watching the disgust grow within his cousin's eyes, he'd rather die than see that same expression on the faces of his comrades—his friends and new family. Imani and Luke didn't judge him, but he couldn't risk it with the others. His heart twisted at the thought of seeing their faces, their opinion of him, plummet.

He straightened his back and washed his face of any emotion. He would hide the watcher as best as he could until his deathbed. He imagined a wall coming down between him and Arakiel, blocking every sensation and thought from entering his own.

Imani frowned at him but he ignored her too, focusing on Luke and the other rangers. In his opinion, the rangers had every right to object to helping the spaceheads in the Spirit realm. The angels from their home world had only shunned or ridiculed anyone different than themselves. He understood, yet a part of his heart twisted at the vision Arakiel had shared with him:

Rows and rows of demon soldiers lined in formation, marching to a portal that'd lead them through Belli Causa. Demons in long red cloaks fanned Satan as she made her way to them. The vision caused the hairs on the back of his neck to stand on end. However, the part that spurred him to Malachi was when Arakiel explained that Satan wanted to rule over as many realms as she could cast her mind control over, expanding her empire far beyond her reach.

With Matthew, Mikael *and* Arick under her control, their chances of survival were slim to none if the rangers fought alone. However, if everyone united, Spirit realm and all, they stood a better chance.

He and Luke needed to convince the others to fight but…

"Even if we help them, those jackasses would leave us to die and you know it!" Another voice jeered from the sidelines.

Many others shouted in agreement.

"And we'll all die if we don't!" Flynn shouted.

The flames in his veins simmered and grew in size. He took a calming breath while all eyes turned to him.

Everyone quieted as he stepped forward. "The watcher was clear about this! If we don't help them, we lose any advantage we'll have when Satan decides to conquer us!"

Murmurs and uncertainty stretched among the masses. He used that to his advantage.

"I understand your hesitation!" He yelled across the stadium. "Everyone has just cause to not help. But please! My comrades! We'll need their numbers to survive."

Silence fell upon the crowd as they listened to him.

"I'm not telling you to like it!" He continued, "Nor am I telling you to forgive them for how they've wronged you. All I'm telling you is to fight under your own free will! Because once *she* gets here, she'll use you to fight for her own."

The silence shifted to rumbles and whispers amongst themselves. Imani nudged him with her wing.

"Didn't know you had such a way with words," she mumbled under her breath.

"I don't," Flynn replied, "I just spoke the truth. If you saw that vision, you'd say the same thing."

"Hmph." Imani grinned. "I'd probably crack a few skulls in. So you're doing better than me."

Flynn's lips twitched. Luke stepped forward, causing voices to fall again.

"I hear you, rangers, and I understand your frustration and anger with the spaceheads." Luke looked around the stadium. "But I'm going to the Spirit realm, not for the Archs but to fight for those around us now and our right to free will. I ask, as my chosen family: will you fight with me?"

Luke put a hand to his chest.

"The *choice* is yours."

More silence followed his words. Flynn held his breath, his eyes searching across the rangers' faces.

One ranger moved from the crowd, walking to the stage. Once the ranger reached the stage, he knelt with tucked wings.

"I fight with you!" The ranger yelled out.

Another ranger approached the stage and knelt. "I fight with you!"

More rangers followed by the dozens this time, kneeling with tucked wings and hand to the heart.

"We fight with you!" The rangers chanted.

More joined in the huddle, chanting as they went.

"We fight with you!"

"We fight with you!"

Warmth bloomed from within his belly, fueling the flames within him. *This. This is why he joined the rangers*, he thought to himself. The unity and sense of belonging were so strong. He would die for the rangers without hesitation, not because of forced loyalty but by choice. His heart ached, remembering his first days as a ranger.

He'd still held a bias against who he'd thought of as lesser angels—especially those born from multiple clans. Luke had sensed his prejudice from the beginning and paired him with Imani. Her parents were lesser angels from the Michael and Gabriel clans. Imani couldn't manifest teleportation or super strength of any kind, but she had the fierceness of any warrior he'd ever met. She'd been cast aside and forced by her parents to join the rangers from a young age. After it became evident that she couldn't manifest her spiritual energy, her mother abhorred Imani mixing her weak genes with the population.

In the beginning, navigating the relationship had been rough and awkward. He'd seen himself as above her and as-signed her menial tasks, but she never listened. In fact, she outright defied him and ordered *him* around. He'd scoffed at her until Luke said she had seniority.

After a life-or-death mission where they had to work to-gether to survive, they'd broken ground between each other. Imani opened up about how growing up in the Spirit realm had been hell for her, providing them the chance to bond. He'd shared his hellish life, which she'd assumed was full of privilege.

He chuckled. Oh, how wrong both of them had been.

"What are you giggling about over there?" Imani scowled at him.

He grinned. "Our mission in Amsterdam."

"Oh," she grimaced, "What the hell made you think about that during a time like now?"

"Just marveling at the home that I have here," he replied, his smile still in place.

Imani grunted in agreement.

The chants died down with Luke standing along the edge of the stage, kneeling with the rangers. Flynn's eyes widened.

Many of the factions stayed in their seats with flared wings. A few of the outpost's leaders stood off to the side with their arms crossed. Out of the hundreds of groups from different countries, not even half joined Luke by the stage.

Flynn frowned. He hoped to recruit more rangers to the cause, to give them a strong fighting chance. How was he supposed to return his cousin with maybe a thousand or so willing to fight? Flynn recounted the numbers. Ten thousand rangers lived within the human realm. Was there anything he could do to recruit more?

Panic settled in his stomach at their numbers. His wings ruffled. He opened his mouth to plea further but Luke beat him. Luke shouted the next instructions for those willing to follow. They all were to meet at midnight to teleport to Aqua Caput in the Spirit realm. Three horns would blow to announce the time for departure.

"All decisions will be respected." Luke gave him a pointed glance. "After all, we're fighting for free will when we march to Aqua Caput."

His stomach clenched at the mention of the city. He prayed Malachi held up his end of the bargain or else they were doomed. The Head Archs needed to unite for the upcoming battle. If Arakiel's intel was correct, Satan's army would make it to the portal by tomorrow night. He shuddered.

Her puppets worried him the most. Mikael, Matthew and Arick. All three skilled warrior angels. His mind flashed back to Atarah, Arick's younger sister. She'd been healing the last time he'd seen her.

His wings twitched, catching Imani's eye again.

"What's up?" Imani inquired, glancing back at him.

"Atarah," he whispered, with wide eyes. "I completely forgot about her."

Imani frowned. "What about her?"

"Could she hold off—"

"No." Imani interrupted. "She's not strong enough to go up against her father, uncle *and* brother."

"I'm not saying that," Flynn pinched his chin between two

fingers. "But what about distract one of them?"

"I doubt it, but it's worth a shot." Imani's frown deepened. "I feel sorry for the girl. She'll have to realize soon enough that she'll fight someone in her family."

"Hmmm," Flynn mumbled, his mind reeling. "Before disappearing, Arick mentioned that Atarah's growing stronger."

"Against regular, everyday Michael angels, sure. She's strong. An average Michael angel has the strength to lift a car here in the human realm." Imani scoffed and faced him. "But an Arch Michael can lift entire ships and cause earthquakes with a single punch. I don't think she's *that* strong yet."

Flynn sighed. "That's why her father and brother worry me so much. They could devastate us. I still think it's something we should consider."

"That's a lot to put on the poor girl."

Flynn glanced at the dwindling crowd of rangers who moved to pack their few items. Living a nomadic lifestyle created perks of mobility and ease. They'd be ready to move out soon. He glanced back at Luke, seeing a few surround him.

"Luke!" He called out, jogging to his side.

Imani quietly cursed before following him.

Luke's black eyes found him immediately. "Yes?"

Those around Luke quieted as Flynn approached. Rangers weren't ranked, but a few of them were natural born leaders. Jose and Sahra stuck out the most in the small circle.

"When we arrive at the summit meeting, I'd like to include Atarah in the discussion. She could be very valuable in the upcoming battle."

"Atarah?" Sahra chimed in from the small huddle. "I remember her."

"Same here," Jose interjected. "She was…nice from what I remember."

"I remember you reported she'd been severely injured," Luke frowned. "Have you heard from her since?"

Flynn shook his head.

"Then how do you know she'll be present?" Luke raised an eyebrow.

Flynn froze. The last place he'd seen her was in Malachi's villa. *Surely she was still there, right?* His wings twitched. *What if she'd gone back to her home region in Belli Causa?* He'd never be able to find the capital city.

He opened his mouth to respond but Imani beat him to it.

"We can find her if need be," Imani spoke out. "I'm familiar with her home region so she won't get far."

Luke's frown deepened, but he nodded. "Very well. She may be useful but we aren't putting our basket in eggs."

Imani's lips twitched. "The saying is all our eggs in one basket."

Luke huffed a laugh. "Tomato, Tamato."

Flynn bit his lip to resist a smile. Now wasn't the time.

"Now, get your things and figure out which weapon you'll bring." Luke raised a finger in the air. "Also, prepare yourselves mentally. Without our minds, we're nothing."

Imani pulled Flynn away before he could say anything else. Sahra and Jose followed behind them.

"Luke always says the wisest and strangest things." Jose shook his head.

"He's not wrong." Sahra sighed, peering at Flynn. "What are you bringing? The rest of us don't have enough spiritual energy to blast things through our fingers."

He shrugged. "Probably a bow and arrow. You?"

Sahra sighed, sending a gust of cold air in his direction. "Probably the same."

"I'm bringing my axe." Imani chimed in.

He raised an eyebrow. "It's fixed?"

Imani smiled. "Yep, finally! I'll never break it again."

"You should use a barbed net like I do." Jose interlocked his fingers behind his head. "Makes it easier to catch things."

"You won't need to catch demons running straight at you," Sahra pointed out.

Jose frowned. "Oh, you're right."

They walked behind the stadium where they left their packs.

"Switch to a sword or axe," Flynn drawled. "And definitely your shield."

"Should we leave our serums behind?" Sahra pulled out two vials from inside her pack.

Flynn paused for a moment before nodding. "It never hurts to bring them. They won't take up too much space anyway."

They fell quiet as they worked through their bags, picking what to bring and leave behind for now. Other rangers did the same all around the outside of the stadium. Hundreds more flew out to relay the message to the rest of their squads around the world. Hopefully, that would rally more rangers to fight with them when the horn blew at midnight.

A few hours more, he thought. A tingling sensation ran through his scalp.

"*I agree with you on the girl,*" Arakiel whispered inside his head.

Flynn jumped. The others looked from their bags with raised eyebrows.

"Nothing," he mumbled with a small wave. "It was nothing."

The others went back to their bags while Imani inclined her head with a small frown. He needed to keep it together if he was going to keep this secret.

"*Quiet!*" he shouted inside his head.

"*Oh, so you will speak to me,*" Arakiel murmured.

Flynn shook his head. He refused to say or "think" anything else.

"*Don't you want my expertise on this subject?*" Arakiel purred. "*After all, I know a thing or two about fighting Michael angels.*"

Flynn paused.

"*That's right, I heard you talking about fighting against*

the Michael Archs."

Flynn silently cursed. They did need all the help they could get.

"Yes, you do." Arakiel drawled.

Flynn resisted the urge to hang his head.

"What do you know?" he asked Arakiel.

"Let's lay some ground rules before I answer anything," Arakiel answered in a stern voice.

Flynn inwardly groaned. *Did he really have to deal with this?*

"For the rest of your life. Yes!" Arakiel growled. *"Now, will you finally give me the time of day or not?"*

Flynn gave the smallest of nods, looking around to ensure no one else saw his internal struggle.

"Rule number one: we have open and honest communication because you have no other choice," Arakiel started.

Alarm bells rang in Flynn's head. *"What do you mean by no other choice?"*

"I'm in your head," Arakiel explained. *"There's very little you can hide from me. When you sleep, I can explore the vastness of your mind and find old memories."*

"Have you done that already?"

"Not yet," Arakiel huffed. *"Next ground rule is that we have* equal *exchange of the body. You have control for a certain amount of hours and then I have control for the same amount."*

"Not gonna happen." Flynn narrowed his eyes. *"I can't let the other rangers know I'm possessed."*

"I'm trying to be polite here," Arakiel replied. *"I don't technically need your permission to take over."*

Flynn froze. *"What does that mean?"*

"It means if I have a strong enough resolve, I can take over the bodily functions."

"But if my resolve is strong, you can't."

"If we fight over the body, it'll be obvious to the rangers

that something's wrong with you, and you'll have no choice but to tell them."

He ground his teeth together. *"Fine, we'll try to keep the time as even as possible as long as you keep the secret as well!"*

"Agreed," Arakiel answered quickly. *"You see, that wasn't so hard."*

"Anything else?"

"Yes, one last thing. No purposely damaging the body. That includes bad health habits. No alcohol—"

"Wait, what?"

"Various drug substances and junk food," Arakiel continued without a hitch. *"It feels awful living inside an unhealthy body so WE are going to keep it as fit as a fiddle."*

Flynn pondered this for a moment. *"That does sound reasonable, but what about a celebratory drink or two?"*

"That's fine, I guess, but within reason." Arakiel shuddered inside their mind. *"Alcohol alters the control we have over our body so not too much."*

"Anything else, your highness?" Flynn scoffed, shaking his head.

"A decent conversation every now and then wouldn't hurt. I've had centuries of tortured silence, so any subject is on the table for discussion."

Flynn scowled. *"I'm not your friend. If you want conversations, go to someone else."*

"Testy, testy." Arakiel sighed. *"But beggars can't be choosers."*

"Now that the 'ground rules' are done," Flynn moved on. *"What do you know about fighting against Michael angels?"*

"Oooh, I wouldn't recommend it," Arakiel replied. *"It's like trying to charge against an elephant head first. Not a good idea, but the girl with the familial ties is a good psychological idea."*

"That's all you have?"

"*Look, every Michael angel's different with different strengths and weaknesses. Azazel was a Michael angel but his weakness was his speed. He was slower than many others.*"

"*Is Mikael slow?*" Flynn tilted his head, pondering.

"*It depends. Is he slower than that girl Atarah?*"

He raised his eyebrows. *That's it! We could use that to our advantage.*

"*Also, one more idea you should use.*"

"*Yeah?*" Flynn asked with caution.

"*Use the serums on them.*"

Flynn's wings flared and his whole body—his feet, his hands, the air in his lungs—froze.

"*The serum stops them from being about to use their powers. If the chit can get her father and brother to consume it—*" Arakiel continued.

"*We'd have the upper hand!*" Flynn finished.

"Flynn?" Sahra furrowed her brow. "Are you ok?"

He whirled around, eyes wide with excitement. "I have an idea!"

Imani leveled a concerned look. "What is it?"

"Pack as much serum as you can! We can use it against them!" Flynn said excitedly, unzipping his pack.

"Flynn, you—"

Three horns blared across the sky. All of their heads shot up to the stadium. He'd already run out of time? Had that many hours passed?

"Quick!" he said, lifting his lightened pack onto his chest. "Trust me and bring it! We can present this to everyone at the summit meeting as a plan to take them down."

Sahra and Jose exchanged a glance but nodded nonetheless. "Ok."

Imani placed a hand on his shoulder, stilling him.

"Hey!" She shook him slightly. "Remember to keep it together."

He put a hand on hers. "Don't worry, I've got it under

control."

After a beat, she nodded, releasing him from her grip.

"Let's move out!" someone yelled.

Everyone cheered, launching themselves into the sky and over the stadium's edge.

Flynn opened his wings wide and jumped into the air. His heart raced as the plan formed in his head. Anticipation built within him while the others followed behind, flying to the stadium.

Chapter 15

Cold water splashed against his face, bringing Azazel back to reality. He jerked awake, sputtering and coughing. His shackles' jingle rang through the air as he wiped his face. The cold desert wind cut through his thin blanket without mercy.

"Ughhh," Arick groaned. *"What the hell's going on?"*

"I don't know yet, kid."

He looked to his left. Mikael sat chained beside him, still asleep. His wings slumped in relief. *Good, the kid's dad is safe.*

Arick gruntled in their shared mind. *"I haven't had a chance to talk to him yet. I need to tell him I'm sorry and so much more."*

"Not now, kid," Azazel grumbled. *"It's not safe."*

Following their conversation with Satan, they were chained to a post near two adjacent curtain-draped rooms for the night. One held Satan's sleeping quarters while the other led outside.

"Now then," a high-pitched voice startled him.

He blinked, his vision blurred and obscured by fog. He had to rub his eyes a few times before she'd come into focus.

Satan stood with an empty bucket in her hands and a smirk stretched across her face. Her long nails scraped against the bucket as she tossed it to the side.

"Glad you're awake. It's time to get ready for the day. Soon, we'll arrive at the portal site and between now and then, you—" Satan pointed a manicured finger at him. "—will tell me all about what my brothers have said."

Her green eyes narrowed at him.

Fog drifted into his mind and shrouded his thoughts. A warm, fuzzy feeling washed over him, giving him the sudden urge to confide in her. Satan wasn't so bad…right? She took them into her tent and sheltered them for the night.

"Hey! Hey!" Arick shouted. *"Stop that! She literally tortured and chained you- I mean us- to a post!"*

"But being inside kept us warm."

"Stop downplaying how awful she is!" Arick growled. *"Get rid of this fog!"*

Azazel blinked a few times, shaking his head. Some of the fog in his mind cleared, leaving only wisps of smoke. The odd, fuzzy feeling from earlier shifted back to his normal senses. His body ached and groaned in protest. While his injuries were healed, his body hurt from exhaustion. Her powers acted as a drug, dimming the pain and the severity of the situation. They were still captives in her army, forced to march across the desert.

The kid's right, he thought. *She's using her powers again.*

"Yeah," Arick replied. *"Without me, you'd be screwed."*

Satan scowled at him as his gaze focused back on her. Mikael squirmed from where he lay, waking up. Mikael's eyes locked onto his, scanning him—Arick's body—for injuries before facing Satan.

"You—" Satan lifted a finger at Mikael. "—will be in the front lines when we cross the border. Your assignment is to destroy Belli Causa's defenses, drawing the people out of the mountains and into the open."

She commanded with a hand on her hip, her expression bored and matter-of-fact. Mikael's face paled.

"Matthew will join you later on." Satan pivoted back to Azazel with a more determined look. "You'll tell me what you know or die."

The absoluteness of her tone sent shivers down his spine. He doubted she'd keep him alive once he'd served his purpose. She couldn't control him, like the others, which made him obsolete in her eyes. Information was the only thing he leveraged. He didn't suffer for so long to find a body to call home only to have her kill him. They needed to make a break for it at the first opportunity, but how?

She clapped her hands, peering at the other servants over her shoulder.

"Chop chop! I don't have all day. Get these two ready for the march ahead." She snapped her fingers. "Have Matthew get my carrier ready too."

Hands yanked him forward and jerked him into a standing position. Servants in red robes flurried around the tent, packing different items.

With a harsh shove, he was pushed outside. The sun hadn't passed over the horizon yet, leaving the stars twinkling in the sky. A faint glow in the distance was the only clue to dawn approaching.

Hundreds of troop and elder formations littered the ground. A horn blared somewhere behind him, alerting the others it was time to move out. A grunt followed by a thud drew his attention.

Mikael had fallen on one knee and an angry guard jerked at the chains around his wrist. Azazel eyed where Mikael's hand had been cut off. The stump looked red and puffy, and it oozed a mixture of yellow puss and blood.

Azazel frowned. Mikael needed medical attention. He didn't have the same healing capabilities as Arick.

"We gotta get him to Mom when we escape through the portal," Arick chimed in.

"No," Azazel drawled. *"We gotta solidify a plan to escape first."*

"And stop her army from going through!"

"One thing at a time kid." Azazel sighed. *"There's only*

one of us."

"Two," Arick corrected.

"Well, it's one body kid."

"Do you actually know anything useful or were you just bullshitting her to buy us some time?"

"A combination of both. Her brothers don't want her to follow through with this plan. But I'll have to embellish some details to keep her occupied."

"They know about her plan?"

"Kinda. They know how ambitious she is and how much she wants to expand her own territory and reach."

"Maybe we can recruit them to our cause."

"Naw, kid. It doesn't work that way."

"Then what's your plan?"

"Our plan is to stay alive."

"What about my dad and family at home?" Arick exclaimed.

"Are you sure we need to help them? I mean they've pretty much turned their backs on you since you're a halfling."

Images of Atarah, Canaan and Noah fighting to help Arick flashed through his mind. They believed in him and who he was.

"No!" Arick shouted.

Memories and hurt of the night before flashed by, including the harshness of Mikael's words.

"Ok, ok," Azazel answered.

Azazel scanned the distance, spotting the mountain range. They were close to the portal site. His goal since Arick ventured into the demon realm was getting to that portal, but now he dreaded every step. He peered behind him. Easily 10,000 soldiers and maybe a hundred elders marched with them. Their eyes glazed over, stuck in whatever vision she'd created.

"My plan is…well it's barely a plan at all," he started, *"I keep her busy with gossip I remember her brothers saying, then create a distraction. Once the distraction happens, we—"*

"We run?" Arick beat him to the punch.

"Yeah, kid." He sighed. *"We run 'cause we're not winning by staying around."*

"What about my dad?" He heard the alarm in Arick's voice and winced.

"We could take him and run, but kid—"

"There has to be a way!"

"Kid, if she puts him under another illusion, there's nothing we can do."

"We could get him away—" Arick argued.

"We could take him to the far corners of the realms and it still wouldn't break the vision." Azazel frowned. *"Your dad will fight you the whole way too. You gotta face it, kid. The only thing we can do is to save ourself."*

"Isn't there a medicine or something? My dad isn't gonna become like Matthew!" Arick yelled.

"Kid!"

"I'm not gonna lose my dad next!"

A sharp pain pierced his chest as images flashed through their mind. Memories of Atarah's face, full of shock, as a dagger plunged into her heart. Another popped up of Mikael cradling Arick, comforting him after her body became lost in the rubble.

A deep ache developed in his chest, restricting his airflow. His breathing grew labored and a strange tingling sensation traveled down his legs. The feeling of numbness while hyper-aware of his body clashed. His heart galloped. *Was Arick fighting for control?* He wondered.

"No," he realized. *"His body's reacting to his distress."*

"Distressed? Distressed?!" Arick scoffed. *"That's all you're gonna call it?! I've lost over half my family right before my eyes! My home region—No, the entire world I grew up in—will see me as a monster because of something I couldn't control!"*

"Arick, calm down!"

"SCREW YOU!" Arick bellowed in their mind. *"I've lost everything and all you can say is calm down?"*

He winced. *"You're right, kid. You have every reason to despair right now. Every right. But there's no way to your dad unless I get him away from Satan before she casts another illusion on him."*

A beat of silence passed before a calmer-sounding Arick spoke.

"Then that's what we need to do." Arick's voice sounded thick with emotion.

"She's shackling him to her travel carriage," he reasoned.

"During the distraction." Arick elaborated. *"We free him, make our escape, then–"*

"On your feet!" a harsh voice commanded.

A rough jerk pulled him to his feet. An elder pushed him closer to the travel carriage, Mikael already chained and gagged. Matthew waited for them with open cuffs in his palms.

"Remove the old ones, so I can attach these," Matthew said, devoid of any emotion.

The elder completed his work quickly before scurrying off. Matthew secured the cuffs, tightening them to the point of pain. Azazel searched his face for any sign of self-awareness or *something*.

A faint light in Matthew's dark, golden eyes flickered. A muscle twitched along his jaw but otherwise he remained expressionless.

"Are you really on her side?" Azazel whispered, after ensuring no one was close.

A hard jab to the side brought him to his knees. His ribs creaked from the attack, and his breath stopped. His wings curled in as if to protect him. Another shove knocked his head into one of the poles along her carrier.

"Keep your mouth shut, *watcher!*" Matthew hissed. "We'll reach the portal in a few hours so don't try anything stupid."

Azazel tucked his head under his wings. Tenderly, he prodded along his forehead, feeling a new bump form but no blood. His restraints gave him enough length to touch his head but nothing more. Breathing turned into a chore after such a punch, but it was worth the information.

"What information?" Arick asked, his thoughts sounded scattered and chaotic.

"Matthew said we have a few hours to figure out how to escape and grab your dad."

Satan burst through her tent folds in a new outfit. This one dressed her from the neck down in a green, embroidered dress with two slits running up the sides to her hip. The fabric drifted in the wind as she sauntered to them.

"Leave that part of the plan to me while you keep her occupied," Arick said with more confidence.

"I'd rather have your job," Azazel drawled with sarcasm.

Satan used the elders' backs to climb aboard the carrier. Cushions, drapes, and various pillows lined the center along with a tray of fruits and snacks. Once she settled into her seat, the whole campsite fell silent. Everyone looked to her, breath held, waiting for her next command.

"Forward!" She shouted, her eyes flashing green for a second.

With that, four large elders lined the sides, lifted the carrier, and marched. The chain attaching him to the post pulled him, forcing him to keep up with the pace the elders set.

"Now talk," Another command from Satan caused the hair on the back of his neck to stand. "What did my brothers say?"

"Well," Azazel started. "To begin with, Beelzebub sounded the least pleased with the idea of you expanding your territory."

Satan scoffed. "He probably wants it all for himself."

"While Leviathan was harder to read on the matter," Azazel recalled the demon lord's behavior. "He was high at the time of the conversation."

"Figures." She scoffed again. "What else have they said about me?"

"Tell her something gossipy that'll keep her mind rolling," Arick whispered.

"Remember kid, you don't need to whisper in our mind. No one can hear us except the Selaphiel angels."

"Oh, right."

"What else, *watcher*? I'm not a patient woman."

"Your biggest threat may be Leviathan," he continued. "He plans on rehabilitating the halfling population stuck in between the domains. In helping them, that creates a loyalty to him rather than to you or Beelzebub."

"Rehabilitating them?" Satan raised an eyebrow. "What do you mean?"

"He's providing them shelter, food, and resources. An admirable trait from afar but possibly self-serving in the long run." He huffed, his breathing picking up as they marched uphill.

"He's helping those weak halflings?" She scrunched her nose in disgust.

"You don't like halflings?"

"I don't like weak ones. The ones like the body you're occupying are nice, but most of them are useless since they don't have the full strength or utility from either side." She sighed. "Certain halflings have their uses. If he is—what did you call it—rehabilitating certain halflings, are there more than others?"

"I mostly saw halflings of aquatic descent. Many have tail fins and small wings on their backs." Azazel panted.

The terrain changed, from sinking sand to firm clay. The mountains grew closer but no trees were in sight to provide shade as they moved uphill.

Satan narrowed her eyes. "I can't tell if he's fooling around again or onto something genius."

"Neither could I," Azazel murmured.

"What about Beelzebub?" Satan leaned back, bringing a hand to her chin. "Did he have the same…disposition to the halflings as Leviathan?"

Azazel shook his head. "No, he's selling them for profit… he's making a lot of money from them. More money than I thought."

"That's 'cause he stole *my* idea," Satan hissed. "It was me who came up with using the halflings as slaves and servants, not him!"

"It was you?" Azazel mentally rolled his eyes.

How many fools thought they'd created something original?

"It was!" She yelled, clenching her fist together. "And he took that from me!"

"Are you seeking revenge against him for that?" A hint of surprise leeched into his voice.

Was she really that…petty?

"It's the principle." Satan pierced him with a glare. "If he's going to take something small; always assume they'll take something bigger next."

"What a…way to live."

Satan scoffed. "You don't have the slightest clue what it means to be us."

Her illusion wavered, rippling like an image in water. Her elongated nose peeked through for a second before the original image was back in place. For a moment, he stared at her, mystified and jaw-slacked. What would she look like if she let herself go? Would she look monstrous or beautiful?

"Were you…?" Azazel froze, his blood running cold.

Crap, he'd almost asked a stupid question. A question that would get him killed if she was in the right mood.

"Was I what?" A muscle in her jaw flexed. "I told you before, I'm not patient."

"Nothing!" he answered quickly. "It was a stupid question."

"Dammit," Satan huffed. "Stupid or not, now I need to know! Say your question or I'll have you killed."

"I've always wondered why you possessed only one ability compared to your brothers," Azazel rushed out. "Were you unplanned?"

Her eyes widened and a ripple of wind blew across the sands in a large gust. Azazel lifted his arms to shield his eyes against the flying sand.

"She has parents?" Arick asked incredulously. *"Never really thought about it before, but probably a dumb question to ask her."*

"No shit, kid!" Azazel grunted, lifting his wings against the wind.

As suddenly as it began, the wind died on the spot without any inkling of return. He peered past his arm to see Satan in her carrier. Though her face remained expressionless, her image rippled and wavered. Flashes of furry ears or a long nose popped out every few seconds only to retreat behind the illusion again. She stared ahead with glowing eyes, not answering his question.

The question had hit its mark.

His heart pounded as he waited for her to lash out against him. However, she sat stoically with a distorted face for an hour. The blazing sun and steep hike upward provided a small distraction from the waiting. She didn't speak or look at him, churning his stomach into knots with each step.

"Crap, crap, crap, crap." He swallowed. *"She's gonna kill us, kid. She gonna wait until we're least expecting it and snatch our head off."*

He peered from the corner of his eye to watch her, sweat dripping down his face.

"We still have a chance," Arick replied. *"She looks distracted."*

"No! She looks...disturbed or upset, I think."

"Either way—"

"Stop here!" Satan commanded in a shrill voice.

He jumped, watching her. Everyone else screeched to a halt.

"We're here!" she yelled out, standing.

He whirled his head around. Just ahead of them, a large, blazing portal sat on one of the mountain peaks. With the high winds and rugged terrain, he'd nearly missed it. The red sand stretched for miles on one side of the mountain while green fields painted the ground on the other half.

"We're out of time, kid!" Azazel yelled, gripping his chains. *"What's the plan?"*

"Move over."

"Wha—"

He felt a sharp yank on his consciousness peeling him away from the body, like ripping off a bandaid. His mind switched to a black nothingness before getting his bearings. A weightlessness washed over him while his mind focused back on Arick.

"Kid!" He groaned. *"That's not part of the plan!"*

"Uggggghhhh, shit," Arick groaned. *"My body does feel like crap."*

"Switch back with me now!" Azazel pushed himself to the forefront of their mind but a thick and heavy concrete wall crashed down on him. *"What the hell kid? How did—"*

"I learned it when you forced the switch when we woke in her camp days ago." Arick shot a mental smirk his way. *"Now, let's break out of these."*

"Kid those chains are made from the strongest metal—"

A creak followed by a resounding snap stopped Azazel in his tracks. He watched as Arick broke the chains with a grunt before darting over to his father. Arick dashed around the other guards so fast, they didn't see him until it was too late.

"Dad!"

Arick grabbed Mikael roughly by the collar and jerked him forward while slamming his heel into the chain. The restraints snapped with a loud crunch, pulling Satan from her fugue state and into action.

"Stop that halfling!" She yelled her eyes glowing green.

Arick was on the move, hauling himself and Mikael up the last few boulders to the portal. With one arm holding Mikael, Arick climbed with the other. Azazel pushed against the wall Arick erected.

"*You gotta hurry through the portal, kid!*" he strained.

Looking through Arick's eyes yet having no control over the body sent chills throughout his soul. This feeling of helplessness and restraint brought back horrors best left in the past.

Arick glanced back to see Matthew charging at full speed.

"*Time to try out the wings,*" Arick grunted.

"*Weren't they damaged??*" Azazel asked bewildered.

"*Yep!*"

Arick stretched out his wings and flapped hard to the portal. Intense pain broke through the mental blockade Arick set up, freeing him. Electric agony sizzled their back with each wing flap. Their ribs ached and groaned at the stress Arick put on them to move.

"*Hell, kid!*" Azazel hissed against the pain radiating throughout their body. "*We could pass out from this!*"

"*Not yet! We're almost there!*" Arick strained.

As Azazel pushed further for control, more senses came back. The copper taste of blood filled his mouth. Their racing heartbeat threatened to explode. Using Arick's eyes, he peered over his shoulder. His eyes widened.

Matthew flew behind them, his arm reaching for them with a thunderous expression on his face. Arick whirled their head forward again.

"*There! The portal's right there!*" He flapped his wings one more time, rocketing them forward.

"Kill that halfling brat!" Satan's shrill voice echoed. "Kill him!"

Azazel gasped, giving one last glance behind him as the

portal's light consumed them. Heat and light tunneled their vision, focusing on Satan's glowing green eyes and her triumphant smirk.

"Oh shit, kid."

They tumbled through the portal as if sucked under dangerous rapids. Tremendous pressure and chaos awaited them once they landed.

Chapter 16

Malachi watched the subtle changes in everyone's faces: the shock, the confusion, and worse—the fear that grew within each of them. After he'd explained his part of the tale, Elijah gave his side next. Followed by Sewall and then Fatima and Atarah.

Now back at his villa outside of the city, they waited in the dining hall for the rangers to arrive. While he paced, many clung to their loved ones. Charlotte and Ava clasped a hand on either side of Atarah, ensuring she couldn't leave. Canaan and Amos deadlocked in a private, mind-reading conversation. Sewall and Fatima sat next to each other, silent other than the sound of occasionally pouring wine into Fatima's glass. Joshua joined him in his pacing route, murmuring Barmen's name every so often.

He'd asked Tariel and Farah to keep the halfling children occupied on the opposite side of the villa for now. He would come to an arrangement with Elijah about where Rhea and her little group's boundaries would be later. Until then, he turned to his daughter and current heir for the time.

Isabella curled in on herself as if sensing his gaze. She hadn't relaxed since he'd spoken about Clarissa's predicament. A gust of wind flurried around her, ruffling her feathers and hair. He swallowed his frustration with his daughters. Isabella and Clarissa couldn't be more opposite. Isabella looked like a lost lamb with eyes begging for guidance while Clarissa couldn't wait for him to leave.

Flames flickered through his veins, threatening to sprout from his arms. Why couldn't Clarissa be more like Isabella and ask for more guidance? Why couldn't Isabella be more like Clarissa and be more independent? He'd have the perfect heir if he could combine the two of them.

He shook his head, running a hand through his hair. He vowed that once they were all back at home, he'd stop ignoring them. He'd address their faults and work on a solution later. Much later.

He was so tired of everything coming down on his shoulders. The upcoming battle with Satan hung over his head like a loaded weapon. A shudder ran along his spine.

He silently prayed the rangers were having a better time.

Sewall, Elijah, and Joshua sent messages back to their regions, ordering their citizens closer to the Head Tree's barrier and preparing for a siege. He ran a hand through this hair again and groaned. His people didn't have the same kind of protection as the others. The Head Tree had been decimated after Matthew's first attack.

His people had no shield or proper defense structures to withstand the oncoming attacks. How was he going to keep them safe? Elijah offered his city, Ventus, as a sanctuary, an easier hike than to Chrysi Poli or Mortem. A pang of sorrow cut through his chest. He had no other choice but to accept the help of others.

"Servant!" he yelled. A scrawny angel ran into the room, eyes wide and wings flared. He couldn't remember his name but that wasn't important. "Bring me some pen and paper."

"Right away, Sir!" He scrambled out of the room in a hurry. He returned within the minute, carrying a stack of blank paper and over a dozen pens in his hand. "Is this enough, Sir?"

Malachi nodded and dismissed him with a jerk of his chin.

Once the servant left, he grabbed one sheet and started on the protocol to evacuate his people. Writing as fast as he could.

"Your offer still stands, right, Elijah?" He paused his pen an inch off the page, looking at the Arch.

"Yes," Elijah nodded, pointing to the paper. "I need to send Noah a message to prepare the extra shelters."

He passed Elijah a sheet while scribbling his final commands out. He seared his thumbprint on the bottom to serve as his signature.

"I need to gather the soldiers in Sanctum." Atarah chimed in, standing from her chair. "As the only heir within the realm, it's my job to lead."

"Atarah!" Ava protested. "You're too young to—"

A loud crackle resonated through the room. They all froze before turning to the head of the table. A faint, crackling light glowed, starting off small before expanding into a large, blazing portal.

The rangers had arrived.

"Everyone!" Malachi called out. "Open the balcony doors and move outside."

They all scrambled out of their chairs. Isabella dashed to the other side of the room, yanking the floor-to-ceiling glass doors open to expand the area to the outside balcony. Malachi grunted as he tried to push the table to the side of the room, opening more space for their reinforcements.

Atarah noticed his struggle and shoved the table with one hand. The table shot to the far wall as if she'd pushed a book instead of a 400-lb, solid-wood dining table. His jaw dropped.

Right, he thought. He'd forgotten she was Mikael's daughter, but had she always been so strong? He hadn't been the only one surprised by her strength.

Ava's eyes widened. "You really have gotten stronger."

Atarah glanced at her hand. "Farah thinks it's because of all of the near-death experiences. It's forced my body to rebuild and regrow stronger than before."

Malachi opened his mouth to speak but motion at the portal caught his attention. They faced it, wings flared. Luke was the first one to step through, followed by Flynn. The others that followed all blurred, his focus sharpening to Flynn with an excited glow in his eye.

He waited to greet them until more arrived, but the air in his lungs stalled. As the portal closed, he guessed no more than a thousand rangers filled the room. Where were the rest of them? He knew the rangers' numbers marked in the tens of thousands. Were they coming later? Was there a delay?

His stomach knotted and his wings trembled. Where were the reinforcements?

He whirled.

"What in the Trinity is this Flynn?" Malachi scoffed with his hands raised. "I thought you said you'd rally the troops."

Flynn stiffened, with flared wings but it was Luke who spoke.

"This was as many who were willing to fight for the 'selfish, ungrateful spaceheads,'" Luke drawled.

His eyes darkened, and a shadow twirled around Luke's fingers as he stepped closer.

Luke leaned in close to his face. "Don't prove their point by belittling those who showed up."

Malachi ground his teeth together, flaring his wings. *Damn, this ranger*. He possessed every right to be upset.

"If I'd known the support would be so…*lacking* I wouldn't of—"

"Malachi." Flynn glared at him, with sparks dancing along his fingers. "Think of the alternative! For once, think of others before you speak."

He blew out a long breath, steam bellowing from his nostrils as he willed himself to relax. A small movement caught his eye. Isabella's wings twitched nervously watching them. A gust of wind blew around her, picking up speed as the silence stretched. His wings lowered. Another beat of silence and a stare-off between him, Luke, and Flynn, before he jerked away.

"Servant!" he yelled out.

The young boy scurried around the rangers and to his side.

"Please escort these rangers to the city and have the different groups stationed with each principality. While we're in the meeting." He handed the young angel the paper he'd written. "Have the rangers evacuate my people and head north to the city of Ventus. Tell them all we are expecting another demon attack soon."

The young angel's face paled.

"Ar—are you sure sir?" The angel stuttered.

He nodded.

"The attack will happen soon and my people need to get to safety first."

"Yes, sir!"

A few of the rangers close enough to see them scoffed, shooting disgusted looks his way. Flynn flapped up into the air.

"Rangers!" Flynn yelled above the chatter. He divided the groups, withholding a handful for himself. "Follow this man to the city and help evacuate the citizens. We'll catch up to everyone when we finish here and give an update!"

The looks on the rangers' faces varied from reluctance to admiration when Flynn spoke. A tinge of jealousy spiked through him at the attention Flynn held, but he squashed it. Now wasn't the time. Precious minutes ticked by as the rangers filed out, flying into the air. Malachi hovered by the balcony edge, soothed by the ocean breeze. Finally, a dozen or so rangers were left; however, they'd surely give him a headache.

"Flynn and Luke," he grunted to them. "Pleasure as always."

Luke grinned, taking in the surroundings before stopping at Atarah.

"You!" Luke's eyebrows shot up to his hairline. "You're

alive!"

Atarah chuckled. "Barely, each time."

A woman, Malachi vaguely remembered her name to be Imani, spoke. "Good on you. We'd thought the worst when Flynn said you hadn't woken up yet."

"Oh," Charlotte chimed in, with a hand on her hip and the corner of her lip twitching. "That was the first coma she was in. She's recently come out of a second coma after Matthew attacked again."

Luke's eyes widened. "He doesn't seem to like you much."

Atarah chuckled. "No one seems to like him."

"And Arick?" Flynn stepped closer, his eyes narrowed. "Any word about him?"

Tears sprung to Ava's eyes.

"No other news since he and Mikael were taken." Her voice came out thick and wavered.

"I'm sorry to hear that." Flynn frowned, pivoting around. "What has been done so far?"

The Head Archs gathered closer. Joshua spoke first.

"Barmen and some of the other heirs stayed back in the demon realm." Joshua sighed."They're going to *talk* with Beelzebub again."

Luke jumped, while Flynn's eyebrows shot up.

"Again?" they asked in unison.

Malachi nodded while pinching the bridge of his nose. "Many heirs have been making pit stops in the demon realm."

"It sounds like you've all been busy. What else?" Flynn murmured.

"We sent the word out," he answered, pulling everyone's attention. "I'm evacuating my people while the others are ordering their citizens closer to their Head Tree."

"Have you called for any troops yet?" Flynn flickered between the Archs.

"Not yet," Atarah stepped forward. "As the only Michael heir, I need to be in Sanctum and gather our forces."

"No—" Ava protested.

"Absolutely, you do!" Luke cheered, lifting both arms. "According to our watcher, the portal will open in Belli Causa so we should be flying to Sanctum now!"

Atarah's eyes bulged.

"She's bringing her army and Matthew to Sanctum first?" She stammered, her voice quivering.

Her mother paled. "They're attacking again."

"That's where the portal connects. Their portal aligns with our world that way. Additionally, it's the closest portal to Satan's domain. Otherwise, she'd contest with her brothers." Flynn paused, tilting his head to one side. "That…that explains why she wanted the Michael family under her control. She knew it'd be her first stop."

"I'll have to face…my father, brother, and uncle while under her control? How can we break it?" Atarah asked, wings trembling.

They all turned to Joshua.

"That's a great question," Malachi sighed. "How would we break her illusion, Joshua?"

Joshua frowned and sighed, clasping his hands behind his back.

"The short answer is you can't. Only the caster can break the illusion once it's taken hold. However, there are exceptions." He pointed to Amos. "A Selaphiel angel would have an easier time breaking free of an illusion."

He lowered his hand.

"Additionally, the condition of the receiver's mind plays a role as well." Joshua tapped a finger to his temple. "Take me for example. Without my medication, my mind will start to distort reality and many things become unclear. She can't cast an illusion on me because my mind is—"

"Already too messed up," Sewall interrupted, crossing his arms.

Joshua flexed his jaw. "That's a bit crass, but yes. Sadly,

there's little we can do once the illusion's cast."

"What about me?" Elijah stepped forward. "I can—"

"The mind can't be mended by the wave of a hand." Joshua scowled. "It's complex and delicate."

"So nothing can be done?" Atarah's voice quivered. "I'll have to fight against my family?"

A gust of wind swirled around them. He glanced over his shoulder to see Isabella curling her wings around her as if to shield herself. She tugged a strand of her hair around her fingers, fidgeting.

"Not alone," Luke chimed in. "We'll all be there to stop the onslaught of her army."

"I need to get home." Atarah flared her wings. "Do we know where her army is currently?"

Flynn shook his head. "The last update we received was that her army was three days from the portal."

"How long ago was that report?" Elijah asked.

"Three days ago." Flynn frowned.

Everyone's wings flared. The wind picked up speed. Atarah screamed something but Malachi couldn't hear her over the blood roaring in his ears. His flames ignited from his belly, spreading to his arms and legs. The demon wench was practically right on top of them!

"You're only now telling us this?" he yelled at his cousin.

Flynn flinched but Luke stepped forward.

"If we'd told you from the start, you would've panicked. No other Head Archs were present, and we needed someone to bring them home while we gathered the troops." Luke narrowed his black eyes at him, sending a small shiver down his spine. "Flynn took the best course of action."

He blew out a breath of steam through his nostrils once more. The fire in Malachi's body flickered at the edge of his skin, ready to burst forward.

"Move out now!" Amos commanded Canaan. They opened their wings wide. "We'll meet you in Belli Causa with our soldiers as fast as possible."

Amos lifted into the sky.

"Malachi." Sewall stepped closer. "Fatima's getting my daughter now before we fly out. However, I'll be sending my troops north as soon as we land."

"Wait, wait, wait." He raised his hand. Other than the rangers, he had no defenses. "I—"

"First things first!" Gabriel Sr. clapped his hands; a crackling sound came from his glowing hands. "Atarah, I'll open a portal for you to return to Belli Causa, but Luke's right. You can't go alone."

"I'll go!" Isabella and Charlotte said in unison.

Elijah froze, his wings faltered as if unsure.

Malachi whirled around, flames sprouting from his head. "You can't!"

Isabella flinched.

"Y-y-yes I can!" The wind swirled around her at high speed; a faint tornado could be made out around her figure. "I-I-I've fought there once and I can do it again."

"Bella, don't be daft," he scoffed. "You need your sister before you can go anywhere."

"No! I need *her* help in this fight." Atarah stepped closer to Isabella, ignoring the growing tornado around her. "Please come, Isabella."

Isabella's wings twitched before she jutted out her chin. "Yes, I can do this."

He opened his mouth to protest but Joshua cut him off by putting a hand on his shoulder. He glared over his shoulder to see Joshua curse under his breath.

"Dammit, I'd forgotten how hot you can get," Joshua huffed, shaking out his hand. "I suggest we all return home to send our troops north. In the meantime, you and Isabella should join Atarah on the front lines of battle."

"Why is it always me who gets dragged into the thick of things?!" he growled, a few more fires sprouting along his shoulders.

"Your people are being escorted now to Silva, and it'd be pointless for you to stay here. Up in Belli Causa, you can buy us time to send more troops."

Bitterness filled his mouth.

"The same amount of time it took for all of *you* to send your aid? The last time there was an attack, no one made it! My city lies in ruins because of your tardiness!"

Sewall stepped forward. "It is not like that this time. We were all struggling. Now we can all unite and attack together."

"Cousin," Flynn's tone was soft. He had both arms raised. "I'll go instead and use my fire there so you can lead your people to safety."

Malachi ground his teeth together for a minute; the sting of past failures faded as he took another calming breath. He didn't like the thought of Isabella alone but with Flynn, maybe he could trust her.

"Very well," he grumbled. "I'll go north with my people to Silva."

"I'll join Atarah!" another voice joined.

Tariel marched forward with the halfling children following after her. Farah hovered behind them, clutching Jack.

"I'll fight against those demons."

Sewall's face turned thunderous. "You absolutely will *not*!"

"Yes, *we* will," Fatima stepped past the door, closing it firmly behind her. "And *you* will return home to bring the troops."

Sewall paled.

"My shadow…" he whispered. "No, I can't."

His shadow tendrils wrapped around her shadow. Fatima clasped his face between her hands, bringing his forehead to hers.

"My shadow," she murmured. "You can. Remember our promise: we'll always return to each other. In this life and in the afterlife."

She gently pulled his head back to look into his eyes.

A sharp pain lacerated Malachi's heart as he watched the Azrael couple. *Liliana*...His wings curled in on himself as the tender memories damaged him.

Sewall's wings trembled. "For you, I can do anything."

His shadows unraveled from hers with reluctance.

"It appears I'll need to open a few more portals," Gabriel grunted, cracking his knuckles. "It's been a while since I've had to open so many. One for Belli Causa, another one for Mortem, and.."

"Silva!" Malachi chimed in quickly. He whirled to Flynn. "My people could get to Silva faster through the portal."

Flynn exchanged a glance with his brethren. Imani stepped forward.

"I'll stay behind with you to direct everyone through the portal." Imani volunteered.

"The rest of us will go fight," Luke exclaimed. "We've been inching for a fight."

"It's itching, not inching for a fight." Imani corrected.

Luke waved a hand. "Tomato, potato."

"Very well. The last portal will be to Silva," Gabriel grunted, spreading his hands apart. Sweat fell from his brow as two glowing circles grew. "I'll make the three after I close these two. The one on the left is to Belli Causa and the one on the right is to Mortem."

After one last tender embrace with his wife and a kiss on the head for his daughter, Sewall jumped through the portal leading him home, followed by Farah and Jack. The portal promptly closed as soon as he passed, leaving only one option left.

Atarah leapt through first, followed by Charlotte. Ava hung back, her brow furrowed as she turned to her father.

"What about you?" She asked in a low voice.

Elijah's face softened as he reached for the halflings behind Tariel. "I'll return to Silva and settle Malachi's people as well as these young ones."

He picked up Bugs. Rhea, behind Elijah, held Alan, who glared at everyone. Both looked wary.

"Once they're settled, I'll go help on the front lines." Elijah finished.

"I'll go with you." Ava gave a half-grin and spoke to the halflings. "I'll show you the best places and make sure you're all safe."

She glanced once at her father, offering a small, reassuring smile.

Tariel and Fatima jumped through next, holding onto each other's hand. Leaving Isabella and Flynn to go through next. More wind swirled around her body, throwing her hair in all sorts of directions.

Her hands shook but she clasped them together as she walked to the portal. Malachi's eyes widened as he recognized the look on her face. A mixture of doubt and determination shone in her eyes, an expression he'd seen on Liliana's face many times before. He wandered after her in a daze. His chest ached as more memories of Liliana drifted through his mind.

"R-r-ready?" Isabella asked Flynn, breaking Malachi's fugue state.

Flynn grinned and patted her head. "We're ready."

A swift flash of irritation washed over him. His flames threaten to burst through his skin at the brutal reminder of loss.

"Go," Malachi barked, feeling bad when she flinched.

The wind picked up speed around her, lifting her and catapulting her into the portal, leaving him behind. Flynn and the other rangers followed suit without a backward glance. As the light engulfed them, Elijah leaned over to whisper in his ear.

"Take it from me," Elijah murmured. "Don't push your daughters too hard."

More irritation fanned the flames in his veins until a spark flew along his fingertips.

"I'll parent the way *I* want to parent," he mumbled, watching Elijah, Ava and the halflings launch into the portal leading to Silva.

That old geezer and him weren't the same and neither were their daughters.

Now it was just him, Imani, and the rangers left to lead the people to Gabriel's portal. He ran a hand through his hair. *One more task*, he thought to himself. *One more.*

He turned to Imani, opening his mouth to give a command but froze. His eyes widened as something stepped out of the shadows and into the light. The sound of sloshing water echoed in his ears.

"What?" Imani cried out, following his gaze.

Gabriel's portal fizzled out as he whirled around. His wings flared.

"Who is *that*?" Gabriel raised an eyebrow.

"Oh?" Paul's dark laugh echoed around them.

Paul stepped into the light on the balcony, donned in an emerald green robe. *His* emerald green robe, which signified him as the Head Archangel. His heart pounded in his chest and his blood roared. A sharp stab of betrayal hit his heart as he stared at his half-brother.

"I'm the new Head Arch angel of the Uriel Clan." Paul's eyes glittered as he grinned. "I told you, Malachi. You'd be sorry if you didn't bring Clarissa back to me."

The water crescendoed around them. Imani gasped as the ocean waves lifted into the air, in tandem with Paul's raised hands. The water loomed over them, like a dark force about to crush them.

"Don't do this, Paul," Malachi pleaded, calling his fire to his hands.

Paul widened his eyes, feigning the look of innocence.

"I didn't do anything," Paul purred. "I'm simply doing what's best for the people, my people." Paul chuckled, darkly.

"You can't even bring your own daughter back home. That's how useless you are."

Sweat fell down his brow.

"Paul!" Malachi yelled. "Now's not the time to start a coup. Our people are in danger! Satan and her army are nearly here!"

"Oh, I know."

Malachi paused, and his jaw dropped. Paul's grin widened.

"I cut a deal with her brother, Beelzebub. Giving him the free labor of our people while he promised us protection from Satan."

Malachi's eyes widened. "You sold our people out…to slavery to betray me?"

Surely he wasn't that daft or reckless.

Paul cackled. "Our people will be grateful I've kept them safe, unlike *you*."

"Dear Trinity," Gabriel mumbled. "He's insane."

"He's a traitor!" Imani spat.

"All that's left to do is for you and Clarissa to die." Paul clenched his fist.

He blared his flames high and hot. Imani screamed while Gabriel attempted to make another portal.

"Take cover!" He bellowed before Paul slammed the 50-foot wave on top of their heads.

His flames extinguished.

Chapter 17

Flynn scanned the infamous living mountains that shifted every few hours to ensure Sanctum's defense.

Maybe Malachi should incorporate that into Caput's infrastructure during the rebuild. He spotted the others with ease and flew over to them. Atarah flew ahead, leading the way to the city with Tariel, Fatima, and Charlotte following behind. Isabella hovered close to Tariel and Atarah. He frowned. *Did she get close to those two? Without Clarissa?* He remembered Isabella struggling to make friends when she was little.

He shook his head. No, he needed to focus. For now, his troops were ok and the citizens of Aquam Caput were moving to a safe location. At any moment, an army could attack them. He scanned the area with fire blazing in his hands, ready. No sign of any demons yet.

Atarah must've slowed, for she peered over her shoulder once he'd caught up. With a single nod, she flapped her wings hard, maneuvering through the mountains with ease.

Within minutes, sweat dripped from his face, but not because of the fire in his veins. The muscles in his back ached as he flew against the strong winds. Making matters worse, the high altitude made him feel as if he was breathing through a straw.

While he struggled to keep up with her pace, in front of him Isabella stretched out her arms. Suddenly a wall of air slammed into him from behind, propelling him at a high speed. He opened his mouth to scream at Isabella to stop when he noticed it was on purpose. The effects weren't limited to him but extended to everyone except Atarah.

Isabella's extended arms tilted in line with Atarah's wings, guiding them through the sky at breakneck speed. Following Atarah's movements, she maneuvered everyone through the mountains. In fact, Tariel tucked in her wings to glide along the current Isabella provided. Had Isabella done this before? Pulling in his wings, he loosened different parts of his body, trusting her to not drop him. Weaving through the mountains, the wind roared around them, making communication impossible.

The others followed his example, stiffening their wings to glide. They zoomed across the snow-topped mountains. The temperature dropped as they flew higher, cutting into his bones. His teeth chattered together as Isabella guided them. His wings shivered despite his best efforts to stiffen them. Using his breathing techniques, he circulated the fire in his belly to his extremities, warming his blood. Steam rolled off his arms and legs as his flames reached just beneath the surface of his skin. He glanced over his shoulder to see the others shivering.

Luckily I have my fire to keep me warm, he mused.

Despite the distance, time flew by as the sense of urgency grew within him. As he prepared his mind for battle, suddenly Atarah veered down, arms drawn back with clenched fists. Isabella followed.

He heard the deep thuds and booms first, like rocks colliding with each other or thunder rolling off the clouds. Within a few seconds, he saw where the sounds came from. A small clearing in the mountain valley came into view. A mixture of rocks, grass, and moss covered the ground, while a stream zigzagged along between the peaks. A faint opening off the side of each mountain made him wonder if the enemy would come through tunnels. On the smaller mountainside, two large

Archs appeared locked into battle, struggling to topple one other.

Isabella's wind softened, relinquishing control back to him. He expanded his wings and circled the two, assessing. However, Atarah leaped into the fray, her eyes wide. He barely heard her voice above the wind.

"Stop!" Atarah screamed at the behemoth in front of her.

Flynn nearly fell out of the sky. It was Mikael!

A dazed look fell over Mikael's eyes as he tossed Atarah to the side and dove after the other…

His eyes widened.

Arick was the opponent. The halfling and host of a watcher.

Someone gasped behind him.

Flames erupted from his hands, ready to attack before he paused. Arick wasn't attacking; he was deflecting Mikael's attacks. Arick yelled something at Atarah, but all he heard was a grunt as Mikael landed a punch to Arick's gut.

"I said STOP!" Atarah propelled herself forward, delivering a jab to Mikael's side.

Mikael careened in the air and crashed onto the ground several yards away. Luke jumped into action, landing on Mikael's back. His eyes darkened and a ripple drifted over Mikael's prone form. Veins popped forward on either side of Luke's head as he held Mikael down. Mikael's face turned gray as the energy was sapped from his body.

They all landed. He kept his flames to the surface, breathing deeply to keep them hot.

"What happened?" Tariel bolted to Arick's side.

Her eyes darkened and narrowed on Mikael.

"I couldn't get him out fast enough," Arick panted.

Atarah knelt down by her father, her brow furrowed.

"What the hell are you talking about?" Atarah asked, snapping two fingers in Mikael's face. His face didn't move or flinch, expressionless. "Is this…?"

"Yeah," He nodded to Mikael. "The illusion's been cast already."

Tariel helped Arick to his feet.

"What's happened to you?" Her eyes searched his body. "How did you escape?"

He scanned the surrounding area with his flames at the ready. Arick tried to speak between his pants and groans, but nothing legible came out.

"Water!" Atarah called out.

One of his rangers, Jose, scrambled to pass his water jug to Arick, who greedily gulped it down. He grimaced. Arick's ribs were peppered with bruises. The halfling's wrist looked raw while his wings were brittle and wilting. One of his eyes was blackened while the other was wide with panic. His breathing remained erratic as he struggled to communicate. He pointed a finger at one of the cave entrances he spotted earlier.

"Fr—from there!" He panted. "They're—they're coming!"

He whirled around to see Matthew, yards away, at the opening. His face was stoic as he crept closer. Flames erupted from Flynn's arms as memories flooded back to him. Visions from Arakiel of Matthew and his demon army destroying his city filled his mind. Looting, burning, and breaking everything he'd held dear. The cheers that had erupted from the demons when he and his citizens were sent fleeing into the night rang in his ears now. His blood boiled. Now was his chance to seek justice for his people.

"It's a bad idea to fight in anger, Flynn!" Arakiel urged but Flynn pushed him to the far corners of his mind.

It's not your turn! he screamed before slamming a mental barrier between them. His flames and anger mixed together perfectly.

"No, Arick," Matthew said so softly, he almost didn't hear. Matthew pointed a finger at the mountain peak. "They're already here."

They followed his finger to see hundreds of figures crawling up the mountain like red ants climbing out of their mound. Demons scurried up the cliffs; their cheers reached his ears. His heart hammered at the sound. The horrific echoes of those chants sent a chill down his spine.

He whirled around and shot his fire out at Matthew. He yelled to drown out the noise of the demons, focusing on Matthew to channel his anger. His flames blazed hot as he fired round after round. Matthew dodged each blow, closing the gap between them with each delivery.

"Atarah!" Luke commanded, the veins on his face blackened. "Get to Sanctum now and rally the troops! Tell them she's here!"

Atarah's face paled. Her eyes flickered between her father and brother with uncertainty.

Arick didn't hesitate. "*Go*, Atarah!"

Without another word, she shot into the sky, Charlotte closing in behind her. Matthew jumped after her but stopped short. Arick dashed ahead, grabbing Matthew's ankle and slamming him back onto the ground.

"You're not going anywhere," Arick growled.

Matthew kicked himself free, backing away.

Flynn jerked his chin at the other rangers to follow and assist Luke. Without hesitation, the rangers darted to his side for backup. Isabella paused, glancing worriedly at Arick. He gave a sharp jerk of his head, to signal for her to go with Atarah. Isabella gave a small nod, darting after Atarah. A large tornado of gusts blew around her as she flew up the side of the mountain.

The demons' cheers died down, making him smile.

Good on her, he thought proudly. Demons huddled closer to the mountainside, seeking shelter from her powerful winds.

Tariel was the only one who stayed back. She darted to Luke's side, whose limbs trembled with fatigue. Sweat dripped from his face as his hold on Mikael weakened until Tariel arrived. Veins popped along Tariel's head as her power crashed down onto Mikael. He slumped to the ground, groaning.

That left Matthew to Flynn and Arick. He sharpened his flames into two daggers in his hands. As he circled Matthew, heat radiated from him in large waves and his fire changed from bright orange to icy blue. Arick flanked the other side of Matthew, his fist raised.

"Ready?" Arick called out, a line of blood dripping from his face.

Flynn raised his fire daggers, glaring fiercely at Matthew. The fire in his belly roared for release.

"Ready."

Chapter 18

Keep breathing, Clarissa's voice whispered through her mind. *You've done bigger things before.*

Isabella nodded to herself. That's right, she'd done this before, that means she could do it again.

But you failed last time, a harsh voice whispered in the back of her mind.

Memories from their failed attack on Ianua flooded her mind. The panic and restrained control pricked at her like fingers poking her. She shook her head, gulping deep breaths to fill her chest and belly. She hissed out the air through gritted teeth, clenching her abdomen and pelvic floor tight. Blood rushed through her body, energized and oxygenated. She was in her element. She was wind, air, and light.

Flying up the mountainside with the wind at her back, Isabella carried the wind current to the cliff sides. Demons ceased their climbing to hold on. Huddled in groups, many demons clung to the side of the mountain; however, several fell off. A scream followed by a thud signaled their demise but not nearly enough came off the mountain. An opening at the base of the mountain gave a faint glow. Flynn approached as close as he could without getting overwhelmed. More and more demons spilled from the tunnel in a never-ending stream. Atarah zoomed up the mountain as if gravity had little effect. Without her wind gust, she never would've been able to keep up with the Michael heir. As they flew past the first line of demons, reaching the mountain peak, Atarah knocked several over the cliff edge. Isabella attacked with her wind.

"I need—" Atarah grunted, kicking a demon's leg. The leg snapped, causing the demon to howl. "I need you to buy me some time."

Atarah pushed the demon into another, sending them both over the cliff and plummeting to the ground.

She whirled on her, eyes so fierce it startled her. "Can you do that?"

Isabella nodded, not trusting her own voice. She didn't know if she'd screamed yes or no.

"You can do it," Atarah reassured her, "Determine your own limit."

Atarah and Charlotte darted to an opening behind them. A pair of lanterns graced each side, their flames dancing at the center. Isabella hadn't noticed the door until Atarah jerked it open, dashing through the tunnel. She was all alone to fight.

Her heart hammered as she threw out another wind current, knocking more demons over the edge. Knots in her stomach formed, tightened, and quivered as more demons scurried over the mountain's edge. A question started in the back of her mind, growing louder as the seconds ticked by: *Can she do this?* A pressure grew within her.

Without Atarah, more and more demons swarmed her. Encircling her. Herding her further back, forcing her to retreat. Fear gripped its way into her heart, not from the demons but from herself. The grasp she held over her powers weakened. As the leash of control loosened, panic within her rose. Something inside her cracked as the pressure weighed her down.

With Clarissa by her side, the nervousness subsided, but with no one, it flourished. Her movements turned jerky and chaotic. Her limbs trembled. Her breaths rushed from her lungs with no uniformity.

She needed to breathe.

The pressure kept building like a weight on her chest. She

needed to breathe. Three demons attacked her at once. She sliced them back with another blast. She needed to breathe. The strain on her lungs felt like she was choking on smoke. She needed to breathe—yet her lungs refused to obey.

Another slash of wind blasted much weaker than before. More demons swarmed, closing in, caging her. *No,* she thought desperately. *This wasn't fair. This isn't fair. I...I...I need to breathe!*

Isabella gasped a deep inhalation. As the air rushed into her lungs, molten ice filled her veins.

She needed to stay in control or—

Isabella paused, tilting her head to one side. *What's the worst that could happen?* a voice from the dark depths of her mind whispered. Something within her soul snapped.

The butterflies in her stomach disappeared. Demons charged at her, weapons raised to strike her down. She lowered her arms as the pressure within her built. The ground rumbled as an eerie calm overcame her. Her heartbeat slowed in her ears. Suddenly everything felt...light.

She exhaled.

An explosion of wind careened most of the demons off the mountain. Dozens were flung back, while many more dug their weapons into the ground to hold on. A large wind tornado formed around her. Up above, the clouds formed and swirled.

Some sort of gate within her exploded. Muffled seismic blasts reverberated from her body in long strokes. The mountain shook. Boulders and rocks crumbled from the sides, plummeting demons to their deaths. The wind currents that were once overwhelming felt moldable in her hands.

The ice spread from her chest to her whole body, empowering her. Her body felt muted in an odd way. Her hands were numb as she lifted them, but her wings had never felt lighter. She jerked her arms down.

Two tornadoes spiraled out of her arms, causing the whole mountain to quake. Her lips twitched into a small smile. Dozens of demons careened through the air before getting slammed into the ground. Over and over again, the wind tossed the demons high into the sky and smashed them into either the mountainside or the ground. She faintly heard crunching and snapping sounds but didn't relent. A small whisper in her mind cautioned her that she'd gone past the point of no return.

"Atarah was right," she murmured. "I was angry."

Once the demons on the mountaintop were nothing but mangled heaps, she floated over to where they'd climbed from. Hundreds of demons scaled the cliff. She must've worn a terrifying expression on her face, for several demons, close to the top, paled.

She erupted another seismic blast at them from her arms.

The strong winds obliterated everything within a close distance. Torn limbs fell to the valley as demon blood splattered across the mountainside along the path of her blast. The demons further down the mountain scurried to the sides to avoid her direct hit.

She smiled and aimed again.

The pressure building within her lessened with each wind current she dealt. She carved the mountainside with her attacks over and over again. Her breaths changed into long-winded pants, but she hardly noticed. The glacial sensation across her limbs heated as she continued her onslaught. Though the sounds were muffled, her attacks' vibrations reached her feet.

It feels so good, she thought. *To finally have release. Relief from this pressure.*

Isabella's movements slowed as a single tear fell down her face. She didn't need to hold back or hold in all her anger and frustration. No one was here to judge her. She wouldn't be shunned or ostracized for using her wind's full ability.

She released another angry slash down the side of the mountain. A rock slide catapulted hundreds to their death, but hundreds more climbed from the tunnel below. Another large quake shook the mountain, enough to cause her to pause.

Her eyes widened.

She'd cut too close to where she stood on the mountain. The surface beneath her withered and crumbled. She jerked back, flaring her wings to catch her, but she underestimated her strength. She flung backward; her wings stiffened and buckled from the pressure, unable to open. A scream lodged itself in her throat as she waited for the impact. She closed her eyes, bracing for the pain, but none came.

Warmth wrapped around her body, melting the ice in her veins. Slowly, sensations came back to her. Her limbs felt heavy and exhausted. Her lungs ached as if she'd overused them. Heat seeped into her cold body like feeling sunshine after a long, cold night. Firm hands lowered her to the ground. Hands?

Her eyes shot open.

Flynn released her, concern etched into every corner of his face. His flames erupted from his wings, back, and hair but not his arms. Normally his fire was scathing hot, but this time it was a comforting warm. She stepped away to see one side of the mountain had collapsed from her wind blast.

Her eyes widened again. *Did she really do that?*

Lifting a hand to her chest, the pressure from before was nowhere in sight. Her whole body ached, but she'd never felt so light. As if someone had removed a 100-lb backpack from her back. The clouds dissipated into smaller wisps, no longer thundering and storming. The wind dancing around her gathered in her hand much easier than before.

"I—" Flynn stopped.

She jerked her gaze back to him, almost forgetting he was there.

"I didn't know you had it in you to do that," he finished.

Tears gathered in her eyes as anger coiled in her belly.

"I've always had it in me," she sniffled, glaring at him as he took a step back. "I knew no one would accept or love me if they saw."

Bitterness coated her words. The sting of his retreat hit its mark on her heart.

"No," He frowned. "I—"

"Don't deny it!" she yelled. "My father took away my training lessons because he couldn't stand the sight of me using my wind power. No one could! He always pushed me off to Sissy because he couldn't stand to be around me. You've seen him do this! Admit it!"

Flynn's eyes widened. She never raised her voice at him. In fact, she never yelled at anyone. She'd repressed so much, and she couldn't live with that pressure again. If that meant she'd be all alone in this world, then so be it.

"He'd never let you do those lessons," Flynn started, tears shining in his eyes. "Because you look so much like your mother when you do."

His voice cracked.

"I was there when your mother, Liliana, died. She was the air he breathed to keep going. Against all of the bureaucracy and bullshit our society liked to uphold. When she died, he couldn't function for a long time, so we selfishly left Clarissa to take care of you. I was about to be called back to duty for the rangers, so I thought she could give you the love and attention you needed." He knelt to her eye level. "None of that was your fault, and I'm so sorry, Isabella. I never realized how much that hurt you."

Tears fell in rapid succession from her eyes. Isabella bit her lip to keep it from quivering. She didn't want to cry now! She wanted to shout and rant about how awful and unfair it'd all been.

She wanted to stay angry. She pushed Flynn. Or tried to. Her exhausted limbs didn't move him a single inch. She landed weak punches on his chest as she sobbed.

He encased her in a hug with his arms and wings.

"It's not fair!" she yelled, struggling to break free of his hold. She was so tired.

"It's not," Flynn mumbled. "You don't have to hold back anymore, Bella. I swear it."

Her limbs fell to her side. All the energy she possessed sapped out of her. Relief consumed her to the point where she went limp. She didn't have to hold back anymore. She hiccuped, letting her tears run down her face.

"I'd thought…" Flynn released her, wiping her tears. "It looked as if you and Clarissa handled yourselves." He gave a small chuckle. "I had no idea you were so strong. I'm proud you stood up for yourself."

Something bloomed in her chest. Instead of molten ice, warmth spread to the rest of her body. He wasn't ashamed but proud of her. In the distance, the sounds of battle echoed closer in her ears, bringing their attention back to the task at hand. She wiped the tears from her face, sniffling and feeling better than she had in years.

"Come on, Flynn," she exclaimed, calling the wind back to her side. "Let's show them what it's like to fight against an Ignis."

Chapter 19

"Hold him down, kid!" Azazel yelled inside their head.

Arick grunted as Matthew twisted to break the arm hold. Tariel continued to hold Mikael down, draining his energy. Flynn assisted him in tackling Matthew, but a thundering blast drew him away. Ominous clouds covered the mountain, swirling like a tornado.

"I'll be back! Give this to both of them," Flynn called out to him, tossing a bag to his side.

That left Arick alone to deal with the two strongest Michael Archangels in the realms. He scowled at the discarded bag.

"What in the Trinity am I supposed to do with this?" Arick grunted.

"I don't know, kid," Azazel exclaimed. *"But we gotta figure out something fast. Demons are pouring into this realm like a flood."*

"I'm trying here!" Arick argued, gritting his teeth. His arms burned with the need for release. *"We gotta wait for Atarah to alert the citizens."*

"And then what?"

"Keep everyone, especially Atarah, away!"

"Kid, we need to figure out what we're gonna do with these two. Satan's mind tricks have latched onto them. You can't fight them both, and Tariel can't hold on forever."

Arick groaned as the muscles in his arms weakened. If he

let Matthew go, he was dooming hundreds, if not thousands. He willed his arms to tighten but the lack of food and his injuries caught up to him.

"Long time, no see, my fellow seeker," a voice called out.

A fist slammed into Matthew's jaw with a loud thud. Matthew's escape efforts stopped. Arick jerked around to see Luke and two other rangers with rope. Luke stood over him with a triumphant smile.

"Never thought I'd see you again." Arick chuckled.

Luke opened his mouth to speak but Matthew lunged again.

"Crap! He waited until I was distracted," Arick thought.

"Jose! Grab the bag!" Luke jumped on Matthew, locking down his legs. "We need the serum."

"Serum? What for?" Arick grunted.

"Before we left, Flynn came up with a plan to take down Matthew and Mikael for a while." Luke groaned when Matthew delivered a kick to his side. Arick heard the faint sound of a crack. "Damn, that hurt!"

"I got it, Luke!" The angel Luke named, Jose, approached, with the bag in hand. He yanked out several vials. "How many do we need?"

"Give him two!" Arick yelled.

One dose of the serum puts his power level at that of a human, so two would weaken him to the point of being harmless.

"It's not going to work," Matthew sneered, twisting again. "I'll die before I'd let that happen."

"I mean...that's a convenient offer. I think we should take him up on." Azazel scoffed.

"I have no qualms with that," Luke moaned.

Matthew jerked, stabbing one of the taloned-ends of his wings into Luke's side. Luke cried out in pain, releasing his hold. Kicking his way to freedom, Matthew reared on him.

"Here he comes, kid!" Azazel exclaimed.

Matthew swung his wings wide. Arick ducked, reaching a hand out to grab the wing. Tucking his own wings, Arick rolled to his side and took Matthew down with him. The bastard yelled in frustration, but Arick wasn't done yet.

He picked up a jagged rock.

"This is payback," Arick sneered.

He slammed the rock into Matthew's wings, scrapping as he went. Matthew bucked beneath him, screaming in pain, but Luke and the other rangers held the luciferian down. With reinforcements, Arick tore into his wings. He didn't hear Matthew's wails nor see the rangers' pale faces. All Arick saw was red.

"Kid."

Arick hacked away again and again.

"Kid!"

He froze. Azazel's voice carried an urgency. He blinked, seeing blood covering his arms and legs. Matthew lay limp on the ground, unconscious and bleeding.

"I beat him," Arick murmured. "I finally beat him."

"You didn't beat him yet," Luke grumbled, nodding to the rangers. "Let's roll him over!"

With a unified grunt, they heaved Matthew onto his back. Blood pooled around them. Matthew's ashen face was devoid of any life.

Arick jumped. *"Did I... kill him?"*

Luke tilted the Luciferian's head back, pouring the serums down his throat.

"Not quite," Azazel answered, *"But after having his wings torn, I bet he wishes he was dead. You did good, kid."*

"I—I almost lost myself again."

"But you came back this time on your own. Last time you fought him, your mind was like a hurricane."

"If my dad hadn't stopped me—Wait, Dad!"

Arick jerked to see Mikael shoving Tariel. *No!* He darted to her side, his wings flaring around her protectively.

"I'm fine," Tariel groaned. "Get the serums in his system before he attacks anyone else!"

"Guys!" Luke called out, pointing a finger at the portal opening. "We got incoming!"

Demons charged them on the ground as his father launched into the air. Mikael flew to the mountain's peak, to the entrance to Sanctum. He tightened his hold on Tariel.

Dammit! What was he supposed to do?

"You gotta go after your dad, kid!"

"I can't leave them here!" Arick argued. *"They're outnumbered!"*

A hand smacked his forehead. He blinked down at Tariel. Her fierce black eyes glared at him.

"Get your ass up there!" Tariel yelled above the demon's war cries. "We'll be fine."

"What if something happens?" His brow furrowed.

Every time he turned his back, someone he loved died or was taken from him. Tariel scowled, shoving his wings away.

"Don't lose focus," Tariel hissed, pointing toward Mikael's figure. "If we don't stop him, you'll doom us all. Now go!"

Her eyes darkened. Veins along her face protruded. Smoke and shadows whirled around her, draining the life of the grass she stood on. Standing before him, she was an avenging angel, death personified. Though the hair on the back of his neck stood on ends, she'd never looked more beautiful to him.

"Go," she commanded again, turning around to face the charging demons. "You'll find no damsel here. Now go!"

Something in his chest tightened. His lips twitched, despite himself.

"Yes'm," he grinned, lifting a hand. "Jose! Toss me some serum."

Jose didn't hesitate, throwing the bag with the remaining serums. Arick caught it midair, launching himself into the sky.

"Come back to me this time," Tariel called over her shoulder.

Her shadows withered the ground, spreading decay. Like whips, the shadows and smoke lashed out at the demons, drying them out. The demon soldiers dropped like flies.

"I will," Arick whispered, flying after Mikael.

His father's flight pattern faltered. He hadn't fully recovered from Tariel's draining effect, giving Arick an advantage.

He flared his wings wide, climbing in elevation fast. Clouds whirled ferociously while thunder echoed in the background. Mikael stumbled along the rocky edge, opting to climb instead of fly.

Arick flew higher and higher.

"Kid, what are you doing?"

"I have an idea," he replied.

Above the mountain range, he saw everything: the scampering of demons, the whirlwinds from Isabella and fiery blasts from Flynn. However, he focused on his dad.

His wings trembled.

"I'm sorry for everything," he murmured.

Arick tucked his wings to his side and dove.

"Trinity, kid! You're going for an air strike?" Azazel exclaimed.

The deafening wind crashed against this face. He knew air strikes were risky attacks. The chances of death upon impact were high if he didn't time his landing correctly, but a strange sense of calm certainty flowed through him.

He wouldn't screw this up.

Mikael's figure grew as he descended. Time ticked by slow and fast. Sounds faded to the far corners of his mind. He readied the serums, clutched in his hand.

He had one shot to redeem himself. As the details of the ground sharpened, he flared his wings wide. Mikael whipped around, his eyes widening, but it was too late.

Arick collided with his father, the impact shaking loose rocks along the edge. He closed his eyes as they made contact with the ground, landing with a loud, echoing thud. His ears rang, and air lodged itself in his throat.

But he couldn't stop now. His father lay immobile, gasping beneath him. With trembling limbs, he popped open the vials and drained the contents down his father's throat, clamping a hand quickly over his mouth.

Arick waited a beat. Then another.

Mikael choked back the serum.

Slumping to the ground, his heart pounded. Slow, painfully slow, breath returned to his lungs. His vision tunneled as the agony encroached. In the far corners of his mind, Azazel called out his name, but he was fading. A horn blared in the distance; black wings poured from the mountaintop.

The last thing Arick saw before the darkness consumed him, was an armor-clad, ivory-winged warrior flying to him. An outstretched hand.

"I'm proud of you, kid."

Chapter 20

The inferno raged. The intense heat melted everything within a few feet of Malachi. He blasted his way across the balcony, evaporating the water Paul sent his way. Shoving Imani and Gabriel behind him, he unleashed the built-up pressure in his veins. His fire collided with Paul's water, creating an instant implosion.

Hot steam and fog bellowed around them when the two elements clashed. The force of the blast pushed Gabriel and Imani back, but Malachi held his ground.

"Get to my people!" he yelled.

The steam obscured his vision of Paul, giving him a few precious seconds.

"We can't leave you alone," Imani roared, pulling out an ax.

Gabriel's hands buzzed with energy, his hands already glowing. "I'll make a portal so we can escape."

"Portal yourselves out of here." Malachi created flame daggers in each hand. "This fight should've happened between me and Paul a long time ago."

A portion of the steam thinned out, giving him a glimpse of his opponent. Paul stood in the same spot across the balcony, smirking back at him. The blood in his veins boiled with anger. Gabriel glanced between them before nodding.

"Come on," Gabriel murmured, creating a small portal.

Imani sized him up as if unsure. Malachi nodded. He'd

handle Paul even if it cost him his life. Imani's gaze softened.

"Imani," he called out, keeping his eye on Paul.

She paused, one foot suspended in the air.

"If I don't make it, tell Flynn I know who the real bad guy is now," he finished, glaring at his brother.

Paul's grin widened. "You think you're *so* noble?"

"I will," Imani called out before jumping through the portal.

Gabriel gave him a reproachful look filled with regret.

"Go," Malachi urged. "Warn my citizens, please."

Gabriel's face twisted with conflict. After a beat, safety won out.

"Don't die," Gabriel whispered, disappearing into his own portal.

The portal sizzled out, giving him no way to escape. Malachi held his glare. For the first time in many years, sweat dripped from his brow from the heat of his fire. Heat rolled off him in waves.

Seldom did he feel hot, and it wasn't a good sign when he did. He was pushing his body to the limit.

"That wasn't a good idea," Paul purred. "You're going to die here tonight."

"I won't die—" Malachi grunted. "—until I drain all your poison from my city."

Paul laughed, the water rose once more, compressing into whips. "This hasn't been your city for a long time."

The whips lashed out. Tucking his wings close, Malachi raised his body temperature. The whips evaporated upon the attack, however…

He groaned. The impact of the whip struck his sides like a hammer.

Paul cackled when he fell to one knee. "Pathetic. You can't fight on your own."

A gentle breeze caressed his face.

Liliana…

He took a deep breath, feeding the fire in his stomach. Flames sprouted along his wings. Paul's wings faltered as he rose to his feet and lashed out again, gathering water from the ocean below. The attacks disintegrated before making contact with his body.

Paul's eyes widened. "I'm not done yet!"

He clenched a hand, draining the surrounding trees and vegetation of their liquid. He hurled the water at him like a spear.

Malachi took another deep breath, distributing the flames through his arms. He slashed through the attack with laser focus. Steam erupted around him as he approached.

Paul's wings trembled. His movements turned frantic as he cast another water blast. Paul switched his water source back to the ocean, drawing in more and more.

"You know, Paul," Malachi murmured, walking slowly. Paul backed away, not stopping in his strikes. "You're right about two things. I can't fight on my own."

Paul doused more water at him. His arms jerked with each motion. Malachi's flames were so hot now the water evaporated before it reached the balcony. Sweat poured from Paul's face. His eyes grew frantic as Malachi backed him into a corner.

The balcony groaned and cracked beneath their feet. They wouldn't last much longer on this structure. Malachi knew he should change their battle surroundings, but he couldn't bring himself to do it.

He wanted to feel the breeze. Liliana's last gift to him.

"I need my family to help me fight," Malachi continued, "Even if *you* have an ocean at your disposal, it'll never be enough. Because angels like you, who only take, will never know the strength of giving."

He grinned and Paul's face paled. He flared his wings to fly away, but a fire dome from Malachi's wings closed off any escape route.

"The second thing you're right about—" Malachi lifted a hand. "—is that this city hasn't been mine for a long time. Clarissa's the heart and strength behind this city."

"No!" Paul cried out.

He desperately tried to reach any water source to keep from overheating. The more water he pulled their way, the more steam developed. The air grew thick and heavy to breathe.

Malachi gave a sad smile.

"She saw your true colors from an early age, but I denied her. I'm still denying her, but not anymore." His flames changed color from bright red to white.

Malachi's heart raced to keep up with his body's demands. His sweat stopped and his skin turned cold and clammy.

"I hope I get a chance to thank her for opening my eyes," he finished.

"NOOO!" Paul bellowed.

He erupted, surrendering himself to the flames, the heat. A bright white light consumed them. The balcony they stood on crumbled from the cliffside into the crashing waves of the ocean.

Chapter 21

Butterflies fluttered in Clarissa's stomach as they took their seats on the couches. Ben took the lone chair facing Beelzebub, while she sat on the loveseat. Barmen took the spot beside her, spreading his wings behind her. Crossing one ankle over his knee, he leaned back as if to appear relaxed. However, the tension around his jaw told her a different story.

He was nervous. She was nervous too.

The fire in her belly expanded to her limbs. Taking deep breaths, she brought her flames closer to her skin's surface to reassure herself. Heat radiated off her in waves, but Barmen didn't appear to mind. In fact, he inched closer.

"Now," Beelzebub growled. "Speak."

The demon lord's eyes narrowed on Ben, who clasped his hands together.

"What is love?" Ben rasped, with an unwavering gaze.

"You came all this way back to ask me *this*?" Beelzebub scoffed.

Ben unfolded his hands.

"I've come all this way to figure out what your real goal is." Ben squinted his eyes together, leaning forward. "Now, what's love to you?"

Beelzebub gave a humorless laugh, glancing at Barmen. "You're paying for this?"

"You're stalling," Barmen drawled, pointing to the ticking clock on the desk. "Time is money, right?"

"Love is…" Beelzebub huffed. "Love is something you either have or you don't. If you can't create it, you take it from somewhere else."

"Not profit?" Ben raised an eyebrow.

"Despite what you think of me—" Beelzebub glared at Ben. "—profit's important to gain love."

"Is that why you weren't really trying to stop your sister?" Ben fired off.

"What makes you say that?" Beelzebub lowered his voice. "Did I not provide you the staffs to stop that Matthew fellow?"

Ben re-clasped his hands together, a vacant expression in his eyes. "You knew her next move, and that the staffs wouldn't be of real use to us."

Beelzebub stilled.

"In fact, you knew the staff would almost immediately lead her right to us." Ben tilted his head. "You wanted her army and minions to cross the realms."

Beelzebub didn't contest but brought his elbows to the desk.

"Why?" Ben asked, his face stoic.

Beelzebub smirked again. "You've seen the halflings in our realm, yes?"

Ben gave the smallest of nods.

"Then you'll know how profitable slave labor is," Beelzebub lifted a gloved hand. "Sending her out on this 'mission' she believes in as a way to prove herself only helps business in the end." He lifted up a sheet of paper. "Everything across the realms has profited from slave labor at some point in time. It'd be ridiculous to not take—"

"There's that word again," Ben interrupted. "Take."

Beelzebub lowered the sheet of paper. "*Everything* in this world takes. I made the deal with you because I thought you understood this fundamental concept. If you can't create it, take it."

Ben raised an eyebrow.

"I saw the hunger in your eyes to take whatever it took in the name of love." Beelzebub pointed a finger at him. "You didn't know it at the time, but you held the same belief as me. Even if you don't acknowledge it, you still uphold it."

"No, I did." Ben agreed. "What's unfortunate for you, is that I learned from that belief when it failed me."

A sharp bell ding signaled the end of the five minutes. The clock on the desk rang again. Beelzebub stood from his desk, buttoning his jacket.

"As much as I'd love to chat more, I have other business to attend to." Beelzebub pivoted around his desk, making his way to the door. "Now, get out."

Barmen rose, offering her a hand. She took it with trembling legs. A quiet question, in the back of her mind, of *why* pestered her.

Why would Beelzebub manipulate his own sister for gain? Why did Ben want to talk with him if he knew it was all a setup from the beginning? As the questions plagued her, the fire in her belly withered. They were almost out of danger.

"Of course," Ben murmured, not moving an inch from his seat. "But one last thing."

Beelzebub opened the door, half turning with a raised brow. "What?"

Ben raised a glittery, bedazzled staff from the folds of his tunic. Blood dripped down his ears once again as the staff glowed. Beelzebub's eyes widened.

"Love is giving," Ben mumbled.

A bright light illuminated behind Beelzebub's desk. A large portal blazed an array of colors around the room. Clarissa's heart hammered as an intense hum filled the room. The hair on the back of her neck rose. Something powerful was coming.

"Stop!" Beelzebub's jaw dropped as he slammed the door shut.

"I hope you heard everything you needed," Ben spoke to

a glowing figure, emerging from the portal.

Blood pooled in Ben's eyes as the creature stepped forward.

"Stay close to me!" Barmen jerked her back to his chest, engulfing his wings around her tight. He whispered, "Stay quiet."

A ripple formed around them. He held her close, shielding her from the new arrival.

A seraphim floated into the room. Her face was obscured by a hood, leaving no clues as to what she looked like. Three pairs of wings expanded from her back. One pair covered her feet. The second pair lifted her off the ground while the last pair circled around her head and neck, hiding her face further. A silver tunic draped loosely around her frame like a long robe.

Power vibrated off the seraphim in waves that sent tremors to Clarissa's knees. Her legs would've buckled if she hadn't clung to Barmen. The glow around the seraphim was like a bright bioluminescence. Looking directly at her was like looking at the sun, painful for the eyes.

"I have heard enough," The seraphim spoke.

Her soft voice sounded distorted, making Clarissa feel lightheaded. Being in the seraphim's presence created a dangerous high, despite her thundering heart warning her danger was here. Barmen tightened his hold on her, a sheen of sweat sprinkled along his forehead. Clarissa glanced at Ben, ready to yell at him to take cover but froze. Ben continued to sit in the chair with a faint smile on his lips.

Beelzebub's face paled. With trembling knees, he buckled to the ground in a low bow.

"Please," Beelzebub whispered. "Have mercy on us."

The End

ACKNOWLEDGEMENTS

Thank you so much for continuing to read the stories of Arick, Atarah, Clarissa, Isabella, and so many more. I hope you have enjoyed reading their journey as much as I enjoyed writing their adventures. I am truly grateful for the opportunity to share their stories and couldn't have done it alone.

I want to say thank you to my husband, Malcomn, for cheering me on from the sidelines. You have been my number one fan and supporter. Thank you to my amazing and supportive friends and family! Love ya'll! Every like and share and social media has meant the world to me. Thank you to everyone who's purchased my book!

Thank you to my editors, Catherine Kopf and Nichloe Heydenburg! Thank you Terra Hitzing for format and design work! Thank you Jessica Cameron for the book cover! Lastly, thanks to you, the reader. I truly hope you enjoyed this story!

If you did love the book, please leave me a review. :)

GRACIE MITCHELL is a yoga-loving, caffeine addicted writer currently based in Georgia. When she is not working endlessly as an Indie author, she can be found curled up on the couch, with her husband, reading a new book or watching a new tv series. On top of her love to read and write, Gracie enjoys going on adventurous hikes, painting, spending time with her cat and traveling to different countries.

Follow her for more at: https://graciemitchell.com/
Insta: @clanofthearchseries
@gmitchell505

Thank you so much for reading! Hope you enjoyed!

Please leave a review on Amazon, Goodreads and Barnes & Noble

Also by Gracie Mitchell

<u>True Wings (Book 1</u>

<u>True Spirit (Book 2)</u>

<u>True Strength (Book 3)</u>

<u>5th book in the series: Pending</u>

www.ingramcontent.com/pod-product-compliance
Lightning Source LLC
Chambersburg PA
CBHW021211310726
48971CB00006B/1519